A SACRIFICE OF BLOOD
AND STARS

a Sacrifice of Blood and Stars

JENNIFER BRODY

Podium

To all those brave enough to seek the stars, and to those who protect this Earth. We honor your service.

Copyright © 2024 by Jennifer Brody

Cover design by Yoly Cortez

ISBN: 978-1-0394-5365-4

Published in 2024 by Podium Publishing
www.podiumaudio.com

Podium

A SACRIFICE OF BLOOD
AND STARS

The Ambush

The sky blisters red with the ambush.

Usually . . . it's gray, icy, and dusty. The distant sunlight casts this stars-forsaken surface with a bleak veneer. But now the sky burns red and angry. I only have time to yell one thing—before the first spray of blaster fire rains down, forcing me to dive behind the rocks. My helmet helps me breathe, but I still smell sulfur from the blasts. I taste it on my tongue, acrid and bitter.

"Incoming!" I scream.

But it's already too late.

The next cascade of enemy fire drowns out my voice and shatters the thin air, kicking up dust and ice crystals. This dwarf planet doesn't have enough atmosphere or oxygen to breathe without assistance, but at least it has some semblance of Earth-like gravity.

Once it lets up, I run over to my friend and fellow guardian, bouncing and hopping in the lighter gravity, assisted by my reinforced suit. I hope my warning is enough. I spot her silhouette over the next ridge. But before I can reach her, I hear the sharp whistle of blasters.

"Incoming, duck now!"

I dive behind a rocky outcropping, but I keep my eyes pinned to the ridge. My friend hears me—and drops down into the icy dust, but the next round of fire stuns us both.

My ears ring, and my head spins. I feel nauseous. I want to puke.

I'm dizzy and on the brink of unconsciousness, but I scramble to my feet and rush over to my friend. I see blood, so much blood, too much blood. I struggle with the weight of the prone body, so much heavier than when conscious, dragging it over the pockmarked landscape that's blistered with blaster fire, feeling the hot wet slick of blood dripping down my shoulder.

It's not slowing.

It's gushing.

Harold, check vitals, I say even though I already know it's dire.

I can feel the blood both on my skin and in my head through the neural connection. The steady throb of each weak heartbeat, pumping too little blood. The rush of looming unconsciousness clouds my brain like cotton. The dampening of sight that comes right before . . .

Death.

I know with certainty. It's about to claim us both. I crest the next ridge. I try to call for help . . . but it crackles uselessly. The base's commlink is too damaged.

The rain of enemy fire has paused, but I only register briefly how strange that is. Then I understand. Faceless enemies deploy to the surface around us, parachuting down and landing in the icy dust. There is nowhere to run, not with the unconscious body weighing me down.

Their suits are black. Tinted masks shield their faces. Their breath hisses out through the air filters in smoky tendrils. Their boots kick up ice crystals. Twenty of them. Maybe more. They retract their parachutes and raise their blasters.

They pull the triggers.

PART 1

ENLISTMENT

Appear weak when you are strong,
and strong when you are weak.

—Sun Tzu, *The Art of War*

CHAPTER 1

KARI

TWO MONTHS EARLIER

I dream of a vacuum that sucks me in—austere, dark, endless as the universe. It pulls at every cell of my being until I implode, crushed to death by the singularity's intense gravity.

When I wake with a jolt, I'm gasping for breath and sucking down oxygen like water. "Bea," I gasp, reaching for the mound next to me under the scratchy covers. Warm and still breathing. Thank the stars, I didn't wake my little sister with my nighttime thrashing.

This calms me, but only a little—before it all comes rushing back with that same black hole-sucking sensation from my nightmare. It's my last day of high school.

And that means one thing—

The Pairing Ceremony.

Realizing sleep is a lost cause, I glance out the window of our tiny bedroom. Through the dingy, screened-in glass, the sun cracks the sky and paints it bright orange. The only other thing I can see is the trailer right next to ours, permanently parked on the artificial, fluorescent green turf. It's supposed to look like real grass. Heavy emphasis on the *supposed to* . . .

The Park is where we live in identical dingy, tin-can-like trailers shaped like boxes and parked on a grid pattern. They were mass manufactured during the housing shortage after the Great War. That means they're old and decaying . . . and the only home that we've got left.

I wasn't born here, I remember with a pang.

But remembering hurts too much . . . because then I also have to remember why we got evicted, so I shut it out of my mind and try to focus on my sister's steady breathing.

Steady like a heartbeat.

I stay in bed for a few moments, waiting for Bea to settle and savoring this last regular morning before everything is about to change. Then I climb out of bed carefully. She needs her rest more than me. My bare feet smack the worn carpet, feeling the rough, synthetic fibers.

I'm even going to miss those, as crazy as that seems. I run my hands through my tangled, long hair—something else I'm about to say goodbye to—and catch sight of my reflection in the dressing mirror. It's the old, standalone kind that swivels. The glass warps and elongates my appearance. The rising sun sends light slanting across my features—my striking oval face and sharp nose; lanky, muscular body; and almond-shaped eyes the color of burnt sugar.

Cat eyes, my sister calls them. We both have them. So did my father, though I try not to think about him . . . well . . . *ever.* We also both have rich brown skin and high cheekbones like our mother. But that's where our similarities end. I also notice how tired I look.

I don't have to wonder why I keep having that nightmare. Two months ago, on my eighteenth birthday, I enlisted in Space Force. I ship out to basic training tomorrow.

That's right, I'm going to be a guardian . . . though it hasn't sunk in yet.

But first, I have to get through my last day of school today. And it's more terrifying than leaving home for the first time and blasting off into space. More terrifying than not getting leave to see my friends or family for four long years. Okay, *friend . . .* singular . . . I only have one, and Rho's not coming with me. More terrifying than Bea being a foot taller and edging past twelve to almost-teenager status, and Ma even more wilted from age the next time I see them.

Enlisted.

The word echoes through my head, both thrilling and terrifying me. It doesn't feel real yet, even though it's the most real thing in the whole blasted universe. But I know why I'm doing this. Who wouldn't want a first-class ticket off this stars-forsaken rock? And to trade the Park for the excitement of the Proxy Wars? And experience the great expanse of interstellar space?

The truth is that I've dreamed of enlisting . . . well . . . since I was old enough to want anything. Plus, this way I can protect our federation from the Proxies and the Raiders. Just the thought makes my heart skip. But then my sister Bea stirs next to me as if to remind me—

You're leaving me, too.

My excitement shrivels instantly, deflated by a shot of pure guilt. I swallow hard, trying to contain the deep swell of emotion flooding through me and drowning me.

I can't change it, I remind myself. *I already signed the contract.*

Right on cue, I hear a groggy stirring behind me.

"Kari, I baked you something."

It's Bea.

Her voice sounds as sweet as her cinnamon hair, even when it's crinkled and scratchy from sleep. I feel guilt stab at my heart again. I'm going to miss these quiet mornings together while Ma is still at work, finishing up the night shift at the factory, and before the sun rises more and promises to heat the city blazing hot, scorching anyone who dares to set foot outside.

"All by yourself?" I ask in a knowing voice.

"Well, Ma helped before she left for work last night," she hedges. "Uh, I guess she's still afraid . . . I'll burn the house down."

"Well, that's 'cause you almost did," I tease her. "You little psycho."

I say that with love, of course. My little sister annoys the stars out of me on a daily basis. But I can't help it. She's my greatest weakness. No matter what, I can never stay mad at her.

"Don't you mean . . . *pyromaniac*," Bea says, sounding far older than her eight years. She's always been a whiz at anything school-related, unlike me. "Not psychopath."

I pull out a fresh T-shirt from the beat-up trunk stowed at the foot of our bed. Well . . . kind of fresh . . . in that I've only worn it a few times since I last scrubbed it in the kitchen sink with our soap rations. I sniff it, then shrug and deem it passable, pulling it over my messy bedhead.

"Oh, and it wasn't my fault," Bea goes on, sounding offended. "I was just . . . *hangry*. That's hungry *plus* angry at the same time. I learned about it at school."

"*Hangry* . . . for cupcakes?" I say, cocking my eyebrow.

"Uh, who doesn't get hangry for cupcakes?" she asks with a feisty pout. She catches my eye through the mirror and smirks. "Now that would be a total psychopath."

We both laugh, savoring these moments like we savor her home-baked treats. Despite us being related and sharing a bedroom since she was born—a squalling red-faced baby who I had to watch, so Ma could work the night shifts at the factory while Dad was deployed—I'm reminded once again of how different we really are. I'm pragmatic and serious, while Bea flits around like some wild and exotic bird straining against the bars of her cage and yearning to fly free.

Plus, she's right—it wasn't her fault.

Our trailer doesn't have a proper stove or heater, so we use a portable gas range and jerry-rigged oven for both when we've got enough propane rations, which isn't often. It's a fire hazard, and that's on a good day. Everything comes out half-baked—partly soft, partly burnt.

But it's better than nothing. I remember what that was like, too.

"Fine, you little *pyro*," I say, reaching over to smooth down her unruly curls.

"Besides, that happened when I was only six," she points out, swatting my hand away. "Two years ago. I'm much more mature now. Ma's just been acting overprotective since . . ."

She trails off. She doesn't have to say it.

We both know the rest—*since I decided to enlist.*

"Why do you have to remind me?" I ask, feeling guilt stabbing me again.

Bea shimmies out of the blanket and starts jumping up and down on the bed. She aims her fingers like a gun and fires them. *Pow. Pow. Pow.* "I can't wait to enlist when I turn eighteen! Blast off to space! Get the bad guys! Keep Earthside safe . . . take that, Proxies and Raiders—"

I press her hands down, pulling them apart so they're no longer imitating death and destruction. "No, you're going to college. Like the kids across town. And that's final."

"But space battles sound *way* more fun than studying all the time . . ."

I shake my head. "It's better than risking your life, trust me."

"But that's what you're doing." She hops off the cot, sashaying over to the mirror. She swivels it back and strikes a diva-like pose—and glares at me through the reflection.

"Plus, I snuck a look at your intake form," she adds with a sly expression.

I glare back at her through the mirror. "You little spy! That was private. As in . . . none of your *blasted* business—"

"Well, if it was so top secret, then why did you leave it out?" she says with a sassy cock of her eyebrow. "It was practically begging me to read it. Like I had no choice."

"Snoop," I declare.

"Liar," she shoots back.

We stare at each other through the warped glass.

It's a sister standoff.

We each wait for the other to blink or look away from our twisted visages. Finally, Bea crumples. Her shoulders sag, folding in on themselves like the wings of a tiny, fragile bird. Now she looks closer to her actual age. Despite her antics and preteen attitude, she's still only a kid.

"Kari, you promised. But you requested . . . front lines."

Busted. I can't deny it.

"Front lines provides double," I say instead, busying myself with tugging on my ratty, ill-fitting sneakers and lacing them up tight so they don't slip off. "Plus, the Golden Gate Attack . . . remember? Well . . . maybe I can help catch the terrorists who killed those kids."

I flash back to the heinous attack that happened a few weeks ago. The newsfeed footage ricochets through my head—the school bus exploding, then plunging off the bridge into the dark, sloshy waters of the frigid bay. The first terrorist attack Earthside in over a hundred years.

But then Bea sets her lips.

"I don't want *double*—I want a sister," she says slowly, making me feel every single word like a knife stabbing my heart. I flinch at her verbal assault. "Plus, stop pretending and admit it already," she adds. "You want to fight up there—you've always wanted to fight."

Busted again.

She's right. I'm a confessed adrenaline junkie. And I've got the battle scars to prove it, from jumping off ledges and trailer roofs, to broken bones and cracked ribs from sneaking off and tussling with Park kids in the back alleys, imitating guardians by fighting with sticks and broken glass and *stars knows what else*. It's a miracle I've survived to adulthood.

I'm not like Bea, or my best friend Rho. I struggle in school. Words skitter across the page and turn back on themselves, doubling over and blurring together. Numbers battle each other, not adding up right. Fighting is the only thing I've ever been good at. It's my one gift.

But I look away from her pointed gaze, trying to hide the guilt painting my face. I don't want Bea to know the truth and worry about me . . . well . . . any more than she already does.

"But I'm coming back," I say in a soft voice. "I promise—"

She waits for a beat, knowing this will hurt— "Dad didn't."

Her words burn me like blaster fire. I fight back tears.

"But I will. I swear it—"

"Your promises don't mean much," she huffs and turns away.

Tension hangs in the air. I hate it when we argue like this. When we were little kids, our fights took physical form, brawls that left us injured with angry, red streaks on our flesh and bitter tears piercing our eyes. But now we stab with words—and I think it hurts worse.

I try to lighten the mood, blinking back my frustrated tears.

"So . . . what'd you bake for me?" I ask, my mouth already watering.

She only bakes for special occasions, saving up rations for our birthdays and federation holidays. But this time is different. A part of me knows this is her way of saying . . .

Goodbye.

"Well, it's a surprise—for the last day of school," she says, turning shy all of a sudden. She fidgets, twisting her toes into the scuffed carpet. "And no guessing this time."

"Well, show me already, silly."

Bea fishes a tidy bundle out from under the bed. It's wrapped in an old dish towel. With a flourish, she unwraps it and brandishes the chipped plate.

"*Chocolate* chip cookies," she says proudly.

I look at the lumpy treats in surprise. "Wait, how'd you get . . . *chocolate?*"

Bea grins, making me think she did something dangerous. My heart hammers again like in my dream. Nobody's had real chocolate since before the war. I mean, I've heard rumors of ancient stashes of cocoa hoarded by the Raiders and sold on the black space markets.

But then she confesses.

"Obviously, it's not real," Bea says. "It's only carob. I've been saving up our rations. But I thought we could make believe it was real. Pretending helps, you know. Helps forget . . ."

She trails off, looking down. But I know what she's thinking—*forget that I'm leaving tomorrow.* So I put on my most cheerful smile, even though the mirror contorts it into a dreadful scowl. I snatch the plate of cookies from her outstretched palms, making her giggle.

"Dibs on the *chocolatiest* chocolate chip cookie."

• • •

I ride the school bus with the chalky, metallic taste of carob still coating my tongue. But at least it's sweet, and Bea was right—pretending does help, even if I'm too old for that rubbish.

Each lurch over the pockmarked pavement sends the bus flying into the air, spewing out black exhaust into the hot air, while nervous tension electrifies the mood on the bus because it's the last day of school. Registering that thought, my neural implant pipes up. *Pairing Ceremony. Lompoc High School auditorium. 3 p.m. Ms. Skye, do you want to set a countdown timer?*

I flinch at the interruption. I hear my neural implant in my head, but nobody else can hear it. Every recruit gets one. I rub the metal stub on the base of my neck. I've only had my implant for a little over a week, and I'm still not used to it disturbing my thoughts.

Uh, thanks a lot, I think back with sarcasm. *Like I could possibly forget.*

You're welcome, says the robotic male voice.

Clearly, sarcasm isn't in the programming.

As promised, the countdown timer flashes in my retinas. Just under six hours until an important part of my future is decided. I should feel excited and grateful. This is supposed to be a good thing. But the numbers counting down make me feel like my life is ticking away.

"Jeez, make it stop already," I mutter under my breath.

Countdown canceled, says that stilted voice again as the numbers vanish.

This voice is the default setting, but you can change it. However, I decide right then and there to name my implant—*Harold.* Somehow giving my implant a dorky, lame name makes me feel better about it controlling my life.

Acknowledged. Name preferences updated.

Thanks, Harold, I think back. *Work on sarcasm detection. I'd really appreciate it.*

Sarcasm (sar kazem/), noun

The use of irony to mock or convey contempt.

The definition flashes in my retinas. I groan inwardly and sink lower in my seat, catching a potent whiff of bus BO. While programming is impressive, clearly we've still got a long way to go toward true . . . artificial intelligence. *But I'm not artificial,* says Harold without any irony.

Over his head again. I wince in annoyance.

Nor are you very intelligent, I think back, then quickly add, *Wait, don't reply to that.*

Blessed silence descends for the rest of the ride. We leave Lompoc's derelict downtown with abandoned storefronts, some empty since the war, and hit the nice side of town where the veterans live, marked by real grass and oak trees shrouding two-story houses. I picture the air-conditioned interiors with hardwood floors and double-paned windows. I know it well—because I used to live there, after all. But that was a lifetime ago, back when I still had a father.

Another starless thought . . . I push it away quickly before it can spawn into more terrible memories. A few minutes later, the bus screeches up to the curb, exhaling a fresh gasp of exhaust that burns my throat and stings my eyes. The squat, industrial buildings of Lompoc High School loom through the grubby windows with their barbed wire and chain-link perimeter fencing. The whole effect makes it look more like a penitentiary than an institution of "higher learning."

Across the campus, I spot the parking lot, where fleets of sleek transports in a variety of bright colors—self-driving cars that levitate a foot over the pavement— glide into marked parking spaces. Ringer kids each get their own personal transport to ferry them to school.

I feel a sharp pang of envy for what I used to have—a transport just like that, loaded up with my favorite playlist or trending shows and the fresh blast of filtered air. Instead, I pull my gaze away and clamber from the ancient school bus. I wave to the driver on my way off.

"Have a nice last day, Kari," the driver says with a wave and toothless grin. Xena's face is sunbaked and prematurely creviced, framed by tufty white hair that spikes out in all directions like a wild cactus. "Oh, and don't get into too much trouble today," she adds with a smirk.

I cock my eyebrow. "How do you define . . . *too much*?"

"You're a lost cause, ain't ya?" She laughs with her eyes twinkling, but then it transforms into a wet, raspy cough. "Thank the stars you're shipping out soon."

"Thank the stars . . . is right," I reply, feeling a surge of affection.

Unlike most of our neighbors, Xena has always been kind toward my family and looked after us. She's one of the main reasons our eviction wasn't more painful.

"Now get to class before you're marked tardy," she says, gripping the hand crank that operates the door. "Can't have you getting expelled on your last day. Not on my watch."

"Yes, ma'am," I say, mock saluting her. "Or should I say, Drill Sergeant?"

She bursts out in a raspy laugh. "Oh stars, don't push your luck. I'm a pussycat compared to them . . ." She trails off as her face darkens from the memories washing through her.

Suddenly, I regret saying that. Of course, I was just joking around.

But it was in bad taste. I know she enlisted, and I know she washed out and ended up in the Park, and I don't know anything else, mostly because she refuses to talk about it. But thankfully, she brightens back up, returning to herself as if snapping out of a bad dream.

"See you after school," she says. "Good luck with the Pairing today."

"Uh, thanks," I say, feeling the lump form in my throat. Before I can say anything else, the door slams shut with a hiss. As soon as my boot touches the curb, Harold pings me.

First Period. Mr. Egbert. California Federation History.

Another reason I won't miss school. I love my science classes, even if my grades don't reflect it, but everything else can ship out as far as I'm concerned. Don't get me started on English . . . or worse . . . math. All of a sudden, getting through today feels impossible.

Anxiety seizes me, gripping my heart like a vise. My eyes dart to the chain-link fence topped with barbed-wire sensors that encircles the campus. Even though it's my last day, I contemplate ditching school and crawling under the fence. I know where the weak spots are. I've skipped before. I could wander around my old neighborhood just for the stars of it.

The urge seizes ahold of me and won't let go, even though I know it's crazy. Why risk everything and jeopardize my enlistment over one measly day? But the thoughts keep tugging at me. *I could go on the run,* I think wildly. *Leave this all behind. Make a fast break for it.*

The bus and Xena roar off in a thick plume of exhaust, leaving me alone on the curb. The urge to flee tempts me, as the other kids ignore me and disperse toward the school's entrance. They mostly pretend like I'm invisible anyway. Nobody else around here cares about me.

Nobody would even miss me.

Except . . .

"Hikari Skye, don't you dare."

CHAPTER 2

KARI

I scan the area for her face, even though I'd recognize that voice with my eyes shut. *It's Rho.*

I spot her in the assigned parking lot. Rho lives in the nice part of town and has her own shiny, silver transport. She speed-walks toward me, tightening the straps on her overstuffed backpack. There's no need for real books anymore, but Rho loves them. Something about the feel and smell of the paper. Her flouncy, flowery dress contrasts with her fishnet stockings and knee-high pleather boots. Her shock of neon pink hair glistens, cascading down her back.

Suddenly, it shimmers and starts shifting colors to . . .

Red.

Her fiery eyes lock onto me. She recently got contacts to match her ever-shifting nano hair implants. The colors change depending on her mood. Red is . . . *angry.* I've spent enough time with her to decode it. Plus, she used my full name. That means she's onto me and my antics.

Now I can't ditch.

"Rhodiola . . . *Raven,*" I greet her with her full name when she reaches me, though it annoys her. It's a dose of her own medicine. "Aren't you just a burst of sunshine today—"

"Don't *sunshine* me," she shoots back. Her hair is fully red now, and it flames like the wrath lighting up her crimson eyes, almost giving her a demonic appearance.

"Uh, what do you mean?" I dig my toe into the sidewalk marred with old chewing gum.

She frowns. "I saw that *look* on your face."

I feign innocence. "Right, what look?"

"Ditching. You were gonna skip, weren't you?"

I can't deny it—especially not under her fiery gaze. Rho knows me too well. She's my best friend, well . . . aside from Bea. But sisters don't count. She's stuck with me.

"Not on the last day of school," she goes on, as we fall in together with the other kids streaming toward the school's entrance. The campus is made up of several concrete buildings linked by worn pathways probably older than the war. I won't miss it, that's for sure.

"If I've gotta tough it out," Rho goes on, "then so do you."

"Fine, but you're such a nerd. You love school. Admit it."

"Ugh, I know," she says, patting her overflowing backpack. I spot several thick books peeking out. "And I'm gonna miss it, too. But not as much as I'm going to miss you."

That hangs between us as we thrust open the double doors, feeling the blast of cool air and taking in the familiar smells—antiseptic cleaner, burnt rubber, dried sweat, and a whiff of old bubble gum. It's a special aroma caked into the old linoleum floors, busted metal lockers, and acoustic ceiling tiles. Her hair darkens to shimmery blue . . . I know what that means.

"Getting sentimental already?" I say, nudging her side.

"Don't rub it in," she says, swatting me back. "But yeah, I guess it's sinking in finally. I can't believe you're going to be a guardian. Just like you always dreamed . . ."

"And you're going to Berkeley . . . to continue your reign as top nerd."

She smirks. "I prefer *nerd-in-chief*. Thank you very much."

I can't help it. I laugh hard. But then we turn more serious. I can tell we're both thinking the same thing. It's hard to believe that it's our last day together.

Rho is the only friend who stuck by me after my family got evicted from the neighborhood. I won't miss school. Or the bus ride. Or my teachers. Or my homework.

But one thing is certain—I will miss the stars out of her.

She catches my eye with her blue gaze. "So . . . nervous about today?"

"You mean the Pairing Ceremony?" I say, feeling my urge to flee flare up. *Not now, Harold,* I think before he can ping me with another annoying appointment reminder.

"*Hikari Skye . . . your Sympathetic is . . .*" Rho intones like the announcer at the ceremony. She's trying to be funny and lighten the mood, but it still jolts me with anxiety.

"Ugh, don't remind me," I say, swallowing the bile down. I tick my symptoms off on my fingers. "Let's see . . . I feel like I might puke. Acid-in-back-of-throat situation. And I'm kind of dizzy. Even Bea's cookies made me feel queasy this morning. Does that mean I'm nervous?"

She frowns. "Pretty much the textbook definition."

"Okay, so yeah. Guess I'm nervous. Think you'll get paired?"

This is the big question on everyone's mind today. I feel it running through the hallways around us like an electric charge. Everyone seems jumpier than usual. For me, it's a sure thing. All recruits get paired with a Sympathetic back Earthside. But these days, fewer kids enlist than enroll in college or stay back home to work in the factories. So, not all of them get paired.

Regardless, attendance at the ceremony is mandatory for all seniors. And the results are announced live. Let's just say . . . it's a perfect recipe for massive bouts of angst.

"Well, a part of me hopes so," Rho says with a shrug. "I'd like to do my patriotic duty. And a part of me secretly hopes . . . I'll get paired with you." She shoots me another starless look. Her hair darkens bluer if that's possible. "But I know . . . the odds are against it."

While there's no rule about it, we both know it's unlikely. Pure math tells you as much, but it's more than that. Superstition, I guess. I'm not used to good things happening to me.

"Ah, look at you . . . still acting all gushy on me," I tease her back. "I like this midnight blue look on you. It suits you. And there's something else . . . it means you care."

"Shut the stars up," she says, sounding exasperated. Her hair and eyes flash bright pink again. *Feisty.* She's back to her normal self. "You tell anyone—and I'll kill you."

"Well, the Raiders and Proxies already have dibs," I say with a grin. "Oh, and maybe my drill sergeant from what I've heard. But I'll add you to the *Murder Kari* list." But then I soften my voice and add, "Also, just for the record . . . I'd love to get paired with you, too."

We both fall quiet. Our divergent life paths fill the space between us. We began in the same place, on the same oak-lined, shady street, but now we're destined for completely different lives in completely different places. I'm shipping out to space, while she goes to college. Can our friendship survive that? The awkward silence that hangs between us is answer enough.

Finally, she clears her throat.

"Space Force, huh? Think you'll run into any sexy Raiders up there?"

Space pirate jokes.

They might be in bad taste, but it's our thing. We both giggle at that thought.

Suddenly, the warning tone sounds. Harold also chimes in to remind me—I'm going to be late for class. Knowing my luck, I'm probably close to my implant giving me an electric shock.

"Hurry up, or we'll be marked tardy," I say, pulling her through the crowded hallway.

It's packed with a rowdy mix of Park kids from the bus and Ringers from the parking lot. They don't want to be late either. And they don't mix. Park kids stick with Park kids, and Ringers stick with Ringers. That's how it goes. Rho and I are the exception to this unwritten social rule.

Suddenly, a cruel voice echoes down the hall.

"Hey, kid, watch your step."

I jerk my head over. Farther down by the lockers, I spot a commotion and hear jeering laughter. Through the tangle of bodies and backpacks, I zero in on the cause. Rho sees it, too.

"*Draeden Rache*," she whispers in disgust. "Blast him, why is he always such a prick?"

"Prick . . . to the extreme."

He's the worst of them—and that's saying a lot. I glare at his face. Dark skin, yet pale eyes and hair. A wide grin paints his face with that cocky confidence, the kind that comes from knowing that you've got a ticket to college and never have to enlist and fight for your life.

More commotion and metal banging from the lockers ricochet down the hall. Then I hear his sharp voice again. "Hey, kid, I'm talking to you! Whatcha hiding in your bag?"

The crowd thins a little, so I can see him clearly now. Drae and his crew are picking on a kid fresh out of middle school, from the looks of him. Drae shoves the skinny kid into a locker, while Jude and Loki sneer at him. The kid drops his backpack—and it spews out old comics, withered and dog-eared, but unmistakable. They land with a wet smack against the linoleum.

A sudden hush falls over the hall.

Shocked whispers ripple through the crowd.

"*Comics . . . Park kid . . . contraband . . .*"

The kid scrambles to shove the evidence back into his bag, but Drae snags them first. He passes them out to his asshole friends, then they start flipping roughly through the pages.

"Hey, where'd you get these?" Drae asks, shoving the kid again.

The locker rattles as his back thumps into it.

"My gramps . . . gave them to me," the kid stammers. Snot is running down his nose. His eyes are red. "Give 'em back. They're mine . . ."

Jude thumps the kid's chest. Unlike Drae, he's pasty pale with blond hair and icy blue eyes. He rips out a page, displaying a flash of red and gold. I recognize the plated body armor, long twisty braids, and twin-holstered golden blasters. My breath catches in my throat.

Wait, that kid's got *Estrella Luna* comics? How did he get those?

I've only heard rumors about the old, vintage comic book. But I've never actually seen a copy in real life. They're super rare and from the early days of Space Force.

"Park Rats can't have comics," Jude spits at the kid. His face twists up with hatred. He rips out another page and dangles it in the kid's face. "You stole 'em, didn't you?"

"No, my gramps . . . they belonged to him," the kid tries again. His upper lip trembles. "Please, I wasn't supposed to take them to school. But I wanted . . . to show my friends . . ."

I dig my fingernails into my backpack straps as I watch them from down the hall. *Not today*, I tell myself. I try to calm my racing heart. *You've got too much on the line. Don't do it. Don't do it. Don't do it.*

But then Drae glares at the kid.

"Hey, kid, you could get into real trouble for these," he says, while his crew starts disassembling the comics, tearing out the pages one by one, crumpling them up, and stomping on them. "Don't get upset . . . they're contraband for kids like you. We're just doing you a favor."

The kid starts to full-on sob now. Ugly sobbing full of snot and shame. He's only a little older than Bea. His body wracks with tears. I've had enough. I can't take it.

Blood pounds in my ears. Black spots dance in my vision. My body tenses up. I lurch toward them.

I feel Rho tug at my elbow. "No, they're not worth it!" she hisses in my ear. Her hair shimmers and turns fully white. Pure fear, I'm guessing. "You've got too much to lose—"

But I shake her off as the heat of anger crashes through me, pouring like molten lava from my heart and engulfing my body in a blazing inferno. I'll never forget what happened last year when Draeden . . . when he . . . tried to . . . in the hallway . . .

Yeah, I'm not thinking about that.

Ever.

Again.

I feel Rho grip my elbow harder, trying to pull me back.

"Kari, don't! You could damage your enlistment. Didn't you see the announcement on the newsfeeds? The secretary-general himself will be here for the Pairing Ceremony—"

But I push her off. There's a roaring sound in my ears that drowns everything out. *The shuffling of feet. The fidgeting of backpacks. The clanging of lockers. The shocked whispers.* It's like it gives me superpowers. Everything seems to move in slow motion, but somehow I fly across the hall at the speed of light. One second, I'm on one side of the hallway with Rho tugging on my arm, and the next I'm standing smack in between the kid and the bullies.

I snatch the comic—or what's left of it—from Drae's outstretched hand.

When our gazes lock, he looks stunned.

"Hey, coward," I snarl at him. "Why don't you pick on someone your own size?"

CHAPTER 3

DRAE

Stars, it's her, I think when Kari yanks the comic from my hands and tells me to blast off.

I stare at her in shock.

This isn't how it's supposed to go.

All year, I've been trying to talk to her. But she always walks the other way when she sees me coming in the halls. Won't meet my eyes. Avoids me like a bad case of the Pox. But ever since I laid eyes on her at the start of this semester, I've been mesmerized by her presence. Something about her had changed and felt . . . *different*. It was like she had absorbed all the space dust and grown into her own planet with a powerful gravitational field that sucked me in.

I was caught in her gravity, and there was nothing I could do about it. Most girls were thrilled if I expressed the tiniest hint of interest in them, or if my friends did . . . let alone kissed them. That's how it went when you were at the top of the social hierarchy. And we were the elite.

We had privilege—and we wielded it.

Our parents were important. They worked for the government in cushy government positions, and my mother was a decorated war hero. But the problem was . . . Kari was the only girl who I felt any attraction to now. I wasn't sure why it happened, how she sucked me into her orbit. I didn't know what to do. How could she pull me in like that, but also resist my charms?

So, I cornered her in the stairwell before third period and . . . well . . . tried to . . . *Kiss her*.

Yeah, that didn't go well.

I rub my jaw. She socked me so hard, it still clicks when I chew. *Entitled asshole.* Those were her exact words before her fist connected with my face. I can still remember how my vision blacked out and danced with starbursts—not the good, lovey kind; the passing out from a bad concussion kind. It was my fault, of course. I know that now . . . and my jaw does, too.

I shouldn't have done it, plain and simple. I was wrong—very, very wrong. The screwy thing is, most of the girls at school are dying for me to kiss them like that.

But Kari isn't like most girls. Trust me . . . I'd take it back if I could . . . but that's not how life works.

The past is like a scar.

A permanent one.

Especially in high school. That was two weeks ago. It's the last time we spoke.

Suddenly, her voice jolts me out of my thoughts.

"Hey, didn't you hear me?" Kari says. She glares at all three of us.

The halls fall silent, as if the sound was sucked into a black hole. Now everyone is watching us. Loki drops the comics and raises his fists like a boxer. He's ready to fight.

"Back off," he grunts at her. He's a big guy, built like a school bus. Kind of looks like one too, with reddish-blond hair and seemingly more freckles than there are stars in the sky. Plus, he's about a foot and a half taller than her with a longer reach. He dwarfs her petite frame.

Kari returns his glare. "Sure you wanna do this?"

Her voice doesn't waver, not even a little. Loki takes a step toward her, towering over her. But she squares her shoulders and sets her feet, getting into a proper fighting stance.

I glance from Loki back to her, feeling a rush of dread. "Loki, she's not messing around," I hiss in a low voice to him. "Didn't you hear me? It's time to let it go—"

But he takes another step toward her.

"You're gonna pay for this! Don't interfere with our business."

Meanwhile, Jude joins him and squares off against her, too. It's two against one now. They both outweigh her by at least one hundred and fifty pounds. She's out-matched in this fight. But before I can intervene and hold my friends back, Loki swings hard at her midsection.

It's a sucker punch, aimed to knock the wind out and take her down hard.

Everything happens lightning fast.

In two swift moves, Kari dodges the punch and flips Loki onto his stomach, stomping on his shoulder blades. He groans and stops struggling. Then she pivots and slams Jude into the locker with a loud *clang*, thrusting him into a tight headlock. She presses on his neck.

"Hey . . . lemme go . . ." Jude pants with red-faced fury.

But the headlock keeps him from reaching her or inflicting any real damage. She holds him still with seeming ease. *Where'd she learn to fight like that?*

"Hey, kid," Kari says, glancing down at the boy cowering a few feet over by his shredded comics. In the chaos, I'd almost forgotten about him. "What's your name?"

"Uh . . . Trevor," he says, glancing at Jude, who's stopped struggling in the head-lock. "From two trailers over. I know Bea . . . your sister. She's one grade below me."

"Trevor . . . from *two* trailers over," Kari repeats. "Grab your comics and scram. Got it? They're contraband. You know what the teachers will do if they catch you?"

The kid doesn't need to be told twice. He scrambles around, shoving the deci-mated comics back into his backpack, and then sprints away. The squeaking of his sneakers fades out as he vanishes into the crowd. The volume seems to rise in the halls to gossip level.

Only then does Kari release Jude.

He reels away, gasping for breath and clawing at his neck. Angry, red streaks mark his pale skin. But he hasn't learned his lesson yet. And worse, she humiliated him. I've known him my whole life. We grew up next door to each other. I've seen him in all kinds of intense situations—losing games, explosive fights with his parents, fallings-out with friends, the usual teen stuff. But I've never seen him look the way he does now . . . just short of murderous.

He spits at her, narrowing his eyes.

"You're gonna pay for this! You're . . . *deserter spawn.*"

A soft gasp escapes her lips, as Kari staggers back as if someone punched her in the gut. The hallway falls silent—too silent—eerily silent from the shock of that awful slur.

"Jude, that's enough!" I react like a bullet and grab his jacket, feeling the costly faux suede crinkle under my fingers. "You went *too* far this time. You owe her an apology—"

"Are you crazy? She's a . . . well, you know what she is . . ." he sputters. "She doesn't care about that kid. She's just looking to cause trouble. That's how *they* all are—"

"No, I don't know," I say, feeling furious at him, but also at myself for having gotten involved in the first place and picking on that kid. "And you crossed a major line."

That's the *worst* thing you can call someone in our world. Even if it's true. That's why Kari's family got evicted and relocated to the Park. But we're not supposed to say it out loud.

It's like some unspoken rule.

I glance over and catch Kari giving me a strange look—*a mix of confusion and surprise*—but then her face hardens back into her usual steely mask. She wipes the sweat from her brow, then squares her stance and raises her fists again. She glares back at him.

"Let him go—I can fight my own battles."

"Ha, bring it," Jude says, twisting out of my grip and turning to face her.

Right when they're about to brawl again—*and really, it's Jude I'm worried about this time*—an angry voice reverberates through the hall. Everyone clams up instantly.

"What in the blazes is going on here?"

I recognize that nasal voice. That's Mr. Egbert.

My first period teacher. He marches out of his classroom, looking incensed. He's short and squat with a bushy mustache specked with gray. He wears the usual boring teacher uniform of a blazer, slacks, and button-down shirt, only he sports a silly bowtie with ducks on it.

His eyes flash over the hall. The students part quickly to let him through. His eyes pass over us—me, Jude, and Lokl—and land on Kari.

They narrow.

"Kari, causing trouble again?"

"No, sir," she says, looking down. "It wasn't my fault."

"May I remind you . . ." His mustache has a funny way of making his voice sound nasal and high-pitched. "This isn't your first *incident* this school year."

Her cheeks flush with shame. She speaks in a low voice. "I know, sir. But I swear, this wasn't my fault. They started it—"

"Good kids like this?" Mr. Egbert cuts her off. "From nice families? I highly doubt it."

Defiance flashes in her eyes, replacing the fear.

"But, sir, it's the truth—they started it."

That's when Jude and Loki step in.

"Sir, she's a liar!" Jude bursts out. He makes his voice tremble. "Look at these marks on my neck. She's unstable—a total menace. Seriously, she could've killed me."

"Yeah, you should expel her already," Loki chimes in. They both do their best impressions of being terrified, though I can tell it's an act and they're faking it.

Mr. Egbert looks exasperated. He tugs at his mustache. His ill-fitting blazer pulls against his paunchy midsection. "And exactly what were they doing . . . *to start it* . . . as you claim?"

Kari opens her mouth to defend herself, but then snaps it shut. I realize the reason right away. She doesn't want to rat that poor kid out. For having contraband comics. We're allowed to possess comics and other valuable reading material, but they're forbidden for Park residents.

Like this poor kid.

I'm about to say something, take the blame, betray my friends—but she beats me to it.

"*Nothing*," Kari says in a small voice. It catches in her throat. "Sir, you're right . . . it was my fault. I started it . . . I'm sorry . . . I don't know *what* came over me . . ."

I catch her sarcasm on that last part. She can't help it.

"That's what I thought," Mr. Egbert says in a triumphant voice, while Loki and Jude smirk that their ruse worked. "I should report you to the principal—"

"Sir, please don't," she says. Her eyes search his face. "I'm sorry . . . I don't know what happened. Probably nerves over shipping out . . . they warned me at my orientation."

Mr. Egbert still looks irate, but then he softens.

He lets out a measured sigh. "Right, nerves are perfectly normal before shipping out. I remember them, too." He tugs at his mustache, thinking it over. "Look, I'll let it go this one time. I won't report you to Mr. Rigby. But you're on thin ice. Is that understood?"

"Yes, sir," she says. "And thank you—"

"Don't thank me—just get into my classroom. You're about to be tardy, in addition to starting this mess." He turns his irate gaze on the kids loitering in the hall. "Why does the last day of school bring out the worst in my students? All of you, get to your first periods. Now."

His voice is more effective than the final bell.

The crowd starts to disperse as students stream into their classrooms. The squeaking of sneakers and chattering of voices die down. The girl with the mood hair rushes over to check on Kari. I recognize her, though we're not friends. She lives a few streets over from me.

They both head to their classes, vanishing into the crowd.

Jude and Loki follow the flow. We're in the same first period. So is Kari, but her friend with the hair has a different class. Probably because she's the top student at school. I notice—*not without a small amount of satisfaction*—that my friends are both limping a little bit.

Kari took down two of the biggest kids like it was no big deal.

How'd she do that?

Jude turns back and waves for me to follow them. But Mr. Egbert catches me.

"Draeden, you're better than this," he says in a low voice. "I expect that sort of behavior from kids like her. But not someone like you. Now, what would your mother think?"

My mother. *The war hero*. Deep sigh.

Everyone knows my mother. Lompoc is a small town. She's practically a celebrity around here. If only he knew what it was *really* like to be in my family. But I push that thought away as always, burying it deep. Just like nobody believed Kari, nobody would believe me either.

We have that in common.

"Sir, my mother wouldn't be very pleased with my behavior today," I say on autopilot. I make my voice sound contrite. He claps my shoulder, giving me a warm smile.

"Son, it's not your fault," he says, ushering me into his classroom as the final bell sounds. "I've got your back. Your mother was in my platoon. Took blasts for my buddy in that horrible Raider attack. I'll never forget her sacrifice . . . blood and stars, as the saying goes. Right?"

I want to shrink down. Vanish. Dematerialize. If I could have a superpower, like in that kid's comics, then it would be . . . *invisibility.*

"Thank you, sir," I say out loud. But inwardly, I'm cringing. The urge to disappear is so strong that it consumes me. "I appreciate that. I'll let her know what you said."

"Good kid," Mr. Egbert says with an approving nod. "Now get to your desk. We've got a lot of important material to cover today. Federation History isn't going to teach itself."

Mr. Egbert drones on about "how we rose from the ashes after the Great War, forming from parts of the United States and the western edge of Canada." Or what was left to them, to be more accurate. Large swaths of Earth remain radioactive, uninhabitable wastelands. He's recapping the most important lessons from the year—and it's more boring than watching paint dry.

A holographic map levitates in the front of the classroom, materializing out of thin air and displaying the outlines of the federation territories, slotted together like jigsaw puzzle pieces. Then it superimposes what Earth used to look like before . . . well . . . we blasted it to pieces.

"As you know, the Arctic used to be largely uninhabited," Mr. Egbert goes on, gesturing to the map. "But climate change and the melting icecaps changed all that. Now, a wealthy conglomerate controls the invaluable natural resources there—and many in space, too."

But no matter how hard I try, I can't pay attention for all the stars in the universe. I sit at my desk fidgeting around and tapping my foot, but my mind pings around like space debris flung out of gravitational orbit. It's not just the boring class. I keep hearing her voice in my head.

Hey, coward . . . why don't you pick on someone your own size?

My mind keeps replaying what happened over and over. I tap my foot harder. I shift behind my desk. I try to ignore the nagging voices in my head, but fail miserably.

"After the California Federation united together," Mr. Egbert drones on, gesturing to the map, "we signed the Peace Treatise to disarm Earth and deploy our military forces to space."

The 3D map morphs into footage of our Space Force ships rocketing into space, then shifts to our interstellar military occupation. Far-flung moon bases, enclosed cities, spindly space stations, our impressive fleet of ships zipping around with warp drives, headed for distant galaxies to expand our stellar realms and defend them from the Proxies and Raiders.

I shift around in my seat, trying to forget, trying not to feel anything. I tap my foot faster and faster. *Tap, tap, tap.* I wish I had some of my mother's meds to numb me, the ones the government prescribes for her. Not that she'd share them. They're too precious for that. She hoards them like candy. *Ugh, my mother.* Thinking about her definitely isn't helping.

I risk a glance at Kari two desks over. She looks just as miserable as me. Okay, maybe more miserable, now that I think about it. She hunches over her desk, looking smaller than the girl who just walloped both of my big friends in the hall. Her long hair sweeps down her back like a curtain. Her fingers doodle on her tablet, almost in rhythm with my thumping foot.

Where'd she learn to fight like that? I wonder again.

I study her face, secretly watching her, feeling my heart speed up and blood rush to my cheeks, as usual. She doesn't know it—but she's like my gravity. My axis tilts toward her, slightly off-center, whenever she's around, but always in her direction, orbiting around her like the most luminous red giant. Those types of stars have shorter lives, burning too bright, before they go supernova and destroy everything in their vicinity when they implode into black holes.

So yeah, I guess Kari is like my red giant.

But she's about to explode out of my life. This is our last day of school, and it's no secret that she enlisted. Her name is on the Pairing Ceremony roster that went out to all the seniors last week. And I'm bound for UC Berkeley like my friends, headed in a total other life trajectory, a privilege bestowed upon me by my parents and their military service.

My heart sinks. But then I remember, it doesn't matter. She hates my guts already. I totally blew it. Even if she were going to college with me, it's not like I'd have a shot of dating her, or even being her friend. Regardless, I want to do better and be better. Berkeley is my chance to start fresh and change my life. Make new friends. Do the right thing, for once.

But doubt seeps into my heart when I remember what happened earlier. Why can't I change my behavior? Why do I always revert to my old, bad ways? Especially when I'm around my jerky friends? And worse yet, why is it so often rewarded by teachers like Mr. Egbert?

The questions ping me like blaster fire. Regret eats away at me, as Mr. Egbert drones on about Raiders—deserters from Space Force who stayed up there and survive by raiding our supply lines. I shouldn't have bullied that kid today. I was the one who started it . . .

Trevor. From two trailers over.

I know his name now, thanks to Kari. Questions ricochet through my head, torturing me. Why did I mess with him in the first place? Why didn't I stop my friends when it started getting out of hand? Why did I rip up his comics? Why . . . why . . . why . . . why . . .

But I already know the answer.

And so does Kari.

That's right—I'm a coward.

The thought floods through my core being. I know it's true, and it kills me. Kari is right about me; I'm not good enough for her. And one thing is certain—I never will be.

CHAPTER 4

KARI

Recruits, line up by height to get your gowns!" barks the stern-faced guardian. He brandishes a tablet like it's a weapon, pointing us toward the tables where they're handing them out. He's wearing a Space Force dress uniform emblazoned with the usual military sigils and Space Force logo. It's only worn for special occasions—like today.

We're gathered backstage in the school auditorium. Of course, I've been here a million times before, usually bored to tears by some school proceeding, but everything feels different today, heightened, nerve-racking . . . and worst of all . . . permanent.

Pairings can't be annulled or changed.

Everyone knows this. I signed the scary-looking legal disclaimers before I took the Sympathetic Pairing Test—or SPT, for short—at school a few weeks ago.

On the other side of the curtain shrouding the stage, I hear muffled voices and footsteps, the slap of the folding chairs, as the rest of our class filters in and takes their seats.

My heart skips a beat as I listen—

One of them is my Sympathetic.

We haven't lined up fast enough, so the guardian is at us again.

"Hurry up, recruits!" he orders. But then he flashes us a conspiratorial grin and lowers his voice as if he's confiding something. "First *unofficial* rule of Space Force. Time is valuable, so don't waste it. Second rule—your drill sergeant won't be nearly this understanding."

Soft laughter ripples through us. I glance at the kids around me, wishing I'd tried harder to make friends. I recognize them, of course. But I feel awkward and like an outsider, as always.

"Hurry up—means *now!*" he barks again, all humor gone.

The laughter dies out instantly. We all jolt into action, moving quickly but chaotically, to identify which table best matches our height. I wonder if the lack of specificity is designed to unnerve us and force us to surrender to the system. But maybe I'm being paranoid.

I line up behind the "medium" table and receive navy blue robes emblazoned with the California Federation seal—a single red star shining down on a grizzly bear, even though they've been extinct for more than a century. I pull them over my head, donning the silly hat.

"Alphabetical order," the guardian orders. "Line up behind the curtain."

It's harder than it sounds and produces quite a bit more chaos, which invites more admonishments and deep sighs of disappointment from the guardian in charge of us.

"You're seniors, right? You do *know* the alphabet?"

I'd be tempted to laugh if I wasn't so anxious. I find my spot near the back of the line, then stuff my hand down into my pocket. My fingers stroke the crumbling remnants of cookies. Bea insisted that I take what we didn't scarf for breakfast. They're brittle in my pocket, but they make me smile anyway. They offer me comfort as we march toward the stage.

Real chocolate, I whisper to myself to calm my nerves.

We stand behind the red velvet curtain. Suddenly, the lights backstage dim, casting us into shadow. We wait in hushed silence. Nerves crackle through our ranks like electric shocks.

In front of me, a petite, curvy girl with curly brown hair and freckled cheeks named Genesis fidgets with her robes, trying to get them to drape properly over her sneakers.

She catches my eye. She knows me from third period.

Math. Ugh.

"You ready?" she whispers. "Getting paired, I mean? Or any of it, really?"

We've shared some classes and ridden the bus together, but we're not exactly friends, so I'm surprised that she's talking to me. It catches me off-guard, and I forget to respond.

"Nobody's ever ready," Percy cuts in, glancing back at us. He's a strapping kid from the nice side of town. He has sharp cheekbones and long, shiny black hair . . . soon to be buzzed off. "Same goes for Basic. They're going to break us down up there. That's the whole point."

"Well, if that's their goal," I say, noticing how we blend together now in a sea of navy blue robes. "This ceremony certainly works. Paired together, possibly with a stranger?"

"Yeah, like major trigger warning," Genesis says with a nervous laugh.

"Indeed, works like a charm," Percy agrees. He taps his temples. "Total head-screw, right? And what about these neural implants? Feels so crazy when they talk to you."

"*Harold*," I say without thinking. "Yeah, he's super annoying."

Annoying . . . I don't understand that command, my neural implant pipes up on command. I wince and think back harshly, *Mute, please! You're proving my point.* He obeys, thankfully.

Percy gives me a strange look, so I quickly add, "Oh, that's what I named my implant. Makes it easier whenever he bugs the crap out of me. Which is pretty much always."

"Harold?" Genesis says, swallowing another laugh.

I shrug. "First thing that came to mind. After I heard his voice. *Private Skye, you're late!*"

"Harold, the neural implant," Percy says with a smirk. "Ha, that has a nice ring to it." Then he lowers his voice and leans in. "Have you gotten the *shock* treatment yet?"

"Oh yeah," Genesis says, rubbing her neural implant jack on the back of her neck. "I got it yesterday when I was late to second period. No joke, it hurt like the blazing stars."

"You got that right," Percy says. "I was late to school. Learned my lesson. *The first unofficial rule of Space Force. Time is valuable—don't waste it,*" he parrots the guardian.

We struggle not to giggle, lest we draw the ire of the guardian. He parades past us, double-checking our names against his tablet, then continues to the front of the line.

"I heard if you ignore the first warning," Genesis whispers, once he's gone, "your implant will shock you so hard . . . you'll foam at the mouth and pass the stars out."

Percy nods sagely. "Oh yeah, you don't wanna push it."

"Asteroid fires," I curse, feeling my neck itch where the nub pokes out.

"Yup, best to accept it already. Harold runs your life now," Percy says in a sage voice. "It'll get more intense once we ship out. Bet you wished you picked a better name."

I shake my head. "Nah, I'll stick with Harold—"

"One-minute warning," the guardian calls out. "Recruits, get ready."

I feel the seconds ticking down, like my life is ticking away. The urge to run away hits me again, but I fight it and force my feet to shuffle forward behind Percy and Genesis. Abruptly, she bumps into Percy's back, jerking to a halt and making me step on her heels.

"Thirty seconds," the guardian announces.

My breath catches in my throat, and I think I might puke. My breathing turns short and jagged. Genesis glances back in concern, catching the petrified look on my face.

"Don't worry," she whispers. "Try to think positive. It might be someone you know," she adds hopefully. "A friend even . . . or maybe . . . it's a chance to make a new one."

I shake my head. "That's the crazy part. Nobody knows how the SPT or the algorithm work. Why do some kids get matched, and some don't? What makes a suitable Sympathetic?"

"Yup, another head-screw," Percy agrees. "It's all super hush-hush."

Before I can respond—or worry any further—the lights die out altogether, casting us into darkness, and a deep hush falls over the auditorium. Orchestral music swells over the loudspeakers. We fidget nervously, fiddling with our robes and shuffling our feet.

"Buckle up, recruits," Percy whispers in my ear, but then his voice is drowned out as the music grows louder. It's our national anthem—"All the Blazing Stars of California"—designed to make you stand up, place your hand over your heart, and feel a surge of patriotism for our federation. Automatically, we all put our hands on our chests, as we're trained to do so since birth.

That's when I see it—

Out of the corner of my eye.

Flashlights illuminate a path through the backstage area. The beams flick around, catching on our alphabetical line. A second later, a trim man in a tailored suit flanked by a cadre of guardians marches our way. Hushed whispers and gasps shudder down our ranks.

"Look . . . it's *him*," Genesis whispers in a breathless voice. "It's really him. I can't believe it. I didn't think he'd actually show up."

"Wow, never seen him in real life," Percy adds. "Only on the newsfeeds."

"Why did he come in person today?" I ask, sharing in their thrill.

"No idea, but it's highly unusual," Percy says. "Must be important though . . ."

We shut up as his procession passes, heading for the stage. I catch a whiff of expensive cologne and glimpse his thin, sculpted mustache and round, wire-rimmed spectacles refracting the bluish beams. Sure enough, it's Secretary-General Manual Icarus in the flesh.

For a brief moment, my nerves are blotted out by a singular feeling—*reverence*. I mean, I've watched him on the newsfeeds since I was a kid, where he's often speaking at grand military processions, but I've never been this close before. I could reach out and touch him.

But I don't.

I stand stock-still and watch as the velvet curtain sweeps aside—*whoosh*—and the spotlight shines down on him, and then the crowd bursts to their feet in jubilant applause.

Secretary-General Icarus waves mechanically and marches up to the podium, the spotlight hugging his every move. We watch from backstage, waiting for our moment under the glare, as the music drops away and a hush falls. Then, he leans into the microphone.

"The California Federation rose from the ashes of the Great War," he says in a deep voice, as a holographic image materializes behind him of Earth. Nuclear warheads sail through the air and explode, igniting large swathes of the planet in mushroom cloud explosions.

The holograph shifts to footage of the aftermath. Mass graves. Demolished buildings. Smoldering ruins doused in radiation. Whole cities leveled to dust. And then, the gathering in Beijing to sign the Earth Disarmament Peace Treatise and the old footage of our first secretary-general, Yaron Trantor. He's the reason we survived the war; he founded our federation.

With one great pen stroke, Trantor seals our fate in the famous archival footage. He looks directly into the camera with a serious expression on his grizzled, bearded face. Poking through the sleeve of his military uniform, I can see the robotic prosthesis that replaced his left arm.

"Earth is hereby disarmed," Trantor intones in his famous speech. "Our wars will now be fought in space. All we require is a sacrifice of blood and stars . . ."

The crowd cheers at the footage, drowning out his voice. We all tap our right hands twice over our hearts—our federation's official salute. At the podium, I notice that Icarus breaks into a sly, catlike grin. He's a pro and knows that he's got the crowd right where he wants them.

Why is he here? I wonder again. Usually someone beneath him but still important, like a war hero general, would conduct this ceremony. But I have a feeling we're about to find out.

"Thanks to Secretary-General Trantor, our great federation has remained peaceful on Earth more than a hundred years," Icarus speaks into podium. "Until this fateful day . . ."

That's when the footage abruptly shifts—to something else.

The patriotic music swells over newsfeed footage of a school bus of kids bursting into flames from an explosion. The burning bus plunges over the Golden Gate Bridge and plummets into the murky bay, extinguished by the waves and subsumed by their frigid depths.

Dead kids.

One bomb.

No survivors.

So much carnage.

"The first terrorist attack Earthside since the Peace Treatise," Icarus says in a mournful tone, punctuated by the staccato flickering of photographers from the newsfeeds.

Now I know why he's here. He's about to deliver an important message to the Proxies. I know from Military History it's called . . . *saber-rattling*. It's a psychological military strategy to flex your military prowess and intimidate your enemies. The press will capture it all.

"Make no mistake," he goes on in a commanding voice. "We will catch the terrorists responsible for this atrocity—and make them suffer. This is why we honor our Peace Treatise. This is why we fight our wars in the stars. To keep Earth safe from heinous attacks like this one. Those kids won't be forgotten—*and mark my words*—they will be avenged."

His voice echoes darkly through the auditorium, delivered with great hubris and gravitas. And it works. The cameras flash like fireworks, while raucous applause breaks out.

Everyone is on their feet.

It's brilliant strategy, too. Talking about dead kids to a fresh-faced batch of recruits for Space Force. I bet it plays nonstop on all the newsfeeds and delivers his message.

I find myself cheering along, wiping away tears. I didn't even realize how emotional I felt until I saw that footage and heard his words. It's one of the reasons I chose to enlist, and I've heard I'm not alone. Recruitment numbers had been flagging, but they're back up now.

Once the applause quiets, Icarus shifts his gaze to us.

The fresh-faced batch of recruits.

"Thank you to those who enlisted," he says, tapping his heart twice. "Your sacrifice keeps Earthside safe from the Proxies. We are here to honor your commitment today."

On that cue, the holograph shifts to a state-sanctioned info blast about the Sympathetic Program. I've seen it before, but today it hits different—because it hits home. Basically, in the early days of Space Force, many guardians struggled with the isolation and long tours of duty. This resulted in high levels of desertion. But even soldiers who didn't desert had trouble readjusting to Earthside after returning home—or *recalibrating,* as our government delicately calls it. Space trauma became a serious epidemic. Hence, the reason we're here today—

The Sympathetic Program.

Now when you enlist, you're paired with a civilian tasked with keeping in touch with you and helping you stay oriented to Earthside. Kind of like a glorified pen pal from back in the old days, when civilians wrote letters to soldiers who were deployed during wartime.

We both get neural implants, but here's the important part. The communications aren't like regular messaging. Due to the great distances of space, we've had to revert to a hard mail system called warp mail. We have a whole Space Force Postal Service and fleets of mail ships. It all sounds quite technical and a smidge boring. But essentially, it boils down to this . . .

You're paired with a potential stranger, then forced to share your deepest, darkest, innermost thoughts, secrets, fears, insecurities—all uploaded by your implant and transmitted to your Sympathetic, every week. Then, they record and transmit a response for you. The neural link means you don't just hear their words, you actually experience everything they're experiencing. And vice versa. Like texting times a million. Plus, angst and humiliation.

Sounds pretty horrifying, right?

Especially if you're me and prefer to stuff everything down and pretend it doesn't exist until you explode and want to punch something, anything . . . just to make your feelings go away.

Right when I'm considering backing out, no matter what the cost, the official info blast finishes—and the lights flood up suddenly. I flinch, blinking at the sudden stark clarity.

"Now for the first Pairing," Icarus says. "Delia Atlas, please step forward."

His voice booms out as a hush falls over the auditorium. The first recruit in line steps onto stage under the spotlight, staggering a bit from the intensity and shock of it all, and then Icarus announces their Sympathetic. "Your Sympathetic is . . . *Lyla Walters.*"

A girl screeches in the crowd, then rushes onto the stage to greet the recruit. Vaguely, I recognize the girls, but we didn't have the same classes. They're quickly swept offstage.

My heart thuds faster. I scan the crowd, searching the expectant faces. Finally, I catch a glimpse of Rho as the lights flare over the audience. She's sitting in the back row. Her hair is ghostly white—*nervous white*—matching her wraithlike eyes. She's worried about me.

Inching forward as each pair is announced, I remember what Genesis said. *You could get paired with someone you know.* That hopeful idea is so unlike me that I want to dismiss it. Good things don't happen to kids like me. But maybe—*just this one time*—fate will smile at me.

It's not impossible, right?

I could get paired with Rho, I tell myself. It's happened before. It's not always a virtual stranger; it could be your best friend or next-door neighbor. Mystery shrouds the program. Nobody knows exactly how the algorithm works, or why certain people get paired together.

Then it hits me . . . *Of course I'll get paired with Rho.* It's the only thing in this stars-forsaken universe that makes any sense. She has to be my Sympathetic, right?

I tick through all the reasons in my head, as we keep creeping forward toward the podium. *Reason number one.* She's my best friend. I don't get along with anyone else. We're total opposites, yet somehow we meld together in this strange alchemy. *Reason number two.* She always keeps me on track, even when I want to do something bad like ditch school. *Reason number three.* She knows me better than anyone else. Except for my sister, of course.

But unlike my sister, Rho is my friend by choice. She's always been there for me. It's her.

It has to be her.

Relief floods through me at the realization. I focus on Rho's face in the audience and how great it will be to keep in close contact, while I ship out to basic training, and she adjusts to college. Now I'm three kids back from the front. Percy is next, then Genesis . . .

Then . . .

Me.

My heart thumps faster, making my body tingle with adrenaline. *Remember, this is a good program*, I remind myself. It's designed to prevent what happened to my father.

"Percy Quan," the secretary-general says. "Please step forward."

He strides out, displaying confidence, making me wonder how he can appear so calm when I'm freaking out and want to jump out of my skin. Percy gets paired with a slim, gangly boy with stringy, blond hair named Rhode Watkins, who cheers and runs to the stage like he won a prize.

They embrace like old friends, pose for a photo op, then rush offstage in a flutter of gowns. Now I'm standing in position, while Genesis gets paired with a girl, Suzy Viola. She lives a few trailers over. I wouldn't mind a match like that, I think. They'd understand me at least.

That's my last thought before—

"Hikari Skye."

My name blasts out through the auditorium.

It's my turn.

My legs wobble and my heart stutters as I stumble up to the podium. The overhead spotlight blinds me. I blink in confusion. I want to hurl. My stomach lurches in protest.

Rhodiola Raven . . . Rhodiola Raven . . .

I think her name over and over, trying to wish it true, trying to manifest it into existence. The secretary-general taps on his tablet, revealing my match. This all probably takes mere seconds, but it feels like a lifetime. Or two. Or three. Time is relative when you go faster than light, but it feels relative right now, too. Finally, Icarus looks up and leans into the podium.

The auditorium falls silent, as if sucked into a black hole.

"Your Sympathetic is . . . *Draeden Rache.*"

CHAPTER 5

DRAE

I hear my name—then the spotlight hits me full blast.

The secretary-general's voice still rings in my ears. I struggle to process everything. This can't be happening. I'm supposed to make my way toward the stage, but instead, I freeze.

How in the blazing stars did we get paired? From the look on her face when they announced my name—shock that quickly morphed into pure disgust—I know Kari would agree with me. Applause rises around me like a high tide sloshing around and threatening to drown me. I need to move, but I'm stuck in place.

Jude and Loki look equally shocked when the spotlight finds me and my name reverberates through the auditorium. "You got paired with . . . *her*?" Jude jeers.

"Oh wow, my condolences," Loki adds, like it's some kind of sick joke. Then they both break into mocking laughter. Suddenly, it feels like the whole auditorium is laughing at me, even though it's just my dumb friends. And everybody else is cheering excitedly, as expected.

I want to run away, but I don't have a choice. Forcing my limbs to unfreeze, I stagger down the aisle and to the stage on weak knees chased by the applause, the oblivious crowd swayed to celebratory adoration by the patriotic music swelling through the auditorium.

She locks eyes with me—then grimaces—before forcing on a smile, kind of like a costume she has to wear. She strides rigidly across the stage to greet me. How does she make her feet move like that? I'm still stumbling forward, surprised I don't fall flat on my face.

Now what? Oh right, first I have to shake her hand. I reach out—it's stiff, unbending in my grip, but also cold and sweaty—and then we pose and force-smile for the cameras.

Flash. Flash. Flash.

Black spots dance in my vision; applause rocks my ears. I'm still disoriented from the shock, focused on remaining upright. Meanwhile, Kari stands as far from me as possible while we pose for the newsfeed cameras, as if I'm radioactive. The grin stretched across her lips more resembles a scowl, like she caught a whiff of something repugnant. And that putrid smell is . . .

Me.

The morning rushes through my head again, fresh as the moment it unfolded, full of shame, embarrassment, and regret. Well, if she hated me before, she certainly hates me now. Even so, my crush on her thumps my heart and flushes my cheeks. But despite that secret held tightly in my chest, I know this is terrible. The look on her face tells me as much.

Before I can get comfortable or process anything, we're rushed backstage and quickly separated to sign our official paperwork and sit through the program briefing, then I'm scheduled to get my neural implant installed before I leave for Berkeley tomorrow afternoon. Kari already has one, jacked into her neck shortly after her enlistment. I know how it goes. My mom also has one since she's a veteran, though it's been deactivated since her medical discharge.

I go through the motions, but it all seems so surreal, like it's happening to someone else. I mean, I knew I could get paired. I had to take the SPT, along with all the seniors. But somehow, I felt I'd slide through. And never in a million light-years did I imagine it would be with . . .

Her.

The rest of the ceremony and proceedings remains a blur broken up by awkward moments—changing into a gown, shaking the secretary-general's hand, posing for a staged picture with Kari and the other recruits and their new Sympathetics. The cameras' staccato flashes blinding me again. My friends don't get paired, skating through without attention. That doesn't shock me, even though how the test works remains a closely guarded secret.

There are more seniors than recruits, so only part of our class receives this "great honor," as Secretary-General Icarus calls it when he congratulates us privately backstage afterward (though I notice a few newsfeed reporters and photographers still covering the proceedings). Then he's quickly escorted away by his entourage, while we're left to . . . mingle.

Yeah, it sounds as horrible as it is. It's worse than a middle school dance, when we all stood on opposite sides of the gym, pretending not to notice each other. Kari knows she has to behave. There are guardians and federation officials everywhere. She has a lot on the line. We both do now. But from the jumpy expression on her face, I can tell she wants to bolt.

At least, we have something in common, I think ruefully.

"Uh, I'm sorry . . . about that kid earlier . . ." I tell her while we're standing uneasily close, though still a few feet apart, as the last vestiges of the ceremony wind down. The crowd disperses from the auditorium, leaving the Sympathetics. I want to apologize for more.

For the kiss.

For getting paired with her.

For my entire existence on this planetary realm.

But I can't form the words on my lips. Instead, I look down and swallow my feelings, going through the motions like I've been doing my whole life. That's when Kari grabs my arm. Her fingernails dig sharply into my skin, while her smoldering eyes grab my gaze.

My heart leaps—maybe this is going be the moment she forgives me, and we can move forward to build our Sympathetic relationship. But then a scowl twists up her face.

"For the record, just because we're paired and about to share a neural link," she says in a low voice, careful not to be overheard, "doesn't mean we're friends now. Got it?"

That's not what I want to hear, but I cover my disappointment.

"Just Sympathetics?" I say, feigning indifference.

I try flashing my trademark smile, complete with dimples. It usually charms . . . well . . . everyone. But it only makes her scowl deeper. And look like she wants to punch me.

In the face.

Again.

"Exactly, because we don't have a choice," she says, tugging at her baggy robes. "This wasn't my choice—and I'm pretty sure it wasn't yours either. But we're stuck together, right? This program is . . . *mandatory*. But don't get any ideas or think I'm going to start liking you."

"Agreed," I say, dropping the stupid smile. It was only making things worse. "Just Sympathetics. Not friends. Not even acquaintances. More like . . . uh . . . coworkers?"

She looks relieved at that. Better yet, less likely to punch me. Though it's the total opposite of how I really feel. But none of that matters now. She despises me . . . period.

"Great, glad we cleared that up," she says with a stiff nod.

We lapse into uncomfortable silence, despite the official brochure they handed us encouraging us to "bond." Meanwhile, the other pairs are chattering happily, if a bit awkwardly, exchanging pleasantries and getting to know each other, under the careful watch of the guardian in charge. I spot Percy Quan from my fifth period bro-hugging his new Sympathetic like they're already best friends. In short, they don't appear dysfunctional . . . the polar opposite of us.

"Asteroid fires, this can't be happening . . ." she mutters under her breath, still coming to terms with it. "It's a total nightmare. Please tell me I'm going to wake up any second . . ."

"Uh, need me to pinch you?" I quip, trying to lighten the mood.

"Touch me ever again," she snaps back. "And you're . . . *dead.*"

"And I thought you had the dangerous assignment," I try joking back, but realize my mistake. She's completely serious. I remember her trouncing my friends earlier today. "You're right," I backpedal. "This is a disaster. They must have made some kind of mistake . . ."

"Exactly!" She shakes her head in dismay. "But that's the problem. They don't make . . . *mistakes*. This program is the core of Space Force. Worse, it can't be annulled or changed."

"Well, maybe we can convince them to make an exception," I say, trying to find a way to make everything better. "You never know, crazier things have happened—"

"Not a chance," she cuts me off. "You're used to getting exceptions. But I know how the real world works. Trust me, I already signed my life away to Space Force. This is irrevocable."

Her words hang in the air with finality.

We both know it's true—*we're stuck with each other*—for the rest of her military career. While that could span two tours, which is eight years total, it could also occupy a lifetime. That's kind of the point. I'm supposed to be there for her no matter what unfolds, something she always can count on, while she makes this sacrifice and risks her life to keep our federation safe.

"Five-minute warning," the guardian announces. "Say your farewells . . . for now. But don't worry. Once your Sympathetic arrives at basic training in a few days, the program will commence. And then, you'll have plenty of time to bond on a . . . *much deeper level*."

Good-natured laughter ripples through our little group. But Kari and I both wince, like we're awaiting a death sentence. That's when we have to begin our Sympathetic exchanges.

"That's right," the guardian goes on with a knowing look. "From personal experience, I know that those exchanges are life-changing—and a lifeline for our guardians. So, start wrapping it up now. You'll have plenty of time to bare your souls to each other in the near future."

Everyone starts to say their farewells, while we stand there staring at each other awkwardly. The tension ripples between us like static electricity. This is the last time I'll see her in person before she ships out, and I head for Berkeley. I heard somewhere that back before the war, kids got whole summers off after graduation. But that hasn't happened in generations.

"Remember our agreement?" Kari says, instead of farewell.

"Just coworkers," I reply in a formal voice. "Who don't really like each other."

She nods, thinking it over. "But we have to communicate?"

"Exactly," I say, then quickly add, "but only because we don't have a choice."

We shake on it to seal our deal, as if that makes it any easier, and then the guardian orders us out of the auditorium. Her school bus is waiting for her, and my transport idles in the parking lot. The next time we speak, it will be through the program in a little over a week's time.

"Asteroid fires, this is the worst thing that's ever happened to me," she mutters as we pour toward the doors behind the other Pairings. "And trust me, that's saying a lot."

Before I can respond, she bolts through the exit like she's being released from space prison camp, leaving me in her gravitational field. I stay back, knowing better than to follow after her, or try to say anything else, though I wanted to wish her farewell, or good luck, or to stay safe up there, or some other cliché nonsense . . . or maybe all of the above.

I step out into the sweltering late afternoon heat. School lets out right on schedule with the bell. Boisterous students throng the pathways, ecstatic to be released from class. In the middle of the crowd, I can just make out Kari. She boards her bus with her long hair swishing behind her. I notice the grizzled-looking bus driver welcoming her aboard with a grin.

But Kari looks . . . despondent. *All thanks to me*, I think ruefully.

Tonight, we'll both be packing up for our futures. She ships out from Vandenberg tomorrow. The location of our basic training facility is a kept secret to protect it. But we both know the truth—it lies in the stars far, far away from here. And I'm headed up the coast to Berkeley. This morning, I thought this was the end of our story. I thought that she was about to blast off into space—and out of my life. But now I realize, this is only the beginning.

I should be excited, but it sinks my stomach and torpedoes my heart. That staged photo op with the other pairs was bad enough. The fake, plastic smile contorting her face still haunts me. I've seen what Kari looks like when she laughs—really and truly laughs. It's a rare occurrence that emanates from deep inside her belly, cascading across her cheeks and lighting up her eyes with joyous fire. I've been studying her for the last semester, secretly crushing on her, watching her in the halls, sneaking sideways glances her way during classes, wishing that she would turn that bright beam of a smile on me, that I could be the object of her core radiance.

She's my red giant—my center of gravity.

Even though she doesn't know it. My friends don't even know it. Oh, and my parents certainly don't know it. They'd never approve of her. Her family has a black mark on it.

You could say . . . this is my biggest secret.

But I was prepared to leave her behind, along with Lompoc and the rest of my life. But now, we're stuck together. I wish it felt like a good thing, and not some ghastly tragedy.

The way she looked at me before that photo? Well, there's no mistaking the disgust that lit up her eyes like starfire. Knowing the truth only makes it hurt that much worse—

She really does hate my guts.

And just like our Pairing, there's nothing I can do to change that.

CHAPTER 6

KARI

The military transport jerks to a halt in front of Vandenberg Space Force Base. The door pops open, while the guardian from our Pairing Ceremony climbs up the steps and announces—

"End of the line! Recruits, this is your cue to disembark."

What he doesn't say is . . . last stop before space.

I drag my sleeve across the window, taking in the massive air hangars with sleek spacecrafts being serviced and fueled, smooth runways crisscrossing the base, and military transports zipping around with armed guardians patrolling the premises. This is the main headquarters of Space Force, and it shows. Everything looks pristine and high-tech.

I also spot the makeshift stage erected on the tarmac for our shipping-out ceremony, complete with the California Federation flag draped behind it. There's also a wood-paneled podium waiting for our officiant. It still doesn't feel real.

But it's happening—and it's happening soon.

I ship out today.

And I should be focused on that. And everything that lies ahead. But all I can think about is . . . *Draeden.* And the horror show that unfolded yesterday at our high school auditorium.

Draeden Rache is your Sympathetic, Harold chimes in helpfully.

Like I could've forgotten.

Mute, please, I think back with a wince. *You're not helping. You're making it worse.*

Thankfully, he falls silent. For now. The shock of our Pairing hasn't worn off. If anything, it's only grown worse. For the millionth time, I wish there was a way to change it, or better yet, annul it. But like most things in my life, it's not fair, and there's nothing I can do about it.

My only consolation is that he seemed equally horrified.

On that dour thought, I heft my rucksack over my shoulder and lug my way off the transport and across the sweltering tarmac over to the check-in table. Guardians armed with tablets mark us down. As I take it all in, I feel a jolt of adrenaline chased by a shot of fear.

One recruit—a stout boy with a blond buzz cut—gets upset and tries to back out, but the guardians quickly change his mind, reminding him about the contract he signed and his Oaths of Enlistment. Backing out sends him to one destination . . . space prison camp.

He's still whimpering, but he stays put. Regardless, it's a somber reminder.

I keep my head down and try to quiet my churning thoughts. But they rebel and want to think about . . . *Draeden* . . . of course. Sometimes I hate myself and my psychotic brain.

After we check in, we're herded onto the makeshift stage with the other recruits shipping out today. Farther down the line, I spot Genesis and Percy. Reporters hurl questions from the roped-off press pool, while cameras flash, fishing for juicy, patriotic stories for the newsfeeds.

"Private Skye, what's it like to get paired with your old neighbor?" shouts a reporter with red lipstick and a large microphone thrust at me. She squirms my way, jostling for position.

More reporters yell questions.

"Private Skye, do you miss him already?"

"Excited for your first exchange?"

Flashbulbs pulse faster, blinding me. They all clamor around the stage now, surging en masse, trying to get closer to me. I flinch back, shocked by the sudden attention lobbed my way. More questions shoot out, along with camera lenses, flashing and recording my every move.

"Glad your family's moving back there?" another reporter asks.

"How'd you feel when they called out his name in the Pairing Ceremony?"

The questions keep coming rapid-fire. They're all asking about . . . *Draeden*. My heart plummets in my chest. Somehow, they've picked up on the story about my family's eviction, and how I used to live in the same neighborhood as my Sympathetic and his family.

"His mother is one of our greatest heroes," shouts the red lipstick reporter, not giving up. "Aren't you thrilled to be paired with someone from such a patriotic family?"

All I can do is force a smile, hating myself for doing it. Words escape me in moments like these. But thoughts assault my brain. I want to tell them—*No, I am not happy about our Pairing, thank you very much.* Oh, and add in a nice little bit about how *he's a cowardly jerkface and tried to kiss me without consent. How would his famous war hero mother feel about that?*

But Genesis saves me from myself.

"Oh, it's an honor for Kari to be paired with such a wonderful Sympathetic," she jumps in, after exchanging a worried look with Percy. "As you know, the Sympathetic Program is the backbone of Space Force. We're all thrilled with the quality of our official Pairings."

"Skye, look over here," a photographer yells, desperate for a better shot.

"Lean in closer," yells another one, shoving the first one aside.

Just then, an armored transport *whooshes* into the parking lot, breaking off their interrogation. I breathe a sigh of relief as all the attention shifts in the other direction. Percy and Genesis wriggle their way over to my side. *Thanks,* I mouth to her with a grimace.

Don't mention it, she mouths back.

The armored transport glides soundlessly up to the stage. Blue-and-yellow California Federation flags adorn the tinted windows. It's about twice as long as a normal Ringer transport.

Everyone's watching the transport now—the press, the photographers, the Space Force bigwigs who have wandered down from their offices, all awaiting what comes next. Our federation's national anthem blares out from the speakers propped up next to the stage.

"Whoa, looks like it's showtime," Percy says.

When the orchestral music reaches its peak emotional impact, two guardians in dress uniforms with white gloves rush over to the special transport and open the door—

Out steps Secretary-General Icarus.

He's been on a full-blown press tour the last few days, starting with our school's humble Pairing Ceremony. The recruits around me burst into applause, drowning out the blaring music. I've heard whispers that enlistment numbers are down, so he's trying to drum up support.

The secretary-general climbs to the stage and reaches the podium, unleashing a shriek of microphone feedback. So many technological advancements, yet they can't fix some things.

He launches into his speech.

"We are gathered here today to celebrate these recruits as they embark on the next phase of their lives," he says in a commanding voice. Flashbulbs go off on cue. "First, I want to honor your families for producing such a fine bunch of guardians— and handing them over to us."

A smattering of laughter from us this time.

"Also, I want to acknowledge your Sympathetics for stepping up when called upon to serve our great federation," he continues, sweeping his eyes over the crowd. "This program has become the bedrock of Space Force and vital to our continued peaceful existence on Earth—"

Suddenly, he's interrupted as a man in the crowd charges the podium, screaming.

"Liar, you're a filthy liar!"

The guardians in his security detail attempt to tackle the protester, but he's slippery—maybe even trained—and he evades them. He has a patchy beard and stringy hair that hides his face. He tears off his shirt, revealing a message scrawled on his chest . . . in blood.

No , , , not scrawled . . . *carved.*

The wounds look fresh.

DISARM THE STARS!

"Our federation isn't peaceful," he shrieks, wheeling around so the crowd can see his chest with its bloody message. "Don't listen to him. He's a filthy liar. Disarm the stars! Long live the Resistance!"

He jerks his head around. His wild eyes lock onto my face and widen. Without warning, he lurches onto the stage. He grabs my wrist, clenching it tight. He's so close that I can smell his putrid breath, slick with whiskey stink. His fists are bloody. I'm so surprised by all of it—*the disruption, the protester, but most of all the attention*—that I completely freeze.

"You're fighting for a lie!" the protester rasps in my ear. "I saw you on the news-feeds. They're using you . . . be careful . . . can't trust anyone—"

Suddenly, Percy and Genesis are right there.

"Leave her alone," she says, pulling me away from his ironclad grasp, while Percy lunges in front of me. He shields me with his large body—and shoves the deranged man back hard.

But the protester leaps off the stage, landing in a crouch. He's so agile that I wonder again if he's military trained. "Disarm the stars!" he shrieks as the guardians finally tackle him, yanking his hands behind his back. "It's a filthy lie . . . kids are still dying up there—"

One of the soldiers finally gets a gag over his mouth. They cinch his wrists behind his back with electronic restraints. He's still writhing around on the ground, but his cries have become muffled. Meanwhile, the reporters and bigwigs have scattered. Secretary-General Icarus has also disappeared in the chaos. They probably rushed him away for his safety.

Over by the check-in tables, I spot the military police confiscating camera equipment from the reporters, taking out their digital chips and erasing their tablets. The reporters don't object. They have to hand everything over . . . it's for the good of our federation.

"Hey, you okay?" Genesis asks, now that the threat has passed.

We watch the military police load the gagged and bound protester into an armored transport. He still struggles and tries to escape, but they force him inside and zoom away.

"Yup, I'm fine . . ." I say, flexing my wrist where he grabbed me.

Angry, red streaks mark my forearm, but they're superficial. I've had far worse from tussling in the back alleys. I'm more embarrassed by it than anything else. And all the attention from my new friends. I'm not used to anyone caring. Well, except for Rho and my family.

Percy shoots me a concerned look.

"That guy was scary," he says. "Did you see his chest?"

That hits us all hard. The jagged letters. How he probably did that to himself.

"Think he's military?" I ask, swallowing hard and looking down at my wrist. "Did you see the way he moved and evaded those guardians?"

"*Ex-military*," Percy cuts in. "Bad case of space trauma."

"Probably from before we had Sympathetics," Genesis adds. She watches the armored transport vanish from our view with him on board. "Well, I hope he gets the help he needs."

"Good thing he wasn't armed," I say, with a sick feeling in my gut. "I heard, back in the day, they used to shoot up crowds . . ." I fall silent. We all know this dark history.

Everything that passes after that passes quickly. I don't know if it's the adrenaline and shock from the protester—I didn't even know they existed anymore since Secretary-General Icarus clamped down on dissenters—or just the reality of shipping out. Or maybe, they run it faster to gloss over the incident. Regardless, the events come at me in staccato bursts, almost like the flashes from the cameras. The press packs up their equipment and leaves the airfield.

Now, it's just us recruits left.

Oh, and also our ride.

The shuttle emerges from the hangar in all its sleek, mechanical glory with *Stargazer* painted across the hull. The ship is a feat of engineering loaded with all the latest tech, including warp drives that can take us interstellar, though we still don't know where we're headed for basic training—if it's in our solar system, or somewhere in distant galaxies. I know it's a machine, but something about the spacecraft feels kinetic . . . and almost like it's alive.

Guardians load our rucksacks onto conveyer belts, then herd us up the gangplank. I watch my bag as it's whisked away and dumped into the ship's cargo hold, feeling misty-eyed. It contains everything I own that complied with the strict packing list. It's not much. I shoved my belongings in this morning in a last-minute packing binge, then wished Bea and Ma tearful goodbyes. I thought Ma was going to miss it, but she got home from the night shift just in time.

"No crying," I remember telling them as the military transport glided up to the dilapidated Park bus stop. I set my rucksack on the rusted bench and turned back to their tear-stained faces anyway. "Now, you're going to make me cry, too. And I've gotta be strong to get through today."

"Can't help it," Ma said with another wet sniffle. Her face looked tired and prematurely aged, but her eyes remained bright and alert. Her cropped, dark hair was wrapped in a colorful scarf, her usual embellishment, while her coveralls were stained with cleaning chemicals and bleach. But the smell brought me comfort. I mussed Bea's unkempt hair, always a lost cause.

"Take care of her, you little pyro. Don't burn the trailer down."

And just like that, it was time to go. I tried to stifle my tears, but some insisted on leaking out anyway, staining my cheeks as the transport carried me away from my only family.

But I don't have time to dwell on that. I did this for them.

I'm about to blast off.

With that thought, I snap out of my memory. I cast one glance at my boots still standing firmly on Earth—the last time that will happen for four years—then I board our ship. Breathing in the recirculated, chilled air of the cabin, I realize my life is never going to be the same again. The cabin is outfitted with high-tech sling chairs, waiting for us. They're essentially fancy seats with built-in give. They're also cushioned with a special gel to withstand the acceleration. They're supposed to make you more comfortable, while your body slingshots through warp.

I claim one in the second row with a good window view. Despite my excitement, a few things still nag at me. Secretary-General Icarus never reappeared to send us off. It's probably a safety protocol. He's too important to the federation. But still, it bothers me. Also, something else . . . the way they confiscated the reporters' equipment to hide what happened today.

I'm sure they had a good reason. The secretary-general probably doesn't want to look weak in front of the Proxies. The protester almost reaching him . . . well . . . it looks bad.

But there's something else I can't seem to shake. I look down at the angry, red marks on my wrist, as I flash back to that moment when the protester lurched onto the stage and grabbed me. All I can think is . . . why did I freeze like that? Why didn't I fight back?

I just hesitated for a second, I reassure myself. *That's all.*

But I keep wrestling with myself, even as I buckle my harness and settle into my sling chair, feeling the gel mold to my spine and cushion me. Even as the cabin door shuts with a great sucking of air that pops my eardrums. Even as the engines roar to life, shaking the whole cabin and drawing excited gasps from the recruits strapped into their sling chairs around me.

"Wow, it's really happening," Genesis says in a jittery voice. She's sitting next to me, while Percy is on her other side across the aisle. "Can you believe it?"

"Of course—I can believe it," Percy cuts in, leaning across the aisle and flashing us both a cocky grin. "This is what we signed up for, remember?"

Genesis rolls her eyes. "Sarcasm, really? Please, like you've been to space?"

"*I've only blasted off in my dreams,*" he sings softly, from the hit song by Zelda Fitzgerald and the Starliners. "*But dreams can be real—if only you believe in the stars.*"

That makes Genesis swat him playfully. And he deserves it. But I notice something else underlying their interactions. *They're flirting*, I realize with a smirk. And it's kind of cute, yet foreign. I have no idea what it feels like to crush on someone like that, let alone want to flirt with them. If I have a superpower—it's repelling any potential suitors. Like the opposite of gravity.

That's what Rho always says jokingly.

I gesture to the window. "Any guesses where Basic is?"

"They haven't told us yet—for good reason," Percy says, tightening his harness. His broad shoulders strain at the straps, while he sinks into the sling chair. "It's a federation secret, like the rest of our outposts and bases. Keeps them safe from the Proxies and Raiders."

Genesis scowls. "Yeah, but you got a guess?"

"Look, we shouldn't even be talking about this," Percy says, lowering his voice. "NTKB—*need to know basis*. They'll tell us when it's time. Better not to ask questions, or you won't last long." With that, he busies himself by double-checking his chair's settings.

"Ugh, he's such a stick in the mud," Genesis complains, lowering her voice and flashing me an exaggerated pout. "Like lighten up already. I was only having a little fun."

I shoot her a conspiratorial smile. "Well, if you ask me . . . I bet it's a secret underground moon base," I say in a low voice. "Maybe even a forest moon—or a volcanic one."

She giggles, reminding me of how young we are. "I'm guessing . . . giant interstellar space station. Solar powered, like a whole floating city. Maybe even with a cantina bar."

We immediately fall silent as guardians parade down the aisles, checking our harnesses and handing out anti-nausea and sleep meds in little plastic cups. After making sure they're secure and we're properly medicated, they exit the cabin. A few minutes later, a deep shudder emanates through my sling chair as the shuttle begins to rocket down the long runway.

"Recruits, prepare for takeoff!" says that same voice via my neural implant.

Suddenly, I miss Genesis and her jokes. My thoughts drift back to that protester. How he grabbed my wrist. The deranged message carved into his flesh. His shrieks— *You're fighting for a lie . . . they're using you!* But on the upside, I guess it's better than obsessing over Draeden. That's when the ship rockets even faster, thrusting me back.

"3 . . . 2 . . . 1 . . ."

I hear the countdown in my head. Finally, the protester's screams—*Don't trust anyone!*—fade away in the propulsive rush of blastoff. My body slams back against my sling chair.

Genesis reaches over in a fit of panic, clutching for my hand. Her palm is sweaty, but I don't care. I squeeze back, but then we're thrown back harder. My vision shutters and vibrates, while my consciousness struggles to remain alert. Black stars dance in front of my eyes.

But then the gel shifts around my spine, transferring the kinetic force and softening the blow. Still, the rockets chatter my teeth and rattle my bones. My vision remains shaky, too.

But the real show is outside the window. I keep my eyes fixed on it, no matter what, as Vandenberg recedes into the distance, the ocean spreads below us like an endless blue expanse, and everything goes miniature. The buildings, the roads, the transports, the cities, and our federation grow smaller and smaller, then clouds and atmosphere envelop our shuttle and block out everything until we shoot out into a void so dark and vivid that I can barely breathe.

We tilt slightly, and then I see it—

Earth.

Blue-and-green puzzle pieces slotted together with white swirls clouding them, rotating under the unceasing, life-giving glare of the sun. Tears burst into my eyes unbidden. It's the most stunning, unreal, awe-inspiring thing I've ever seen. These words come to mind, but they don't do it justice. I've never felt so small and insignificant, yet so big at the same time.

Then I hear a stern female voice broadcasting from the bridge through my neural implant. "Recruits, hold on to your sling chairs! You're not in California anymore."

I feel mine tighten around my body as the warp drives kick in full force and we accelerate away from Earth, leaving it far behind in our space dust. Her voice echoes out again.

"Next stop—basic training."

PART 2

BASIC TRAINING

It is easy to love your friend, but sometimes
the hardest lesson to learn is to love your enemy.

—Sun Tzu, *The Art of War*

CHAPTER 7

KARI

Recruits, welcome to Ceres Base," I hear a female voice say via my neural implant. It jolts me from my deep, nightmare-ridden sleep, where a black hole sucks me in and crushes my body into nothing. I pop my eyes open with a gasp—confused and disoriented. Where am I?

"Home of the California Federation's basic training facility," the voice goes on in my head, rousing me further. "Arrival in T minus thirty minutes. Prepare for docking."

I wriggle upright in my sling chair, feeling the gel molded to my back. That must be what triggered the nightmare of getting crushed to death. Around the cabin, I count about twenty-five recruits. Percy and Genesis are the only ones from our school. I yawn and glance through the window. The blackness is so unfathomable, so velvety and deep, and as dark as my nightmare. My heart hammers faster as my mind struggles to comprehend this vastness, this emptiness.

"Sure messes with your head, doesn't it?"

I jerk around at the voice.

Instead of Genesis and Percy, two unfamiliar recruits occupy the sling chairs next to me—a boy and a girl. The voice belongs to the boy, who sits in the next seat with a dreamy look on his face. Meanwhile, the girl across the aisle has nodded off to sleep. I scan the cabin for Genesis and Percy. While I was out like the dead, they shifted up a few rows. Probably so they could sit closer. They're huddled together watching our ship's trajectory on a monitor.

The landing countdown ticks as we near our destination. Even with warp drives, space travel isn't instantaneous. It's still taken us over twenty-four hours to reach our destination.

"You can say that again," I say, still groggy and disoriented. "Ceres Base?"

"Yup, welcome to the asteroid belt," the boy confirms.

"Oh, that's right. Ceres is an asteroid," I say, trying to recall my astronomy classes. My thoughts swim toward me as if through a murky depth, while my tongue feels thick and clumsy.

He shakes his head. "Nah, more like a dwarf planet."

"Uh, that sounds made up."

"Well, it's all made up if you think about it. Someone had to discover it and name it, right?" he says thoughtfully. "Anyway, we left Mars in our warp dust a while ago. I don't know how everyone can *sleep* through this. It's the most remarkable thing we've ever experienced."

I study my new seatmate. He's scrawny and bony, with a pinched, rodent-like face and wistful gaze, while the girl next to him has lean muscles packed onto her sturdy frame. The boy looks diminutive in comparison. Aside from that, they appear nearly identical. They both have freckled faces and shockingly red flames of hair that remind me of struck matches.

"The God of War looked stunning through the viewfinder," the boy goes on in that dreamy way. "Sorry you missed it, sleepyhead. But don't worry. The asteroid belt is pretty incredible, too. Basically, a massive void with millions of asteroids between Mars and Jupiter."

He points to the window, but all I can see is intense darkness peppered with stars blanketing our ship. Behind us, solar sails unfurl to collect power and slow our approach.

"You're right. It looks like . . . *nothing*," I say, shivering a little at the emptiness.

"Yup, but that's precisely what makes it so cool," he says, perking up in his sling chair. "I mean, there's loads of mind-blowing stuff out here. The remnants of the early solar system."

"What do you mean?" I ask, struggling to understand.

"It's like looking back in time. These asteroids are the product of violent collisions, so instead of fusing together to form planets like Mars, the protoplanets shattered into millions of pieces. And well, these asteroids are all that's left from that extraordinary cosmic violence—"

"Anton, lay off the lame astronomy lesson," the girl next to him says, play-punching his shoulder. She's awake now and glares at him with her piercing sapphire eyes. He still winces from the jab. She didn't pull her punch fully. Then, she turns her intense gaze on me. "What my *little* brother here means is—welcome to the most depressing spot in the cosmos."

"Nadia, how can you say that?" Anton says with genuine dismay, pointing to what looks like a smaller version of Earth's moon that looms closer and closer. Now that our ship has started rotating for docking, our destination spins in and out of view. It's both riveting and nauseating.

"Because it's *true*," Nadia says. "I thought we'd at least warp somewhere exciting for Basic. Even Mars would be better than this asteroid junkyard of the solar system."

"Junkyard?" he gasps in horror.

"Fine, that's too kind," she says. "*Landfill* . . . of the solar system."

"Didn't you hear what I said?" Anton says. "About the protoplanets? Looking back in time? Not to mention, Ceres is a dwarf planet with an icy mantle and interior ocean—"

"*Translation*," Nadia cuts in, shooting me a look. "It's a frigid rock about the size of the Texas Federation. But on the upside, it's got some water. So, we've got that going for us."

I can't help it. I chuckle at their sibling banter. It reminds me of my sister.

"You're a funny pair," I say with a laugh.

Nadia snorts and jerks her thumb at Anton. "Sorry about my brother. He's a space nerd."

"*Certified* . . . space nerd," he says, raising his hands in a guilty gesture. He whispers to his sister, "But maybe our new friend loves astronomy, too. Did you think of that?"

"Well, did you even bother to ask her?" Nadia says, pursing her lips. "Before you started blabbing your mouth off with boring factoids?"

Anton nods. "You're right. That was pretty rude." He fixes his gaze on me. It's eerie how much it matches his sister's visage. "So, do you like space nerd stuff?"

They both peer at me expectantly. Nadia looks skeptical, while Anton looks so hopeful that I hate to break the truth to him. "Not really," I say in a sheepish voice. "Sorry, I wasn't much of a student. My best friend Rho is the only reason I didn't flunk out of high school."

Anton's face falls. "You're right, Nadia. She's a jock like you."

"Told ya," Nadia says with a triumphant grin. She turns back to me with a knowing smirk. "So what's your name, recruit? Unless you like being called . . . *recruit*."

"It's Hikari, from Lompoc. But my friends call me Kari."

Anton gives me a mock salute. "Nice to meet you, Kari from Lompoc," he says. "We're the Ksusha twins from Fresno. I'm Anton, and this is Nadia. My folks wish I was more like my sister. Proud military family and all that space junk. Well, they'd probably like you, too."

Nadia sighs. "They like you, Anton. Don't act so emo."

"So says the favorite twin," he says, brushing his curly red hair out of his eyes. "Nadia, don't deny it. You're like the perfect recruit. And I'm the . . . well . . ."

"*Certified* space nerd?" I offer.

"Exactly," Anton says with a faux bow. "I rest my case."

"So, why'd you enlist then?" I ask, already knowing that he's a Ringer. Even if he didn't mention his military family, I could tell by the way he talks about it. Like he had choices. "Why not go to college? And study all this space nerd stuff you love so much?"

"You're right," he agrees. "I don't give a comet's tail about being a guardian or the Proxy Wars. This was my ticket to see the stars for myself. Civilians can't travel off Earthside."

"True, this is the only way," I say, glancing through the window at the view rotating clockwise outside our ship, thankful for the anti-nausea meds. "All I dreamed about as a kid was enlisting. It sounded so thrilling. Basically, like the total opposite of my life in Lompoc."

"Maybe you're a secret space nerd after all?" Anton says with a grin.

I blush. "*Jock space nerd?*"

"Well, it does have a nice ring to it," Nadia says.

But then, we're all thrust forward as our acceleration slows. My heart lurches along with my stomach. The sling chair adjusts, tightening my harness and cushioning my body. The anti-nausea meds are probably the only reason I'm not puking my guts out right now.

"Watch—this is the cool part," Anton says, tapping me excitedly.

I follow his gaze. Docking gear spirals out from our transport as Ceres Base looms closer and closer on the surface of the dwarf planet. Through the window, I can spot the spindly, artificial structures jutting out of the icy crust, all enclosed against the extreme elements.

Farther away from the main base, mining equipment drills into the surface. The pumpjacks hammer up and down in a rhythmic fashion. Only, they're not mining oil; they're mining fresh water. This is the main reason Space Force colonized Ceres in the first place.

"The base doesn't look like much," I say in disappointment, squinting at the tiny structures, thinking Nadia was right. "I thought it would be more impressive."

Anton grins. "That's because . . . that's *not* the base."

"Wait, what do you mean?" I ask in confusion.

"Think of it like the tip of an iceberg," Anton explains. "What you see poking out is for docking purposes. But that's only the miniscule top of a massive underground structure."

"Oh, it's a subterranean base?" I ask, trying to picture it.

"Yup, better to build underground," Anton says with an eager nod. "To minimize exposure to the extreme elements. Luckily, Ceres does have some gravity, so you can walk around out there. But it's also got extreme temp shifts. During the day, it's about *negative* one hundred degrees Fahrenheit. And at night, it drops another hundred degrees or more."

"Yeah, you don't want to be stuck outside at night," Nadia says. "Even with a proper space suit, you'd eventually freeze to death. And during the day, you'd still freeze to death."

"Yup, and no breathable air," Anton adds. "So, that would kill you, too."

"Sounds charming," I say with a wince. "What's that over there?" I gesture to the strange rocky formations jutting out from the planet's icy, dusty surface.

"You mean, the ice geysers?" Anton says with a quick nod. "They're like volcanos, but they emit vapor jets. Oh, and sometimes they erupt and spew out mud and ice. They're also called . . . *cryovolcanos*. I prefer that name. What do you think?"

"Cryovolcanos?" I laugh. "Well, they're right. We're not in California anymore."

That makes them chuckle. He might be a certified space nerd, but I have to admit, the kid does have some useful info. Suddenly, I regret not paying better attention in school.

That's my last thought before we start the complex landing process, descending and matching our spin motion to dock with the port on Ceres Base. Finally, Nadia and Anton stop their bickering. In fact, all the recruits have lapsed into silence, as if the oxygen was sucked out of the cabin. I know why—it's finally real. We all feel the significance of this moment.

There's no going back now.

Not unless we wash out.

My sling chair grips me tighter as we spin faster. Nausea flips my stomach, bringing the acrid tang of bile to my throat. Finally, right when I think I might hurl, the transport locks onto the port with a deep shudder. Despite the cushioning gel, it rattles my bones down to the depths of my soul. Before I can swallow back the stomach acid, a blast of cold air hits me. *Whoosh.* The cabin decontaminates and pressurizes. I cough and shiver, tasting antiseptic on my tongue.

"Recruits, disembark in an orderly fashion."

The same disembodied voice reaches us through our neural implants. Right on cue, our sling chairs release us from the harnesses. I stagger to my feet despite the artificial gravity, feeling wobbly after all that spinning and landing maneuvering, not to mention the heavy-duty anti-nausea meds. I almost trip, but then I feel an arm grab my elbow and stabilize me.

"Steady there, recruit," Nadia says. "Gotta get your sea legs."

Her grip is ironclad, and it signals one thing—we're in this together now. Before I can mutter *thanks*, the disembodied voice barks for us to "hurry up and get our asses in gear."

This time, she sounds pissed off.

In lockstep behind the twins, I jam the aisle with the other recruits hustling to disembark. In a chaotic jumble, we clamber down the gangplank, as another rush of dizziness hits me from the artificial gravity and thinner air, despite the pressurization. I'm not adjusted yet.

The twins seem less bothered by everything, making me worry that I'm already shaping up to be a headcase. They've started bickering over the theory of relativity—and which twin is older. "In another multiverse, I could be the *older* one," Anton says. "It's theoretically possible."

"Theoretically—but you've got *zero* proof," Nadia shoots back. "Plus, we live in *this* universe, not that imaginary multiverse you just made up for your dumb argument."

"Einstein didn't think it was dumb," Anton mutters stubbornly.

I can't help it; I burst out in giggles. They keep coming, probably because I'm punchy from space travel and the meds. It's a potent brew, and it's messing with my head right now.

Suddenly, a dark shadow falls over me.

It's accompanied by a stern, rapid-fire voice.

"What's so funny? Think you're on a California Federation–funded vacation to the stars? Is that why you're loitering on my gangplank and not following direct orders?"

It's a drill sergeant.

I clam up instantly, fear strangling my throat. I recognize her voice. She's been making all those disembodied announcements in my ear. But this is the first time I've laid eyes on her. The drill sergeant is a tall and imposing figure, towering at least a foot over my head. She sports the signature pressed fatigues and stiff-brimmed hat that all the drill sergeants wear, which makes them resemble glorified park rangers. Her brown eyes narrow to slits—they bore into me.

That's a bad sign.

"Sorry . . . sir . . ." I say, feeling my cheeks burn with heat like lava flow.

"What did you just call me?" she demands. "Did you say—sir?"

I realize my mistake right away. "Uh, I mean . . . ma'am?"

She taps at her tablet angrily, scrolling through the roster. While her attention is diverted, Nadia leans over and hisses in my ear. "It's . . . *Drill Sergeant, yes, Drill Sergeant.*"

The drill sergeant looks over. She glares at Nadia.

"Recruit, mind your own business. Is that clear?"

"Drill Sergeant, yes, Drill Sergeant," Nadia says quickly, popping off a salute. She rushes past me, casting a worried glance back. Anton follows after her, more reluctantly.

Sorry, he mouths, before they continue across the docking bay, a huge warehouse-like structure filled with military transports like *Stargazer*, smaller fighters, and postal ships. They grab their duffel bags from the belt, then continue across the way with the other recruits.

Meanwhile, the drill sergeant taps violently on her tablet. My picture flashes across the screen. It's my official military ID photo taken at my enlistment. And it's not flattering.

She snaps her head up.

"Private Skye, let's get something straight. You just made my official shit list," she says, checking her watch. "By my count, you've been at Basic for . . . less than thirty seconds. That's gotta be a new record. Now get your ass in gear—and stop holding up my line."

"Drill Sergeant . . . yes, Drill Sergeant," I force out, trying to sound confident. But my voice wobbles. Other recruits are piling up behind me. I'm slowing everyone down. I hadn't even realized it . . . but for some reason, I'm frozen in place. I can't make my legs move.

The drill sergeant barks at me again.

"Ass in gear, recruit. What about that didn't you understand?"

This time, I keep my mouth shut and force my legs into motion. I lurch the rest of the way down the gangplank, feeling like all the blood has deserted my extremities. I'm not sure if it's from the thinner air or artificial G—or maybe just my complete and total mortification.

On shaky legs, I stagger across the docking bay, snag my heavy duffel bag and hoist it over my shoulder, and trail after the recruits. More drill sergeants in their traditional hats wave us into the waiting cargo elevators. Soon, we're all loaded inside the claustrophobic spaces.

Whoosh.

The doors shut with a rush of cold air, then they whisk us deep beneath the surface, proving Anton right. That was only the docking area. The real base is underground, and it must be enormous. We keep plunging, making me feel like everything is moving in fast-forward, and I can't get a handle on any of it. The drill sergeant's voice keeps echoing through my head.

Private Skye . . . you just made my official shit list.

My ears pop, and the dizziness gets worse. I grasp the railing to keep my knees from buckling. Desperately, I search for a familiar face in this sea of strangers, but the Ksusha twins and my friends from school must have boarded the other cargo elevator.

We keep plunging downward, picking up speed. My ears pop again.

With another sick lurch of my stomach, I realize that this is the moment when basic training really started—with a healthy dose of public humiliation, heaped with a topping of paralyzing shame. I made the drill sergeant's *official shit list* in less than thirty seconds flat.

Even factoring in relativity—she's right.

That's gotta be a record.

CHAPTER 8

DRAE

Stars, where's my *stupid* dorm?" I mutter under my breath, dragging my suitcases behind me. The hefty bags thud against my calves, sending pain radiating up my legs into my back.

It's my first day at college—and I'm already completely lost. Feeling self-conscious, I scan the area for some clue. It's so perfect, it almost looks fake. Freshly manicured lawns of *real* grass and paved footpaths make up the expansive central courtyard. Upper-class students stroll around, gossiping and chitchatting, without a care in the world. But I'm sweating, and I'm stressing. I wish my transport could take me to my dorm, but they're not allowed on campus, so mine is parking itself back in the structure. I'm not used to walking like this . . . well . . . anywhere.

Suddenly, a female voice echoes through my head and makes me jump.

Draeden, would you like my assistance?

It's Estrella, my neural implant. I named her my favorite comic book character. I haven't gotten used to her constant presence in my head. My thoughts aren't my own anymore.

"*Yes—and hurry it up*," I hiss under my breath, even though I don't have to speak out loud. She can understand my thoughts. *"I look like an idiot sweating out here."*

I don't mean to be condescending when I reply, but I can't help it. I'm so uncomfortable.

My imposter syndrome is rearing up. Her warm voice intrudes into my head again.

Starting route to Foothill Housing Residential Complex. A map of the Berkeley campus flashes in my retinas, along with the route. I breathe a sigh of relief, and follow her guidance.

Other students lug their bags across campus, searching for their dorms. We all look a little lost—and a lot nervous. But these new, unfamiliar faces fill me with a buzzing sense of hope. I run through my secret plan to reinvent myself again. This is my chance to start over and leave my past behind. I want to forget about Jude, Loki—and everyone from my hometown.

Sure, the Pairing Ceremony threw a little wrench into my plan. *Okay, maybe a big wrench,* I remember with a wince. But actually, Kari is the one person that I'd want to stay in my life, even if the last time we spoke right after the Pairing Ceremony, she still hated me. Regardless of that hiccup, this is my chance to make new friends—who didn't grow up on my little block.

Starting with my new roomies.

I checked "no preference" on my housing form, but kept it a secret from Jude and Loki. It felt liberating when I selected that box, like my future was a wide-open, blank slate for once.

Buoyed by that thought, I follow Estrella's guidance across Memorial Glade, the large central courtyard, and past Sather Tower with its impressive clock face. Brick buildings and stately lecture halls stare down at me, framing the campus like imposing sentries.

A few minutes later, after stopping to rest and flex my hands to return the circulation, I finally reach my dorm. It's a wood-paneled housing complex that overlooks a peaceful, tree-filled courtyard. The branches rattle in the breeze. This is exactly how I pictured college life.

Despite my jumble of nerves, I swipe my key card, then lug my bags up to the second floor. Rolling my bags behind me, I pad down the carpeted hallway and stop at the door that matches my key. I take a deep breath to still my nerves about meeting my new roommates.

I swipe my card. *Time for my new life,* I think as my heart races with anticipation. The lock beeps, and I push the door wide open. A rowdy voice reverberates through it.

"Drae, what took you so long?"

And not just any voice.

A familiar one.

I cringe as my eyes land on Jude. He's lounging on a new futon with a burgundy cover with his feet resting on the coffee table. Both look brand new, probably supplied by his parents.

"Did you take the scenic route? Took you long enough to find it," he rambles on, grinning at me like a fool. "Look, isn't this dorm super sick? We scored a triple."

"A . . . triple?" I repeat in shock, feeling dread bubble up in my chest. I can't believe this is happening. This is my worst nightmare. "Wait, three rooms. You mean—"

That's when Loki pops out of the bathroom, confirming my fears.

"But how did we get roomed together?" I force out in a halting voice, trying to make sense of this horrible turn of events. I blink at them a few times, hoping that they'll vanish.

But they don't.

Instead, they both grin at me, mistaking my horror for happy surprise.

"Yeah, we put you down on our housing forms," Loki says, clapping me on the shoulder. "Gotta keep the Lompoc crew together. That was our plan, remember? Didn't you put us down?"

"We talked about it all year," Jude adds, looking suspicious.

"Uh, right . . . of course," I say in a thick voice. "It's just . . . I didn't know if it would work. The application says they can't always accommodate student housing requests."

"True, they don't have many triples," Jude says, appearing relieved at my explanation. "And usually, they're reserved for seniors. So that's why I had my dad pull some strings. Grease a few wheels, you know how it works. Look at what he hooked up!"

With that, Jude shows me around the carpeted suite. There's a private bathroom with a shower off the common room—another perk—a little kitchen area, and three bedrooms, each furnished with a twin bed, a wooden desk that looks like it's seen its fair share of coursework, a modest side table, and an empty bookshelf. The bedrooms overlook the leafy courtyard.

"Isn't this great?" Loki says, trailing after us. He points to the unclaimed bedroom at the end of the hall. "That's your room. Sorry, we already picked ours. First come, first serve."

Room choice is the least of my concerns right now. I plop my suitcases down on the bed, feeling demoralized. I have my own bedroom, I reassure myself. I can close my door whenever I want and drown out their lame banter. It could be worse, right? But my heart sinks anyway.

I start unpacking, trying to avoid them. But Jude barges in, my solitude broken.

"Hey, it's frosh orientation time," he says, dragging me toward the door. "I wanna get there early and score choice seats. You can unpack later. How many comics did you bring?"

"Uh, I dunno." I blush at my extensive collection of vintage *Estrella Luna* comics. They're all sheathed in plastic. My most prized possessions, collected over the years.

"Yeah, hurry up," Loki adds, donning a new blue-and-yellow stitched Berkeley cap and tilting it sideways. He admires his reflection in the bathroom mirror. "Maybe score you a girlfriend who isn't made of paper," he adds, wiggling his eyebrows at his reflection.

"Berkeley is supposed to have some choice ladies," Jude adds with a salacious look. "That's why we gotta get there early and scope for hotties. Stake our claim now."

I cringe inside (and maybe outside, too). I should keep my mouth shut, but I can't help it. "Uh, maybe you shouldn't objectify our new classmates like that—"

But Loki rolls his eyes. He exchanges an annoyed look with Jude.

"Ugh, the buzzkill strikes again," he says with a deep groan. "What's gotten into you since the Pairing Ceremony? Can't you loosen up a bit? Try to have some actual fun for once?"

"Yup, that's like the whole point of college," Jude agrees, pulling me toward the door. "Just watch and learn from the experts. By the end of freshman year, we're gonna own this campus."

My dark mood doesn't improve during the orientation. It's not Dean Thatcher in her stiff pantsuit with her droll voice, though that doesn't help matters. Or the mundane details (*What if you lock yourself out of your dorm? Call campus security!*). It's the two jerks sitting next to me.

"Just pray you're not butt naked." Loki snickers as the campus security number flashes across the screen at the front of the wood-paneled lecture hall. He catches my eye and smirks. "That happened to my cousin Louie," he goes on in a low voice. "Twice."

"Unless you're that girl in row two," Jude says, nodding to a blonde student sitting a few rows up. "Then consider it a high-class problem. One that requires immediate intervention."

Loki cranes his neck. "Yeah, in that case, forget campus security. She can call me for assistance." They both laugh and crack more crude jokes as the orientation continues.

I want to scream—*Get away from me!*

Instead, I shrink down in my seat in mortified silence. I was so excited about my plan that I can't believe I'm right back where I started. I can't concentrate on anything except their jarring sniggers and crude jokes. I'm counting down the minutes until I can escape.

Finally, right when I'm about to lose it and bolt for the exit, the orientation concludes with a reminder about the mixer tonight. Everyone starts filing out, packing the aisles. I immediately begin rattling off excuses about needing to be somewhere else, but Jude and Loki won't hear of it. They start dragging me back toward our dorm to get ready for the party.

"No way you're missing that mixer," Jude says, ignoring my lame protests about needing to unpack and get a good night of sleep. "This is phase one of total campus domination."

Suddenly, a sharp voice cuts through the crowd noise.

"Gentlemen, a word with Mr. Rache?"

I recognize her right away. I jerk around to find—

Rho.

Really, it's impossible to miss her with her neon yellow hair and matching eyes. She's Kari's friend from back home. But we weren't exactly close, so I'm surprised to see her.

Loki frowns. "Hey, it's the fluorescent weirdo. She must've gotten lost."

"Looks like a highlighter shat on her head," Jude adds with another jab of laughter.

I cringe, but can't find my voice to tell them to shut up. Rho catches that last comment and does it for me. Her nano implants flame bright red. "Are you like . . . *five*? Seriously, scram, losers. Leave us alone already. A word with Mr. Rache means . . . *without you.*"

She doesn't look like she's messing around. Her hair smolders bright red like the inferno lighting up her eyes. Jude and Loki don't budge, so Rho places her hands on her hips.

"Losers, didn't you hear me? Scram."

Jude's face flushes crimson, reminding me of her implants. He looks like he wants to throw down and fight her right then and there—in the middle of freshman orientation.

"Hey, Jude, it's cool," I say, stepping between them and trying to calm him down. "She's Kari's friend. I gotta talk to her about . . . uh . . . important Sympathetic stuff."

A few tense seconds pass.

Rho's hair darkens from fiery red to somber burgundy with black tips.

"Fine, have fun with the weirdo," Jude says finally, gesturing for Loki to follow him. "Just remember, she hangs with Park Rats. If you're not careful, you might catch the Pox."

I cringe at the petty slur as they storm away. Watching them leave, I'm slammed in the face by our shared history. Sure, I had fun with them when we were kids. I'll admit it. They also pushed me to be braver than I felt. Three rambunctious boys terrorizing the block with toy blasters and pretending to be guardians—a fate that our family status would save us from when we came of age. But growing up next door? And playing together because your parents considered their family a strong political alliance? Is that a reason to stay friends for life?

The truth is they were chosen for me, and I've never been able to change that.

"Sorry about them," I say to Rho, who still looks quite . . . enflamed. "Thanks for saving me from them. They've been driving me crazy since I got here. Really, they're the worst."

She plops her backpack down on the folding seat next to me and perches on the armrest. Her pleather combat boots scuff the back of the chair. She's wearing black fishnets paired with a soft, red velvet baby doll dress. She stands out from the buttoned-up Berkeley crowd.

"By the *worst* . . . do you mean your best friends?" she says, pursing her lips and staring me down. "Who you never go anywhere without? Guessing you probably use the loo together, too," she says, slipping into a fake posh accent. Her hair and eyes brighten to light pink.

"Loo? Are you from British Federation?"

She shrugs, brushing her rosy hair away. "Nah, just a fun affectation. But back to your statement of gratitude . . . *you're welcome*. I agree, they're the absolute worst. They've always been the worst. They will always be the worst. Seriously, you're only realizing that now?"

Her pinkish eyes blaze into me. The whole effect is unnerving.

"Right . . . that's fair." I fumble for words. "I just can't seem to get away from them."

I give her a relieved look, finally feeling like I can breathe. Rho misreads it as being potentially into her. She unleashes a practiced scowl and thumps the seat with her boot.

"Don't think this means I want to be friends. Also, it doesn't mean I forgive you for all the lame shit you pulled in high school. It just means you're paired with my only friend in the whole *blasted* universe. So, you're my best shot at finding out how she's doing up there."

I frown. "But can't you send her messages? Berkeley has a post office."

She rolls her eyes. "Yeah, but the civilian communication schedule is limited. And it's also redaction city. Plus, I don't have a high-security clearance. Not like her Sympathetic."

Her eyes turn dark blue, matching her hair. They study my face.

I sigh, dragging my hand through my hair, feeling the stiff, wiry curls. I've developed a punishing headache. It stabs at me with a gentle *throb, throb, throb* behind my eyeballs.

"You know I can't tell you anything," I say, lowering my voice and glancing around to make sure we're not overheard. Thankfully, the hall is mostly deserted now. I also muted my neural implant at the beginning of the orientation, so I hope she's not spying on me. But my nerves flare at the thought. "I signed scary-ass papers swearing on my life not to divulge classified military secrets. If I'm not careful, they could toss me into space prison camp."

Rho lowers her voice to barely a whisper. "But they won't do that. Don't you know how the system works? Your dad works for the head Federation honchos, and your mom's—"

"*A war hero.*" I groan at the mention. "Don't remind me."

"Not just any war hero—one with a purple star and a stellar reputation. She's practically famous. So, you're safe. Or rather, safer than most," she adds with a frown.

"Right, well . . . I'd rather not test that theory."

Her hair morphs bright red again, as her eyes burn with liquid fire. "Look, you don't have a choice. Because I'm gonna stalk you up and down this lovely campus if you refuse."

I flinch back. Rho can be scary when she tries. She was like this even back in kindergarten, long before her nano hair and implants that amplified her mood swings. I've always steered clear of her for that reason. But then she softens, her hair flushing deep blue.

"Plus, I don't want military secrets. I just want to know that my friend is safe and happy up there. Or at least, semi-happy," she revises her statement. "Well, Kari-level happy."

I smile a little. "I know what you mean. Her baseline is a bit of a downer."

Rho nods in understanding. "One of her most endearing qualities."

That shared remembrance hangs between us.

"You're her Sympathetic," Rho goes on. "So, that means you're going to know her better than anyone. And if she's in trouble . . . well . . . you're going to know that, too."

Blue washes through her visage. Her voice cracks on that last part.

"Even those details might be classified," I backpedal, feeling uneasy again. "Plus, won't it be obvious, meeting in broad daylight to discuss classified secrets? Somebody's sure to notice."

Rho grins. "That brings me to my next genius idea. We've both got Great Books of the Federation tomorrow morning. I pulled up the class list. All incoming freshmen have to take it."

"Great Books?" I say with a groan. "Sounds torturous. Kill me now."

"Exactly, except I'm not planning to murder you," she says with a cock of her eyebrow. "Though that would be pretty satisfying. Congratulations—you're my new study partner."

"Study partner?" I repeat in confusion.

She nods. "Your grades in high school? Well, they sucked like a supermassive black hole. The only reason you're here is the teachers back home gave you a free pass. But that nepotism won't fly at Berkeley. You're going to have to study for once in your privileged life."

"No way," I say, shaking my head. "We don't get along. You don't even like me, remember? I make you turn red. Plus, it's too dangerous. For both of us . . . and Kari."

"Yeah, true facts," she agrees. "But I'm an ace student. My GPA was 4.3. And we can use our study sessions to exchange info on Kari. You rub my back, and I'll rub yours. But not literally, like gross. Don't get any ideas." Her hair turns puke green. So do her eyes.

I'm not used to the unnatural colors that morph and light up her countenance. She holds out her hand to shake on it, and at least it's normal colored. Her green eyes bore into me.

"So, do we have a deal?"

This doesn't fit into my reinvention plan. Just like Jude and Loki, Rho is also from my old life. The one I want to forget and leave behind in my space dust. She knows every shameful thing that I've done since elementary school. Asteroid fires, maybe even preschool.

And now, we're going to be study partners? Not to mention, committing high treason on a regular basis? This is a terrible idea—and a terrible way to start my college life.

"I will stalk you, remember?" she says, turning all fiery and scary again. "Like a vengeful wraith. I might even start following you into the loo—"

"Okay, fine," I say, throwing my hands up in surrender. It's what I always do. I give up and give in without a fight. "I'll do it, just stop threatening me for one *blasted* second."

"Great." She nods in satisfaction. I breathe a sigh of relief, but then she lowers her voice and leans in. "You can start by telling me: When is your first Sympathetic exchange?"

Even the thought of that makes my heart skitter. So much is already going wrong, and I haven't even dealt with the fact that the Sympathetic Program is about to begin for real.

"In two days . . . in the afternoon."

"Perfect," Rho says brightly, grabbing her bag and springing to her feet. Relieved of the weight, the seat slaps back into position. "That's our first study date. Also, you're buying. I'm guessing Mommy and Daddy set you up with a nice ole commissary account."

"And yours didn't? You're just as privileged as me. You grew up around the block."

For the first time, she doesn't look so confident. Her shoulders sag, and everything about her turns bright pink. That's the only way to describe it. *Embarrassment*, I realize after a moment. I'm starting to catch on and learn to decode this mood fashion stuff.

"Yeah, I kind of screwed that up," she says, pointing to her eyes. "They hate these nano retinas. My folks told me not to get them on, like . . . *actual pain of death*. And, uh, I sort of . . . did it anyway. So they cut me off. I guess they want to teach me a lesson via total starvation."

"Don't be so dramatic. There's always the dining hall," I point out. "It's open to all students on campus. Comes with our room and board package. Three hot meals a day."

She shudders in disgust. "Exactly, like I said. Total starvation. Have you seen what they serve in there?"

I tick off what I spotted when I peeked my head in there on the way to my dorm. "Gluey potatoes. Reconstituted textured protein. Wilted, overcooked broccolini—"

"Enough," she says, turning puke green again. "I can't eat that stuff. My body totally rejects it. Just trust me, it's a mega TMI situation."

I smirk at her. "Now you sound like Jude. Welcome to the club."

"Ha ha, touché," she says. "Very funny."

A moment passes between us—and it's really weird. It almost feels like . . . *friendship*. Or maybe, the start of one. Like the delicate tendrils of real grass sprouting up in the campus courtyard. But I don't want to mess it up by letting the silence drag on or saying something lame. I know how easy it is to kill delicate tendrils of grass. I watched Jude and Loki stomp on them on our way to orientation, despite the signs saying, "Keep Off the Grass."

I clear my throat and meet her gaze.

"How does pizza sound?"

She beams, her hair gushing out sunshine yellow, and her eyes gleaming like gold coins to match. They shine at me.

"Perfect."

CHAPTER 9

KARI

Grunts, this is your first test," the drill sergeant barks from the front of the transport when we jerk to a halt. "Now get off the bus in alphabetical order. You have thirty seconds—"

Bang.

I jump as someone slaps the window by my head. I snap my eyes outside. They fall on what looks like a track field carpeted with fake turf. A domed, concrete ceiling stretches overhead. Other drill sergeants surround the personnel transport and bang on the windows.

I stumble to my feet. My new boots feel stiff. I run my hands over my freshly buzzed head, still surprised by what I feel. I'm still not used to the lack of hair. They shaved it off when we arrived into a military-approved buzz cut. I'm also wearing my newly issued uniform that we had to change into after landing. Pressed green fatigues with the Space Force logo.

I don't feel like Kari anymore. I scan my nametag, reading the name printed on it. I'm officially *Private Skye* now.

Bang.

The drill sergeants keep pounding the windows and yelling at us.

Bang. Bang. Bang.

"Alphabetical order, you heard the orders! Get off the transport!"

What happens next isn't pretty—a chaotic stampede to get off the vehicle, with recruits frantically calling out their names and trying to get in alphabetical order. But the aisles are too narrow for us to get into proper order, and nobody knows anyone's names yet.

"Asteroid fires, it's impossible," I grumble, shouldering my duffel bag amid the banging by the drill sergeants and the shoving of the recruits. "It's like they want us to fail!"

"Right, you're only catching onto that now?" Percy says, rescuing me and dragging me toward the back. Genesis is forcing her way ahead of us. We're always near the end with our "S" last names. But the aisle is too narrow and we get logjammed. The recruits behind us push us off the transport. I stagger down the steps and onto the turf, almost dropping my duffel bag.

Before I can regain my balance, the drill sergeant in charge of us—the one with the shit list—is screaming in my face. "Took you over forty-five seconds to get off that transport!" she yells in my ear, spittle flying at me. "Just like you jammed up my gangplank!"

"Drill Sergeant, yes, Drill Sergeant," I manage, fighting back frustrated tears.

"Last time I checked, *Skye* comes near the end of the alphabet," she continues her rant. "Or has the alphabet changed back Earthside? Recruit, did you get off in the proper order?"

The drill sergeant stares me down from under her hat. Her eyes glower with dark fire. I try to keep my lip from trembling and sound strong. "Drill Sergeant, no, Drill Sergeant."

But I fail miserably. I drop my head in shame.

Triumphantly, she wheels around to face everyone. "You're the sorriest bunch of recruits to ever grace my field. Especially Private Skye here. Grunts, now drop and give me thirty push-ups. Then give me another twenty for Private Skye failing to follow my orders."

We all throw down our duffel bags and dive into the push-ups. I don't even have time to feel embarrassed. My cheeks scrape the rough turf, stabbed by the blades of fake grass. It seems so out of place on this desolate, frozen asteroid a few long astronomical units from Earth.

After the push-ups, we're given more punishing exercises—sit-ups, burpees (they seem easy, just going down and then up, but they almost kill me), running in place, then more push-ups. I spot the Ksusha twins across the field, while Percy and Genesis struggle next to me.

"Recruits, what were you expecting?" the drill sergeant barks, parading down the line as we cycle through the impossible exercises. "To get issued fancy blasters? Cool tech gadgets? And go on interstellar adventures to fight some Proxies and Raiders?"

"Drill Sergeant, yes, Drill Sergeant," we chant in unison.

"That's what I thought. Well, I'm in charge of this platoon now, so what I say goes. And I say—*you're as green as this turf grass.*" She stomps on the turf by my sweaty face as I struggle through the push-ups. "I wouldn't trust you with a butter knife, let alone blasters."

Another cycle of brutal exercises is hurled at us, accompanied by plenty of berating and taunts from our drill sergeant. They're the exact opposite of pep talks. Before long, my muscles are quaking, my breathing comes in ragged, desperate gasps, and my sides burn with cramps that feel like getting stabbed repeatedly. In short, I'm dying. And nobody else is faring much better.

The drill sergeant stalks over to me. Her long shadow, cast by the fluorescent lights overhead, stretches over my prone form. She bends down to glower at me from under her hat.

"Private Skye, stand up . . . *now.*"

I'm not the only one struggling. Anton is puking his guts out on the side of the field, while Nadia collapses onto her stomach. But she's singling me out. It's not fair, but there's no arguing with her. That will only make it worse. So, I struggle to my knees, but bend over and retch on the field, though there's nothing left in my stomach. Just bile, acrid and burning.

"I can't . . . please . . . I'm sorry . . ."

"Private Skye, what did you just say?"

Her irate voice hits me like blaster fire. I realize my mistake right away. I only have *two* choices of proper responses, both versions of the same thing. Any deviation is a huge error.

The drill sergeant wheels around to the rest of the platoon.

"All of you—on your feet! And hold your duffel bags over your head."

Groans run up and down the line. Everyone staggers up and hoists their heavy bags over their heads. I do the same, forcing my knees to lock and hefting my arms up, but they're already shaking from the push-ups. My bag wobbles in my grip, growing heavier and heavier by the second. Suddenly, I regret everything that I packed. I should have brought nothing, just myself.

The drill sergeant plants her feet right in front of me, daring me to fail. *Don't drop it, don't drop it, don't drop it,* I think to myself over and over. *She wants you to fail . . .*

"You feeling tired, grunt?" she asks with a cruel smirk.

"Drill Sergeant, no, Drill Sergeant," I gasp, but it's a complete lie.

I want to flop down and never get up again. My arms shake harder. I can feel my legs, every single muscle screaming in agony. This is the longest few minutes of my life. *Just hold on,* I tell myself. *Don't drop it.*

But it's futile. My body starts to rebel against me.

Finally, my arms buckle and my legs give out in one horrible, ungraceful collapse. I sit down hard on my ass. My duffel bag tumbles to the turf, landing in a sorry heap next to me.

I hear other duffel bags thumping the turf around me. I'm not the only one who failed. It was an impossible task, like everything else so far. But I'm the one she's targeting.

"Private Skye, you're a yellow-bellied coward," the drill sergeant screams in my face. She's so close to me that spit lands on my cheeks. "Just like your . . . *father.*"

Those words hit me like a sucker punch.

I gasp and almost double over. *How does she know about him?*

The shock and terror must shine in my eyes because the drill sergeant smiles in satisfaction. This was exactly the reaction she wanted. She was hoping to get a rise out of me.

"That's right, Private . . . *Skye.*" She sneers my name like it's a slur. She kneels and whispers in my ear. She's only inches away. "Oh, I knew your father. You think this is bad? I'm going to make Basic your worst nightmare. You're gonna wish to the stars you never enlisted."

"I'm sorry . . . I'm nothing like him , , ," I mumble, tasting puke on my tongue.

"Recruit, did you just disagree with me?" the drill sergeant yells so loud my ears ring.

"No, I'm not like him! I swear—"

"What did you say?" she cuts me off.

"Sorry . . . I'm so sorry . . ." I blather on like a fool.

"Say *sorry* one more time. I dare you."

This time, I keep my mouth shut. Angry, frustrated tears spring to my eyes. She flashes me a taunting grin, begging me to defy her again. "Did you want to say something?"

"Drill Sergeant . . . no, Drill Sergeant," I say in a soft voice.

"That sounded hesitant to me," she says, fiddling nonchalantly with the baton on her belt. "Not that I expected anything better from the likes of you. Recruits, you should know something important about Private Skye. She's a yellow-bellied coward just like her deserter father."

Shocked gasps roil through our ranks. I hear their whispers.

"*She's deserter spawn . . .*"

There's no worse crime in our world. Even sweet Anton looks like someone slapped him. Nadia, who was always friendly before, if a little feisty, shoots me an ice-cold glare that could freeze the sun. Percy and Genesis both give me pitying looks, since they already knew the truth about my family. Suddenly, I become aware that all the sound has drained from the field like we're standing in the vacuum of outer space, not the pressurized interior of Ceres Base. Only the hissing of the air vents and the screeching of the bots cleaning puke off the turf remain.

The drill sergeant keeps that sick smile plastered on her face. She's enjoying this. "Last thing we need is *deserter spawn* in this platoon," she barks. "Isn't that right, Private Skye?"

"Drill Sergeant, but I'm nothing like my father."

Rage sweeps over her face, barely contained.

"Disagreeing with me again? You're a yellow-bellied coward who would desert your watch and let most of your platoon die, just like your father. I can see it in your eyes."

I recoil from that. It's the most I've ever learned about what my dad did. His military records are sealed. Ma never wanted to talk about it. Also, it's possible that she didn't know the truth. He deserted—and let most of his platoon die? Even I'm disgusted by this fact.

I catch Nadia gaping at me, only her whole demeanor has changed to revulsion. There's nothing a proud military family hates more than deserters—and their spawn.

The drill sergeant lets that hang in the air before she calls us together. "Recruits, now it's time to assign battle buddies. Does anyone know what that entails? Permission to speak."

Silence, then Nadia pipes up. She can't help being a boss.

"Drill Sergeant, you work out with them. Eat with them. Get dressed with them. Shit with them." Chuckles ripple through our ranks. "And if they mess up—then you mess up."

"That's right, Private Ksusha," the drill sergeant says with a pleased nod. "Your battle buddy is attached to you like a space parasite. They're a reflection of you. Their purpose is to keep you on schedule and on top of your game. If they're late, then you're late. If they dress in the wrong uniform, you dressed in the wrong uniform. If they fail, then you fail. Is that clear?"

"Drill Sergeant, yes, Drill Sergeant," we chant back. The words are coming easier now with repetition, but my voice still wobbles over them. I'm red-faced and humiliated.

The drill sergeant wheels around and gestures to me.

"Who volunteers to be Private Skye's battle buddy?"

Silence.

Like we're in that space vacuum again. No, it's worse than that. It feels like I'm being sucked into a black hole and crushed to death by the extreme gravitational forces.

More long seconds pass in silence.

Still nobody volunteers.

It's confirmed—they all hate me.

I shrivel. I shrink. I want to vomit. I think death would be a mercy. My muscles quake, but it's nothing like the quaking of my heart. I risk a glance around. Even Anton won't meet my gaze. Nobody will. Not Percy, not Genesis. And certainly not Nadia, the boss of our platoon.

The drill sergeant marches down our ranks with a satisfied twitch of her lips. She keeps pacing, her eyes sweeping over our faces. Nobody meets her gaze; nobody wants to summon her attention right now. And still, nobody dares to volunteer. Anton almost buckles, but Nadia slaps his wrist, and he gives in without a fight. I see her mouth, *Don't even think about it.*

"Nobody wants to volunteer to be Private Skye's battle buddy?" the drill sergeant says, still pacing in front of us. "I find that hard to believe. Are you sure? Last chance to step up."

Silence again.

Somehow it feels deeper, darker, and longer, though I know the rules of sound haven't changed, just my perception. The drill sergeant paces back, but then she stops in front of—

Nadia.

"Private Ksusha, since you know so much and love sharing your vast knowledge with everyone," the drill sergeant says. "You're assigned as Private Skye's battle buddy."

Nadia's mouth drops open to protest, but she quickly clamps it shut. Her face turns bright red. "Drill Sergeant . . . yes, Drill Sergeant," she forces out in a strained whisper.

"I'm sorry, Private Ksusha. I couldn't hear you," the drill sergeant says with a cruel smirk. "For not speaking up, everyone drop and give me another twenty push-ups."

Groans ripple through our ranks. I don't dare complain. I just drop, despite the protesting of my poor, shaky arms. "Groans earn you another twenty," the drill sergeant adds.

This time, everyone stays silent, aside from our ragged, shallow breathing. Nadia pumps up and down next to me in perfect form. "I'm sorry—" I whisper in her direction.

But she cuts me off. "Look, you'd better not screw this up for me," she hisses in my face. "This is about *both* of us now. And I don't intend to wash out on account of your deserter spawn ass. So quit wasting your breath talking to me—and use it to finish your set ASAP."

I shut the stars up and focus on my push-ups, my arms trembling in pain, but I can't shake the way Nadia is treating me now. It's like somebody flipped a switch. Her friendly banter and bravado from earlier are all gone, replaced with pure loathing.

The worst part is that it's not because I messed up today. I could live with that.

It's because she knows what my father did.

CHAPTER 10

DRAE

Freshmen, welcome to Great Books," Professor Trebond says from the podium at the front of the wood-paneled auditorium filled with folding seats. "This is the class you will either love to hate—or hate to love. That depends on you."

We're in a different lecture hall than where we had orientation yesterday. This one is named Wheeler Auditorium. It's bright and early on Monday morning—my first official day of classes—and I'm majorly struggling. My eyelids feel like lead weights, while my brain feels sluggish and foggy for one reason. I look over at Jude and Loki. They kept me up late, partying and carrying on in the common room after the mixer. Even my bedroom door couldn't block it out.

They're sitting to my right, while Rho has claimed the seat on my other side. She sashayed into class bright and early with the buoyant declaration, "Hey, study partner!"

Jude looked suspicious of her friendly tone, while Loki wanted to know if we were . . . well . . . he made a crude hand gesture that I had to swat away, hissing, "Stars, no!"

Meanwhile, Professor Trebond lets her dark eyes sweep over the lecture hall, waiting for us to settle. She sports a boxy gray pinstriped pantsuit that gives off a vintage vibe, paired with worn combat boots. She also wears round spectacles, while her hair juts out at all angles. A plastic hair clip hangs on for dear life, struggling to contain her rebellious black curls.

"Students, let this be a warning," she says from the podium, unleashing a hellish squeal from the microphone. She waits for it to quiet before continuing. "Your privilege may have gotten you through upper school with inflated GPAs and pats on the back, but it won't fly in my class. You're going to have to earn your grades in here." She pauses to let that sink in. A few groans ripple through the auditorium. "Maybe for the first time in your entitled little lives."

Now the class is paying attention.

The thrum of chatter dies out at once. I feel a nervous flutter start in my chest and work its way through my body. The same nervous energy shoots through the lecture hall.

I realize two things fast. This professor wasn't always like us. She had a noticeable hitch in her gait when she ascended to the stage. Probably an old war injury. Medical discharge, I'm guessing. She used that opportunity to enroll in university and then grad school. Two, she might be one of us now, technically speaking, due to her service, but she hates our privilege.

"Let me guess," Professor Trebond continues. "You probably think Great Books is an antiquated area of study? That has nothing to do with your real lives? Raise your hands if you had that thought this morning."

Yup, busted, I think, cringing inwardly.

Feeling lame, I put my hand up in the air, along with a few other brave souls willing to publicly confess their sins. Oh, and Jude and Loki . . . only they seem proud of it. Rho keeps her hands firmly on her desk, where they're busy tapping at her tablet and taking meticulous notes.

Professor Trebond nods, pushing her glasses up her nose. "Maybe you're wondering why it magically appeared on your freshman schedule? Or why it's a requirement for graduation?" More hands go up, one by one. "Possibly, you're speculating that it might be some elaborate prank the dean concocted to torture you?"

Rho raises her hand on the last question, smirking and whispering in my ear. "Busted . . . I had my money on *elaborate frosh torture method.*"

Now almost the whole class has their hands thrust in the air.

We all look around. Nervous laughter ripples through Wheeler.

"That's what I thought." Professor Trebond flashes a knowing smile. More laughter cascades through the auditorium. "Okay, you can put your hands down now."

She walks over to the whiteboard and writes the name of the class in all caps.

GREAT BOOKS

"Great Books is the most important class you will take all year," she goes on, circling the name. "Maybe all four years, if you make it that far without flunking out." More laughter, then she turns back to face us, all business. "Now, pull out your syllabuses and let's dive in."

Then she starts spewing off our reading assignment, before digging into the syllabus and all the books that we have to read this semester. I try to keep up, but my head starts to pound. Next to me, Rho scribbles furiously on her tablet. She catches me watching and scowls.

Why aren't you taking notes? she mouths.

Oh right . . . because Professor Trebond is right. I've never had to apply myself in school before. Minimal effort always got me by with a little help from teachers like Mr. Egbert.

Following her lead, I pull out my tablet and try to take notes, but I can't keep up with the professor. My hand moves too slowly. I miss words and fall behind. I glance over at Jude and Loki. They're not taking notes and they look furious. It wafts off them like a wave of heat.

Jude jams his meaty hand into my side. "She's a Park Rat," he hisses in my ear, gesturing to the professor. "How can Berkeley let her kind onto their faculty? That should be illegal."

"She *was* . . . past tense," I whisper back. "I think she's a veteran."

"No, *they* never change," Loki chimes in. "You know that—"

"What was that?" Professor Trebond says, whipping around and zeroing in on us like a targeting scope. Her lips set into a deep frown. "Care to share that with the whole class?"

Silence falls over Wheeler.

Uncomfortable silence.

All the other students stare at us with rapt attention. But Jude doesn't seem fazed by it. Rather, he seems encouraged. He stands up, grins widely, and proudly declares—

"I said . . . *you're a Park Rat.*"

Snickers and shocked whispers shoot through Wheeler.

Professor Trebond stays calm.

Too calm.

"Stand up," she barks. "All three of you. That's right, on your feet."

Her voice reverberates through Wheeler. She waits for us to obey her orders. I find my feet somehow, despite the dread shooting through my body. The folding seat slaps back behind me with a sharp noise. Now, we're on our feet—and the whole class is staring at us.

Professor Trebond smiles warmly, and that worries me more than if she'd started berating us, or kicked us out of class. "Now, take a bow," she says, still smiling widely. "Go ahead, don't be afraid. You wanted attention, right? Praise? Accolades? Well, here's your chance."

We follow her suggestion and start bowing. I feel stiff and mortified, but Jude and Loki relish their moment. They bow with dramatic flair, flinging their arms wide and facing the class.

"Why aren't you clapping for them?" Professor Trebond says, turning to the class. She raises her hands in a mocking gesture. "Don't be shy. Give them a nice round of applause."

The class starts clapping, reluctantly.

The pitter-patter of applause echoes through the lecture hall. Jude and Loki get into it, and the clapping drums up in response. But as they keep bowing, they start to get uncomfortable. Every time we try to stop our performance, the professor demands that we keep bowing.

"Come on, don't stop now," Professor Trebond says, that same eerily calm smile plastered to her face. "You know, it takes a surprising amount of muscular strength to bend over, not to mention balance and core stability. I learned that in basic training. Simple actions, like holding your duffel bag over your head, can become excruciating given enough time."

She's right.

After a few more minutes, my back starts to clench up and ache like I've been lifting weights, not simply bending forward. Jude starts breathing hard and sweating, while Loki's cheeks flame bright red with exertion. Even the students clapping look pained from the effort of smacking their hands together over and over, their palms red and stinging, their arms trembling.

Right when I think I can't take another bow—

She finally signals for us to stop.

"Gentlemen, I hope you enjoyed your applause," she says, still smiling in a friendly way. Her tone is breezy and light, but her eyes remain narrowed and sharp. "Because that's the last time you're ever going to speak out of turn in my classroom again. Is that understood?"

But Jude looks furious. He *hates* being humiliated.

"I'll tell the dean," he spits out in a venomous voice. He's still breathing hard. Sweat has soaked his baggy, button-down shirt and khaki chinos. "I'll report you for . . . for . . ."

She arches her eyebrow. "For asking you to take a bow in front of your fellow students? And suggesting they give you a round of applause?"

When she puts it that way, it does sound silly. Whiny and weak. All the things that Jude hates the most. She's called his bluff. He's got nothing. Even his parents would probably think he was being lame for reporting that. But it doesn't stop him from digging a deeper hole.

"Yes . . . exactly," he says, less certain now. "You tortured us . . . on purpose."

"Well, the dean is a busy woman," Professor Trebond replies, shuffling the papers on her podium. "Runs this whole university. And you're gonna bother her with a round of applause?"

Silence engulfs the auditorium, peppered by a few nervous titters.

It's a standoff.

Jude looks more heated than I've ever seen him, and that's saying a lot. His lips purse like a fish gasping for air, only he's searching for something to say. But nothing escapes his lips.

"That's what I thought," Professor Trebond says when he doesn't respond. The smile has now evaporated from her face. That's when she does something completely unexpected.

She hitches up her jacket, revealing her prosthetic arm in all its mechanical glory. She's not wearing the flesh sleeve to disguise it. Either she doesn't care, or she wants people to know how she suffered and almost died serving our federation. I'm guessing it's both.

"Go ahead," she says. "Take a good, hard look at it."

Hushed whispers ricochet through the room, the shuffling of bodies, a general racket of unease. But it's impossible not to stare at it, even though it feels shameful and wrong.

"It's a feat of engineering, connected to my neural implant," she continues, flexing her arm. The gears shift and whir, working seamlessly and clenching the fist. "It responds to my thoughts. We have great body armor tech. That's why I'm not dead, just slightly maimed."

Without the flesh sleeve, I can see the inner workings of the mechanical tendons and joints. I can even see where machine meets flesh and bone at her shoulder. She clenches her mechanical fist and leans forward over the podium. That's when it dawns on me . . .

She's a war hero. Like my mother. With a purple heart.

"That's right, I fought for this federation in the Proxy Wars," Professor Trebond says after a long moment. "I did things that I can't repeat in civilian company. They're classified, for a reason. But as far as you're concerned—I'm untouchable. Even by Mommy and Daddy."

Jude and Loki keep their mouths shut. They almost seem to have shrunk down. *They're afraid of her*, I realize all of a sudden. And there's more. She wasn't just a regular guardian. I bet she was special ops, the most elite forces who work on highly sensitive and dangerous missions.

"Mommy and Daddy also can't get you through my class," she continues. "And if you fail, you can't graduate from UC Berkeley. This is a required course. All freshmen must pass it. Now, does anyone else have any additional comments they'd like to share with the class?"

Silence.

It's so strong, it's almost like noise.

Even Rho has stopped scribbling like a maniac on her tablet. Shame surges through me, making me want to curl up and disappear. This is my first class, and the professor already despises me thanks to my lame friends. Worse yet, if I don't pass Great Books, then I flunk out of Berkeley. The scenarios rush through my head, making me dizzy, each worse than the last.

How can I already be struggling? I haven't even been here a week.

Suddenly, a message pops up on my screen. It's from Rho, who's sitting next to me, having returned to her furious notetaking as the class resumes. She flashes me a smirk. I scan it.

Glad I'm your study partner now?

After class, I return to my dorm with Jude and Loki. I wish I could erase the horrible first day of classes from my memory. I head straight to my bedroom, needing desperately to shut the door and be away from them. I have loads of homework from my calculus and geology classes, not to mention a whole book to read for Professor Trebond this week. But I can't face any of it.

Suddenly, my neural implant pings me.

Reminder, Estrella communicates. *Sympathetic exchange with Private Hikari Skye tomorrow.* The details about the time and campus post office location pop up in my retinas.

"Dismiss," I mutter back, making the reminder vanish.

After what happened today, I can't think about that. My head throbs more, spiking the headache I've had since the morning. It's not quite dinnertime yet, not that I'm hungry. My stomach churns with anxiety. I flop onto my bed, crawling under the comforter, and bury my head in the unfamiliar pillow, shoving my arm underneath it—

Suddenly, my fingers brush something wedged under there. *Weird,* I think, yanking the object out from my pillow. It's an envelope made of thick paper stock, cream-colored, and sealed with red wax. A symbol is stamped into the seal of a grizzly bear pawing at the sky.

I bolt up straight, gripped by curiosity. My fingers slide over the rich, textured paper. It's old-fashioned stationary. I flip the envelope over . . . my breath catches in my throat.

Written in elaborate calligraphy is my name—

Mr. Draeden Rache

I try to slide open the wax seal, but it won't budge. *Extra weird,* I think. I feel around, then finally press my thumb into the seal. It conforms to my thumbprint, almost gripping it. Suddenly, the seal lights up, the grizzly bear glowing with golden light. I gasp and almost drop the envelope. Then it opens and unfolds like origami, revealing a card nestled inside.

I slide it out, feeling the thickness of the paper. The top is embossed with the same symbol—the grizzly bear pawing the sky. The note is handwritten in more fancy calligraphy.

You've been chosen.
Don't tell anyone.

Tomorrow
Midnight
The Campanile

Don't be late—or forfeit your chance.

My heart races as I read the mysterious message. It's not signed by anyone—it's totally anonymous—but a crazy thought occurs to me. Could this be for a secret society?

My friends were talking about it just yesterday. They're both planning to pledge frats, something that doesn't interest me, and this topic came up. Apparently, UC Berkeley has a secret society called the Order of the Golden Bear—and it's old, dating back to before the war, and considered a great honor to join. But you have to pass an initiation test first.

Jude was particularly hoping to score an invitation to pledge. But neither he nor Loki had any idea how to get chosen, well . . . since it's secret. But could this be for it?

I stare at the mysterious card again, as my heart thumps faster. I flip it over, searching for more clues, but there's nothing else written on it. Another crazy thought occurs to me. Whoever delivered this invitation had to get into my dorm . . . but how?

Our room locks automatically, of course. Even the windows are sealed. I get up and double-check. I peer down at the courtyard below. We're three stories up, so it's unlikely someone could climb up here in broad daylight without drawing attention. I can hear Jude and Loki sniggering in the common room. I poke my head out. They're slumped on the futon.

"Oh look, the buzzkill emerges," Jude declares when he sees me.

"Don't tell me you're actually studying?" Loki adds, cracking open a beer. They've already stocked the fridge. Technically, we're underage. But we're funded and protected. We can get away with anything, probably even murder. Though I'd rather not test that theory.

"Uh, did you let anyone into our dorm earlier?" I ask, holding the card behind my back to hide it. I remember the admonishment on the note . . . *don't tell anyone.* I don't want to mess up.

Jude frowns. "Nope, just us . . . the Lompoc crew!" He breaks into a goofy grin. "But tonight, we're gonna change that. Rush parties are kicking off up and down frat row."

"Yeah, wanna pre-game?" Loki asks. I can tell that he's already had a few. He plucks another ice-cold beer out of the fridge. He tosses it to Jude, then reaches for one more.

But I wave him off. "Uh, no thanks. I think I need to study," I say and duck back into my room, quickly shutting the door against their protests. I click the lock into place.

I know them well. If they'd gotten invitations to the secret society, they wouldn't be able to shut up about it. I flounce back onto my bed to study, but not for class. Instead, I examine the cryptic note, running my fingers over the embossed seal. Whoever delivered it didn't sneak in through the window, and Jude and Loki didn't let them in. That means only one thing—

They had access.

My breath catches. This secret society must be really connected. The message is clear enough, stating a day and time. That must be for the initiation test. But one thing stumps me.

What's the Campanile? I wonder.

My neural implant pipes up, startling me. I'm still not used to it.

Accessing dictionary, Estrella says, then a few seconds tick by. *Definition of Campanile. Origin: Italian. Meaning: A clock tower with bells in it.*

I feel a rush of excitement. *Is there a campanile on campus?*

Accessing campus records, Estrella replies. *Yes, it appears so.*

Images of Sather Tower flash in my retinas, along with the history of the building. It's a moment before she continues. *Sather Tower is a campanile, named for its resemblance to the Campanile di San Marco in Venice, Italy, destroyed during the Great War.*

Images of the Campanile di San Marco appear, and the resemblance is striking to the building on campus. It's sad how so many amazing places were obliterated during the war. The campus map flashes, with an arrow pointing to Sather Tower. Well, that solves one mystery.

That's the meeting place. And I also know the date and time, I think.

Estrella pipes up. *Would you like me to set a reminder?*

"*No!*" I practically yell at her.

My paranoia has spiked. I don't want to ruin my chance to join . . . well . . . whatever this is. I have to keep it a secret. I picture the imposing tower that looms over campus like a vigilant sentry keeping watch. The pleasant sound of the bells chimes through my head. I remember walking past it on my first day, when I was trying to find my dorm. It's impossible to miss.

Feeling a flutter of excitement, I replace the card in the envelope and press the wax. It glows and seals the envelope. I was dreading tomorrow, with a full load of classes and my first exchange. The last thing I want is to confess to Kari how badly I'm already failing.

But now, I have something to look forward to . . . something private . . . that's all mine. If the secret society picked me, then I must be doing something right. I must not be a total failure. The warning message printed at the bottom of the card races through my head again.

Don't be late—or forfeit your chance.

"I won't be late," I promise myself in a low voice. "If it's the last thing I do."

CHAPTER 11

KARI

Greetings, recruits, I'm Postmaster Hugo Haven," he says with a salute. Even his hands look floppy and soft. "As you may have gathered, I'm the head of the Ceres Base Post Office."

A few snickers run through my platoon. I don't join in. From my perch on the hard plastic chair, I couldn't be more miserable—for one reason. My first exchange with Draeden is today.

Kill me now, I think with a wince. I notice some recruits don't look nearly as despondent. Percy really hit it off with his Sympathetic, while Genesis also looks shyly excited.

The drill sergeant shoots us a warning look, and everyone clams up fast. We're gathered in the lobby, which looks like a mundane government building with a generic lobby and beige carpet. Mail counters span one end, with postal workers scanning digital packages.

"Welcome to the post office, where we deliver the warp mail to the stars and beyond," he goes on with enthusiasm. "The California Federation has one of the most sophisticated postal services in the universe, though I may be biased," he says. "Ceres Base is the main hub in this system. Believe it or not, communication is our *secret weapon* against the Proxies."

That provokes snickers again. This time, the drill sergeant gives in with a resigned sigh and doesn't bother glaring at us. I can tell she thinks this is a bit silly, too. But I like the postmaster already. He's humble, warm, and he even has a sense of humor, which stacks him way above the drillmaster. He's on the shorter side with a cherubic face and piercing blue eyes framed by round wire spectacles. He sweeps his gaze over us before continuing the orientation.

"Recruits, can anyone tell me why we had to revert to a hard mail system?" Postmaster Haven asks. "Like we had a long time ago before digital communication took over?"

Anton shoots his hand in the air, dancing in his seat like a maniac. I don't know how he can wriggle around so much after PT majorly kicked our butts this morning. I'm still hobbling around. The burpees alone almost took me down, not to mention more taunts about how I'm . . . *a yellow-bellied coward like my father.* She even had the whole platoon chant that to my face.

The postmaster points to Anton. "Yes, recruit?"

"It's all about warp drives," Anton says, speaking at a rapid clip. It's like punctuation doesn't exist for him. But I guess that's just how fast his mind works.

Nadia rolls her eyes. "Jeez, can you translate your nerd speak?"

Chuckles erupt. Everyone is used to the twins by now. The drill sergeant looks seriously annoyed, but she doesn't chastise us. She knows we can't keep up with Anton either.

"Oh right!" Anton blushes and looks down at his boots. "Sending communications the regular way would take for-*freaking*-ever. Like months or even years, depending on the distance to our interstellar outposts. Excuse my language, sir," he adds with a wince. "The fastest way to deliver digital communications and hard packages is to load them onto small postal ships and warp them. That allows them to travel several warp factors faster than the speed of light."

"That's correct," Postmaster Haven says. "Here on Ceres Base, we're still close enough to Earth to transmit communications directly. However, you will experience lag time," he goes on. "Can anyone tell me how long it takes for our digital communications to reach Earthside?"

Only Anton raises his hand. He looks so eager that it's like he's about to explode.

"Yes, Private," the postmaster says with an amused expression.

"About fifteen to thirty minutes," Anton replies. "Depending on our position in orbit relative to Earth. But based on our current position, it's about twenty-two minutes, sir."

"And sixteen *point* five seconds," the postmaster adds with a nod. "Nice job, recruit. What's your name?"

Anton grins. "Private Ksusha, sir."

"Private Ksusha, nice to make your acquaintance," he says with a warm smile. "If you decide you don't want front lines duty, you're welcome in my post office anytime."

"Thank you, sir." Anton beams, then elbows Nadia and whispers under his breath. "Did you hear that? Space nerds are good for something."

"Mail duty is lame," she shoots back.

Luckily, the drill sergeant doesn't hear them. She's turned around to set up a screen, which displays Ceres Base's position in orbit around the sun relative to Earth. The postmaster taps on the screen, zooming in on one of the enormous satellite dishes on our surface.

The postmaster points to the screen. "Can anyone tell me how your Sympathetic communications will differ from the ones you transmitted to your families earlier today?"

We had a few minutes to send recorded messages to our families, not nearly enough time. I miss Ma and Bea like crazy. On the upside, it was easier to put on a good front and act like everything was going amazing, even though that's the opposite of what's really happening. But I don't want them to worry, or think I'm going to wash out. They're depending on me now.

Anton raises his hand. *Again.*

"Someone other than Private Ksusha?" the postmaster prompts.

Anton elbows Luna, his battle buddy. She's on the taller side with short, buzzed sandy blonde hair, and heralds from Fresno, from what I've gathered. He whispers into her ear, as she raises her hand uncertainly. Her cheeks flame pink. They're dappled with freckles.

The postmaster points to her. "Yes, recruit?"

"Our neural implants, sir," she says in a soft voice. "We use them to record encrypted messages for our Sympathetics in some sort of special pod. Though I'm not sure how it all works . . ." She trails off, glancing at Anton for more help. He knows the answer but keeps quiet.

"That's right," the postmaster says, then looks at Anton. "Though I think you got some help from your little friend over there."

Anton shrugs and plays innocent. The postmaster points to the screen, which resolves to show a high-tech padded room filled with rows of egg-shaped pods.

"You will use these warp mail pods specially developed for the Sympathetic Program," he continues, pointing to the pods on the screen. "Your neural link will allow you to record more than just your image and words. It will also upload your feelings and emotions. So, your Sympathetic won't just hear you and see you—they'll *feel* you through the connection."

A hush falls over the platoon.

Don't remind me, I think in horror.

"And vice versa," the postmaster continues. "There will be lag time, as discussed. You will record and transmit your exchange, then wait to receive their response. That should take around forty-five minutes. When you jack back in to receive their reply, your neural link will allow you to experience their feelings and emotions. This part is critical to the program."

I let that sink in. *I'll feel him, too,* I think with a shudder of revulsion.

"Recruits, you may feel inclined to hide your true feelings in your exchange," Haven continues in an ominous voice. "But don't attempt to keep things from your Sympathetic."

Genesis raises her hand. "But what if you accidentally forget stuff?"

"Yeah, I space out all the time," Percy adds with a grimace.

The postmaster nods. "Great question, recruit. Your neural implant will monitor your exchange and keep you on track. It can sense if you're not being fully honest or withholding information—like a fancy lie detector—and then prompt you to get back on message."

My stomach flips. That's even worse. I can't lie to Draeden. That alone makes me want to tear my neural implant out of my skull. But I guess I should look on the bright side. This way, he will feel how much I hate his guts, I think wryly. At least I've got that going for me.

Anton raises his hand. "Does that mean it'll zap us? Like if we don't tell the *whole* truth? Like when I was late to an appointment once?"

The drill sergeant cuts in. "Yup, zap and report you, too. Know what that means?"

"More push-ups?" Anton guesses. He flexes his puny biceps, then grimaces.

"Brilliant, Private Ksusha," the drill sergeant replies. "Don't let it go to your oversized head. However, if you continue to withhold information, or worse, purposefully lie to your Sympathetic, then you will be dishonorably discharged and shipped back Earthside."

Her words hit us hard. I flinch in my chair, as Haven calls the first recruit for their exchange. They'll take us back one by one. I swallow hard. Being forced to communicate my deepest, darkest secrets and feelings with Draeden is a punishment almost worse than death.

"Private Skye?" Postmaster Haven says as he hits a button on his tablet to unlock the warp mail pod. "Ready for your Sympathetic exchange?"

The curved siding of the pod cracks open with a *hiss*, revealing the interior. It's outfitted with an ergonomic chair upholstered in velvety gray fabric. It would almost look welcoming, if I didn't know better. I take a whiff and smell something strange that makes my nose crinkle.

"Is that . . . *lavender?*" I ask in surprise.

"Why, yes, it is," Postmaster Haven says with an impressed nod. "It's synthetic lavender oil blended with chamomile and peppermint. Oh, and a touch of sandalwood. It's my special aromatherapy blend, designed to help you relax and let down your defenses."

That's the last thing I need right now, I think. When it comes to Draeden, I need all my defenses. Steel ones reinforced with barbed wire. And maybe electrified, too.

"Private Skye, take a seat and make yourself comfortable," he says, gesturing to the pod. "Don't worry, it won't hurt a bit," he promises, seeing the terrified look on my face.

That's because he doesn't know my Sympathetic, I think in alarm.

But instead, I bite my tongue and say, "Right, thanks."

I try to settle into the chair, feeling the soft cushioning mold to my frame. It reminds me of the sling chairs. But inside, my panic is rising and stiffening my limbs in a fight-or-flight response. I can't make out a screen or anything else. *How do we communicate?* I wonder.

"Okay, almost ready," Postmaster Haven says, swiping his tablet. "There you go, the timer is all set for your exchange. You have to stay in here for a required ten minutes."

"Ten minutes?" I say in a strained voice, dreading every last second.

Postmaster Haven mistakes that for me wanting *more* time. "Oh, don't worry. That's just the first session. For subsequent exchanges, you may request additional time."

I shudder at that thought and decide . . . *never.*

"Have a nice exchange," Postmaster Haven says, swiping at his tablet again. *Whoosh. Click.* The door whisks shut, sealing me inside the pod with a terrifying finality.

Immediately, I can't breathe. I start hyperventilating. The aromatherapy only makes it worse. My breath sharpens when I see the timer cue up in my retinas, thanks to Harold.

Then, my implant pings me.

Hikari, are you ready? Draeden is waiting to receive your exchange.

"Right, I can't wait," I force out, working to control my breathing and slow my racing heart. Having a panic attack right now won't help me get through the next ten minutes.

Was that sarcasm? Harold asks in his stilted voice.

"Ah, yes," I reply. "You're improving, but you've still got a long way to go."

Thank you, Hikari, Harold says, unaware that it wasn't much of a compliment. He also indicates that my elevated heartrate is perfectly normal before my first exchange.

INITIATING SYMPATHETIC EXCHANGE

That message flashes in my retinas. Before I can object, soothing instrumental music kicks on in the pod, more aromatherapy blasts out, and the lights dim, casting me into shadow. The dimensions and curves of the pod recede into pitch blackness. Not like night back Earthside, when there are still stars and ambient light. This is like cave darkness. It's suffocating.

Calibrating neural link, Harold communicates. *Connecting now.*

I feel my neural link jack into the pod, and I can't describe the sensation, except that it feels like my brain is being ripped from my skull. Suddenly, I'm falling through a vast . . .

Nothingness.

My stomach drops as I plunge deeper into the void. It's just like my nightmare. I try to scream, but I can't move my lips. The blackness presses into my eyeballs and snakes down my throat, choking me. Just when I think I can't take it anymore—I stop falling abruptly.

My boots touch down on solid ground. Then stars bloom overhead, millions of them pricking the black velvet sky. Ice geysers spout behind me like mystical fountains. That's when it hits me—I'm standing on the surface of Ceres. It's some kind of simulation, but it feels so real.

I test it out, taking a cautious step. My boots skid on the black ice.

"Wild," I whisper, my breath ghosting out in milky tendrils. There's less gravity here, so each step feels like bouncing on a trampoline. I peer up at the stars, so brilliant without the dilution of much atmosphere or light pollution. I can't help but marvel at the alien landscape.

Ready for your exchange? Harold pings me.

I'm not ready. I'll never be ready.

But what choice do I have?

The red recording light materializes in the corner of my vision next to the timer. It starts flashing, indicating that the exchange is about to begin. Harold counts down the time, but it feels like he's counting down my life. My heart races faster, and cold sweat breaks out over my body.

Three . . . two . . . one . . .

The light turns solid red; the counter starts ticking down.

The exchange has started. I stare straight ahead with a scowl, my breath smoking out, while Ceres spans behind me. I have to be honest, I remember. I have to tell the truth. That means, how much I despise him. And trust me, I have a list of reasons, all culminating in that . . . *kiss.* I picture his stupid face as I remember it from high school. His cocky grin and roguish eyes. The way he carries himself like he's invincible and nothing bad could ever touch him.

Turbulent emotions flood through me. I purse my lips and form the first words that pop into my mind. I force them out through stiff lips. And once I start talking, I can't stop the vitriol. But I know I won't get into trouble for my exchange. I'm just following the rules.

It's completely honest.

CHAPTER 12

DRAE

Sympathetic message loading, Estrella communicates. *Stand by for neural link.*

The warp mail pod seals shut around me as the blonde postal worker retreats. The ergonomic chair contorts around my body. The enclosed space feels so much smaller now. The curved walls press in on me like a vise. My heart starts to beat faster and faster at the prospect of . . . Kari. My cheeks flush, while sweat slicks my palms like I've been running a marathon.

INITIATING SYMPATHETIC EXCHANGE

Before I can back out, the lights dim and extinguish, then the strangest sensation overtakes me, like jumping out of a transport at high speed. Then it feels like my brain is being sucked out of my skull. It doesn't hurt, just feels super bizarre. Suddenly, endless stars bloom overhead, erupting in an impossibly black sky. My breath gushes out like smoke.

Goosebumps prick my skin. Suddenly—I'm freezing and shivering. My clothes are flimsy protection. I cradle my chest, trying to kindle some warmth. I take a stumbling step forward, but slip on black ice. Dusty rocks and fine sand coat my sneakers. Stranger yet, I feel lighter . . . like there's less gravity pressing down on me. This must be some kind of simulation.

But where am I?

That's when a figure materializes in front of me—

A dark silhouette.

She walks closer until the starlight licks her sharp cheekbones and lights up her dark eyes. It's Kari—only she looks different now. Her long hair is shorn into a buzz cut, for one thing. But it's more than that. Something about how she carries herself. She pauses a few feet away, standing on the crystalline surface. Her breath gushes out in smoky swirls, blending with mine. She looks like a space goddess in her uniform, like Estrella Luna from my comics.

One thought shoots through my head—

She's the most beautiful thing I've ever seen

"*Kari* . . ." I whisper in a soft gasp. But that's when I remember the orientation for new Sympathetics. This is only a recording. We can't converse in real time. All I can do is listen.

She stares me down, her eyes narrowing to slits. They lock onto my face, even though this is a prerecorded message. Somehow her eyes still find mine and hold my gaze.

Her lips move, and words shoot out—

"You're the last person in the universe I want to talk to right now."

I cringe as if she struck me. Like that time in the hallway. But the worst part is that I don't just see her—I *feel* her. And how exactly much she hates me. Honestly, I don't know what I expected her to say in our first exchange. I guess some part of me hoped that time and distance would change how she felt, maybe soften it. But now, I know it's the exact opposite.

My heart drops, but before I can worry more—

Her thoughts, her feelings, her emotions . . . her *everything*. They bombard me all at once, overriding my senses. I feel myself receding until . . . it's like I'm inside Kari's head. Or maybe, she's hijacked my neurons, until I am her . . . and she is me . . . and we are like one being.

I lose myself in the exchange. I feel as though I'm the one saying these words, not the other way around. They become a part of me. Kari keeps talking—and I listen, caught in her complicated tangle of emotions.

I'm helpless to do anything else.

"Hey there . . . uh . . . Drae," Kari says, stumbling over the words. Then she steels herself and plows forward. "Everything on Ceres Base is going *great*. Like super-duper, awesome, amazingly great. I'm kicking ass in PT, more than kicking ass, I'm totally acing it—"

She cringes as her neural implant zaps her. I feel the sharp sting in my head, too. Like I got zapped for lying. The back of my neck throbs with pain, and a healthy dose of humiliation.

Hikari, you're not being honest, her neural implant communicates. *Remember the rules? Violate them again—and I'll be forced to report you to your drill sergeant.*

I hear the message from her neural implant like he was talking to me.

"Jeez, Harold, I get it!" Kari says, rubbing her neck. "You don't have to zap me."

Just doing my job, her implant replies in a stilted voice.

"Fine," she says, gritting her teeth. "I'll tell . . . the . . . blasted . . . truth."

She resets her stance, squares her shoulders, and huffs out smoky swirls of breath into the frigid air of the simulation. Then without even talking, somehow she communicates . . . *everything*. Her thoughts come at me in a cascade, colored by kaleidoscopic emotions. They flash through my head like scenes cut together, only layered with sensation and cadence.

I experience her last few days like they're my own in a matter of minutes. *The journey to Ceres Base, where she's stationed for basic training. The grueling exercises that she has to do in PT every morning. The degradation when the drill sergeant taunts her about her dad and singles her out for punishment. How everyone at Basic already hates her, and she's terrified that she's going to wash out in record time.* It all comes at me rapid-fire. Just her thoughts.

But she does talk. She has to talk and get it out.

"Look, let's get this straight," Kari says, staring me down in the sim. "I despise you and everything you stand for. And you don't like me either. This Pairing . . . it's a horrible mistake. And that . . . incident . . . in the stairwell . . ." She trails off and glances down at her boots.

I gasp, knowing that she's talking about . . . *the kiss.* Her cheeks flush with heat even in the frigid air. Blood also rushes to my cheeks. She looks up and has to force the words out.

"So why'd you do it? Why'd you . . . kiss me?"

Her words echo out. She lets them hang there. I experience her shock and anger at me in that moment, boiling over into rage. I feel her fist connect with my jaw, again and again. But I also sense another emotion underneath those surface feelings. Something more secretive. Something deeper and hidden. Something that she doesn't even like to admit to herself.

Curiosity. Intrigue. Desire. Lust.

But also this—

She'd never been kissed before. That was her first kiss.

This catches me off guard. I'm shocked down to my core. Most kids our age have had some kissing experience by senior year. She has such a tough exterior, I assumed . . .

"The kiss . . ." Kari spits out, emitting dragon's smoky breath and fiery words. "Right, please let's never call it that again. Uh, from now on . . . let's call it . . . *the incident.*"

Her eyes flit over my face, even though I'm not really there.

"Anyway, I want to know why you did it," she demands. "My whole life, everyone has always avoided me. Trust me, that's not an exaggeration. Rho practically hooked up with the entire senior class. Remember Percy Quan and Genesis Salerno? From school? Well, they've been attached at the hip since blastoff. Somehow, they even got paired together as battle buddies."

It takes a moment, but I do remember them.

"So why'd you do it?" Kari goes on. "Why didn't you avoid me like everyone else? Did your friends dare you? Was it to humiliate me? A lame prank? Or . . . was it because . . ."

She speaks fast, like she has to get it all out.

"You actually *liked* me?"

Her question hurls out in the thin air. When she stops confessing everything, she's out of breath. Her cheeks flame, while her breath hisses out in short bursts. She stares straight ahead, her chest heaving. I feel the complex jumble of emotions unraveling in the depths of her heart—*shame, fear, humiliation*—but something else, too. Something that's foreign to her . . .

Hope.

That's when she realizes that the exchange timer has almost ticked down to zero. Her face registers this fact. Her eyes widen in alarm. Alarm floods through her whole being.

"Wait, Harold?" she says in a panicked voice. "Don't send that exchange! Delete it . . . now! I want to start over. Please, erase it and let's try again. Talk about something else—"

Only *five* seconds left.

I can see the timer in the corner of my vision. She sees it, too. Her panic grows. "Harold, I'm begging you! I don't know what came over me. Don't send that exchange—"

Sorry, Hikari, her implant communicates. *Sympathetic exchanges cannot be erased and rerecorded. They must be transmitted. You signed the agreement. You know the rules.*

"But Harold," she says, whipping around in total panic. Her boots skid on the ice. "You can't send that message. I don't know why I mentioned . . . that stupid *incident*. It's not relevant. I was supposed to talk about basic training, not old high school stuff—"

The timer ticks down to *zero*.

A message flashes in my vision.

Exchange recorded and transmitted. Disconnecting neural implant.

Kari's panicked, fear-stricken face is the last thing I see before the exchange fades away. The stars dry up; the icy crust vanishes from under my sneakers. I feel that strange sucking sensation, then the lights slowly fade up, blistering my retinas. I'm still in here in the warp mail pod.

I never went anywhere.

I blink hard, shocked by her exchange. She could have told me about anything. But she chose to talk about—*the kiss.* The one I planted on her lips without consent. The one I regret. Even more now, if that were possible. Her first kiss, it turns out. That makes me wince.

But before I can gather my thoughts—or come up with a composed response—it's time to record my exchange for her. The red light starts flashing, the timer starts ticking down.

Abruptly, the exchange simulation unfolds around me. Kari materializes in front of me. Before my neural implant can zap me for withholding, I open my mouth and spill my guts about college and everything going on. But when I finally get to the *incident*, I'm almost out of time.

I freeze up and blurt out the first thing that jumps to mind. The words tumble from my lips in a breathless rush. Immediately, I want to take it back . . . but it's too late.

I have a feeling Kari isn't going to like it.

CHAPTER 13

KARI

Just as my anxiety peaks waiting, and I'm about to lose it in this warp mail pod, my neural implant finally pings me. My heart stops, then basically falls through my stomach.

Exchange received from Sympathetic. Ready?

"Yes, get it over with," I say through gritted teeth. But the truth is—

I'll never be ready, I think as the lights fade out again. But I don't have a choice. The aromatherapy kicks in full blast, then my neural implant jacks me in to receive his exchange.

I experience that crazy, brain-sucking feeling again. Everything falls away, like plunging through a vast nothingness, but then another landscape unfurls around me.

Bright sunlight blinds my eyes, dazzling and strong. I blink hard, waiting for my vision to clear. Soft grass crushes under my combat boots. Real grass, not that awful fake turf. Paved paths curve through the courtyard, framed by stately, pre-war buildings. I'm standing in front of an edifice that skewers the cornflower-blue sky. After a moment, I realize that it's a clock tower.

The bells chime boldly, signaling the hour of the day.

I take all this in, and it hits me all at once in a rush of sensation—sight, smell, touch, feel, sound—even the taste of musty fall leaves tainting the breeze. I can *smell* the fresh-cut grass. I can *feel* the sun warming my skin. I can *hear* the gentle rustling breeze as it tickles my cheeks.

I'm at UC Berkeley.

Or rather, it's a simulation of the campus.

Though it appears to be midday, and the courtyard should be swarming with students, the courtyard is deserted. But then, a door cracks open in the building with the clock tower.

Creak.

A lone figure emerges—it's Drae.

He's silhouetted by bright sunlight, but as he draws nearer, his features come into stark relief. Chiseled nose and cheekbones, dark skin, perfect teeth, the result of quality dental care. But when he draws closer, I notice something else—dark circles under his eyes. He doesn't start talking yet, but already I can *feel* his thoughts coming at me. I relive his first humiliating days at college as if they were my own. I experience his thoughts, his memories, and his emotions.

What it's like to be . . . *him*.

And I'm shocked to learn . . . it's not so great, after all. He might hate his life more than me, and that's saying a lot. How is that possible? I'm up before the crack of dawn every day, getting my ass kicked by a drill sergeant with an extra-special vendetta against my father.

Finally, he starts talking . . . not just thinking at me.

"Hey, Kari . . . so I guess you can tell that my life isn't all it's cracked up to be . . ."

It's like the floodgates open. He tells me about Jude and Loki being his roommates, even though it's the last thing he wanted. How much he hates them and desperately wants to get away and start over, but he can't seem to leave his past behind.

Wow, I know what that's like, I think before I can stop myself. Against my better judgment, my mind unclenches a little. Maybe Postmaster Haven is right. Maybe I just need to give the program a chance. It's so unlike me to trust anyone that it takes me by surprise.

He keeps talking and talking, confessing everything to me about his life. I glance at the timer in the corner of my eye. It's already running down. Only a few minutes remain for our exchange. I can't believe how fast it went after the torture of waiting for his response.

He notices the time is running out, too.

"You asked about . . . *the incident,*" Drae says, looking pained. His lips twist into a grimace. "You should know, I regret it. I know I can't take it back. But I wish I didn't do it. You have to believe me. I had no idea it was your first time. But you asked why I did it . . ."

I can feel his awkwardness, his discomfort, and his regret. I can even feel the shooting pain in his jaw where I punched him. This all passes wordlessly between us like a secret.

"All I can say is . . ."

He holds my gaze, though I'm not actually there. But it almost feels like he can see me—*the real me.* I hold my breath. My heart thumps, sending waves of heat tingling through my body. I feel both tense and like I'm melting at the same time, in defiance of natural laws.

Then he opens his mouth . . .

"Temporary insanity," he says with a cocky grin. "That's the only explanation for why I kissed you. Because believe me, it certainly wasn't your . . . winning personality."

And in that instant, the old Draeden is back, the bully who I despise with every fiber of my being. I should've known better than to trust the likes of him. I curse my foolishness.

Well, it won't happen again. I can promise that.

I scowl back at him, wishing I could blast him to the stars and back, until the timer ticks down to zero. Mercifully, his smug face finally dissolves, and everything fades to black.

My neural implant pings me.

Exchange complete, Harold communicates. *Disconnecting neural implant.*

I wait for that brain-sucking feeling, then for my link to disconnect and the pod to *hiss* open, releasing me from my purgatory. My thoughts knot together in a raging mass of black emotions. One thing is certain—he hasn't changed one bit. He's the same privileged jerk.

Just in a new setting.

"*Winning personality,*" I grumble all the way back to the barracks.

If I could do it over, I'd punch Drae when he uttered that phrase with his stupid grin. Right in his perfect square jaw, like I did back in high school. I clench my fist. Not that you can punch someone in a warp mail message, but the idea still makes me feel better.

When I reach the barracks, I cast myself onto my rack, feeling even worse than I did before our exchange. I bury my head in the scratchy pillow. I'm pretty sure this isn't how the Sympathetic Program is supposed to work. Aren't I supposed to feel more adjusted and grounded—not all *ragey* and *stabby* and *murdery*? But I can't help it. He has that effect on me.

He makes me want to punch things.

He always has. It's like his superpower.

I flip over with a groan, feeling the rough sheets scratch my cheek. Since it's warp mail day, my platoon had the afternoon off from PT. Thank the stars for small miracles. I'm trying to relax and forget about my horrible exchange when I hear the *slip-slap* of flip-flops.

Nadia heads for the showers. I try to hide in my rack, praying that she won't notice my existence. But then, she skids to a halt and jerks her finger to the edge of my mattress.

"Recruit, remake that," she orders, oblivious to my mental crisis. "Those corners aren't right. Get them tucked in. Or you'll fail inspection again—and earn us both extra reps."

She's been extra hostile since that disastrous first day, when the drill sergeant outed me for being deserter spawn, then made her my battle buddy to punish her for acting like a boss.

"Right, sorry, Nadia," I say, scrambling up from my rack and trying to mold my sheets and blanket into perfect military-style triangles. But I struggle to get them to tighten and fold right. They come out all lumpy and misshapen—sure to fail inspection again later.

Why is this so hard for me?

I don't understand it. Lately, I can't seem to do anything right, according to both Nadia and the drill sergeant. Frustrated tears spring to my eyes. But I know breaking down now will only make everything worse. I try to fight back against them, but fail miserably.

Suddenly, a shrill alarm blares through the barracks.

Beep! Beep! Beep!

Strobe lights pulse, illuminating the room with staccato bursts. I leap to my feet, while my rack mate Luna jumps down from above me. That's Anton's battle buddy.

Nadia and Anton come running back from the showers with their hair sopping wet. Other recruits spring up from their racks. Nervous chatter ricochets around the barracks.

"Wh-what's happening?" I hiss to Nadia, who is busy tugging on her uniform and boots. She half hops, half staggers to my side. I shove my boots onto my bare feet without socks. But I don't care that they're rubbing my heels. My heart hammers into my throat in the confusion.

Bang.

Suddenly, the door bursts open.

The drill sergeant comes charging into the barracks. She looks worried but quickly hardens her countenance. The door remains ajar. Outside in the corridor, I spot guardians and recruits rushing around. Their footfalls sound organized, but urgent at the same time.

My brain struggles to piece it all together.

"Threat level increased to RED," the drill sergeant barks at us. Her eyes sweep over our worried faces. "All recruits down to the bunker right away. Prepare for incoming attack."

CHAPTER 14

DRAE

After my late night "study" date with Rho, during which I bought her faux pepperoni pizza and briefed her that Kari 1) is perfectly alive and breathing and 2) still hates me with every fiber of her being, and she helped me through my Great Books reading assignment of *The Odyssey*, which I learned isn't a book at all, but rather an epic poem (let's just say, I barely survived that), I speed walk across campus. I have an important mission tonight—and I can't be late.

My hand snakes into my pocket, feeling the outline of the envelope. I pray that the bells don't chime out twelve times before I make it. *Don't be late—or forfeit your chance.* That keeps me on edge the whole way there, as I cut across Memorial Glade toward the front steps.

The clock tower looms over campus. Quickly, I glance around to make sure nobody is watching, then I dash up the steps and duck into the shadows under the ornate eaves. The only light comes from the thin wisp of the moon hanging in the sky. The night is cold and clear.

I glance up at the wooden doors of the building. They're closed tight.

What do I do now?

I double-check the card, but it doesn't offer directions. It simply says to be here on time—which I am. I reach for the doors . . . but before I can touch them . . .

Creeeeaaaaak.

They swing inward with a groan that cuts through the night.

I freeze and wait. My breath catches in my throat, while my heart races. I don't want anything to jeopardize my chances of making it into the secret society. I hear some distant laughter—*drunken, foolish, slurred*—but nothing to indicate that anyone overheard me.

It's pledge season for the fraternities; no doubt that's where my roommates went. After a few seconds, I relax and slip inside the building, shutting them behind me. It's dark, except for . . .

Candles. Little tea lights.

They line the stairs and lead up the spiral staircase that climbs into the clock tower, casting flickering light over the stucco walls. Somebody must have lit them.

That means, they were expecting me. My heart thumps in my chest, while sweat slicks my palms.

Now I know I'm in the right place. I grip the card tighter, feeling a secret thrill rush through my body. I'm right—it must be that secret society. I strain my ears, but I hear nothing.

It's silent.

Almost too silent.

The soft flicker of the candles dances against the dark. I decide to follow them. My shoes slap against the metal rungs as I wind up the staircase, twisting around. I can hear the ticking of gears from the clock's innards. This ancient technology still keeps perfect time somehow.

My legs start to grow tired, but I keep climbing. Minutes tick by, counted out by the clock. The candles follow me until I push through the heavy door and reach—

The clock tower.

A dusty, deserted, dimly lit, circular room. I can see the blue-green-tinged bells dangling like old relics from a forgotten age. I wonder who maintains the clock, winds the gears, and keeps it all running. Tall, arched windows look out over the sprawling campus. I approach the windows and lose myself in the breathtaking view bathed in moonlight, but then—

Creak, slam.

Suddenly, the door slams shut behind me.

My heart jackhammers against my ribs. I lurch to the door and twist the knob, but it's locked. I crank it again in vain. I bang on the door and yell, "Hey, let me out! I'm stuck in here!"

But it's thick and won't budge. Nobody comes to my rescue.

Feeling rattled and claustrophobic, I back away from the door and desperately search the circular room for another exit. But they're all locked. *I'm trapped inside the clock tower.*

I slump down against the curved wall, trying to slow my breathing and calm my racing heart. It doesn't work, not really. That's when I spot something—

Propped up by the bells, surrounded by a cluster of tea lights, there's another envelope. I climb to my feet and cross the room, my ears pricked for any sounds. *Was it left here earlier—or is someone watching me?* I think, feeling paranoid. As I get closer, I see my name on it in the same ornate calligraphy. The other side is marked with the familiar wax seal of the grizzly bear.

Maybe this is my way out.

I scoop the card up, quickly pressing my thumb into the seal. It glows and unseals the envelope. Carefully, I slide out the thick cardstock. I scan the handwriting, feeling a jolt.

Congratulations on making it this far.
But until you solve this puzzle,

you will go no further.
You have until dawn to free yourself
from this clock tower.

Underneath it, I find this riddle:

What can fly without wings?
What is harmless but can kill you?
What is the question you can ask all day long,
but get completely different answers?

I squint at the ornate text, but it's a riddle. This message makes absolutely no sense. My brain feels fuzzy. *Shit, I wish Rho were here,* I think immediately. She'd know how to solve this mystery and figure out the answer. "Come on, Drae," I say under my breath. "Think . . ."

That's when *something* stirs in the shadows.

The candles flicker and dance with the sudden movement. I whip around and scan the tower, but it's dark and impossible to see anything. Then I hear something that freaks me out—

Footsteps . . . scraping against stone.

Like halting, dragging steps.

My stomach lurches as fear floods through me. If any place on campus is haunted, it's definitely this clock tower. That's when a high-pitched cackle reverberates out from the shadows. I whirl around, trying to locate the source of the laughter. I zero in on the spot . . .

It came from the back. By the ticking gears.

"Wh-who's there?" I stammer. "What do you want from me?"

In response, the horrible cackles come again, sending chills up my spine. They resolve into words, echoing out of the darkness. My fear spikes when I hear what they say—

"Draeden . . . *Raccchhhheeee* . . . your soul belongs to me."

CHAPTER 15

KARI

Recruits, get into the bunker!" the drill sergeant orders, as the alarm continues blaring.

We rush into the emergency shelter, buried deeper underneath the base. My combat boots track prints into the dust covering the floor. The air smells musty and stale. One thing is clear—nobody's been down here in a long time. Monitors span one side of the bunker. They show grainy security footage of the surface. But it's dark outside; night has already fallen.

I scan the concrete room, taking it all in. Non-combat personnel—medical, postal workers, engineers, support staff—plus other platoons at various stages of basic training crowd into the bunker. Everyone looks a little shell-shocked, and a lot worried. One thing is clear—

This isn't a drill. The jumpy energy tells me that much.

Harold, what's going on up there? I think, studying the security feeds. But the footage doesn't provide any clues. Nothing moves or disturbs the exterior darkness.

Stay in the bunker, Harold replies. *Remain calm. Wait for orders.*

No shit, I think back. *I already know that. But what's really going on?*

Stay in the bunker, Harold starts to repeat, so I cut him off.

Message received, I say with annoyance. *Thanks for nothing.*

You're most welcome, Harold says brightly without a hint of irony. *Anything else?*

Mute, please, I think, and realize that I better settle in to wait this out.

The bunker starts to feel cramped as more people rush inside. Meanwhile, the drill sergeant paces in front of us, monitoring her communications and tapping agitatedly on her tablet. She responds to some of the messages. I strain my ears and catch a few muffled words.

"*Siberian Federation . . . Arctic Federation . . . Proxy alliance . . . chatter over the communications . . . threat level increased to RED . . .*"

Finally, Nadia can't help it. She speaks out of turn.

"Drill Sergeant, are we under attack?"

She looks up in surprise, then irritation washes over her face. Nadia just broke the first rule of Basic—*don't speak unless spoken to first.* The drill sergeant marches over to us.

She zeroes in on Nadia. Her words come out like blasts.

"Private Ksusha, are we friends now? This is above your pay grade! Need-to-know basis. But if it'll shut you up, it appears the Siberian Fed just pulled a flyover of our base."

Gasps ripple through our ranks. This is confirmation.

It's not a drill.

"Now sit down—and keep your mouth shut," she adds. "And wait for orders."

Satisfied we got the message, she wheels around and tramps across the bunker toward the other drill sergeants. They're easy to spot with their signature stiff-brimmed hats and stern, *don't-mess-with-me expressions*. Left alone, we hunker down, but that doesn't calm me. Instead, it makes me feel helpless. I'm used to fighting my way out of problems, not hiding from them.

I lean closer to Anton.

"What exactly is . . . a flyover?" I whisper, making sure we're not overheard.

"Oh right, it's a classic military maneuver," Anton says in an equally low voice. "Basically, an enemy ship flies low past our base, but they don't engage in combat . . . yet." He forms his hands into wings to demonstrate, then whooshes them right past my face.

I frown back. "So, what's the point of that? Seems like a waste of time."

"Jeez, you really are green," Nadia butts in. "The purpose is simple—to intimidate us. Sounds like classic Siberian Fed tactics. Probably a show of strength to send us a message."

I swallow hard. "What kind of message?"

"Above our pay grade, remember?" Nadia snaps. "You heard the drill sergeant."

We lapse into silence. But I can't stop my mind from . . . well . . . *thinking*. Ever since the terrorist attack back Earthside, tensions have been mounting with the Proxies.

In this strange limbo, my mind drifts to one thing—

Bea and Ma.

"What if this is only the beginning . . ." I say in a soft voice, barely a whisper before I can stop myself. Doubts rush through me. My words hang ominously in the recirculated air.

Luna looks over. "The beginning of . . . *what?*"

"Interstellar war," I say with a shudder.

"Do you think the Siberian Fed was behind the Golden Gate Attack?" Anton pipes up. It's the question on everyone's minds lately. The newsfeeds have been accusing them nonstop.

"Well, it makes sense, right?" I whisper back. "We've been fighting the Proxy Wars for decades. They're our main adversary up here. Well, and their ally the Arctic Fed."

"Sorry, but I'm not convinced," Luna says with a shake of her head. "I know the newsfeeds have been pushing that theory. But if the Siberian Fed really did it, then wouldn't pulling a flyover make them look guilty? Then why are they bothering to deny responsibility?"

"Well, somebody blew those kids up," Nadia cuts in, raising her head from her knees. "And they're the top suspects—for a reason. Who else would want to attack us?"

"From what I heard, that bomb was super high-tech," Anton says, perking up. "Not to mention, infiltrating our federation and planting the explosive device on that bus?"

"You're right," Luna says with a sharp nod. "Only a few of the Proxies could pull something like that off. Not to mention, get away with it. That does point to them."

"Plus, there's the issue of motive," Anton goes on. "The Siberian and Arctic Alliance has held a grudge against us since we tried to siphon off their natural resources after the Great Melt. That means they have a reason to go after us. So logically speaking, all signs point to them."

"Right—that's what started the Proxy Wars," I say, struggling to remember my Federation History classes. "The Resource Wars after the Melt kicked it off. That led to the Siberian and Arctic Feds forming an alliance. They've been hostile toward us ever since."

"Yup, no wonder the secretary-general blamed them for the GGA," Anton says.

"But isn't it a little too obvious?" I say, frowning. I can't explain it, but something doesn't feel right. "And then, they pull a flyover? Are they trying to start a war?"

Nadia glares at me. "Why are you defending them? Those Siberian bastards murdered our kids! Blast it all, I just wish there was something we could do about it . . ."

"Jeez, don't be stupid," Anton says, shaking his head. "We can't even get through PT without dying. We've only been here for one week. We're lowly grunts—green as the stars."

"I know, I just hate feeling useless—" Nadia starts.

But she's cut off as the whole bunker rocks. The floor rumbles and undulates beneath my boots. My heart jolts in my chest, jackhammering against my ribcage.

"What's happening?" I gasp, holding onto Luna and Anton for support.

Panic ripples through everyone like an aftershock. The drill sergeants scramble around, huddling together and speaking urgently. I'm pretty sure that's a bad sign.

"Those bastards must be attacking us," Nadia hisses, but then we lurch forward as the base rumbles again. But Anton shakes his head, pointing to the monitors of the surface.

"Look, it's not them firing . . . it's us."

"Anti-spacecraft artillery," Nadia says. "Our defenses are fighting back."

Giant arrays of blaster shots explode out to protect our base, designed to take down enemy spacecraft. They have a wide range and can emit rapid-fire shots. They fire in waves, illuminating the surface with brilliant explosions. A quick flash, then darkness cascades back in.

"Stars, know what that means?" Nadia says. Her voice wobbles in fear.

"They're back! It's not just a flyover . . ." Anton trails off.

Suddenly, the black skies outside our base light up again with another barrage of anti-spacecraft artillery fire. Everything turns blindingly white for a split second, completely flaring the security feed. I can't make out anything. My heart hammers faster. And then I see it.

A sleek spacecraft careens straight toward our base.

The fighter speeds closer and closer. Their blasters pierce the black hull, pointing straight at our defenses. My breath catches sharply. This doesn't look like a flyover anymore—

It looks like an attack run.

The enemy fighter flies closer, but it's clearly disguised, maybe even cloaked. It appears to flicker in and out of existence. But then, in the next flash of anti-aircraft artillery fire, the cloaking shields fail for a quick second. I catch a glimpse of the bold insignia marking the hull.

The underbelly glows with—

A red sickle slicing through golden wheat stalks.

There's no mistaking what that means. I find my voice; it comes out strained.

"It's confirmed . . . it's the Siberian Fed . . . we're under attack."

CHAPTER 16

DRAE

Draeden . . . *Raaaccheeee.*"

That creepy voice echoes out again. It's shrill and otherworldly and terrifying.

"Wh-who's there?" I say, whipping around and feeling my heart pound harder. I scan the shadows, searching for whatever ghostly entity haunts this clock tower.

I don't believe in ghosts, but I also don't *not* believe in them. I heard that a lot of college kids died here protesting the Great War. Back then, Berkeley was a hotbed for the pacifist movement (which has all been banned, of course). The legend on campus, though it's considered an urban myth, is that their spirits still materialize in the clock tower to protest the wars.

That voice echoes out again.

"Draeden . . . *Raaaccheeee.*"

Followed by a spine-chilling cackle.

I raise my hands, shaping them into fists. "Stay back! Uh, I'm warning you. Listen, I know how to defend myself. My mom's a war hero. Don't you dare come any closer—"

"Boo!"

A face lunges out of the shadows at me.

"No, stay away," I scream in a high-pitched voice. I cower back, raising my fists to defend myself. The ghost has white hair and eerie white eyes that make it look dead . . . or, well . . . undead. I'm not exactly sure how ghosts work. I shut my eyes tight, expecting to be possessed or maybe killed, and swing my fists wildly—but they don't connect with anything solid.

Not that a ghost is solid.

More cackling laughter reverberates through the clock tower. But then it morphs into something more . . . *normal*. Even familiar. *What's going on?* I crack my eyes open.

"Blast the stars, I *knew* you were up to something," Rho says, stepping into the flickering candlelight. "When you got all awkward tonight at the end of our pizza study fest."

The light catches her face. Her hair morphs from shock white to something more natural. Well, natural for her. Pinkish fading to blonde . . . *delight*. Her eyes transform to match.

"Plus, you said you were going to bed," she goes on. "So, then I knew you had a secret. I figured you were just gonna wank off to *Estrella Luna* comics in your dorm room."

I'm still standing there with my fists raised. I lower them, hoping she didn't notice.

"You should've heard yourself," she says, snorting out more laughter. Her hair and eyes brighten to hot pink. My cheeks burn to match. "What was your plan? You can't punch a ghost."

Shit, she did see my fists.

Now, I feel extra lame. My cheeks flame hotter. Rho skips toward me in her impish way, kind of like a demented fairy, pushing her long, pink-tinted locks behind her shoulders.

But I cross my arms, glaring back at her.

"Rho, what are you doing here?" I demand in a haughty voice. "Did you follow me? This is a *secret* meeting. I'm not supposed to tell anyone. Even Jude and Loki don't know I'm here."

"Relax, study partner," she says with a flirty pout. To my surprise, she holds up a card identical to mine. "I got an invitation, too. I arrived a few minutes before you. When I heard you come through the door, I hid in the back. I wasn't sure who it was, or if I could trust them."

"Wait, you got chosen, too?" I say, unable to hide my disappointment. I'm not sure why this deflates me. I guess . . . I thought I was special. She spies the look on my face.

"Oh wait, you thought you were the only one?"

She stops, bends over, and laughs good and hard.

"Please, these secret societies gotta punch a few frosh," she says when she comes up for air. "I mean, we won't all make it through the initiation, right? And based on your little . . . *come on, Drae, think* . . . I'm guessing you haven't cracked that riddle. You're lucky I turned up."

"Not true—I can do it," I protest, but she holds out her hand.

"Amateur hour is over—give it to the professional nerd," she says, gesturing for the card clutched in my hand. But I dangle it over her head. I've got more than a few inches on her. But she jumps up, swiping the card cleanly from my hand. I let out a defeated sigh in surrender.

"Fine, you can help."

"That's the spirit! But we have to work fast," she says, as we settle down in the flickering candlelight. "This riddle probably leads to another puzzle, and so on . . . until we finally find the key to unlock that door." She jerks her thumb toward it. "And there's a time limit."

"We have until dawn—or we fail," I say in agreement. "The clock tower keeps time."

"*Time*, exactly," she says, grinning at me. Her hair morphs to clear blue like the midday sky. "That's genius. Anyway, don't get cocky. This first puzzle was likely the easy one."

"Wait, you already solved it?" I say.

"No, dummy," she says, rolling her eyes. "You did . . . accidentally, it seems."

"Uh, like what did I say?" I ask, still stumped. "Just refresh my memory . . ."

She grins. "Yup, I figured. You said, *the clock tower keeps . . .*"

"Time," I repeat. "Oh . . . *time . . .*"

I reread the riddle. Now that she pointed it out, the answer does seem obvious. I look up from the card, still confused. "But how does that help us?"

She sighs. "You're completely hopeless. It's the solution—and the location where our next clue is hidden." She leaps to her feet and skips over to the gears of the clock.

She starts running her hands over them, looking for our next clue. They clank away, keeping time, oblivious to her intrusive search of their ancient innards.

I hold my breath, waiting in nervous excitement, while she keeps fumbling around and looking for it. Despite how the riddles mess with my head, now that Rho is here . . . I find myself enjoying the challenge. And there's more . . . I'm actually having fun for once.

Just when I think we made a giant mistake, Rho grins and produces another envelope that was hidden deep in the clock's gears. "Found our next clue. Oh, I can't wait to see what it says."

With that, we hunker down to solve the clues and escape from the tower.

Before dawn, we encounter five more mind-numbing clues, including math puzzles, riddles, and other brain teasers. They finally lead us to a rusty key, hidden inside one of the bells. The rust flecks off onto my hands when I finally snag it, when suddenly, the bells start chiming.

It's six a.m.

I jerk my gaze to the window. The sky is starting to lighten outside. Rho leaps up in alarm. "Come on," she says, grabbing my arm. "We have to get out of here before dawn."

We dash to the door in a breathless rush. I struggle with the large key, trying to fit it into the old, finicky lock. Finally, with Rho's help, it twists—and the door swings open, exhaling fresh air. Or maybe just less stale than inside the clock tower, where we've been locked up together all night. We hurtle down the spiral staircase, taking the steps two at a time.

The tea lights have all burned out by now, but the predawn light is leaking through the windows. Any second, the sun will start to rise, signaling it's dawn. And we'll be disqualified.

"Hurry up," Rho says in a breathless voice, pulling me faster. "If I don't get into this secret society because of your slow ass, then you're officially on my major suck list."

"Wait, I thought I was already on it?" I say, trying to keep up with her, but my legs feel like molasses. I'm exhausted from staying up all night and everything else that happened.

"Let's see, you were on it," she says. "*Past tense.* Then you got paired with my bestie and fed me pizza with your cushy, parental-funded expense account. So, I took you off it. Mentally speaking. It's not an actual list—it's only in my head."

"Well, thank the stars for that," I gasp, feeling my lungs burning.

We tackle the last curve of stairs, winding down, trying to beat the sunrise. Her hair whips behind her, pale yellow like the predawn sky. We burst outside right as the bells finish chiming their morning chorus. The fresh air tastes cool and sweet as I suck it into my screaming lungs. Dew clings to the lawn, a gift from the cool night air. I look up at the sky.

The sun hasn't risen, but it's about time. The sky is brightening in anticipation.

"We made it," I say, trying to catch my breath. "So . . . what now?"

The campus remains deserted, aside from some lunatic jogging in the predawn light. We both scan the area for our next clue. But there's nothing that catches my eye.

Suddenly, Rho jabs my shoulder.

"Look, over there," she says, pointing across the glade.

That's when I spot a figure, cloaked in a blue-and-yellow sweatshirt with an oversized hood. A grizzly bear marks the back of the shirt. The figure tilts their head toward us—but their face remains shrouded by the hood—then they spring away in the opposite direction.

"Hey, we made it," I yell at them. "We got out in time. Look, we passed the test . . ."

But the hooded figure doesn't stop going with that hitching gait, hooking a right and vanishing around the next building. We're left alone. No way we could catch up now.

Rho scowls and kicks the grass.

"Drae, you're officially back on my major suck list—"

"Wait, not so fast."

I point to two envelopes propped up by the door that leads into Sather Tower. In our rush to get out, we overlooked them. One has my name, and the other is for Rho. It's her full name in all its splendor, scrawled in ornate penmanship. She holds up her hand before I can speak.

"Say my full name out loud, then you're back—"

"On your major suck list," I say with an exaggerated eye roll. "Right, I got it."

"That's better." She nods approvingly. "You're inching toward the . . . *you still kinda suck, but you could suck worse* list. You should be proud. That's a serious improvement."

"Sounds like a real honor," I say in a wry voice, scooping up my envelope and pressing my thumb to the wax. My heart beats faster. Golden light leaks out from the seal, then the envelope comes undone just like the last one. I slide out the thick, creamy cardstock.

It's identical to the first one, only there's a new message printed on it.

Congratulations, you made it to the next stage.

"Next stage?" Rho says, scanning her card. She looks up hopefully. "What'd you get?"

"Yup, same. Looks like we both made it."

She dances a happy jig, while her hair sprouts out in excited, hot pink tresses to match her eyes. "So, what does this mean?" I say, squinting at it. "The last one had a place and time."

She stops dancing . . . and actually hugs me. It feels weird coming from her, but also sort of nice. She smells like ripe strawberries, like fresh-cut grass, like pepperoni . . . like *home*.

She releases me and grins, as the sun also rises and spills light over campus.

"It means . . . now we wait."

I frown. "For how long?"

"Like how would I know?" she says, slipping her card into her pocket. "This is the first time I've gotten hazed for a secret society. I'm as much in the dark as you for once."

With that, Rho bids me farewell and skips off toward her dorm with her bright pink hair trailing behind her, while I trudge the other way. I take the increasingly familiar route back to my dorm. When I first arrived, the campus felt like a maze. But now, I'm learning it by heart. I don't even need Estrella's directions anymore. As I stroll along feeling elated, the message runs through my head on repeat, giving me a secret thrill. *Congratulations, you made it to the next stage.* That was actually fun, for once. The most fun I've had since I got to Berkeley.

Suddenly—

My implant pings me with a breaking news alert. It flashes across my retinas in bold font.

BREAKING NEWS ALERT

Siberian Federation flyover in the asteroid belt . . . Threat level increased to RED . . . Report any suspicious activity immediately to federation authorities . . .

My heart drops into my stomach. I flash back to my exchange with Kari . . . the icy crust of that strange arctic tundra . . . the million stars overhead . . . Ceres Base . . . I remember my astronomy lessons. That's located in the asteroid belt. That's where she's stationed.

The location of basic training is top secret, but the Sympathetic program gives me access to all sorts of classified information. That's why I had to sign all those scary contracts that granted me security clearance. I scan the vague newsfeed alert again. But there's nothing else.

But one thing is clear—

Kari is in danger.

That thought is an icy dagger to my heart. It freezes it, as all the blood drains away. I stand there, feeling paralyzed. And the worst part? There's nothing I can do about it.

CHAPTER 17

KARI

A nother rumble shakes the bunker.

I'm huddled with my platoon, waiting out the attack. The security footage on the monitors flares with the barrage of anti-spacecraft artillery lighting up the impossibly black skies. It's still our defenses firing at them. The enemy ship hasn't engaged us . . .

Yet.

The Siberian Fed fighter makes one more pass, flying low over our base and displaying their sigil again. This time, they have their cloaking shield off—they want us to know it's them. Our anti-spacecraft artillery swings around again, tracking their trajectory overhead.

And then before we can fire—

The enemy ship warps and then vanishes in a split second.

But still, we wait. *Was that the only ship? Is it really gone?* The bunker feels tense and claustrophobic with jittery energy.

Right when I'm about to jump out of my skin, the alarms finally shut off. The strobe lights also stop flickering. I'm not sure if that's a good thing or a bad thing.

The drill sergeant speaks to the other drill sergeants, then marches over. I study her face, every crevice and nuance, searching for some clue. But it's a blank mask, completely unreadable. I try to mimic her stone face and act stoic, even though I'm terrified.

"The threat has passed," she says finally, the relief palpable in her voice. "It was just an aggressive flyover. Recruits, you may return to your barracks. But remember, we're on high alert now—RED threat level." She doesn't say it. But we're all thinking the same thing.

The next alarm could signal an actual attack.

Back in my rack that night, ghost alarms ring in my ears. Nobody from my platoon talks or gossips. The usual happy nighttime chatter has dried up in the wake of that flyover.

I lie awake in the semi-darkness. It's never fully dark because of the safety lights. They splinter my dreams. I flash back to the aftermath of the Golden Gate Attack. The images from the newsfeeds jolt through my head. The school bus bursting into flames. Those young children plunging into the bay. Their bodies hitting the frigid, dark water, trailing smoke and ash.

Despite my exhaustion, sleep doesn't come. It feels a long way off. I force my eyes shut and wonder if it will ever come again. My muscles scream with tension, while adrenaline pumps through my veins, preparing me to fight . . . even though I'm not ready for combat yet. All I can do is hide underground and wait it out. Anton is right . . . we're still green as the stars.

I hear soft whimpering in the dark.

"This isn't good . . . I shouldn't have enlisted . . ."

It's Anton. His rack is right across from me.

"Coward, stop your whining," Nadia hisses back in the dark. "Quit embarrassing yourself. This is why we came here! You knew what you signed up for—"

"But Nadia, they could've killed us today," he whispers in a shaky voice. "The Siberian Fed has one of the strongest militaries in the universe. They're second only . . . to us."

"And that's why we're here, remember?" Nadia says, thrashing around with her blanket in annoyance. Her rack is right over the top of his bed. "Stop acting like a crybaby."

"But aren't you afraid?" Anton insists. I hear him sit up. "Even a little bit? *RED threat level.* It doesn't go higher than that."

I sit up, too. "He's right, you know. Higher than that is . . . war."

My words hang in the darkness.

They grow stronger the more time passes without anyone daring to speak. Finally, I hear shifting above me as my rack mate Luna chimes in. She peers over the edge, down at us.

"Well, you'd better hope to the stars that doesn't happen," she says in her soft voice. "We've never had interstellar war before, just smaller Proxy skirmishes. All the feds and their alliances. All that firepower. All those fighter ships. We would destroy each other . . ."

She trails off as those words sink in. Then she adds one last thing—

"It would be the end of us."

Nobody says anything after that.

I hear the shuffling of covers and the shifting of bodies. Then light snoring and deep breathing, as they drift off, one by one. But still, I lie awake in my rack for a long time listening to them snoring, the blood thrumming in my veins, the chatter junking up my brain. I'm too jacked on adrenaline to sleep right now. I keep picturing the Siberian Fed ship flying over us, low and menacing, flashing the sigil with the red sickle slicing through golden wheat.

When I finally fall into restless slumber, terrible images haunt my dreams. Real war, full of fire and fury, full of blood and stars. Limbs severed, bodies obliterated, torn to shreds. Sleek starships reduced to shrapnel and rubble, falling from the sky and peppering the ground like fresh snowfall.

When I wake the next morning, I'm even more exhausted than when I went to bed. I blink in the stark artificial morning light as it washes over the barracks. All I can think is—

I made a huge mistake coming here.

"Who would like to read the passage for us?" asks the drill sergeant.

Of course, Anton shoots his hand in the air. The sparse classroom resembles something from high school. Like everything else up here, it's a no-frills situation. Concrete floors and walls. Not even a lame faux-cheerful poster to brighten the decor. The rest of my platoon occupies the desks around the room. I'm sitting in the back, of course. My usual choice.

"*The greatest victory is that which requires no battle*," he reads from Sun Tzu, an ancient philosopher. I scan the cryptic words in my *Art of War* book. They sound like a riddle.

"And what does that mean?" the drill sergeant asks, scrawling the passage on the whiteboard. The words stare back at me, making my head throb. I thought I was done with school. *No such luck.* Anton raises his hand again. Nobody else even bothers.

"Ksusha again?" the drill sergeant says with a resigned sigh.

"Right, I think it means that war should be a last resort," Anton says, biting his lower lip. "That there are better, more strategic ways to win besides fighting. Plus, if you think about it . . . isn't it way smarter if you can win without casualties or wasting valuable resources?"

Laughter ripples through the class.

"Or that dude's a total coward," Percy mutters under his breath.

"What's that, Private Tran?" the drill sergeant demands, zeroing in on him.

But Percy doesn't back down; he puffs out his chest.

"I said . . . he's a *total coward*," he repeats. "Where's the honor in winning that way? That dude is probably just afraid to fight because he'd get his ass kicked. Am I right?"

More laughter erupts. I'm wondering the same thing.

The drill sergeant angrily taps the board.

"Spoken like a green-ass recruit who's never seen real combat in his life," she says, her face hardening. "Trust me when I say, war should always be a last resort. Once you've had to hold your battle buddy in your arms, dragging them out of a trench, as their guts spill out of their abdomen that's torn open from blaster shrapnel, then we can discuss who's a coward."

Shock ripples through the class.

Her words hang in the air. It was like she was in a trance when she said all that, like she was back on that battlefield. Percy deflates under her glare. All the bravado drains away.

Suddenly, her eyes dart to me.

Your father did that, she mouths.

My stomach drops as I realize something else, something horrifying. She's talking about that terrible night when my dad deserted. She lost her battle buddy because of his actions. I shrink down in my desk even farther, withering under her harsh gaze, wishing I could disappear.

Thankfully, Anton shoots his hand in the air.

"Yes, Ksusha," the drill sergeant says. "Got something else to add?"

He nods eagerly. "Yes, I realized something. Battle philosophers like Sun Tzu imply that . . . our minds are actually our greatest weapons. Not blasters, or warships. That strategy is the most important part. That's how you don't just win the battle, but the whole war."

"Excellent, Private Ksusha," the drill sergeant says with an appreciative nod. "Keep up the good work. You've got the makings of not just a guardian—but a commanding officer. You and your battle buddy are exempt from PT tomorrow. Nice job."

She wheels around and sweeps her gaze over the room.

"Everyone else, you get extra reps."

Nadia shoots her brother a look and mouths—

Suck-up.

But Anton sits there beaming. He might not be the strongest, most physically fit recruit. He still struggles with reps, though he is getting better, mostly thanks to Luna's coaching. She's one of the bosses in our platoon. But he's certainly the smartest. Meanwhile, I sink lower in my chair, pushing my book away. My stomach churns with shame. Not only did I learn something new and horrible about my father, but it makes everything worse. If I can't get a grip on myself—

Then I'm closer than ever to washing out.

CHAPTER 18

DRAE

Let's begin J. R. R. Tolkien's classic," Professor Trebond says, peering at us from the podium as we settle into our seats for class. "Not all great books take place in the real world," she goes on. "Speculative fiction can be just as important and impactful—if not more so."

I'm sitting in class trying to focus, but I'm worried about Kari. Since the breaking alert, I've been scanning the newsfeeds like crazy. But there haven't been any updates. I'll have to wait for our Sympathetic exchange next week. However, the threat level remains raised to . . .

RED.

And the evidence has reached our idyllic campus. On my way to class this morning, I felt a jolt when I spotted the Fed Patrols roving around Memorial Glade. They're drones—sort of like blocky robots on wheels—with a scanner instead of a head. They're about waist-high and fairly cranky, considering they're AI tech. They stop anyone suspicious and scan them to verify their identity. They're also armed with stunners if you decide to resist being scanned.

They're supposed to make us feel safe, but they seem to have the opposite effect.

They make me feel jumpy—and more afraid.

"Please open your copies of *The Hobbit*," Trebond continues from the front of the class, jerking me out of my morbid thoughts. I struggle to focus on today's lecture.

But my friends aren't helping.

"Stupid dwarves and wizards and treasure maps," Loki snorts, thumbing through the book on his tablet. He's sitting between me and Jude, while Rho sits to my left.

"And what in the stars is a . . . *hobbit*?" Jude adds in a stuck-up voice. He doesn't even bother trying to whisper. Everyone can hear him clearly. "This is the dumbest kiddie book of all time. It doesn't belong in a college class. And especially not a Berkeley class . . ."

The class falls silent. Professor Trebond zeroes in on him.

"Anyone care to answer him?"

I raise my hand, ignoring Jude's venomous glare.

The professor nods. "Yes, Mr. Rache."

"Halfling creature, about this tall," I say, holding my hand about waist high. "They live in these holes in the ground. Only they're not gross and dirty and filled with worms. They're like super nice, cozy homes. At first, they don't seem like heroes—in fact, the total opposite. But it turns out that they're the only ones who can save Middle-earth and defeat Sauron."

Rho catches my eye. *Busted.*

Since we started our study dates, I binge-read through *The Hobbit* and all of *The Lord of the Rings,* even though the trilogy wasn't on our reading list. Once I got over the archaic language and far-fetched fantasy elements, the books were surprisingly catchy. I couldn't put them down. Let's just say, I've been spending a lot of time in Berkeley's library.

Loki rolls his eyes. "At least Bilbo likes smoking out."

That makes Jude snicker. Laughter ripples through the auditorium.

Professor Trebond crosses her arms. "Do you have another question to share with the class?" she says, flexing her prosthesis. "Or are you just wasting our precious time?"

"Fine, why should I care about hobbits?" Jude says in a challenging voice. It reverberates through the lecture hall. "This is Berkeley. Aren't we supposed to study important stuff?"

Grumbles ripple through the class, agreeing. Feeling buoyed, Jude goes on. "This class is called . . . *Great Books.* Maybe we should actually be reading some for a change?"

Clearly, he's poked a hornet's nest. Professor Trebond marches over to the whiteboard and writes two words in her boxy handwriting. The marker squeals across the whiteboard.

WHAT IF . . .

She wheels back on the class. "Speculative fiction explores *what-if* scenarios, allowing these authors to conjure new worlds that reflect back on our contemporary issues. It's like holding up a lens to our culture. These are books of possibilities, books that deconstruct society and teach us about our own humanity, even when the characters aren't human at all."

Rho shoots her hand up. Her hair and eyes morph bright pink.

She's excited.

"They're also books of warning," Rho says, flipping through the book on her tablet. "They show us what can happen if humanity doesn't curtail our worst impulses. Actually, Tolkien was inspired to write his books after serving in World War I. He was a veteran."

"Exactly," Trebond replies with a crisp nod. "Couldn't have said it better myself."

That settles the debate for now, but Jude and Loki are still stewing in their seats. I can feel indignation wafting off them. I try to focus on the rest of class and not let it affect me.

I want to change. To learn. To grow.

Plus, I like Professor Trebond, even if she still detests me because of my friends. On our way out of class, she passes out our papers from last week. It's my terrible essay on *The Odyssey*. I pulled an all-nighter trying to get through that cursed book and crank out something intelligible. Even Rho's study dates didn't save me. Unlike Tolkien, reading it wasn't . . . pleasurable.

C+

Not as bad as I expected, but still the worst grade I've ever gotten. Back in high school, I could sleep through class, hand in a sloppy, handwritten paragraph for a paper, and score As. For Trebond, I actually have to try on my homework, and even then I feel like I'm failing.

But then, I spot the note scrawled across the top. The grade is in blue ink, but the note is written in red. It looks like it was added recently—maybe right before she passed it out.

Draeden, I'm seeing real improvement in your work this semester. Keep it up. I look forward to your next paper. —Professor T

I wonder if she wrote that after today's class, where I contributed something substantive. I feel a swell of pride, which I never felt back in high school, even with my steady stream of As. I had to work hard for this grade—and for Trebond's respect. For once, this feels earned.

With class dismissed, we make our way toward the exit, joining the throng of students filtering out. Rho's paper sticks out of her arms with the expected "A+" circled on the top. Meanwhile, Jude glances back at Professor Trebond and narrows his eyes. She's packing up her materials and preparing to leave the lecture hall. Her mechanical arm works flawlessly, the joints flexing and responding to her neural commands. I know that look from him. It's not good.

"Don't worry about Professor *Tre-bitch*," he says in a low voice, keeping his eyes on her. "I reported her to my dad. I don't think she'll be a professor of anything for much longer."

"Yeah, no way this curriculum is approved," Loki adds with a scowl. "These books should be banned. She's gotta be breaking some major regulations by teaching them."

They both laugh in a way that sends a chill up my spine. I like Professor Trebond. She's pushed me hard. But to my surprise, I can do it, and it feels great. I catch sight of Jude's paper with "F-" scrawled in bold ink. He's flunking the class. I bet Loki's failing, too.

People like us can't flunk out of college. Especially not connected ones. Their parents won't allow it. They're supposed to run this federation one day. That's the whole point of Berkeley. It's the finishing school for the privileged, so they can take over the world one day.

I frown, feeling my stomach churn.

Trebond's days here are definitely numbered.

CHAPTER 19

KARI

Today is your lucky day—I've got a special surprise," the drill sergeant says, after marching us into a subterranean corridor with numbered chambers set into the walls. We've never been to this part of the base before. I feel a rush of anticipation turbocharged with adrenaline.

"Recruits, pair up with your battle buddies," she orders as we come to a halt.

Excited whispers cut through our ranks. We skipped PT to come here. Nadia slides next to me, while Anton and Luna move into place beside her. Percy and Genesis pair up on my other side. I know we're all wondering the same thing—what is this place and why are we here?

"Listen up, today is your first combat sim," the drill sergeant says. That provokes more whispers, covered by coughing fits. "Now load into a sim chamber with your battle buddy."

I pivot to follow her orders and find a sim chamber, but Nadia doesn't budge. Worse yet, she shoots her hand up. I hiss at Nadia to drop her hand and keep her mouth shut. Everything that affects her . . . well . . . it comes down on me like a hammer. But I'm too late.

The drill sergeant looks up from her tablet and frowns. "Yes, Private Ksusha." Her voice seethes with annoyance.

"You said combat sim . . . but what about our weapons?" Nadia says, always acting like a boss. "Pardon me for speaking out of turn, but shouldn't we get blasters first?"

The drill sergeant glares back. "Think you're ready for blasters?"

Nadia clears her throat and responds in a firm voice. "Yes, we've been training hard—"

"That was *meant* to be rhetorical," the drill sergeant cuts her off. "First, you're not ready for blasters. You're still as green as the radioactive turf back Earthside." She turns to Anton in exasperation. "Asteroid fires, your brother would probably blast his own foot off."

Laughter erupts from our ranks, quickly covered by more coughing fits, lest the drill sergeant be in an extra testy mood and decide to dole out extra PT reps.

"And second of all, not all combat is about fighting and blasters," she goes on, dragging her gaze over our ranks. "Who remembers Battle Philosophy class yesterday?"

Anton raises his hand, of course. The drill sergeant rolls her eyes.

"Right, someone *besides* Private Ksusha."

After a long moment, Genesis volunteers. The drill sergeant nods to her. "*The greatest victory is that which requires no battle,*" Genesis quotes from Sun Tzu in a strong voice.

"That's correct, Private Salerno," the drill sergeant says. "You saved your platoon extra reps. The purpose of this combat sim isn't to win. Instead, it's to learn an important lesson that might just save your miserable, worthless little lives one day—and that's how to retreat."

Groans ripple through our ranks. The disappointment wafts off us like solar wind.

The drill sergeant picks up on it. "That's right. Today you're going to learn how to run away like yellow-bellied cowards. Now, that shouldn't be too hard for some of you." Her eyes fix on me. I shrink down, knowing that's a dig about my father. Tension grips our ranks.

"For this combat sim, you're getting dropped into enemy territory," she continues. "You've only got your hands, your feet, and your wits to save you from getting blasted."

Percy raises his hand. "Drill Sergeant, what's our objective?"

"Simple . . . to survive, Private Tran," she answers in a solemn voice. "The safety controls will be engaged, but I've left a little wiggle room. You can get hurt—even wounded—in those chambers. It just won't kill you . . . unfortunately, in a few of your cases," she adds.

She looks at me again, just in case I wasn't sure who she meant with that verbal jab, making my mouth go dry and my palms sweat. With that, she taps at her tablet rapid-fire. *Whoosh.*

Before I can dwell on it, the doors behind us retract. In lockstep with Nadia, I enter the closest chamber. The pounding of my heart matches the stomping of our boots. We find our marks on the floor—two red Xs—next to each other. The interior of the chamber looks like a blank canvas, reminding me of the warp mail pods, except we're standing and ready for action.

"Initiating combat sim," the drill sergeant barks.

Her voice pipes into my brain via my implant.

I wait for Harold to jack me in, then that crazy brain-sucking feeling overtakes me, as the sim loads into my brain circuitry and hijacks it. The world blurs and dims in my vision.

One second, I'm standing in the chamber.

And the next I'm—

Blinded by searing sunlight.

"Asteroid fires, where are we?" Nadia asks, materializing beside me and whipping around to get her bearings. She blinks hard, trying to clear her vision. Panic permeates her voice.

"Not Ceres," I hear from my left. "That's for damn sure."

I jerk my head around as Percy and then Genesis materialize into the sim next. We're standing on an unstable surface. My boots slip and slide around. I look down— *Sand.*

Everywhere, as far as the eye can see. Tinged red, shifting under our boots. Dunes ripple out of the desert, rising up like gently sloping hills, waiting to swallow us. They're baking under the intense glare of that hot sun. We don't have helmets or life support tech since this is a sim.

"Where are we?" I ask, kicking the sand with my boots.

"Most likely culprit . . . *Mars.*"

That's Anton.

He and Luna materialize into the desert behind us.

"Where's the rest of our platoon?" Luna asks, scanning the horizon. I follow her lead on recon and finally spot them on a nearby sand dune, a few hundred meters away.

"Nerd bro, how do you know it's Mars?" Nadia asks, turning to her brother.

"Basic astronomy," Anton says with a shrug, pointing to the sky. "The position of the sun. Also, the temperature and geological formations. You know, geeky science stuff. Since we can breathe the air and gravity feels normal, I'm guessing they rigged up the environment for that."

"If you're right—that's bad," Luna says, sifting the red sand. The grains slip through her fingers like our time is running out. "Mars is Proxy territory. See those indentations? They're footsteps—and they're fresh. Anything else would've blown away, or gotten swallowed up."

"Look, more over there," Percy adds, pointing to tracks leading across the dune. I follow his gaze to the prints in the sand, already starting to dissolve. I've got a bad feeling.

"Wait, who controls Martian territory?" I ask with a frown.

"Siberian Fed mostly," Luna says. "They made a big territory grab recently, backed by their alliance with the Arctic Fed. I heard my dad talking about the Proxy skirmish before I shipped out. Basically, it's a war zone. Oh, and there's one other major threat—"

That's when suddenly they appear.

"Incoming Raiders!" Percy yells, cutting her off. He points to a cluster of ships clouding the reddish sky like a swarm of black flies. Their hulls are painted with skulls and crossbones.

Fuck, Raiders. There's no mistaking that.

"Yup, that's the other main threat," Luna says, straightening up with a jerk.

"Blasted space pirates," Nadia grumbles under her breath. "Of course that *sadist we call a drill sergeant* would subject us to a Raider ambush for our first ever combat sim."

"Oh, and you're forgetting. We also have to face them without blasters," I add, trying to count the number of Raider ships. I stop at fifty. They keep popping out of warp.

They bank toward us, circling and landing on the nearest dune. Dust swirls into a mini sandstorm. Their ships are hijacked and stolen from Space Force, but they've been modified over the years. They could easily be mistaken for space junk if they didn't fly like that.

Precise and deadly. Their bay doors yawn open—

And the Raiders swarm out en masse. I spot blasters, also stolen and modified, along with more primitive weapons like swords, pikes, battle axes, and maces, all electrified. They're clad in old federation uniforms, patched over and desecrated with baubles, rocks, crystals, feathers, trinkets, and hand-painted with colorful graffiti. Their faces are smeared with white makeup.

One of the Raiders—their leader, from the looks of him—points to us and gestures angrily.

"Aye, fresh meat!" he yells and pounds his chest. "Go get 'em! Who's hungry?"

They charge at us with shrieking battle cries. Their blaster fire rains down on the dunes. I freeze as they gain precious ground. All I can think is—*Uh, they're cannibals?*

Abruptly, hot wind whips toward me with a blast of sand, and I can smell them strong as the day. It's a putrid mix of body odor, rotting teeth . . . and *stars knows what else.*

A hand hooks my elbow.

"Come on! Are you crazy?" Nadia gasps, yanking me into action. She drags me away as blaster fire strikes the sand. "Didn't you hear the drill sergeant? Run—or we're dead!"

We take off across the dunes with the Raiders right behind us. But it's hard to run. My boots keep slipping in the sand. Sweat runs down my face in rivulets, stinging my eyes and blinding me. I can only see in blurry flashes. But I can hear their battle cries clear as day.

"Technically, we'll only get *lightly* maimed," Anton says, panting next to us. His little legs churn as fast as they can. "She engaged the safety controls, remember?"

Nadia tosses him a glare. "Killed, wounded . . . lightly maimed? Who cares, they're *blasted* cannibals! I don't want them getting their filthy hands or teeth anywhere near me!"

"Point taken," Anton agrees with a grimace.

"Seriously, not in the mood for light maiming either," Luna says, sprinting ahead. She's more agile and fit. "We need to make it to our platoon . . . it's our only chance."

"And then what?" I say in a breathless voice. They're standing on the next dune, but it looks impossibly far away. Blaster fire rains down around us. "They're gaining on us."

"No *fucking* clue," Nadia barks, as sand explodes by her feet.

Luna leads us, while Anton and I round up the back of our crew. Despite PT, my legs start to tire and cramp from running in the thick sand. I wince from pain but keep going anyway.

Suddenly, Anton stumbles—and goes down hard.

"No, get up!" I yell at him. "You can't give up now."

I reach down and yank him to his feet, dragging him after me. The Raiders are only a hundred yards behind us now. I hear their shrill cries and boots pounding the sand.

Luna doubles back to help me with Anton. She grabs his other arm, and together we half carry and half drag him over the dune, slip-sliding down the other side. We scramble up the next one, pulling Anton along so he doesn't fall again, and then we skid to a sudden halt.

"*Screw the stars*," Luna hisses. Her eyes lock onto—

Another bunch of Raiders stands on the other side in front of their idling ship, waiting to ambush us. They're all riled up and heavily armed. And we ran right into their trap.

"Look, Fed scum! Blast 'em," their leader orders. His lips stretch into a sneer, revealing crooked, dirty teeth. They raise their blasters to obliterate us. I open my mouth and yell.

"Watch out—we're trapped!"

CHAPTER 20

DRAE

I'm in my dorm room, avoiding my roommates by hunkering in my bed and burying my head deep in the pages of my new library book—*Raiders on the Star-Seas*, an early anti-war story, about a doomed guardian's first year of enlistment—when my neural implant pings me.

Estrella's stilted voice echoes through my head.

Incoming call.

I grit my teeth when I see the caller ID. It's my parents.

If anything could tank my mood right now besides my roommates, it's them. I've been avoiding their calls since I got to college, replying with upbeat text messages instead. It's not the whole truth, of course. Not even close. But trust me, it's better than getting them involved.

Estrella, I'll call them back, I think back.

The alert vanishes from my retinas.

Through my closed door, I hear the *thump-thump-thump* of upbeat music kicking on. Jude and Loki have started their pre-party ritual. They're getting ready to go out to the frat parties. I bet they're pulling out the hard booze and fruity, caffeinated mixers from our little fridge now.

I sigh in defeat and fall into my pillow, yanking the blanket over my head. Why is it so hard to focus? I try to lose myself in my book again and tune out the thumping of party music and the grating sound of Jude and Loki's jeering laughter. Finally, the music shuts off.

I hear the heavy *clomp-clomp* of footsteps. "Drae, time to party!" Jude calls out. I imagine how they're probably draining their syrupy, alcoholic drinks from those red cups.

Rap. Rap. Rap.

Jude pounds drunkenly on my door.

"Don't be a buzzkill for once. Come out with us."

"Pleasssseeeeeeee," Loki slurs, falling into my door with a thump. They both giggle like little kids. I hold my breath and stay very still, careful not to even squeak my bunk. Yeah, I'm playing possum. I'm praying they'll think I fell asleep, deeply asleep. A few tense seconds pass.

One louder *rap*. Then—

"He probably passed out," Jude slurs. "Books are boring AF."

Loki adds, "Especially Trebond's dumb reading list. Better than sleep meds."

But the next thing Jude says sends shivers down my spine. "Good thing we won't have to worry about her . . . much longer." His voice sounds cruel and devoid of all humor.

Jeering laughter peppers that sentiment. My stomach sinks. That sounded ominous. Clomping footsteps tramp across the common room. Then finally—the main door slams.

Thank the stars, I think, feeling a flood of relief.

They're gone. I flip over on my bed, craning my ears. But our dorm is finally . . . quiet. Then I read all night long, devouring the musty pages of my assigned book for Trebond like I'm a starving man, and it's the most delicious dish in the whole stars-loving universe.

A few hours later, my roommates return to continue partying. I'm still up reading, reaching the final emotional chapters of *Raiders on the Star-Seas*, which fills me with more sadness and longing than I expected. I don't want the book to end. I'm not ready to leave this world yet.

Thumping music kicks back on. I cringe, feeling my head start to pound. It's gotta be after two in the morning, maybe later. I'm hoping they've forgotten about me.

But no such luck. Because suddenly—

Squeak.

Jude cracks my door open. Bright light floods in.

Ugh, I forgot to lock it when I went to the bathroom.

Jude wiggles his eyebrows suggestively. "Drae, we brought the after-party back here," he says in a low voice. "We've got some *serious* hotties over. You can thank me later."

"Buzzkill, leave your dumb books," Jude hollers. "And have some fun for once."

That's emphasized by high-pitched giggles from the girls. I grimace and look up from the last chapter. And yawn. "Nah, I'm gonna turn in. Long day of classes tomorrow."

"Lame," Jude says. "*You only live once.*"

I stifle another yawn for effect. "Really, I'm beat. Maybe another time."

"Suit yourself," he spits back. "You're gonna regret it."

With that, Jude slams the door. I know I pissed him off, but I don't care anymore. I'm sick of their shit. The door mutes the partying. Loud music, giggling, hooting and hollering, probably from Loki fist pumping and raising the roof. But it doesn't silence it.

Blast them to the stars, I think, wishing for the thousandth time that they weren't my roommates. Back in high school, I used to enjoy going to parties with my friends, drinking, and trying to flirt with girls . . . and maybe more. I never went anywhere without them, and now I can't stand to be in their presence. I'm shocked by how much I've changed in a few weeks.

But that's a good thing, right?

Out of nowhere, Rho pops into my head. I wish she were my roomie. Then, we could have library study dates and pizza reading nights. That thought startles me. A warm, affectionate feeling blossoms in my heart. I can't tell if it's friendship, or maybe something more.

Suddenly, a pumping baseline kicks on.

"Hey, it's my song," Jude yells. "Turn it up."

I groan and flip over on my bed, knowing that Rho is a delicate situation, especially with my feelings for Kari. I bury my head under the pillow, trying to block out the noise. But then . . .

My hand brushes *something* under the pillow.

Feeling the sharp edges, I shift my pillow aside, revealing another envelope. The same ornate calligraphy, creamy cardstock, and seal with the grizzly bear—plus my name scrawled in rich pen strokes. My heart thuds faster. I wonder if Rho got one, too. We both made it to the next round, but that doesn't mean we'll face the next initiation test together. But I hope we will . . .

I press my thumb to the seal and yank out the card, scanning the swooping, handwritten message. The words fly past my tired eyes. I feel another secret thrill when I read them.

> *Your next test.*
> *This is the big one.*
> *Don't get too excited.*
> *That last one was easy.*
>
> *Wednesday*
> *Midnight*
> *Sather Gate*
>
> *Don't be late—or you're finished.*

That's in two days. Suddenly, all other sounds drain away—*the partying, my friends hooting, the girls giggling, the obnoxious music.* This is all I can think about. I remember the chiming of the Campanile bells as we solved the final clue. Rho's delighted laughter as we poured out into the crisp predawn air—and discovered that we'd passed the first test together.

As the party quiets down and I finally drift, I dream of Rho and Kari and blazing stars going supernova and destroying everything in the universe, like the big bang in reverse. I also dream of the next test and the thrill of earning our initiation into the infamous secret society.

Two more days, and I'll find out my fate.

I can't wait.

CHAPTER 21

KARI

K ill those guardian bastards!" the head Raider sneers at us.

His gang raises their blasters to fire. We're unarmed and helpless—ambushed in the desert and marooned away from our platoon, who are hunkered down a few large dunes away. Meanwhile, the sky overhead lights up with Raider ships flying over with their blasters aimed.

In a panic, I duck and search for an escape—but we're completely trapped. That's my last thought before they open fire, lighting up the desert. The sand explodes all around me.

Blaster shots hit my body full force, knocking me flat on my back. I land hard on the sand, all breath knocked from my lungs, as searing pain radiates through my entire body.

Dimly, screams shatter my eardrums.

They're from . . . my friends.

I have to help them. Despite the searing pain, I force myself up, spotting Anton also downed by blaster fire and writhing in the sand. I grab his arm and yank him to his feet, though he groans in protest. His face twists up with pain. I shoot him a stern look and yank him ahead.

"I know it hurts like the blazing stars, but we've gotta run for it."

"Ugh, I hate you," he grunts as I drag him across the dune. Nadia and Luna both took hits, but they also scramble up and chase after us. And so, just like the drill sergeant ordered us—we run for it like yellow-bellied cowards. We climb the dune, then half skid, half slide down the loose sand on the other side. Now we have two packs of angry Raiders on our heels.

My body hurts from the blaster fire. Running makes the pain stab at me with each step. But I'd be dead in real life if this weren't a combat sim. So, I guess I'm lucky like that.

"Watch out," Anton yells as a Raider pops out of the sand where he was hiding and swings an electrified mace. The blow is about to connect with my head—

But Anton jumps in front of it.

The mace collides with his abdomen, making him shriek in pain. He crumples like a sack of rocks, going down hard. He convulses and writhes from the electric shock.

Then he goes . . . still. That's worse than the convulsing.

"Oh no," I yell as I lunge for him.

But the Raider wheels on me with his mace. Luna and Nadia flinch back behind me, sensing the threat. We're completely unarmed and helpless. The spiked ball dangles from the deadly weapon, sizzling with electricity. He sneers, revealing his dirty, putrid teeth. They're black from . . . *blood*, I realize with a start. When it dries, it turns black and flaky like that.

Suddenly, I hear something—

"Raider scum, mess with somebody else!"

The familiar voice ricochets across the desert.

And it has the intended effect. The Raider jerks his head around.

Percy shouts from the next dune, jumping up and down and waving his arms. So does Genesis, who sneers and flips the Raider off. "Yeah, come and get us! Over here, Raiders!"

They have the Raider's attention now. He pivots around and raises his electrified mace. He lets out a pitiful howl at Percy and pounds his chest. We don't waste a second—we run for it.

By the time the Raider turns back around, we're already on the retreat. That distraction bought us time. Luna and Nadia help me carry Anton, who remains limp in our arms. I glance down at his ashen, motionless face. He got electrocuted when he took that blow for me.

Harold, check vitals on Private Anton Ksusha, I think in a panic.

It takes a long second for the response.

Abnormal heart rhythm, Harold responds. *Seek medical care immediately.*

That worries me, but it could be worse. At least his heart is still beating . . .

That means he's not dead . . . yet.

Or fake dead, or whatever happens when you die in a sim. But we have to hurry. We take off toward the dune with rest of our platoon. But they're still a few hundred meters away.

"Quick, this way," Nadia yells, glancing back at the Raider.

We keep running—retreating really—while sweat drips into my eyes and my lungs burn from exertion. Even with all the training, my muscles start to cramp and fatigue.

And that's when—

Suddenly, something grabs my leg from behind and trips me. I go down hard, the sand gripping me like a tourniquet. I struggle and flip over, but my ankle is throbbing like crazy. That's when a dark shadow falls over me. It blocks out the blazing sun.

The head Raider stands over me.

I can smell his rancid breath before I can make out his face silhouetted by the sun. He raises his mace to finish me with a death blow. Electricity sizzles through the savage weapon.

"Die, fed scum," he says in a strange accent.

I raise my hands and try to squirm away. But I'm in too much pain.

At that moment, when I think I'm going to die—*when that mace is flying down toward my head to kill me*—I expect my life to flash before my eyes. At the very least, I expect my last thoughts to be about Ma and Bea, or my best friend Rho and Xena, or maybe my deserter father and how I never got to tell him that I hate his guts to his face before he deserted.

But all I think about is . . .

Drae.

And how I'll never get to communicate with him again. How he'll receive an official report, then retire from the Sympathetic Program. Or maybe get paired again. For some reason that I can't fathom, that idea makes my stomach twist and heart lurch in my chest.

The spiked mace swings down toward my head.

I shut my eyes and scream.

"Noooooooooooo—"

Zap . . . whoosh!

Everything goes blurry, then evaporates. I get that brain-sucking feeling. Suddenly, I'm flat on my back in the sim chamber. Next to me, Nadia is screaming and writhing on the floor.

"Get those Raiders off me!" she shrieks in a terror.

Her eyes are shut tight. She's still in the sim, but then she comes out of it, too. That means she finally got . . . *killed.* I lean over and nudge her shoulder gently.

"Hey, it's okay," I whisper, helping her to her feet. "They're gone . . . it wasn't real."

"Well, it sure *felt* real," she groans, blinking her eyes to clear the disorientation. "And that blaster fire hurt like the blazing stars. Light maiming, my ass!"

"You can say that again," I agree. We stagger toward the door, triggering it to open. We're both hobbling and in pain. "But at least we're not dead. The real thing's probably much worse."

On that ominous note, we burst into the corridor. That was *nothing* like I'd imagined it would be, even if it was just a simulation. I shudder again, thinking . . . *that was pure hell.*

"Asteroid fires, that was intense," she says, still adjusting to our reality. She rubs her sore shoulder. That must be where she took the blaster fire. "Why can't I snap out of it?"

"You know how dreams seem real?" I say, thinking it over. The bright light of the corridor stings my eyes. The other sim chambers remain shut. "The mind is powerful."

Nadia smirks. "Yeah, and they sure enjoy fucking with it."

We share a chuckle.

Whoosh.

Suddenly, the other doors crack open down the corridor, as the rest of our platoon emerges, signaling that it's over. I spot Anton and Luna stumbling out, followed by Percy and Genesis.

"Stars, you all made it out," I say in a soft voice, half to convince myself that we're still alive. That we didn't die on that desert planet. *Mars*, I remember. Nadia and I got taken down first, so we got pulled out of the simulation earlier.

"Yeah . . . barely," Anton says, limping over with Luna's help. He pulls his shirt up, revealing a sickening palette of black and blue marbling his ribs. He took that blow to save me. "I should be dead, but I'm only bruised. Still, that hurt like the blazing stars."

Everyone looks rattled, battered, and a little dazed, but also grateful to be alive. I remember the exact moment when I died in there—*well, simulated death*—and how what I thought about was . . .

Drae.

Even admitting it makes my stomach churn with acid. As that mace streaked toward my head, spitting sparks and promising to end my life, I thought about how I'd never get to send him another exchange. Tell him about the Raiders attacking us. But there's more. How I'd never find out how he did in his Great Books class, or how it's going with his horrible roommates. Or the million other tiny things that make up a normal day in his life—a life still lived back Earthside. Our divergent paths unspool before me. Him back home, me bound for distant stars.

I shudder again, trying to block the feelings out. But they churn and swell anyway. I can't believe my brain would betray me in my first near-death experience and decide to think about . . .

Him.

I can pretend it never happened, right?

Memory archived, Harold chimes in right on cue. *Hikari, it's normal to grow attached to your Sympathetic. That's how the program works. The neural connection speeds up the process of a normal relationship, making you gain immense trust and emotional intimacy.*

Shut up! I'm not attached, I think back, trying to inject as much irritation into my thoughts as possible. *I don't even like him. Get it straight. Our Pairing was a mistake.*

A pause, then Harold pipes up again. *But you thought about him right before you died. My programming indicates that therefore he's of great importance to you. According to psychological studies, most guardians think about their loved ones when facing death.*

Oh, barf, I think. *I don't love him—I hate him. Trust me, he's the worst.*

Neurologically, Harold goes on, *love and hate produce the same neural waves. Is it possible you're mistaken? I can run a quick scan to make sure.*

No, that's impossible. I cringe, feeling my gut curl up in disgust at the mere suggestion. *Look, my brain is clearly psychotic. That's the only rational explanation.*

Harold takes a moment to respond.

No indications of psychosis. All neural circuitry is functioning at optimal levels. An increase in pulse and cortisol levels was detected, but that's normal following a combat sim.

Nadia catches my pained expression. Apparently, being attached at the hip with your battle buddy makes you ultra-aware of them. "Uh, everything okay?" she asks in a low voice.

"Just my implant being extra annoying, as usual," I mutter back. "Harold, mute, please."

He follows my orders, thankfully. I turn to Nadia, now that my brain is quiet for once.

"He thinks I have *feelings* for my . . . Sympathetic," I mutter, even though my cheeks start to burn. "When really, I'm not sure who's more annoying—him or Harold."

Nadia grins at me. "The important issues of our time. You know, they say there's a fine line between love and hate—"

"Ugh, that's what Harold said. Forget I mentioned it," I say as my cheeks flame hotter.

Genesis laughs. "Would you rather talk about Raiders? *I'm gonna eat your stars-lovin' guts,*" she says, mocking them and their savage ways.

We all crack up. Humor helps, even when joking about dark things. It really is the best medicine. But then we all clam up as the drill sergeant marches over with her tablet.

"Mess hall . . . now!" she barks. "This is no time to joke around. I went easy on you in that combat sim. Trust me, an actual Raider ambush would be much worse."

Her words hang in the air. *Worse than that nightmare?* I think with a jolt of fear. How could they be worse? Then, I remember. That blow to my head? I'd be dead right now.

I can tell we're all thinking the same thing. Humor deflates from our ranks, replaced by a serious undertone. I know it sounds naïve, but combat—even simulated—is more disturbing and terrifying than I realized. And I signed up for front lines . . . if I make it out of basic.

With that warning, the drill sergeant dismisses us.

"After supper, get some sleep tonight. Tomorrow's gonna be a big day."

We march off toward the mess hall still jittery from the sim, but now I'm wondering . . . what makes it a big day? Knowing the drill sergeant, it can't be anything good.

Darkness engulfs the barracks, shrouding us in shadow.

I hear breathing in the dark. The squeaking of coils. The shifting of rough sheets and blankets. I'm still too juiced to sleep yet, but that's not the only thing keeping me awake.

I'm troubled by my confusing feelings for . . . *Drae.* Blast the Sympathetic program and how it messes with my head. Ugh, even thinking his name makes me cringe.

I shift around in frustration, emitting a loud *squeal* from my rack.

Silence. And then—

Anton's voice echoes out of the darkness. "I didn't like how that sounded. What do you think happens tomorrow? Why do we need to rest? What torture does she have planned?"

"Maybe she's just looking out for our best interests?" I say, injecting as much sarcasm as possible into my voice. Nadia snickers in response from across the way.

"Oh, I hope it's something fun for once," she says, shifting and making her bed squeak. "Like more combat sims? Or maybe, we're finally getting our blasters?"

"No way," Luna says from overhead. "I've got a bad feeling it's something else."

More silence as we all take that in.

"Yeah, something decidedly *un*-fun," Anton agrees in an ominous voice. "The drill sergeant sounded way too cheerful. When she's delighted, it always means the worst."

"Agreed," I say. "She's a glorified sadist. If she's excited, then it's bad for us."

On that gloomy proclamation, we all fall silent. I shift around, trying to get comfortable, but that nagging worry in the back of my head won't let me fall asleep. Also, there's something else distressing me. Why did I think about Drae in that combat sim?

Fuck my life. Why do I care about him?

So what if I've stopped dreading our exchanges? Maybe even started to look forward to them? That's because he's the only person back Earthside that I get to communicate with regularly. Family communications are infrequent and time-restricted so we don't get too homesick and want to desert. I have another week before I can send my next one to Bea and Ma. I suspect that it's also so we bond further with our Sympathetic, though they don't say that.

It's like being kidnapped by a creepy stranger. They keep you locked up, but also they're your only company. You don't have a choice but to confide in them, and so you grow attached, even start to care. *Stockholm Syndrome*, that's what it's called. That must be it.

Despite my best efforts, I still can't sleep. I remain wide awake with my mind racing. I toss and turn. I yank the covers on and off. I'm hot, then I'm cold. Intrusive thoughts bombard my brain. I keep seeing that electrified mace flying toward my head. Sparks hissing and lighting up the air—

Suddenly, the lights in the barracks burst on.

"Up, recruits, time to rise and shine!"

The drill sergeant storms into the barracks, slapping our racks with a pugil stick. *Clang. Clang. Clang.* She marches up the row, ruthlessly hitting each one.

I rub my tired eyes, feeling even more exhausted than when I tried to fall asleep. "What time is it?" I hiss to Luna overhead, hearing her rouse. "It can't be morning yet?"

The drill sergeant hears me.

She marches over and glares down at me. "Think Raiders give you a nice little warning before they attack? Now get up, recruit! No breakfast today—hurry your slow ass up!"

I shut my mouth and climb out of my rack, trying to ignore the exhaustion weighing down my body like lead weights. The combination of the adrenaline crash after the combat sim and no sleep is like a powerful narcotic. As I tug my boots on, all I can think is . . .

Whatever is about to happen—it's nothing good.

CHAPTER 22

DRAE

"Well, you look terrible," Rho says in her usual blunt way when she sees me in the courtyard on the way to class. Her nano implants flash fiery red, then soften to pink when I approach her.

Does that mean she despises me less?

"Nice to see you! You look great, too," I quip back as I stifle a yawn, rubbing my tired eyes. I'm more exhausted than I realized. "Jude and Loki kept me up late partying."

"Ugh, let me guess. Fist pumping. Terrible bass music. Bad dude dancing." She does an impersonation of jerky dancing with no sense of rhythm, then shudders to herself.

I crack up. "Uh, it's like that, only worse. Oh, and you forgot Jude whooping like a stars-forsaken idiot every time *his song* comes on. Which sounds like every other song. Frankly, I don't know if he can even tell them apart."

She gives me a piteous look, as her hair and eyes turn blue. "I'm so sorry you have to witness that abomination on a daily basis. You definitely deserve caffeine for your pain—"

Suddenly, a Fed Patrol zips up, blocking our path to the campus cafe.

"Halt for scanning and identification," the robotic voice barks at us.

We both freeze and thrust our hands up automatically, waiting while it scans our faces. I'm almost getting used to these new security intrusions. *Almost.* This happens a few times a day.

"*Approved,*" the robotic voice barks. "Move along."

Then, it zooms off to scan the next pack of students on their way to class. I don't know if it's my imagination, but more Fed Patrols seem to appear on campus every day now.

Once I'm sure the patrol is gone, I catch Rho's eye and flash the envelope at her—just a glimmer of cream-colored cardstock and ornate calligraphy spelling out my name.

"You jerkface. I got . . . *nothing*," she shoots back with navy tresses and eyes. *Sadness.*

"Oh, I'm so sorry," I say, feeling awkward. And worse, disappointed. "I'm sure it's coming. We both made it to the next phase, right? You'll get one soon—"

Then she breaks into a grin, as her hair morphs fiery red.

"Got you!" she says with a snort laugh. "You should see your face."

I shake my head at her. Then I turn more serious and glance around to make sure no more patrols are zooming over. "Wednesday?" I say in a low voice. "Midnight? Sather Gate?"

"Yup, yup, and yup. That's tomorrow night. You gonna be ready? They said that the last test was the easy one. And it was . . . for me, that is. Don't forget. You struggled mightily."

"Shut up," I reply with a scowl. "I did not struggle."

"Mightily. Like Odysseus."

We continue across the courtyard to class. Suddenly, Estrella pings me.

The alert flashes in my retinas.

Incoming call from Dad.

I groan. Why do my parents keep calling me? I've dodged like three calls in the last two days alone. Usually, they pretend like I don't exist. What's gotten into them lately?

"Send to voicemail," I say back to Estrella. I'm too exhausted to talk now anyway. Plus, it will make me late for class. I catch Rho's curious expression.

"Ugh, my folks keep calling," I say with a wince. "It's almost like they care or something. I'm hoping cheerful text replies will keep them away for the rest of the semester."

She arches her eyebrow.

"Careful, or they'll actually visit. Like in real life."

I shudder at that idea. "I didn't think of that."

"Yup, better to take their calls. Save yourself a surprise campus visit."

I think it over, picturing my mom on her favorite recliner, whiskey tumbler in her hand while the newsfeeds stream in front of her face. Her transport collecting dust in the driveway.

"No way," I say, shaking my head. "Mom doesn't go anywhere."

"Let's see, you're an only child?" Rho asks, catching my eye.

"Yeah, I'm an only," I reply. "Mom's deployment made it hard to have more. That's why there's always that four-year age gap with military brats."

"Yeah, I'm an only, too," Rho says. "Trust me, they all get a little batty when their one and only offspring moves away from home. Your mom might be a complete hermit. But keep dodging her calls, and I bet she shows up at your dorm room door."

"Nightmare," I moan dramatically. "Fine, next time, I'll pick up. I swear it."

"Yup, bite that bullet," Rho says with a sympathetic nod. "You'll thank me later. Might save you from real life parental face time if you're lucky."

I feel my shoulders slump in defeat. If only I could run away for four years like Kari. But no such luck. College doesn't work that way. We get all kinds of breaks, plus summer. And I'm not millions of kilometers away. Just an easy transport ride from home.

"Wonder what all the fuss is about?" I say, my eyes tracking to the commotion across the courtyard. Several Fed Patrols cluster around one of the faculty housing buildings.

A crowd has gathered outside of worried-looking students and professors held back by the patrols. The red and blue lights flash, but their sirens remain silent. Still, it unsettles me.

Rho follows my gaze. "Probably some old professor found an ancient reefer stash hidden in his room and smoked out. All these extra Fed Patrols? They gotta do something useful, right?"

I watch professors loiter outside, held back by the patrols from entering their living quarters. Concern is etched into their faces.

"All that commotion over a little skunky weed?" I say, catching her eye, then looking back at the patrols. "I know they're here to protect us. But I wish they'd blast off campus."

She frowns. "Not likely, especially with the elevated threat level."

"I dunno," I say. "I'm just worried. Something feels wrong."

"Stop being so emo already," Rho chastises me in a shift to feisty pink. She grabs my arm and drags me away. "We still need caff—and we're late for class."

Rho and I settle into our usual front-row seats for Great Books. I'm still rattled by the commotion with the patrols, but I feel better now that my favorite class is about to start.

Jude and Loki stumble in at the last minute, reeking of alcohol and too much aftershave, as always. "Bro, gimme some of that latte," Jude groans, rubbing his unshaven face and reaching for my disposable cup. I start to refuse, but he snatches it. "I'm dying over here."

I watch him slurp my coffee in desperation, glad I'm not hungover. "Late night?"

"Those frosh couldn't get enough," Loki cuts in, looking equally banged up. But he still manages to grin like a fool. "Couldn't disappoint them. You feel me, Drae?"

They both snicker. Rho shoots them a contemptuous look.

"Ugh, misogynists," she says, sinking lower in her seat. "I thought they died out along with the dinosaurs. Guess we need another meteor to take the rest of them out."

"Mysogy-*whats*?" Loki says in confusion. "Is that a bad thing? Well . . . is it?"

"Sounds badass," Jude says. "Like tyrannosaurs, or pterodactyls."

Before I can get into it—or more likely, Rho can tell them off again—a breathless, red-faced woman bursts through the door and marches to the front, placing her tablet on the podium.

I feel shock when I see her face—

It's not Professor Trebond.

"I'm Professor Goode," she says, smiling placidly. Her smile matches her bland gray suit and stiff bun. Her head moves, but her eyes remain overly wide and frozen.

"I'm sorry to report that Professor Trebond won't be able to finish the semester . . . for personal reasons."

Surprise ripples through the class. The way she says that makes it seem like a lie. Rho nudges my arm and shoots me a worried look, while our new professor taps at her tablet.

"The dean has asked me to take over," she goes on, then purses her lips in distaste. "I reviewed your syllabus. Frankly, it was a bit of a disaster. Many of these books have been banned and violate our official education guidelines . . ."

Professor Goode taps again, then projects a new syllabus on the screen. I can't believe my eyes. All the books we were supposed to read this semester are gone, simply erased. In fact, any books from the pre-war period have been removed. The reading list now looks more like California Fed propaganda. Autobiographies by retired generals and state officials and "patriotic" fiction, meaning memoirs from our soldiers about fighting the good fight in the stars.

I look down at the library book clutched in my hands, what's supposed to be our next assignment—*Fahrenheit 451*—and feel a deep chill emanate through my body. The title means the temperature at which books burn. The opening line flashes through my head.

It was a pleasure to burn.

Only my teacher is the one *burning* these books.

"As you can see, I've taken the liberty of preparing a new federation-approved curriculum," Professor Goode continues. "I'm sorry to report that we'll be starting over from scratch. By order of the dean, all your grades will be also wiped clean."

A hush falls over the lecture hall, but also sighs of relief.

That's when she looks up and fixes Jude and Loki with a pointed smile. Her gaze sharpens. There can be no mistaking her meaning. They did this . . . or rather, their parents.

"Don't worry," she goes with a plastic smile. "You'll find that I'm far more lenient with my red pen than my unfortunate predecessor. Especially with students whose families have proven their extraordinary worth to our federation. We must honor their service."

That's met with approving chatter, making my stomach sink. Jude and Loki elbow each other, not even trying to be subtle, while Rho just looks about as miserable as I feel.

"Gross, so much for meritocracy," Rho mutters in a low voice, shoving her tablet aside in disgust. "I mean, it's always been a joke. But Trebond seemed . . . well . . ."

She doesn't have to finish. I know what she means.

Trebond seemed . . . different.

Professor Goode points to the syllabus. "We'll be focusing on military literature, starting with *The Great California Federation Diaries*. You may have perused excerpts in high school, but we'll read the unabridged version. It contains interviews with our most decorated war heroes."

I scowl when I see the rest of the reading list. The usual propaganda they try to pass off as literature. Here we are with the largest library in the federation, all these great books at our fingertips—and instead, we read the same recycled crap over and over.

"One more matter before we launch into the material," Professor Goode goes on. "You've likely heard rumors swirling around campus about this morning's unfortunate . . . *incident*."

She furrows her brow, trying to project an air of grave concern that rings false. There's an underlying haughtiness that gives her away. Rho catches my eye. Her hair and eyes shift to a greenish-blue shade that ripples with worry. I can tell we're thinking about the same thing—she's talking about that commotion outside the faculty housing building we saw on the way to class.

"Let me assure you," she continues. "The feds are working tirelessly to ensure our safety. The situation should be resolved shortly. No need to worry about your old professor anymore."

"Wait, what happened to Trebond?" Rho hisses to us. She clutches her library book to her lap like a lifeline that's about to fray and shred to pieces. But Jude doesn't look surprised.

"Told ya," he sneers at us. "My dad took care of her."

"Your father?" Rho whispers. Her hair shoots out ice blue.

"After I reported her, he launched a formal investigation," Jude says, puffing out his chest. "This morning, they went to her room to arrest her and haul her in for questioning—"

"Wait, they tried to arrest her?" I say with a sick feeling.

"Of course—this is serious," Jude says, looking pleased. But then, he shrugs in defeat. "But turns out, she skipped town before the patrols could grab her."

That makes me feel even more nauseous.

Those patrols were there for Trebond.

"Good riddance," Loki says with a derisive snort. "Turns out, this wasn't the first complaint this semester either. She was already on thin ice with the dean. Not to mention, the grades she was giving out were below average. Tons of families were complaining."

I can't believe what I'm hearing. The new professor notices us talking but completely lets it slide, unlike Trebond. She's a federation stooge here to give us stellar grades and pad our GPAs, so we can glide through college, graduate with honors, and run this whole place.

"But arrest her?" I whisper. "Doesn't that seem a little . . . extreme? It's not like she was teaching us anything dangerous. Just a bunch of old books—"

"Not in these times," Jude cuts me off. "Enemy forces threaten us from all sides. You can't be too careful these days. Plus, Trebond skipped town. Doesn't look good . . ."

"Yeah, she had something to hide," Loki chimes in. "Otherwise why would she run?"

"Yup, she's a fugitive now," Jude goes on. "When the authorities catch her, she'll regret it. It's only a matter of time. Oh, and don't worry. They'll make an example out of her."

His words make me shudder. He's looking forward to her punishment.

"Yup, that's what her kind deserve," Loki says, taking a big slurp of my cold coffee. This turn of events appears to have lifted his hangover. He turns to Jude, furrowing his brow.

"Also, how'd she know they were coming?" Loki asks, actually thinking for once. "Somebody must have tipped her off. You should tell your dad—they've got a leak."

"Oh, he's already on it," Jude says. "Don't worry, they'll find the culprit. The roads around campus are all locked down. Fed Patrols are everywhere. Trebond won't get far."

I don't hear anything else the new professor says for the rest of the class. It's just more federation propaganda anyway about our military prowess and superiority to other Proxies, *blah, blah, blah.* Rewind and repeat. Rho seems equally glum about the shift in curriculum.

When class ends, it's like somebody set us free from prison camp. We both bolt from our seats. On the way out, Rho shoots me a look. Her face crumples in despair, as her hair and eyes flash the darkest of blues. "Asteroid fires, I liked Trebond," she says, careful to whisper.

Her eyes remind me of the richest, darkest blue in the cosmos. Blue like the evening sky bleeding into night. Blue like the deepest depths of the oceans. The blue of grief and sadness and gloom. The blue of loss and regret and defeat. And it encapsulates exactly how I feel.

"Yeah, me too," I reply softly. "Me too."

That's the best I can manage.

Besides, we can't talk too much, or somebody might get the wrong idea. The library books weighing down my backpack only seem to emphasize the loss. They tug at my shoulders, cutting into my flesh and making me feel like I'm drowning. All I know is, this is unfair.

This is wrong. This is horrible. And there's not a single thing I can do about it.

Oblivious to my dark mood, Jude claps his arm around my shoulders. He pulls me close, making me squirm to get free. But he's got me locked like I'm in a vise.

"Ah, buzzkill, don't look so bummed out," he scoffs into my ear. "This class is gonna be a major breeze now. No more reading or lame papers. All thanks to my dad."

"Yeah, we can coast like back in high school," Loki adds with a conspiratorial grin. "Save our energy for partying!" They high-five each other, then turn to me.

I let their hands dangle there awkwardly. I don't attempt to reciprocate. I taste the bite of metal. It concentrates into acid, eating away at my throat and making one thing abundantly clear.

I hate them more than all the stars in the galaxy.

CHAPTER 23

KARI

"Privates, welcome to . . . *the gas chamber*," the drill sergeant says, wheeling around to face us.

Nervous whispers cut through our ranks. We're standing in front of a thick, metal door. I'm exhausted and can barely keep my eyes open thanks to our middle-of-the-night wake-up call, despite the jittery adrenaline pumping through my veins. The drill sergeant fixes her eyes on us.

"Who can tell me the symptoms of chemical weapon exposure?"

I struggle to wake up and snap to attention. But my brain feels foggy since I barely got any sleep. Anton's hand shoots up. "It's a combo of tear gas . . . and something else . . ."

The drill sergeant gives us a grim look. "That's correct, Private Ksusha. Even though it's banned by our interstellar treaties, some Proxies have started adding psychological compounds to their gas that produce a fear response. We call it . . . *fear gas.*"

I let that sink in.

Fear gas.

Banned . . . but of course, we're all using it anyway.

Before we can ask questions, she starts passing out gas masks. Then she orders us into the gas chamber. We step through the thick metal door into the rattrap, a smaller inner chamber that leads to yet another door. She seals the first door behind us with a sickening *thud.*

We wait in the smaller chamber while it pressurizes and filters the air. Then the next door opens with a *hiss*, admitting us into the gas chamber. We clamber inside single file and grab seats on the hard, metal benches that circumvent the rectangular room with a low ceiling.

The thick door seals shut behind us. Suddenly, the air feels staler and thinner, too. We don our gas masks and activate them. We look like aliens with the contraptions shrouding our faces.

"Enjoy the chemical bath," the drill sergeant says. Her voice is piped into our neural implants, but I glimpse her in the corridor. "This compound's a favorite of the Siberian Fed."

I feel the air stiffen and stagnate, then I hear a soft *hissing*.

Fear gas floods into the chamber. It's tasteless, odorless, invisible—but potent. My mask works hard to protect my sensitive eyes and lungs from the poison. I'm grateful for it. We sit in tense silence for what seems like forever. The drill sergeant's voice echoes out again.

"Privates, remove your masks."

Confusion ripples through our ranks as we all register the simple order.

"Asteroid fires, is she crazy?" Nadia hisses next to me. Her voice sounds mechanical through her mask. "This must be a sick joke."

I hesitate. We all do. Paralysis grips our platoon, along with a healthy dose of fear. It's not even caused by the gas. My mask is working overtime, the filters working to clear the air.

"Don't make me ask again—or you'll regret it," the drill sergeant says, sounding irate. Her voice rises several octaves. "Privates, take them off . . . *now*. That's an order."

I know better than to disobey. My hands feel shaky and want to rebel, but I reach for the clasps and unfasten them, then I slide the protective mask from my face. I hear rustling around me and know that everyone is removing their masks.

Don't breathe, I think to myself in desperation with my eyes shut tight. *As long as you don't open your eyes or breathe it in, you're safe.* But then—

"Privates, open your eyes and recite the Pledge of Allegiance," the drill sergeant orders. Such a simple request any other time, but doing this now means . . .

Opening my mouth. Breathing in the fear gas. And somehow remaining focused on the task. I force myself to follow her orders, though every circuit in my brain is screaming at me to put my mask back on. *But I can't be like my father,* I remind myself. *I can't wash out.*

I force my eyes open, and the gas hits and singes them like they're doused in gasoline and lit on fire. I try to speak as fast as I can and not inhale My words rush out in a jumble.

"I pledge allegiance to the flag of California . . . and to the Federation for which it stands . . . one Nation under the Stars . . . indivisible . . . with liberty and justice for all . . ."

I get that far, mumbling around with everyone, but then I have to . . . *inhale.* My lungs scream and spasm from the lack of oxygen. As a reflex, I gulp a big lungful of poisonous gas—

Within seconds, my lungs are . . . *burning.*

I start gagging and choking, doubling over with nausea and pain. My mouth and eyes won't stop watering. All around me, gasps and panicked groans fill the chamber. Just when I don't think the pain can get any worse, the *fear* component hits me like a punch to the gut.

I glance to my right—where Nadia was sitting—but instead, it's the Raider from the combat sim staring back at me. *How can this happening?* My brain screams at the impossibility. I stagger backward in shock and blink to clear the watery film from my burning eyes . . .

But he's there. There's no mistaking him.

He clutches the electrified mace. It sizzles and sparks the air. Terror grips me, paralyzing my limbs. My heart lurches and drops, struggling to keep beating through the panic. *He wasn't real. No, this can't be real.*

But then the Raider grins, exposing his crooked, stained teeth. He raises his mace and swings it at my head. I raise my hands and scream in shock, "Noooooooo!"

That's when everything drops out around me. The gas chamber. The other recruits. And I fall back and back into . . . *nothingness.* Even the drill sergeant's voice can't reach me here.

My stomach drops as I keep falling . . . no . . . it's more like I'm being sucked into the absolute center of a black hole . . . the singularity that crushes everything into oblivion.

And then, suddenly—

I'm back on that sand dune, back in that combat sim, trapped between warring hordes of Raiders. *This isn't real—it's that fear gas,* I tell myself, struggling to hold on to reality.

But it keeps shifting and morphing around me.

I fight back against this terrorist assault on my senses. I work to control my fear and tamp down my panic. "You're not . . . *real,*" I scream at the Raiders. "Didn't you hear me? You're not real! You can't hurt me . . . it's just the fear gas . . ."

But they keep advancing up the dune.

I whip around, feeling the blaze of the sun on my back and the soft sand slipping under my boots. I try to convince my brain that it's just a hallucination . . . I'm not really standing here.

I force my lips to move.

"You're not real . . . none of this is real . . ."

The Raiders have almost reached the dune now. They raise their weapons to strike me down. But I don't run away this time. Instead, I make myself stand and face them.

"This isn't real! It's only a hallucination! You're not . . . real!" I scream until my lungs can't scream anymore. And then I keep rasping the words out in my croaky voice.

Slowly, like puzzle pieces breaking away—

The vision fades from my eyes.

And just like that—like waking from a bad dream—I'm back in the gas chamber, my eyes and lungs burning. But the Raider isn't next to me anymore . . . it's only Nadia again.

And she's panicking, too.

"I'm gonna die," she screams, flailing around blindly. I reach for her, trying to keep my eyes shut against the gas, but she fights back. "Raider scum, get off me."

"No, you're not dying," I choke out, trying to snap her out of it.

But she attacks me like I'm the enemy. Claws at my face. Beats at my body.

"Nadia, snap out of it . . . this isn't real," I choke out, my voice shattered by the gas. "It's Kari . . . your battle buddy . . . hang on . . . I'm getting you out of here . . ."

She keeps clawing at me, but I haul her to her feet, sling her over my back, and stagger toward the rattrap. Somehow, I manage to force the first door open and collapse inside.

Fresh air blasts in. My lungs still burn like asteroid fires, but this feels like gulping cool water on a hot day. I suck down the clean oxygen in short gulps, the most my spasming, singed lungs will allow. Once the gas clears, I burst back into the corridor, dragging her behind me.

We're both choking and gagging. My mouth won't stop watering, while my eyes tear nonstop and blur my vision. My lungs burn like the heat of a thousand suns. Yet, the drill sergeant is suddenly nowhere to be found. *Where did she go?* I wonder dimly.

I lay Nadia's limp body down . . . she's lost consciousness. I call for help, but nobody comes. Checking to make sure she's stable and breathing, I turn back to the gas chamber.

More like . . . *torture* chamber.

Through the windows in the thick doors, I spot the rest of my platoon. They're panicked and stuck inside, overcome by the fear gas. Some have turned on each other, thinking they're the enemy. Genesis and Percy are all-out brawling on the floor, the rest clawing at their eyes and throats, or on the verge of passing out. One urgent thought shoots through my head—

I can't leave them in there like that.

I have to get them out before they hurt each other . . . or worse.

Even though my lungs are still on fire, I force them to take a big gulp of clean air, then I shut my eyes and hold my breath. I charge back through the rattrap and into the gas chamber.

"Everybody, this way," I yell. "We have to get out . . . now."

I pull Percy off Genesis—no easy feat, as he's twice my size. Then, I drag them both kicking and screaming into the rattrap and force them inside the smaller chamber. They're blind to the world, ensnared in their own hallucinogenic nightmares. But something about my touch, about my voice, finally reaches some deep part of them. They calm down, but only a little.

"I'll be back, just stay there," I order them.

One by one, I haul the rest of my platoon into the rattrap, then shepherd them back into the corridor once the gas clears, taking deep gulps of fresh air each time. I keep going back in for more recruits, despite my eyes blurring and burning. Finally, I think I've gotten everyone out.

I count the bodies in the corridor . . . and come up one short. "Wait, who's missing?" I ask, whipping back around. I blink hard, trying to clear my vision. "Who did we leave behind?"

"Anton . . . it's Anton," Luna gasps from behind me, where she's dry heaving on the floor. Spittle dribbles from her mouth. "I left him . . . I don't know how . . . he's my battle buddy . . ."

Panic surges through me. He's the smallest and weakest recruit in our platoon. That means the effects of the fear gas could hit him harder. Despite the screaming of my lungs, I gulp down fresh air and charge through the rattrap and back into the chamber, forcing my eyes open and scanning the compact space. Fear gas clouds the air like an invisible film of poison.

"Damn it, Anton!" I yell for him. "Where in the *blazing stars* are you?"

At first, the chamber looks empty. Dread grips my heart and squeezes it.

But then I hear a weak voice—

"Raider, no . . . get off me . . ."

Violent coughing cuts off the words . . . the kind that brings up blood. But there's no mistaking his voice. I dash to the back corner, where I find Anton crumpled in a tight ball.

When I reach for him, his face morphs and transforms into that Raider. Suddenly, I smell his putrid breath. His hands wrap around my neck and squeeze. "Fed scum, die!"

They choke off my air supply.

I claw at his hands as I start to suffocate. The edges of my vision black out. Tears cascade down my cheeks. Any grip on my fragile reality threatens to evaporate altogether.

You're not real! I think as hard as I can. I try to scream it, but my voice is gone. It's deserted me. I keep thinking it over and over—*You're not real! You're not real!*—until I force the hallucination away.

My vision clears at last.

It's only Anton. His hands clutch at my uniform, his fingers clawing at my neck weakly. His breathing sounds halting and jagged. His skin looks deathly pale. He thinks that I'm the enemy . . . he's trying to strangle me. But his hands barely have any strength left.

"Stars, get up now," I say to him. "You stay down . . . we all fail."

Some part of him hears me. He stops trying to strangle me and staggers to his knees. Then, I sling his small body over my shoulder. He feels like a baby bird fallen from the nest. I carry him to the rattrap, staggering to my knees and dropping him on the cool metal floor.

Hissssssssssss.

Fresh air floods the room, chilling my skin and dousing the fire in my lungs. The rest of our platoon watches through the door. I see their pale, ghostly faces hovering in the window, waiting for us to emerge. Anton lies next to me. He's not moving . . . he's barely breathing.

He looks dead.

That's my last thought before everything goes black.

CHAPTER 24

DRAE

I don't know what comes over me as I cut across campus the next day. Maybe it's everything that happened yesterday with Professor Trebond's disappearance. Maybe it's my roomies driving me crazy. Maybe it's some sense of justice, of wanting to know the truth. Maybe it's that Kari is in real danger up there with the increased threat level, while I'm still the same old lame coward.

But as I pass the faculty building, I remember the Fed Patrols cordoning it off and the commotion. It's a bad idea, but I can't help feeling drawn there. I'm seized by the sudden urge. But I'm not authorized to enter the faculty building, so my key card won't work.

I wait until a professor exits with her head buried in a tablet. Once she passes, I vault up the steps and bolt through the door before it can shut. It clicks into place and locks behind me.

Stars, that was lucky.

That thought is immediately chased by a more urgent one—

What am I doing sneaking in here?

That's when Estrella pings me and flashes a map in my retinas.

Draeden, your next class isn't located in this building. You made a wrong turn. Projecting the correct route now. Federation History with Professor Drake is located in Building—

Estrella, mute, please, I think quickly. *And get rid of that map while you're at it.*

My neural implant falls silent and the map vanishes from my retinas. Making a wrong turn or being late to class doesn't technically violate any official rules, since most kids have a bad habit of being tardy. No electric zap from my implant, just blessed silence.

I refocus on the corridor in front of me. It's empty and smells faintly of rationed aftershave, pungent cleaning products, and that familiar, musty odor that's baked into the walls of Berkeley's older buildings. It's the smell of . . . *time*, I decide, and breathe it in deeper. Doors to the faculty rooms line the corridor on both sides. They all have security pads with locks.

I'm not sure what I'm hoping to find here. Maybe some clue about what happened to her. I should turn back and head to class. I could get into major trouble if I get caught snooping around about Trebond's disappearance, but I can't help it. That's when I spot it farther down the hall.

Yellow crime scene tape stretched across a doorway.

That's gotta be her room. I'm sure of it. I hurry over and notice that the door is slightly ajar. On closer inspection, the police tape has jammed it from closing all the way.

I nudge it open . . .

Creak. It swings inward.

I freeze instantly and recheck the hallway, but thankfully, it remains deserted. Then I peer inside her faculty room, feeling a secret thrill. It's been tossed. Everything looks chaotic. The room has been thoroughly searched. Shoes, clothes, and bedding are strewn across the floor in a messy tangle. The desk drawers gape open, displaying their ransacked contents.

From the looks of it, she didn't take much with her when she bolted. That means one thing—she left in a real hurry. I remember what Jude said about there being a leak. He must be right. She had to have been tipped off that Fed agents were coming to arrest her.

That's when I hear . . . *footsteps.*

They're coming from the hall.

My heart plunges through my chest. I don't have a choice. Without any time to waste, I jump down to the floor and scramble under her twin bed. It's not easy to fit beneath the low frame. I scratch my cheek on the metal coils, drawing blood that drips down my cheek.

But I keep my mouth shut, not even daring to breathe. I just need to wait for the footsteps to pass, then I can sneak out. They draw closer and closer, sounding staccato and official.

I hold my breath and wait.

But—

The footsteps stop at the door.

Blast the stars, I think in alarm.

They enter the room. From my low perspective, all I can see are shiny, black, faux-leather shoes. *Federation* shoes. They're government officials. Just my stars-blasted luck.

"Hey, did you leave the tape like this?" the first man asks. His voice is deep and gruff—and terribly authoritative. But there's something more . . . something eerily familiar.

Fear stabs my heart like a dagger when I place it—

The voice belongs to Jude's father.

Growing up next door, I've spent enough time at his house with Jude and Loki to recognize it anywhere. There's no mistaking him. He's always been like a second father to me. He offered us *real* soda on hot days while joking around with us from the recliner, where he scanned the newsfeeds and sipped his scotch *neat* (unlike my mother, who likes it on the rocks).

I hear them inspecting the tape and the fluttering of plastic. I hold my breath . . . and pray they don't decide to search under the bed. But then, the other man finally speaks up.

"Probably the janitor," he says, sounding bored.

I should be relieved by that statement, but instead panic screams in my ears. *What is he doing here?* I think in shock. I can't believe this is happening . . . but I recognize him, too.

It's my dad.

CHAPTER 25

KARI

When I wake up, I don't know where I am.

Dimly, panic thumps my heart. I try to sit up but collapse back. I blink in the stark light of the room. Gauzy curtains drift down around my bed. Machines beep next to it in steady rhythm. Wires run from them to my arms, snaking into my veins. Outside the door, nurses bustle down the hall in their white uniforms with red crosses. That's when it hits me . . .

The infirmary.

That's where I am. I try to sit up again, quickly regretting it as my body screams out in pain. How did I end up here? It takes a minute for everything to come rushing back. *The middle of the night gas chamber exercise. The fear gas. The Raider hallucinations. How I got my platoon out . . . and went back for Anton. Then collapsing to the ground . . . and blackness.*

I can't remember anything after that.

"Private, how are you feeling?"

I jerk my head to the left—a little too fast.

Pain shoots through my temples like tiny spikes. After my vision clears, I spot the drill sergeant standing at the door. She signals to the nurse. They talk in heated whispers, then the nurse rushes off down the corridor, probably to fetch the doctor.

I'm not happy to see her, and I can't hide it. I know my rage shows plainly on my face.

"Terrible," I choke out. "No thanks to you."

My voice is raspy and grizzled. My throat and eyes still burn like the heat of a thousand suns. My brain feels like a sandstorm blasted it. I know I shouldn't talk back to my drill sergeant like this. That I can be punished brutally in PT. But I don't care anymore.

She abandoned us in that gas chamber after exposing us to chemical weapons. This whole place is psychotic. This isn't what I signed up for. They're not training us—they're torturing us.

I don't care if I wash out now.

"Well, I'm not here for thanks," the drill sergeant says, perching on the plastic chair next to my hospital bed. "That's not in my job description."

Under the brim of her hat, dark circles line her eyes, like she didn't get any sleep. That surprises me. I didn't think she cared. How long has she been sitting by my bedside? Waiting for me to come around?

"Right, you're here to torture us." I try to sit up but regret it as a fresh wave of dizziness washes through me. "Don't pretend that's not in the job description."

I brace myself for her livid response. I half expect her to kick me out on the spot, or at the very least, to berate me for my verbal insubordination. And I'd deserve it, too. Instead, she tosses her head back and laughs. Good and hard belly laughs. Tears leak from her eyes.

I stare at her in shock, which quickly dissolves into worry. I start to wonder if the fear gas got to her and scrambled her brain, too.

"Asteroid fires . . . I needed that," she manages once she gets ahold of herself.

Despite her outpouring of laughter, I still feel furious.

"Why'd you make us take our masks off in there?" I flop my arm with the IV line in my elbow, almost dislodging it. "And breathe that poison? What if I didn't get Anton out in time?"

She levels her gaze on me. "But you did. Get him out."

"But you didn't know I was going to do that," I sputter, taken aback. "I didn't even know I was going to do that. And now I'm in the infirmary. And I'm guessing Anton is down the hall."

She nods. "Room 305. Recovering nicely, I might add."

I sigh in frustration and flop back. "That's not the point."

"Well, you asked," she says with a shrug. "I'm just answering your questions."

I glare at her, angry at how nonchalant she seems over almost getting one of us killed. "Just admit it. You're a sadist who gets pleasure from torturing her recruits. Stop acting so high and mighty already. Why else make us breathe fear gas?"

"Simple, so that in a real combat situation with a chemical weapon attack," she says in an unflinching voice, "you'll never forget to secure your mask and activate the filters. Gas exposure creates a deep muscle memory. One that you'll never forget."

"You can say that again." I snort. "I think putting your mask on is pretty obvious. We've had plenty of classes on chemical weapons and how to use our masks. Isn't that enough? What fool soldier wouldn't remember to activate their filters?"

"This *fool* soldier," she says, jerking her thumb to her face. "And I almost died for my mistake. I'm lucky my commanding officer pulled me out in time."

I stare at her in shock. I can't believe it. "You forgot to put on your mask?"

All of a sudden, her face cracks open. That's the only way to describe it. Human emotions flit across her features. Lines and wrinkles cut into her skin—from stress, from combat, from aging—from everything life throws at you. She looks like an actual human for once.

"Trust me, it's easy to forget your training in the heat of battle," she says after a long moment. "In a combat situation, that deep muscle memory can mean the difference between life and death. Between making it out alive—and losing your whole platoon."

"Training via torture?" I say, still not convinced.

"Pretty much," she agrees with a conspiratorial smirk. "The purpose of the gas chamber exercise is to sear the effects into your body and your brain, so you'll never forget. That type of memory is stronger than any classroom instruction. It's burned into your cells."

I sputter out a raspy cough. "Yeah, my cells agree. And they're pissed off."

That provokes a wry chuckle from her. It's like she's letting her guard down. She passes me a cup of water from the side table. I drink thirstily, even though it burns my throat like fire.

"You did well in there, recruit," she adds with a nod. "You got your whole platoon out. You fought back against the fear effects—and overcame them. Faster than any of my former students, I might add."

I wait for the punchline. The insult.

But it doesn't come.

Was that an actual compliment? Is she proud of me?

"I'm no hero," I mutter, feeling an unworthiness inside so vast and deep that it's like being sucker punched in the gut. "I'm deserter spawn, remember? I'm just gonna wash out and ship back Earthside. Or worse, crack up like my dad and get half my platoon killed."

Tears pool in my eyes. I hate displaying my raw emotions like this. I want to blame the fear gas still stinging my eyes. But I know it's more than that. It's deeper. This is why I never talk about my dad. *Ever.* She passes me tissues, waiting patiently while I wipe my eyes.

"That's your father," she goes on in a gentle voice. "It's not you."

"Then why do you keep calling me those terrible names?" I say through my tears, which keep coming. "Constantly reminding me of what he did? For the record, I hate him, too. He ruined our lives, and I don't want to be anything like him. That's why I'm here."

She gives me a hard look. "Private Skye, do you think you're the first deserter spawn to waltz into basic training with something to prove? Who both loves and hates her family at the same time? Who yearns for something better, but can't help messing up all the time?"

Her words hang in the air. Shock emanates through me. The tone of her voice, the look on her face, and what she said make one thing very clear—

She's deserter spawn, too.

"Wait, you're like me?" I sputter, unable to disguise my surprise.

She nods with a grim look. "Mom couldn't hack it. She deserted her platoon during a Siberian Fed attack that left my family in ruins, too."

Her words hit me like blaster fire. I struggle to square this information with the asshole drill sergeant who's been berating me for the last few weeks.

"But why didn't you tell me?" I ask, unable to make sense of her motives. Why would she taunt me for being the same as her?

"Let's see," she says, letting out a deep sigh. "Do you go around telling everyone that stupid sob story? And how your dad destroyed your family? And betrayed his federation?"

"Right, I don't tell anyone if I can help it," I say, feeling my cheeks flush. I pat my chest over my heart. "I keep it buried, stuffed down."

"Exactly, so we agree on something."

We both fall silent. The only sounds are the soft *hiss* of the vents pumping in recirculated air and the steady *beep, beep, beep* of the bedside monitors. What is unsaid means more than anything we could utter aloud. We're the same; we're both deserter spawn.

"Oh, tell anyone about our little chat today," she adds with a stern look. "And you'll be doing extra PT reps until the end of time. Is that understood?"

She says it like it's a joke, but there's an undercurrent of seriousness.

"Drill Sergeant, yes, Drill Sergeant," I reply in my raspy voice.

I manage a tired, limp salute. But I can't stop tears from slipping out. I don't know if it's the side effects from the fear gas, or this small act of kindness from the drill sergeant who's been hell-bent on torturing me for the last few weeks.

"Sorry, I don't mean to cry," I say in a raspy voice. "It's just that . . . nothing has gone the way I planned . . . starting with my horrible Pairing . . . to Draeden Rache . . ."

Now it's her turn to look surprised.

"Wait, that name. Did you say . . . *Rache*?"

That's enough to stop my tears. I meet her shocked gaze. "Don't you already know the names of our Sympathetics? It's gotta be in our Space Force records. I assumed you knew . . ."

She shakes her head. "We're not privy to that information. It's top secret. The Sympathetic Program is classified. Only the postmasters know the identity of your Sympathetics."

"But you recognize his name?" I ask, feeling curiosity rear up in me.

"Yup, and I'll never forget it as long as I live." She lowers her voice. "Listen closely. Sergeant Rache is the only reason I'm sitting here right now. I'd be dead without her sacrifice."

I sit up a little straighter, trying to process it. "Wait, what do you mean?"

"Well, I shouldn't say anything. But there's more . . . it involves your father, too."

"My father . . ." I say in barely a whisper.

She wants to talk, but she hesitates. Something holds her back.

"Look, just tell me already," I whisper back. "I deserve to know the truth."

"The truth? That's relative," she says with a derisive snort. "I shouldn't say anything . . . but after your father deserted his watch, the Raiders attacked our platoon. We had no warning. Sergeant Rache saved my life that day. I was knocked unconscious after I got blasted by enemy fire. She pulled me out of that crater and to safety. She saved as many of us as she could . . ."

That haunted look flashes across her face again. *How many guardians from her platoon died that day?* I wonder. *Not just fellow guardians, but friends even? All because of my father?*

I think of Nadia and Anton, but also his battle buddy Luna. Not to mention, Percy and Genesis. Sure, we were all assigned to the same platoon. By some combination of luck and secret Space Force algorithms, we were forced together. Despite the tough circumstances and daily drill sergeant torture sessions, we've become fast friends. We're basically inseparable at this point.

"So, you're saying . . . your commanding officer was his mother?" I say, putting the pieces together. "If that's true . . . then you both served in the same platoon with my father . . ."

The drill sergeant nods. "That all computes. The injuries that she sustained in that attack led to her medical discharge. She was awarded a purple heart. Also, it's worse than you think."

"What do you mean?" I ask, feeling my heart sink. "What could make it worse?"

"Listen, I really shouldn't be telling you all this. There's a reason it's classified . . ."

"Well, I already signed my life away," I say, desperate for more information. "Please, just tell me. I promise to keep it to myself. You know how much I hate talking about my dad."

She thinks for a long moment. My heart races, then sinks.

She's not going to tell me, I think in defeat.

But then she leans into my bedside and whispers, "The official report said your father deserted . . . on purpose. That he wanted to help the Raiders. He led them to our platoon."

I stare at her, struggling to process this.

"But if that's true, how can her son be my Sympathetic?" I ask, my mind reeling and making me feel dizzy. Well, dizzier than I already felt. "And you assigned as my drill sergeant? And you both served with my dad? That can't be random. It's too much of a coincidence."

"*Nothing* at Space Force is random," she says, keeping her voice low. She glances around to make sure nobody is listening. "Haven't you figured that out yet? They assigned you to me on purpose. And not just me, but your Sympathetic, too. They had a reason."

"Uh . . . to torture and humiliate me?" I say in a wry voice.

"No, to *rehabilitate* you."

I frown. "Wait, what do you mean?"

"Look, I'm not supposed to talk about this," she says with a frown. "But like I said, none of these assignments are accidental. Space Force isn't being malicious, despite what you think. They're probably hoping that your Sympathetic can rehabilitate you, based on your family history. Same reason they assigned me to train you. They want you to face your worst fears."

My worst fears? I try to absorb and understand this, but my brain feels overloaded and on the verge of melting down. She lets that sink in for another long moment, before slipping back into her official persona. She leans back and straightens her shoulders. The mask is back.

"Recruit, why are you laying around the infirmary and playing hooky?" she barks, climbing back to her feet. She gives me a stern look. "I'm gonna get the docs to discharge your lazy ass."

She marches toward the door, then glances back. "And don't think this little injured act gets you out of PT tomorrow," she adds for good measure. "Private Skye, is that understood?"

"Drill Sergeant, yes, Drill Sergeant," I say before another coughing fit takes me.

Tears leak from my eyes, but this time it's not from the fear gas. It's my stupid feelings. They overtake my body and cloud my mind. Before she leaves, she turns back and says one last thing.

"Good job in there today," she says in a softer voice with a nod of respect. "You might just make it through this torture session we call basic training after all." She even cracks a tiny smile. It looks unnatural on her. I'm so used to glares, frowns, and all varieties of scowls.

"Oh, and one more thing," she says, hovering in the doorway. "What did you see in your hallucination? From the fear gas? It's different for every guardian. It represents the one thing you fear the most. Above all else. It will help your training to target those weaknesses."

"The Raider from the combat sim," I say with a deep shudder. His filthy face flashes in my memory. "The one who almost killed Luna . . . and took Anton out in our combat sim."

"Ah, the Raiders." She absorbs that. "But that also means your friends are your greatest weakness. You fear losing them. That's a good quality in a guardian, but it can get you killed."

With that unsettling proclamation, she marches down the corridor. Her boots slap the polished floors like blaster fire, on her way to fetch my doc and get me discharged.

A few hours later, I'm discharged from the infirmary and limp back to the barracks, caught in a swirl of complicated emotions. Each step brings a new wave of pain to my body.

My lungs still ache from the fear gas, but that's not what's got me so worked up. Everything the drill sergeant says ricochets around like space junk in zero-g.

His mother, the war hero . . . my father, the deserter . . . both from the same platoon . . . both their lives permanently altered by events from the same Raider attack. How could this be true?

The drill sergeant's words reverberate through my head.

Nothing at Space Force is random.

It's almost too much to process. I'm not sure what to make of it all. If anything, this new information leads me to one terrible conclusion. *My father is worse than I already knew.*

Ugh, I didn't think that was possible.

Deserter scum, I curse him. *Good riddance.*

I hate him more than anything. Lost in a tangle of emotions and still physically drained, I stumble into the barracks and push the door open. But it's pitch black inside . . . that's strange. It's not time for lights out yet. My fear response kicks into high gear. Did something happen?

I feel panic in my heart; I taste it on my tongue.

Suddenly, applause breaks out. The artificial lights flicker on, blinding me. My eyes fall on the faces of the recruits clapping for me. Luna, Anton, Nadia, Percy, and Genesis . . .

The cheering grows louder.

"Hip-hip-hooray, Private Skye saved the day," Nadia calls out. Everyone takes up the refrain, filling the barracks with their jubilant voices. She claps me on the shoulder.

"Thanks for pulling me out. And my weakling little bro," she goes on, jerking her thumb to Anton, who shoots me a bashful grin. He's also been discharged from the infirmary.

Percy and Genesis both grin at me.

"Nice job back there!" Genesis says. "I was about to strangle him."

"No, you weren't," Percy says, looking faux upset. "I had you beat."

Luna pops her head over the edge of her rack. "Thanks for saving me and my battle buddy. Sorry, I kinda froze back there. That fear gas did a serious number on me," she says, tapping her temples. "Maybe you can teach me a thing or two about how to overcome it."

The cheering and celebrating continue past our official bedtime until the drill sergeant finally bursts in looking irate. "What about *lights out* don't you grunts understand? Get in your racks! Now! I don't need any recruits winding up back in the infirmary from sleep deprivation."

Everyone shuts up and scrambles into bed as she dims the lights. As I drift off to sleep, the cheering of my platoon echoes in my ears like the sweetest sound. Before I nod out, I remember that I have my Sympathetic exchange tomorrow. I can't wait to tell Drae about how I finally did something *right* up here for once. But something stops my thoughts in their tracks.

What about the stuff about my dad . . . and his mom . . . and what he did to their platoon? I clench up. I know I can't talk to him about it. So, I decide to stuff it back down like always. I'm used to that. He doesn't need to know the truth. The last thing I need is another dirty family secret ruining my life again, right when the Sympathetic Program is starting to work and I'm not dreading our exchanges. Space Force paired us together for a reason, I remind myself.

That's also what the drill sergeant said. That means I should trust the process.

And I can't have what my father did messing up our relationship . . . and both our futures.

Instead, I try to focus on my platoon cheering for me. That happy reminiscence carries me down into a deep, dreamless slumber. No Raiders. No fears of washing out. No memories of my deserter father. No black hole dreams that suck me in and crush me into space dust.

Just blissful, blissful nothingness.

CHAPTER 26

DRAE

Thought we told them to leave the place alone?" Dad says, fluttering the police tape. His voice is filled with suspicion as he inspects the room in his shiny, black shoes. "It's a crime scene."

He's standing only inches from my hiding spot under the bed.

What's he doing here? I think in shock.

He's usually stuck behind a desk pushing metaphorical paper. He doesn't conduct field investigations. The same goes for Jude's father. Not to mention, this is pretty far outside of their jurisdiction in Lompoc. Why didn't my dad tell me he was coming to campus?

But that's when—I remember all the dodged calls. Ugh, I'm so stupid.

That must be why they kept calling me. Dad probably wanted to tell me he was coming to visit for work. Rho was right, as always. Dodging their calls was like setting off a ticking time bomb. Now, I regret not picking up and defusing this whole situation.

"Janitors," Mr. Luther says in disdain. I picture the frown spreading over his sharp face, framed by blonde hair flecked with gray. He looks like an older version of his son, except with a sizable paunch. "Can't trust anyone to do a decent job these days."

"Yup, it's disgraceful," Dad replies, speaking with coded bias. "They can't follow simple directions. There's a reason we keep their housing separate."

"Oh, you've got that right," Mr. Luther replies. They both chuckle. It sickens me, even though that's exactly how my parents always talk at home.

Mr. Luther inspects the room, pushing clothes and bedding around with his shiny black shoes. I hold my breath, trying not to make any noise. He's only inches away.

"Professor Trebond sure took off like the blazes," Mr. Luther says. "Didn't take much with her. You'd think we'd find something good here. Not a bunch of ratty old clothes and books."

"Clearly, she got tipped off," Dad says, picking through her desk drawers. He chucks books and notepads on the floor. They land with a *thud*. "Did they pinpoint the leak yet?"

"Not yet," Mr. Luther says. "But they're working on it. Going through her messages. The leaker probably used an encrypted line—but we'll find them. It's only a matter of time."

"The sooner the better," Dad says. "Someone must be helping her. How else is she staying off the grid? Why haven't we located her? Or more like . . . a lot of someones."

I perk up at that. But who helped Trebond escape . . . and why?

"Well, in that case," Mr. Luther says, slipping into a sinister voice. "It will make it even more fun when we finally catch her. And make her squeak like the filthy rat she is . . ."

Shivers rush through me. I've never heard him talk this way.

Suddenly, my dad pokes at something partially buried under the rug with his gloved hand. It's wrapped in gray linen cloth. I only see the contents for a quick second. It looks like some kind of feather. Long and back. And something else . . . a little black jar with a cork stopper in it.

I try to catch a better look, but he scoops the items up—and out of my sight.

"Walt, what do you think these are?" he asks in a suspicious voice.

"No clue," Mr. Luther says. "Looks like some prewar relics that belong in a museum."

"Maybe," Dad says, his voice stiffening. "It could be contraband."

"Always a possibility with a traitor like her," Mr. Luther agrees in a cold voice. "Trebond was a crazy old bat, that's for sure. I've been interviewing her associates. You should hear some of the stories from the faculty. My son was right to report her. He should get a federation medal."

They're talking about . . . *Jude*. That turns my stomach as much as the thought of them discovering me under the bed. They turn to leave, but then Mr. Luther turns back.

"Hey, did you ever reach your kid?" he asks my dad. "Jude seems to think . . . well . . . that his sympathies might not be in the right place. Something about reading a lot of books lately?"

My heart drops like a stone.

Jude told his dad about me? And my reading habits?

"Oh, right, I spoke to him," Dad says, trying to sound nonchalant, but it comes out a little forced. This shocks me—he's lying to cover for me. "Don't worry about Drae. He's a good kid. I'll get him to lay off the library card. Good thing we rooted out this bad influence."

He kicks a book on the floor. It lands only inches from my face. The yellowing, stained pages stare back at me. I feel their accusations wafting off those printed words like heat.

"Knowledge in the wrong hands spreads like a virus," Mr. Luther replies, "Just keep an eye on him. You said it yourself. You can't trust anyone these days, not even family."

"Of course," Dad says quickly. "I'm sure Jude will keep an eye on him, too."

"Indeed, he plans on it," Mr. Luther says. "Good thing we pulled those strings and got them roomed together. Just like us back in the old days. Remember our legendary exploits?"

His words hit me like a dagger—*I'm being watched.*

My dad gives Mr. Luther a chummy clap on the shoulder. "How could I forget? We tore up this campus. And forget homework. It's a stars-given miracle that we graduated in one piece."

"Don't remind me," Mr. Luther says. "Good thing our parents greased those wheels."

More laughter, then—

"Well, should we leave these here?" my dad asks. His voice sounds uncertain. He must be talking about the strange objects that he found wrapped in that cloth—the feather and the vial.

Finally, Mr. Luther replies. "Bag it and let's take it back to the lab. Can't hurt."

"That way we won't turn up empty-handed," Dad agrees, but then he hesitates. "Don't you think it's strange how little she kept here? No electronics? No personal effects? Not even a computer? Either she covered her tracks, or she was smart and knew we could track her."

"Or maybe she's innocent?" Mr. Luther says.

There's an affected pause, then both laugh heartily.

"Oh, nice one," my dad says between chuckles. "I needed that."

At last, they saunter out of the room. But I don't exhale until the slap of their footsteps fades away.

After waiting a full ten minutes, I finally slide out from under the bed and bolt out of Trebond's room. Luckily, the hallway is empty. It's the peak of afternoon classes. I don't stop, or dare to look back, until I reach my Federation History class, slipping in through the back doors.

I spot Rho a few rows down and slide into the seat next to her.

"What happened to you?" she mouths when she sees me. Her hair turns gray with worry. Her eyes fade to match, as I settle into my folding seat in the large, wood-paneled lecture hall.

"Nothing," I lie through my teeth.

I want to tell her the truth, but it's too dangerous. She gives me a piercing look with her gray visage. She knows I'm not telling her something important. But finally, she gives up.

"Okay, weirdo, whatever you say."

I listen to Professor Drake blather on about how "the Great War was a blessing because it led to the formation of the California Federation and Earth's disarmament." It's just more propaganda, like what they broadcast on the newsfeeds. I tune it out and instead focus on slowing my heart. I'm still jittery and pumped full of adrenaline after what happened.

I think about everything I learned. The authorities are taking this Professor Trebond situation seriously. Mr. Luther and my father are handling the investigation. The fed wouldn't send them all the way here if it wasn't important. But why? It can't just be unapproved curriculum. That much is clear. I try to remember everything I overheard, piecing it into a fractured puzzle.

Trebond kept her room bare, like she knew they'd be coming to arrest her one day . . . like she expected it even. They also insinuated that she did something dangerous . . . treasonous even. Oh, and one more thing. Whatever she did—she isn't working alone. Questions rush through my head one after another, each more vexing. Clearly, this whole thing is bigger than I thought.

Another puzzle piece tumbles through my head. What was the weird feather and bottle that my father found in her room? The more I think about everything, the more confused I feel. All I know is . . . Trebond's in major trouble . . . and they won't rest until they catch her.

And worse—

My father is the one searching for her.

I sink lower in my hard-backed seat, feeling another jolt of dread as I recall something else that they said. Jude didn't just report on her—he reported on me, too. That means I need to be careful around my roommates, or I could be next. I'm just lucky my dad covered for me.

Sneaking into Trebond's room was risky. I had Estrella on mute, but that doesn't mean that she wasn't silently documenting it all. I can't do something like that again. It would be easy to pull my records and discover that I broke into her room. That I dislodged the crime scene tape, not the janitors. That alone could get me into major trouble. Luckily, my father being the lead investigator does buy me some protection. But that won't last if I get caught doing anything.

The boring class ends with my panic still silently building. I follow Rho outside into the fading afternoon sunlight. But I shrink back as a Fed Patrol whirs past and beeps at us.

"Stay on the sidewalks," it barks in a robotic voice, making me jump.

Rho shoots me a worried look. "Hey, is something wrong? You've been acting super weird and jumpy since the whole Trebond thing."

"Uh . . . it's nothing," I say, trying to keep the panic from my voice. I glance nervously at the patrol, which continues away. "Just nervous about my exchange with Kari this afternoon."

"Ah, yes!" she says and brightens. "Study date later?"

"Yup, I'll see you after," I add with a wince.

I don't feel ready to talk to Kari right now. My mind feels jumbled and frazzled. Plus, she already has enough to stress about up there. I don't want to add to her problems. That's the last thing I want. I try to keep my heart from sinking with worries. But I fail miserably.

As I trudge away and take the familiar path toward the post office, winding through the center of campus, all I know is . . . nothing makes sense anymore . . . and worse . . .

I'm in danger . . . we all are.

CHAPTER 27

KARI

Postmaster Haven seals the pod shut.

The lights dim and the aromatherapy kicks on full blast. I feel that brain sucking sensation as the artificial environment envelops me. One second, I'm in the post office—

And the next, I'm standing on the surface.

Slick ice stretches beneath my boots, a glistening black expanse that gleams under the undiluted starlight. I glance up at the night sky, as glittery and endless as the universe. It's so much clearer and darker without the atmosphere to filter it.

A lone figure materializes in the middle distance. He walks toward me. Though his face remains shrouded in shadow. Starlight dances in his dark eyes. My breath catches in my throat.

Drae has never looked more handsome. I know it's only a projection—an amalgamation profiled and generated by his implant. But something about his presence catches me off guard . . . and makes chills rush through me.

This person who I hated so much back in high school. *How can I be feeling this way?* I think in alarm. *No, he's the enemy!* I want to tell him how much I hate his guts—

Suddenly, I feel a painful zing. That's accompanied by a stilted, robotic voice.

Hikari, he's not the enemy. He's your Sympathetic.

Harold always has the worst timing.

Well, could've fooled me, I think back with zero sarcasm. Only extreme annoyance.

My neural scans indicate that's not the truth about how you feel, Harold goes on obliviously. *You must be honest about your feelings. Participation in this program is mandatory.*

Ugh, that's the very last thing in the whole universe that I want to do. But I don't have a choice. Or Harold will zap me again. But there's more. I search my heart and my head. He's right. I don't hate Drae, not anymore, though that confuses the ever loving stars out of me. But Harold is right about one thing. I'm all alone up here. I need to talk to someone, even if it's Drae . . . especially after everything I learned from the drill sergeant . . . or it might eat me alive.

But nothing feels more terrifying.

I take a deep breath, open my mouth. I have to dig deeper.

"Drae, there's something I've never told you . . ." I start in a soft voice, but then trail off. The words feel clunky in my mouth. They make it hard to talk, but I force myself to continue.

"Actually, it's something I've never told anyone."

I feel the usual dread spiked with a hefty chaser of shame. But I force it down and work to excavate the memories. *How deep did I bury them all those years ago?* But then I remember the gas chamber and what happened in there. How fear didn't stop me from acting then.

I draw on that confidence. I force my lips to move.

"It's about . . . *my dad.*"

I cringe the second that leaves my mouth. Regret churns in my gut stronger than starlight. Those terrible words hang in the frostbitten air. My breath hisses out like smoke, curling around my face and freezing in this strange tundra.

I wait for shame and humiliation to overwhelm me and strike me dead. I wait for my worst fears to come true. But strangely, nothing *bad* happens. It's only me talking to Drae about something that happened a really long time ago. Something that can't hurt me anymore. It's only me and this tundra and this virtual message that will travel many AU units to reach Earth.

What was I so afraid of?

I keep talking, and so much pours out of me like a deluge of buried memories. I tell Drae about my father. I tell him . . . *everything*. I don't hold back at all. I've never talked to anyone about this stuff . . . not Ma or Bea . . . not my best friend Rho . . .

Nobody.

I tell him how it felt to get evicted from our comfortable house and bused across. How after my dad deserted, they showed up at the crack of dawn with eviction papers. How we had to march past all of our "confiscated" belongings, haphazardly strewn across the front lawn for our neighbors to gawk at and even pillage. How they gloated and basked in our utter humiliation.

How they whispered loud enough to hear it.

"That family . . . those little girls . . . *deserter spawn.*"

How that was the first time I heard that slur uttered about . . . *me*.

Not just me, but my tiny baby sister, still in swaddling clothes. How neighbors came out to watch our pity parade to the waiting bus. Xena drove us to the Park that day. She volunteers on her days off for eviction runs. She was the only thing that made that day slightly bearable.

"Don't cry now," Xena said in a gentle voice, helping me into a bench seat padded with old blankets and ratty stuffed animals. She'd collected the donations and brought them to help kids like me adjust. She knelt down, while Ma tried to calm Bea, who was fussing fretfully, and handed me a sad-looking, fraying rabbit with most of the stuffing crushed down.

"Wh-where are we going?" I stammered as I hugged it to my chest. It hung limp in my arms, stained and faded, nothing like the crisp, new toys from my childhood. Those were great, big plastic atrocities with mechanized parts and blinking lights and shrieking noises.

"The Park," she said simply, patting my leg. "Oh, don't worry. It's not so bad there. And guess what? You're gonna be my new neighbor. Isn't that cool? The trailers are pretty cozy. The one they cleared out for your family even has *window*s in both of the bedrooms."

It didn't stop the tears that day, but it helped.

"Thank you," Ma said to Xena, settling across from me. She clutched Bea to her breast and she suckled listlessly, rooting around for milk. "I'm sorry . . . I don't know your name."

"Xena. *Period*. No last name. No prefix. No suffix. I keep it simple these days. I left all that behind when I moved into the Park." With that, she climbed behind the driver's seat and caught our gaze in the rearview mirror. "By the stars, that was practically a lifetime ago."

Ma's eyes flicked to the lawn and the gawking neighbors. They were staring daggers at us on the bus. Some were pilfering our confiscated belongings strewn across the front yard.

Worry flashed in Xena's eyes.

"Don't listen to me prattle on like an old fool," she said, grasping the worn, oversized steering wheel and shifting into gear. "Let's get you folks settled into your new digs."

With that, Xena gunned the bus and shot us out of there faster than you can say . . . *asteroid fires*. But we couldn't outrun the shame and humiliation that followed us everywhere. Thanks to the busing program, I still went to school with all the same kids that I grew up with. Even Xena driving me there in her bus couldn't make it better. My former neighbors and playmates now shunned my family like we had the Pox. All except for Rho, of course. Somehow, she's always been immune to caring what other people think. That's why she's my one true friend.

Deserter spawn.

That became my new name. My prefix. My suffix. My surname.

I tell Drae how it felt to never see my dad again.

What that did to Ma.

How it made her crumple and shrivel up, and then fade away like a ghost. How it felt for my family to lose everyone and everything all because of my father's pathetic actions.

Then, I confess something that I've never admitted to anyone—not even myself. Knowing that my father is probably dead doesn't make me sad. In fact, it's the opposite. It brings me satisfaction that he likely took his last breath not long after he deserted his platoon.

Revenge tastes sweet on my tongue.

As these words tumble from my mouth, I relive it all like it's happening again, though I thought I'd left the pain behind back Earthside. I experience the trauma like it's the first time.

"Now you know the truth—I *hate* my father," I say in a searing voice, feeling white-hot hatred sweep through me like lava fire. "I don't miss him—and I'm glad he's dead."

There, I said it out loud. The dreadful thing that I carry around with me, buried in the deep, dark recesses of my ever-beating heart. The thing that fuels me when I have to fight.

My worst secret.

When I finally stop to catch my breath, the timer has almost ticked down to zero. My face is slick with salty tears. I'm out of breath and sobbing; I'm sweaty and spent. Despite all that, I feel strangely exhilarated and lighter, like I just touched down on a planet with less gravity.

Sure, I'm a total mess—but it feels amazing to let my defenses down for once, not have to guard these terrible secrets, always walking around like my heart is a sealed vault, that at any minute, I might get ambushed and cracked open and exposed as the deserter spawn I really am.

It feels good to just be me in this exchange with Drae. Not deserter spawn. Not the former Ringer turned Park kid. Not the Space Force recruit. Not even Private Skye.

No prefix. No suffix. No surname.

Just Kari.

CHAPTER 28

DRAE

Kari's tear-stricken voice fades out as the exchange ends, jettisoning me out of the simulated stellar environment, out of Kari's head, back to myself, back to Berkeley. I blink in the stark, artificial lighting, completely disoriented. I'm stunned by everything that I just absorbed.

But especially this part—

Kari told me about her dad.

Of course, I knew that he was a deserter, but I never knew how it *felt*. Now, I understand her in a way that I never did before. Why she was always so guarded back in high school. Why she walked around with her fists clenched like she was always itching for a fight.

However, before I know it, Estrella is pinging me to record my exchange for Kari all those AU away in space. At first, my heart races and makes my brain freeze up. But then, I open my mouth and the craziest thing happens. I start telling Kari all my worst secrets, too.

How growing up with privilege isn't all it's cracked up to be. How the pressure can drive you insane, so all you want to do is hide under your covers and read *Estrella Luna* comics and never come out again. How my friends are complete assholes, and I have to live with them at Berkeley. How I walk around campus with imposter syndrome, feeling like I don't belong. How I don't deserve to be here. How I worry constantly that I'm going to fail my classes and flunk out.

And that would be the single worst thing.

Because then, I'd have to go back home and live with *my parents*. And that's the last thing in this star-loving universe I want to do. I'm privileged to have these options, so it probably sounds lame. But it doesn't change the way I feel on the inside . . . and it's awful.

When I finish, the timer is ticking down. I only have a few minutes left. My heart pounds. This is my moment to spill my guts and tell her everything. I know I shut her down in our last exchange, but this is my chance finally to come clean. So, I take the brakes off my thoughts and let it all out. I tell her something I know deep down, something that has grown steadier and stronger with each heartbeat of knowing her—that I'd never leave her. That I couldn't abandon her like her father, even if I tried. And it's not just the Sympathetic Program. It's so much more.

I talk and I keep talking and talking and saying everything until—

The timer ticks down to . . . *nothing.*

When I stumble out of the pod, through the busy post office, and step outside into the warm afternoon sunlight, I feel both dizzy and terrified, but also liberated. If I had feelings for Kari before, they're stronger than ever now. They feel like something hot and burning. Something dangerous and crazy and all-consuming. Something that burns brighter than the hottest sun.

Blazing stars, I'm falling for her.

Here's the proof. At the end of the exchange, right before the timer ran out—I told her the truth about why I kissed her in that stairwell. It wasn't because I liked her, as in a lame crush or the way Jude and Loki talk about girls. I told her how she's my sun, how my gravity tilts around her, drawing me toward her center with impossible attraction. How she always lit up the halls like the heat of a thousand blazing stars, even if she wouldn't wave back or utter a shy . . . *hello.*

Her bravery. Her fearlessness. Her strength. Her impossible beauty.

How she made me *want* to be a better person. To do better for her. Even if she was right about me, and I'm still a total coward at heart. And worse yet, I'll never be worthy of her.

I kissed her because . . .

I had to kiss her, the same way I had to breathe.

But I said that I was sorry for doing so without her permission. That was totally wrong, and she had every right to punch me in the face. Well, maybe it didn't have to be . . . *in the face.*

But I'd still do it all over again.

All of it.

Just to feel her lips one more time.

I confessed everything about my own fears and regrets. How I always hide behind witty put-downs and act superior, but really inside, I'm afraid that if I open up and make myself vulnerable, that she'll be the one rejecting me, not the other way around. But that I really did return her feelings. That my heart ached to be around her. That it had been aching for her the whole year.

When the lights finally came on in the pod, my first thought was—

What in the stars did I just do?

I wanted to run to the postmaster and ask her to stop transmitting the exchange. But it was too late. My neural transplant told me. *Message recorded and transmitted to Private Skye.* I have no idea how she'll respond . . . or even if she'll respond. This could be our last exchange.

But I feel a strange buzzing as I cut across campus to meet Rho. I feel like I'm high . . . or about to pass out . . . like I'm both floating and falling at the same time . . . like I'm in . . .

No, I can't say it. Not even in my head. It's too crazy.

Kari is hundreds of millions of kilometers away and not coming back for four long years. And worse yet, there's not a chance in the galaxy that she feels the same way about me.

"You look positively radiant," Rho says when I burst through the swinging door into the warm, pizza-scented air. She's sitting in our usual red vinyl booth at the back of the packed Berkeley hole-in-the-wall restaurant, "Pie Hole." It's the post-class pepperoni rush. Well, *faux* pepperoni rush. I slide into the booth, but then her face twists into a grossed-out expression.

"Oh stars, did you get laid?" she grumbles.

"Sorry to disappoint," I reply. "But that's a major no."

She scrutinizes me, her eyes tinting dark crimson. "I don't buy it," she says, speaking at her usual rapid clip. "Let's just say, I'm pretty experienced in this arena. I know that look."

"Uh, what look?" I say, avoiding her heated gaze, which makes her look demonic, like an evil Cupid. Her retinal implants still throw me off sometimes. "I don't know what you mean—"

"Now you're gaslighting me!" she cuts me off. "You have that *look* blasted all over your pathetic face. It's unique in the whole cosmos—and there's only one possible culprit."

I keep my face blank. "Oh, and what's that?"

"When you're totally falling for another human being—*mind, body, and soul,*" she goes on in a whimsical voice. "And they're all you can think about and talk about and all you want to do is spend every freaking second with them until the end of time. Ideally, *sans* clothing."

I'm busted, but I can't admit the truth. Not to Rho. And especially not when it's about her best friend. Saving me from total mortification, the waiter slides a wire rack on the table and places a steaming pepperoni pie on it. It's so hot, the faux cheese is dripping all over the crust.

"Trust me, that feeling fades so fast," Rho goes on, dousing the pie with enough chili flakes to singe the sun. Then she stuffs a large hunk in her mouth. "Enjoy it while you can."

"I told you. It's nothing," I mutter, fumbling for a piece. Upbeat conversation fills the air all around us, coming from all the tables and barstools. It only makes my stomach sink.

"So, who's this *nothing* person that's got you all twisted? Or should I say . . . *unlucky*?" She bats her eyelashes. Her hair streams out darker red.

"Fine, you're right. There might be someone, but I can't tell you," I mumble, stuffing pizza into my mouth. It singes my tongue, both from the temperature and the chili flakes.

"Still holding out? Wow, then it must be pretty serious." She shuts her tablet and pushes it away. "No way I'm getting any studying done until you fess up."

"Rho, you're wasting your time," I say, shredding the crust into tiny dough balls. "Like I said, I can't tell you. I really can't. You have to trust me. You don't want to know."

She raises her eyebrows. "Drae, you've already broken major rules by telling me about Kari in our little study sessions. And now you won't tell me who you're crushing on?"

I take a deep breath, then let it out slowly.

"*Kari.*"

It comes out as barely a whisper, but Rho heard me. I know because her hair turns shock white, and so do her eyes. She looks like a wraith. The kind that's about to haunt me forever.

There's a long pause. Then she lets it out.

"Oh you poor, sad bastard."

After that, we sit in silence for a long while.

The pizza congeals on the wire rack to an unappetizing texture. Rho's tablet sits unused in sleep mode. Her white hair and white eyes look unnerving. Finally, she breaks the silence.

"Asteroid fires, that Sympathetic stuff must really do a number on you," she says, trying to make sense of it. "That's the only explanation. Maybe that neural implant hijacked your brain. Like it makes you experience what you think is love, but it's really the programming . . ."

I shake my head, feeling miserable. "No, it's more than that."

"How do you know? I've heard the Sympathetic Program messes with you."

"Because it all started *before* the Pairing Ceremony," I say, looking down at my demolished pizza slice. "That's how I know. Did Kari ever tell you . . . about the time . . ."

"You assaulted her in the stairwell at school?" she finishes. "Oh yeah, we spent a solid hour laughing about it. And how she socked you in the jaw? I'd say you got off easy."

"Yeah, you're right," I say with a grimace. "I made a big mistake. I know that, of course. But seriously, did you ever stop to think about . . . *why I kissed her?*"

"Uh, that's a no-brainer," she replies. "Because you're an entitled asshole who thinks he can go around school kissing any girl who crosses his path without their permission."

I blush harder, feeling deep shame seeping from my veins. When she puts it like that, I realize how bad it sounds. But I know the truth. I force the next words from my lips.

"Or maybe . . . it's because . . . *I love her.*"

There, I finally said it.

Out loud.

My heart starts to pound, and my ears ring. I feel like the world's about to end. Like the Earth is going to stop spinning around the sun. Suddenly, the smell of pizza nauseates me.

Rho blinks in disbelief, while her visage turns stark white.

"You. *Love*. Her."

"That's right."

"Asteroid fires, you're crazier than I thought!" she says, giving me a pitying look. "You know this is a doomed love story, right? Not the kind where everyone marries at the end, but the sort of tragedy where everyone dies horrendously at the hands of their loved ones."

"Right, it's not like that," I say, trying to find the proper words. "This isn't some lame crush. It's deeper than that. I need her like the Earth needs the sun to keep spinning in orbit. I need her more than I need to breathe. Without her, I'm pretty sure I'll suffocate to death . . ."

I trail off, feeling stupid and embarrassed. Rho studies me for a long moment. Her eyes darken from stark white to the darkest blue of the deepest oceans. "Listen, I want to give you a hard time and talk you out of this insanity. But you're telling the truth, aren't you?"

I nod slowly, solemnly. "I swear. It's all true."

Rho lets out a worried sigh. "You know Kari's enlisted for the next eight years, right? That this isn't some short-term vacation? That her next leave is in four years? Unless . . ."

She trails off. She doesn't have to say it. We're both thinking the same thing. *Unless . . . she gets injured and shipped back Earthside—or worse, comes home in a body bag.*

Rho gives me an understanding look. This is what we share.

Her best friend . . . is the girl I love.

"Listen, I wish I could tell you it's going to be okay," she says, still turning that deep, endless blue. "Those were just the logistical problems. Kari also hates your privileged guts, remember? Best-case scenario? You're completely and totally screwed. And not in the fun way."

"Ugh, tell me something I don't know," I say, feeling everything in my body deflate. She's right, and I can't deny it. I know that Kari opened up to me today, but that's probably just her implant zapping her to stay on the program. But then, Rho says something unexpected.

"Okay, I'll do whatever I can to help you."

I stare at her in shock.

"Wait, you're going to help *me*? Like out of the goodness of your heart?"

She shoots me a feisty look, her hair jetting out bright pink like her old self. "Listen, you're many things that annoy me to the *blazing stars* and back, but you're not a liar. So, if you really feel that way about my best friend, then I have to help you. It's my sacred duty."

"That's not sarcasm?" I say, wondering if I missed something.

"Nope, I'm being serious. Also, you've seen the newsfeeds. I've got a bad feeling that Kari is going to need all the friends she can get. Even if they're privileged jerks like us."

"Uh, thanks . . . I think," I say, feeling more confused than ever.

"Just enjoy the ride all the way to the top, before you plummet over the cliff. She's still going to break your heart into a million tiny shards," she says, then reaches for her backpack.

"Wait, is it study time?" I ask, but she shakes her head.

"Not today. You've got too much on your mind to focus, you lovestruck fool. Plus, we haven't talked about this," she says, pulling something out of her backpack.

She slides it across the table. I feel a secret thrill at the sight of the thick cardstock, printed with ornate calligraphy. With everything else going on, I'd almost forgotten about it.

"You ready?" she says in a low voice, tapping the card. It reads, *Midnight. Sather Gate.* "You'd better not flake with all this romance mega-drama."

"Ready as I'll ever be," I say, but then I add, "Even in my lovestruck state."

With that proclamation, we get up to leave. We make our way across campus toward our dorms. We've still got a few hours to kill before meeting up at midnight. I should be thinking about the final initiation test and what lies in store for us, but all I can think about is—

Just Kari. Just Kari. Just Kari.

Her words repeat in my head like a drumbeat, like a heartbeat, like a mantra. Rho's right—*I am a lovestruck fool.* But there's nothing I can do to change it. Once you fall, you keep falling . . . until you hit bottom . . . only I'm not sure if my feelings for Kari have any end.

That should scare the living stars out of me.

But instead, it makes me feel tingly and floaty. I keep tingling and floating all the way back to my dorm room, after promising to meet Rho later tonight for the final initiation test.

Whatever that may be.

CHAPTER 29

KARI

That soul-sucking feeling levels me, then I blink in the semi-darkness of my warp mail pod. My brain whirs in a tangled swirl of emotions. I just experienced Drae's return exchange. That's the only word for it. I felt his thoughts, emotions, the surging of his heart struck with . . .

No, that can't be true.

I try to dismiss it and stuff it down. He didn't say the word directly. But something pounds hard in my head telling me that the potent emotion that I felt surging from him into me . . . well, there's only one thing in the entire universe that could be . . . even if it's too crazy to think . . .

But I can't deny what I felt from him.

One thing shoots through my head—*he loves me.*

My first reaction is shock. My second is complete and total mortification. The kind that flips your stomach and makes your heart pound like crazy. My third impulse is to explain it away. But that's the strange magic of the Sympathetic Program. His implant would've zapped him if it detected him lying. Plus, I could feel everything he felt, so I know that he was telling the truth.

He loves me.

That's why he kissed me.

It wasn't some random, fleeting crush.

I think over what he told me in the exchange. The way he described me as the sun with his planet orbiting around me, pulled toward my heat and gravity . . . well . . . he meant it.

He said something else, too. He experienced what my father did to me from my exchange and promised that he'd never leave me like that . . . and there it is. My deepest fear at the core of my being . . . that in the end . . . everyone will always . . . abandon me . . .

Hiss.

Abruptly, the pod cracks open and allows light to stream in. I blink in the stark glare of the post office. Dimly, I'm aware of other recruits emerging from their pods as their exchanges wrap up. But still, I sit there in shock. I'm pretty sure that falling for your Sympathetic has to be against the rules. Also, I hate his guts, I remind myself. I wait for that familiar surge of revulsion that follows that thought to churn my stomach and spark hatred in my cerebral cortex.

But then I realize . . . it doesn't.

A different sensation erupts inside me. It's just as heated and passionate as hatred, but to my surprise—it's the opposite. *No,* I think in horror, *this can't be happening . . . not . . . him!*

Of all the billions of people in this whole stars-blasted universe, I can't fall for that privileged jerk. I try to fight back and quash it down. But my heart rebels and beats back against me. I feel tingly and light-headed, and it's not from the disorientation of pulling out of the exchange.

The truth of everything flows through my veins, as it flows through his now.

I swallow hard in disbelief. My tongue feels like sandpaper.

Silently, I wish for a redo and a chance to take it all back and start over again, maybe all the way back to the moment of my birth. But unfortunately, time doesn't work that way. It only moves forward. You can't travel back to the past, despite all those stories. The only kind of time travel that's theoretically possible is into the future, or some multiverse iteration of it.

Ideally, one in which I don't . . . *love* . . . Drae.

Ugh, even thinking that nauseates me. I'm just grateful nobody is around to witness my humiliation. Then I remember that our exchanges are recorded and archived. Double *ugh.*

But before I can worry any more—

Suddenly, alarms blare through the post office.

They shriek in the pods. A strobe light pulses in a staccato rhythm to the cacophony. *Evacuate to the bunker immediately* flashes through my retinas. Harold repeats it in my ears.

Despite my training, I freeze in my pod.

That's when Postmaster Haven rushes over. His eyes go blank as he scans his implant for the emergency alert. "No, it can't be," he mutters, still scanning his retinal display. "That's impossible . . . highly irregular . . . we're a remote outpost . . . a training facility . . ."

"Postmaster, what is it?" I ask, dread flooding my voice.

"We have to evacuate to the bunker immediately," he says, yanking me from my pod. He drags me away while other recruits stream around us. Panic subsumes the post office.

We rush into the lobby, while postal workers evacuate from the docking bay, abandoning their mail bins by the idling postal ships. The alarms blare louder in here.

I glance at the postmaster's face, which gives nothing away. He's so kind and affable that it's easy to forget that he's a trained guardian. All the postal workers are. He's holding back and not telling me the whole truth. But his eyes give him away. They look . . . spooked.

"What's happening?" I demand, planting my heels and refusing to budge. Postal workers rush past us toward the exit. "They don't tell grunts anything, but I deserve to know the truth."

The worry on his face deepens as he scans his retinal feed again.

Then he utters three words that shock me to my core.

"*Incoming . . .* Raider attack."

"Wait, what? Raiders attacking Ceres Base?" I stammer as he pulls me from the lobby toward the exit. "But I thought they stayed out of our system and mostly plundered our interstellar supply routes? Maybe it's a training drill . . . or like that flyover—"

Boom.

That's when a blast roils through the base. The floor buckles and heaves under my feet. I clutch at the nearest mail bin to keep from falling. But it makes one thing very clear.

This isn't a drill.

It's a real Raider attack.

"Private Skye, this way!"

Haven gestures to me, and we start running for it. But the corridors are blocked, jam-packed with bodies. It's a total impasse—we're trapped. That's when the base rocks again.

Dust shakes loose from the concrete ceiling.

Despite my weeks of training, my heart thumps like blaster fire. Fear freezes up my legs and wants to root me in place. "We're stuck . . . what do we do?" I ask in a panicked voice.

But Haven remains calm. He turns back toward me.

"This way—and fast!" he says, pulling me back into the post office. "There's a mail service elevator that can take us down to the bunker. Hurry, the whole base is under attack!"

PART 3

ESCALATION

If you know yourself but not the enemy,
for every victory gained you will also suffer a defeat.

—Sun Tzu, *The Art of War*

CHAPTER 30

DRAE

I jolt awake to my alarm.

Draeden, time to wake up, Estrella chimes in. *You're going to be late.* I rub my eyes, still half asleep. They land on the invitation still propped up by my bed. It's time to meet Rho.

My book rests on my chest. I must have nodded off reading. I slide it aside, careful to mark my place. I'm in the middle of tugging on my sneakers when suddenly, I hear the shuffling of feet—actually more like *staggering*—in the common room. Followed by a slurred voice.

It's Jude.

He must be back from the frat parties. And he's had more than a few drinks from the sound of it. *Nothing new.* Then I hear a different voice. Higher-pitched, also drunk. He's not alone. *Also nothing new.* Their voices sound muffled, but then the girl speaks louder.

I can hear it through my door.

They're in the hall right outside.

"*No . . . I don't want to . . . I wanna go home . . .*" She's slurring her words. "*No . . . please don't . . . no . . . I wanna leave . . . let me go home . . .*"

The hairs rise on my arms, my neck, my whole body.

Then I hear his voice respond. It sounds like a snarl. "Hey, don't be such a tease . . . please just come in my room . . . don't embarrass me . . ."

Suddenly, he sounds dead sober. He's not slurring anymore.

That chills me even more. I rise from my bed, my feet thumping down.

Sounds of physical struggle reach my ears, then the girl speaks again. "*I'm sorry . . . I don't feel comfortable . . . I want to go back to my dorm . . .*"

That's followed by soft sobbing.

Barely audible through my closed door.

"Shut up, you're embarrassing me!" Jude snaps at her. "Don't you know who my father is? Trust me, you don't want to get on my bad side. Get inside—"

More sounds of struggling.

I can't listen anymore.

I fling open my door. In the dim light of the hall, Jude has the girl lodged against the wall by his room. He's pulling up her skirt and trying to force her toward his bed. She's crying softly. Mascara runs down her cheeks in dark rivers. Her blonde hair tangles into clumpy mats.

She whimpers, "Please . . . no . . . I don't want to . . ."

That's enough to make me snap. That's the only way to describe it. All that pent-up fury and hatred stored up over the semester comes pouring out of me at this very moment. It flames through my arms and makes my hands bunch up into burning fists.

I lurch across the hall, grab Jude's shirt roughly, and pull him away from the girl. I throw him to the ground. His shirt rips in my grasp. Shreds of fabric hang from my knuckles.

"Get off her!" I growl at him.

He looks up at me, dazed, incredulous. "Drae, are you crazy?" he says in shock.

"Let the girl go!" I shoot back.

"Now, you're *both* embarrassing me," he says in a furious voice. His face flames bright red. He looks sharply from me, then back to her. "Don't you know who my father is?"

"I do," I say in a cold voice. "And I don't care."

What happens next all happens in a blur, as if on fast-forward. He staggers up and shoves me back—*hard*. My back hits the wall with a *thud*, pain radiating through my neck.

I blink to clear my head as he reaches for the girl again, manhandling her and trying to force her back into his room. She cries softly but goes limp in his arms. That's when I hit him.

And I keep hitting him.

And hitting him.

Until Loki pulls me off. I'm still struggling to punch as he holds me back. Jude's nose is crooked and broken. Maybe his jaw, too. I can't tell. There's too much blood . . . everywhere.

The girl is shivering, cowering down. Her shirt is torn, and her skirt is askew. She scrambles up, bolting from the common room. I try to go after her, but Loki grabs me and holds me back.

"Drae, what in the blazing stars happened in here?" Loki asks.

He has a look of horror on his face. His bedroom door is ajar. His date sits on his bed, blurry and half-clothed, watching everything in awkward silence. From the floor, Jude sputters, spitting blood, maybe a tooth. His face looks stained and swollen, beaten beyond recognition. His date is gone already, I realize dimly. I wanted to help her, but I'm too late. She fled from our dorm.

Loki finally releases me. I back away in shock. I can't believe what happened.

Oh stars, what have I done?

"You'll pay for this!" Jude screams, but it comes out jumbled due to his broken teeth. "You're dead to me! Wait until my father finds out! You're dead, Rache!"

I cover my ears and stumble toward my room to grab my backpack. Then I bolt across the common room. I can still hear Jude raging, but my ears ring, making it sound distorted.

"Dead!" he yells at me. "You're dead . . ."

I don't stop to answer him. I dash from our room, down the carpeted hallway, and hurtle down the stairs, taking them two at a time. I burst out into the crisp night air. And I keep running across the deserted courtyard, trampling over the grass. I tell Estrella to summon my transport.

A few minutes later, in the dark of night, I abscond toward the parking lot and slip into the back seat, sweaty and pale. The doors shut softly. My knuckles hurt. I look down.

They're torn and bleeding. There are blood splatters on my shirt.

Jude's right—*I'm dead.*

Deader than dead.

I can't go back there. Ever. I think about his father poking around Trebond's room. And my father trying to protect me. I was already under suspicion—they'll come for me now.

What's your destination, Draeden? Estrella asks. She's synced up with my transport.

The vehicle idles, conspicuous. Streetlights pool down around us. I'm mired in shock and indecision. It's only a matter of time before the Fed Patrols find me here and arrest me.

I feel the hard outline of the card stuffed into my pocket. I recall the message for the hundredth time. *Midnight. Sather Gate.* It's all I have left—my last lifeline. I drag my finger over the sharp edge, feeling the thick cardstock slice into my tender flesh. But I'm so numb.

Draeden, your destination? Estrella tries again.

My transport purrs softly. I slice another cut into my finger. I crave the pain. At least it's something. I deserve it, too. The streetlights cast an eerie glow over the empty campus. It's shadowy and quiet. But that won't last. The Fed Patrols are everywhere. They'll spot me.

I have to make a decision—and fast.

Jude could've already reported me. One quick call to his father, and I'm finished. The dashboard clock shows two minutes to midnight. I look up in desperation at the stars blistering the night sky. Kari's face flashes through my mind. I wonder what she would do in my position. *You coward,* I think to myself, *she wouldn't be in it.* So instead, I do what I always do.

I run away again.

But I know with deep certainty—

I'd do it again. Okay, maybe I didn't need to hit him that many times. But he deserved it . . . for what he was doing to her. My only regret is that she vanished before I could help her.

But something is very clear. There's only one place I can go now. I don't have a choice. And there's only one person I can trust. I steel my gaze ahead. I inhale, then let it out slowly.

"Sather Gate."

CHAPTER 31

KARI

Anton and Nadia rush toward me when I storm into the bunker. "Kari, thank the stars," she says when she reaches me, exchanging a relieved look with her brother. "You're okay."

The shelter appears the same as I remember it from last time. But I suppose that's the point. They don't change or alter; instead, they preserve all hidden inside until the end of time.

"Good as new," I proclaim, trying to keep my voice light, though I feel rattled to my core. "I was at the post office when it happened. Just shaken up, literally. Did you feel those blasts?"

I keep expecting the floor to lurch and shudder under my feet again. My heart twitches with adrenaline, but seeing familiar faces calms me a little. They lead me over to my platoon, clustered together on the far side of the shelter. On the other side, the drill sergeants stand with the other non combat officers. There are quite a few, as Ceres is primarily a training base.

"Newsfeed alert . . . I'm alive," I say when I join everyone, trying to joke around.

But Nadia glares at me. "Don't ever do that again, Skye. It sucked like a black hole to evacuate the barracks without you."

What she really means is—she cares about me. And it annoys the stars out of her.

"Sorry, we wanted to look for you," Genesis chimes in. "But the drill sergeant ordered us down here on penalty of death, or maybe just more push-ups. Not sure which is worse. I couldn't hear over the blasts—"

Just then, another one rattles the shelter. They're not as strong down here. But we're still pitched around as the floor ripples and shakes.

"Know anything about what's happening up there?" Nadia asks in a low voice.

"*Raider* attack," I whisper back, not sure how much we're supposed to know about the situation. Postmaster Haven told me more than my alerts. I don't want to get him in trouble.

"Raiders . . . here?" Nadia says in shock. "They're firing on us?"

"Negative," Anton says, crumpling his brow. He thinks for a moment. "Actually, I think those blasts are coming from our defenses. Anti-spacecraft artillery fire, probably."

"Then that means they must be close," I say, feeling unsettled. "If we're firing back."

"Too close," Nadia agrees. "They'd have to be in range."

Luna glances around and lowers her voice. "But why would they attack here? They hit vulnerable supply lines in interstellar space. They don't usually venture this far into our system. This is a remote base in the asteroid belt. There are no valuable resources here."

"That's right," Nadia agrees. "Anything in our system is usually Proxy saber-rattling. Just trying to flex and scare us. Like that last flyover from the Siberian Fed, remember?"

Anton nods to his sister. "That's a good point though. Maybe the instability emboldened the Raiders. Like a power vacuum. They feel like they can invade our system now."

"Nah, Raiders don't care about Proxy tensions," Luna replies. "They're glorified pirates, remember?"

"Who cares?" Percy says with a shrug. "Why are you trying to understand their motives? We're the good guys—they're the bad guys. They hate our guts. Enough said."

"Because it's never that simple," Genesis cuts in with a roll of her eyes. "Remember what we learned in class from Sun Tzu? *If you know yourself but not the enemy, for every victory gained you will also suffer a defeat.*"

Percy snorts. "What does Sun Tzu know? He lived like a bazillion years ago."

"Right, it's philosophy," Genesis mutters. "Time is irrelevant. The concept still applies to this situation. Plus, you don't think they had pirates in ancient times?"

Just then, another blast shakes the bunker.

We brace ourselves, then fall silent again. These jolts do feel different, however. Anton must be right. They emanate from our foundations, coming in steady waves, almost like pulses that shudder the floor under our feet. It must be our defenses firing back again.

I lock eyes with Postmaster Haven across the room, as he tries to keep the postal workers calm. He offers me a grim smile and mouths something. I read his lips—

Stay strong, Guardian.

I glance away, ashamed at how frightened I feel right now. My stomach churns with worry. I turn to the thick door, sealed and locked. I keep picturing Raiders storming our base and blasting into the bunker with their shrill battle cries and electrified weapons.

"Something's bugging me," I whisper to our group. "Even if they're attacking because they need supplies, we have bases farther out in other systems, where it would be safer."

Anton nods, picking up the tangent. "Kari is right. Why come all the way to Ceres Base? That's dangerous, even for them. Our military defenses are strongest in our home system."

Percy groans. "I told you, they're crazy. That's all you need to know."

"*Crazy* . . . is too simplistic," Genesis says with a frown. "To survive for this many generations in the hostile reaches of space, they must have tough survival instincts . . .

coupled with intelligence and strong leadership. Otherwise, they would've died out years ago."

"Yup, that's dead on," Nadia says, stopping her pacing for a moment. Absently, she runs a hand through her buzzed hair. "Why take the risk of attacking a well-defended base?"

"Because they *want* something," I say, my mind flying through ideas at high speed. "They act in their own self-interest, right? They're pirates, like Percy said. They're greedy and self-interested. That means there must be *something* they want . . . here on Ceres Base."

"But . . . what?" Anton says. "There's nothing important here. Just a bunch of lame recruits like us. Basic is held here for a reason. It's like the boring sticks of our solar system, so to speak, where nothing exciting ever happens. They can't exactly train us on the front lines."

"*'Cause we're greener than the turf back Earthside,*" Percy says, parroting one of the drill sergeant's favorite taunts. Despite the tense, somber mood, that provokes laughter.

But then, more blasts make the floor lurch and shake. I slump down and put my face in my hands. "Maybe I'm overthinking it," I say in a defeated voice. Frustration, coupled with fear, overwhelms me. "None of it makes any sense. Maybe Percy's right—they are just crazy."

But that nagging feeling won't go away.

A few tense hours pass as we wait out the Raider attack in the bunker, bracing ourselves against the intense blasts from our anti-spacecraft defenses. And then, finally, for a long spell—

Silence.

No more blasts. Even the tension seems to deflate from the room. The officers talk into their neural implants, then the drill sergeant finally calls us over.

"The threat has passed," she informs us in her stiff voice. She's all business. Her face remains an expressionless mask and gives nothing away. "Back to the barracks, recruits."

I feel disappointed. I'd hoped for more information. I know it's dangerous to *think* too much . . . but questions rush through my head. Did we suffer any casualties or damage to the base? How many Raider ships attacked us? And most importantly, why did they target Ceres Base? But that's all we're gonna get from her. Her clipped voice made that crystal clear.

Those questions all have the same answer—

It's above our pay grade. We're lowly grunts, not even official guardians yet.

They don't tell us shit.

But on our way back to the barracks, marching in our usual tight formation, I can't shake this terrible feeling. The Raiders came here for a reason. And it had to be a good one.

At the front of our platoon, I study the guarded look on the drill sergeant's face. I think back to her talking to the other drill sergeants in the bunker. Are they not telling us anything about the attack because they don't want to scare us? Or is there more to it?

One question rushes through my head—

What if there's something the drill sergeant doesn't want us to know?

CHAPTER 32

DRAE

My transport shoots out into the dark night. It's almost midnight. I scan the campus for patrols, but it's late and deserted. Even so, I sit low in the passenger seat with my hoodie up.

Outside the tinted windows, the stoic Berkeley buildings blur past like silent sentries keeping watch over the university. I glance down at my bloody clothes again. *Jude's blood*, I realize with a deep shudder. I try to block it out.

Being on campus is dangerous right now. They could be looking for me. Jude could have already reported me, not to mention all the extra security since the RED threat level. But I don't know where else to go, except for one place, where I already directed my transport.

I blocked Jude on my neural implant, of course. But I'm tempted to message Loki for some intel. However, I decide that it's too risky. In fact, I should block him, too.

Contact blocked, Estrella replies, reading my thought.

Thank you, I say, then think of something else. *Please disable GPS.*

Estrella beeps and confirms the location tracking is disabled. I don't want Jude—or worse, his father—to be able to find me. I know they can probably turn it back on if they want to. But it might buy me a little time.

Silently and hovering a foot off the ground, my transport approaches Sather Gate from the streets on the outskirts of campus. I spot the familiar arched, turquoise metalwork of the historic entryway. Beneath it, a dark, hooded figure kneels down by the gate.

My heart thumps faster. I keep expecting the Fed Patrols to blare their sirens and pull me over. But as we draw nearer to the gate, my transport's lights catch the figure's face.

Black hair and matching eyes—*seriousness*—it's Rho.

She bends over as if inspecting something, then straightens up in the glare of the headlights. She recognizes my transport. Her hair and eyes soften to light pink tipped with black.

She waves me down. I instruct my transport to pick her up. We pull over, and then she slides into the back seat next to me.

"You're *two* minutes late," she says, her hair flashing from pink highlights to angry red accents. She waves an envelope at me in annoyance. "I already found our next clue . . ."

But then she trails off.

Her eyes widen with shock as she focuses on my appearance. There's still blood on my shirt. Blood on my face. Blood on my torn-up knuckles from hitting Jude over and over.

Her face crumples with worry, as her hair and eyes ripple dark blue.

"What in the stars happened to you?"

I consider making up a cover story. The truth feels so horrible. But I can't deceive her. She'll see right through that. She knows me too well. I take a deep breath.

"*Jude* . . . happened," I say, then proceed to tell her everything.

It comes out in a shaky voice, all at once. The more words spill out into the filtered air of my transport, the darker her red hair and eyes become. They remind me of molten lava.

"I didn't think . . . I just reacted . . . it's all my fault," I finish with a shake of my head. "I should've called security. Or found another way to stop him—"

"No, you did the right thing," Rho cuts me off in a fiery voice. "He always gets away with everything. And it would keep happening. He'd just talk his way out of it."

"Or his father would cover it up. He's the king of avoiding responsibility."

"Also, you know what?" Rho says with a dark look. Her eyes flash to black. "I've got a terrible feeling this wasn't the first time . . . and it wouldn't have been the last."

"I know," I say with a grim nod. My stomach sloshes sickly in agreement. "I've never witnessed him doing anything like that before. But I have a bad feeling that you're right."

"Well, maybe you taught him a lesson this time," she says. "The kind he'll remember, judging by your fists. He deserved far worse, by the way."

"I know, but he'll come after me," I say, feeling bile backing up my throat and choking my voice. "He'll gaslight everyone and twist the incident around. Make it seem like it was all my fault. And Loki will back him up, like always."

"What about the girl?" Rho asks in a soft voice. "She's a witness."

I shake my head. "She ran away before I could get her name or help her back to her dorm. I just hope she's okay. But she's probably afraid. I mean, we all know who his dad is."

Rho reaches over and clasps my hand. My knuckles sting, but I don't pull away. Her touch is comforting, exactly what I need right now. My transport continues to idle by the gate.

"Listen, it's not fair," Rho says, pressing her red lips together. "People like him should be locked in space prison camps. But instead, they run the whole *blasted* federation."

I take that in. I know she's right.

"Look, it's dangerous to be around me right now," I say in a thick voice, pulling away from her, though it's the last thing I want to do. "I should bow out of this initiation test. I don't want to ruin your chances. As it is, I'm probably getting expelled anyway . . ."

I trail off as my thoughts darken.

I slump back into the seat, engulfed in a complicated swirl of emotions. But there's something else that's bothering me now. And it's more confusing than quantum physics.

My heart still beats for Kari, but also . . . I feel something . . . for Rho . . .

I quickly push that away. "Listen, I can drop you off back at your dorm," I say, looking away from her. "You should continue the test without me. I'm putting you in danger—"

"Drae, with all due respect," Rho says. "Shut up."

"Wait, what do you mean?"

Rho lets out a deep sigh. "I mean, *shut the stars up with your pity party sob story* nonsense. Jude's the worst. He's always been the worst. We'll find a way to clear your name. You're crazy if you think I'm going to let him jeopardize us getting into this secret society."

Her hair flashes red again, like her lava eyes. They practically sizzle.

Feisty, angry, loyal.

"Are you sure?" I say, still hesitating. "This could put you in danger. If Jude finds out you're helping me . . . well . . . he's unpredictable. There's no telling what he might do."

"Well, I'm not scared of him. And I'm not abandoning you. Oh, there's something else."

"What's that?" I ask, still feeling uneasy.

"Remember how Kari tried to beat the *ever-loving stars* out of him back in high school?" she says, smirking at the memory. I can't help but smile, too. "Guess you finished the job." She lets out a snort chuckle before she continues. "Seriously, I can't wait to tell her about this. If she didn't have feelings for you before . . . let's just say, this might change her mind."

That's enough to make my cheeks flush. I know, I shouldn't care about that stuff right now, given my dire circumstances. But somehow . . . suddenly . . . it's all I can think about.

"Okay, last chance to back out," I say. "Jude's dangerous and unpredictable. Helping me could get you expelled, too. I know how important Berkeley is to you—"

"Dead sure," she says without hesitation. Then, she tears open the envelope and pulls the next clue out. "Now, get over yourself and help me with this clue already. It looks hard."

I force myself to read the card, despite the sick feeling in my stomach. It helps to focus on something other than Jude, and the complete and utter ruin that's my college career.

The ornate calligraphy flashes before my eyes.

The Final Hunt Begins HERE.
You have until dawn to reach the final location.
This is your last chance to prove yourself.
Only those brave and worthy shall succeed.
Did we mention—your lives depend on it?
Good luck. You'll need it. Again.

"Our lives depend on it?" I say, a little taken aback. "Uh, that sounds intense."

Rho rolls her eyes. "Probably just having a bit of fun. You know, to add to the drama."

"Oh, right," I say, although something about this final test feels more real. But she's probably right. I'm not thinking straight. I'm still jittery and jacked up on adrenaline from everything.

I flip the card over. On the back, there's another riddle. We both scan it.

I'm old as dust, old as rock.
From long before the Great War,
Thrust up from the Earth's core,
On waves of molten lava born.
A gift from those who came before,
To those who wish to learn.

"Oh, this one's easy," I say right away. "I already know the answer."

Rho squints at the clue, then back at me. "How is that possible? I still have zero clue. And for the record, that's highly abnormal."

"Well, maybe you should brush up on your UC Berkeley history," I say with a wicked grin. "Wow, I can't believe I know the answer to something that you don't know."

She glares daggers at me. *Blazing* daggers.

"My Berkeley history?" She sounds skeptical.

"That's right. You heard me."

"And you're some kind of expert now?" she says in a huff.

"Not an expert exactly," I backpedal. "But I've been spending a lot of time in the library. The other day, this book on pre-war Berkeley landmarks and history caught my eye. It was on display in a glass case in the lobby. So I guess . . . I kind of . . . read it."

Rho looks at me like I've sprouted a second head, or maybe a third eyeball. "First of all, you went to the library?" she says in an incredulous voice. "Like of your own volition? And then you read a book? Like on purpose? Not because some professor made you read it?"

I nod sheepishly. "Yeah, I read it . . . for fun."

An expression of pure joy cascades over her face. She thrusts her arms around me, hugging me tight. "I'm so proud of you. Jeez, I'm just mad you didn't take me with you."

"Uh, thanks . . . I think," I mumble, trying not to smell her . . . when she smells so *freaking* good. And especially not when she's only my friend. Or supposed to be . . . only my friend.

Not to mention, I'm in love with her best friend. Who is also my Sympathetic. *It's a terrible idea.*

"So, what's the answer?" she says, pulling away. I breathe a sigh of relief.

We're only friends, I remind myself. I'm just confused. It's been a really long night. I'm not thinking straight. I realize now that I've never had a real friend like her before, that's all.

"The riddle means . . . Founders' Rock," I say, gesturing to the card. "It's this natural outcropping of rock where the original Berkeley trustees met to dedicate the new campus. The part about *the gift from those who came before to those who wish to learn* tipped me off."

She grins at me. "Brilliant."

Our eyes meet again, and she holds my gaze. Everything about her fades to light pink—her hair, her eyes, even her cheeks flush that beautiful, soft shade. My heart skips a beat.

"Estrella, take us to Founders' Rock," I say, and my transport slides into gear.

We find another envelope hidden at Founders' Rock that leads us to more locations around campus, each with a new clue. It's like a scavenger hunt through our college. Despite what happened earlier, I'm having a blast solving these riddles with Rho at my side.

Finally, the last card leads us to the library, right smack in the middle of campus. It's closed and locked, of course. But we find a basement door that's been left cracked open.

"Clearly, this was unlocked for us," Rho says, thrusting it open.

With a rusty creak, it admits us into the dark basement.

Inside, we find little tea candles lighting the way up the stairs. It reminds me of the Campanile and our first initiation test. We creep down the dusty stacks like fugitives as Rho pulls me along in search of the next clue. She reaches up and grabs an ancient-looking book from the shelves. *The People's History of the California Federation*, reads the gold-embossed title.

Wedged into the dusty pages, we discover the next clue. I recognize the book, but only because it's been banned from most libraries. I'm not sure how this copy survived.

Maybe it was forgotten in the stacks amongst this trove of tombs? But then another, far more dangerous thought occurs to me. Or maybe it was placed here for this test?

That gives me a thrill. And it makes me wonder again—what exactly are we getting ourselves into? What if this isn't a secret society at all? What if it's something else?

But I push those questions away. I'm just being paranoid after everything I've been through tonight. Rho fishes the clue out of the musty pages, but then suddenly—

We hear rustling in the stacks.

A flashlight beam bounces around, lighting up the library.

"Watch out, it's a security guard," Rho hisses in my ear. We flee from the library stacks, back downstairs, and through the basement door where we slipped inside.

We burst outside into the brisk night. The excitement gets to both of us. We're giddy and laughing, arms linked and sprinting like wild creatures across campus. We step onto the manicured grass. And that's when, unexpectedly, the sprinklers spout on and drench us.

But we giggle and run through them like carefree children, all the way back to my transport, avoiding the Fed Patrols still circling the campus. They're easy to notice with their lights. We climb into the back seat, drenched and giddy.

Our eyes lock. We stop laughing instantly. Tension hangs between us.

An awkward silence falls. And it lingers.

"Hey, not so fast," Rho says, pulling away. "You're not my type. I prefer bi girls, or genderfluid boys, or anyone covered in tats with an affinity for bondage and fishnets." She lists them off on her fingers. "For the record," she goes on. "I'm sex-positive and not against casual hookups. But you're mind-melded to my best friend. So, that would be all kinds of creepy."

"Extra, super-duper creepy," I agree quickly, stiffening and pulling away. We both start shivering from being wet. "We're just friends, nothing more."

She sticks out her hand. "To staying in the friend zone. *Sans* benefits."

We shake on it.

With that settled, we turn our attention back to the new clue. Rho does the honors, ripping open the envelope. The ornate script flashes before our eyes. We both scan it.

Wheels over me roll, water under me flows.
I connect all things, without me you can't go.
In times of war, I'm always the first to go.
Destructive fury makes me spark and explode.
Many lives lost, drowned in the great below.

We huddle together and both study it for a moment. I glance at the sky. It's still dark, but the sun will start to rise and tint the sky pale yellow soon. That means dawn isn't far away.

We have to hurry, or we'll fail the test.

Suddenly, Rho brightens. "Oh . . . oh, I think I've got it."

I squint at the clue. "Uh, spit it out already. We don't have much time."

"I think it means like a . . . bridge," she says, pointing to a line in the riddle, and reads it aloud. "*Wheels over me roll, water under me flows.*"

"Yeah, but not any bridge," I say, as it clicks together.

She looks up in excitement. "Oh, you're right!"

"Yup, the Golden Gate Bridge," I say, meeting her excited pink gaze. My heart flutters in anticipation. "Only the most iconic landmark in San Francisco. That's our next stop."

CHAPTER 33

KARI

Privates, this is your final test to graduate from basic training," the drill sergeant says, halting in front of the sim chambers. We clutch our newly issued blasters tighter.

A chill zips up my arm and through my entire body, though that could be from the blaster's security mechanism locking in my unique DNA signature. I've never felt more like a soldier than at this moment—when my hand wraps around the handle and feels the weight of my weapon. It's lightweight and ergonomic, yet balanced. Seemingly wielded from one solid piece of silver metal with a special security feature on the handle, so nobody else can fire it.

Security features activated, Harold communicates in his stilted voice. *Weapon synced with neural implant. All systems go.*

Technically, they're called PEPs, which stands for "pulsed energy projectile." That's the fancy techie way of explaining—*they shoot lasers.* Plus, saying PEPs over and over is a major tongue twister, so everyone just calls them blasters.

In the bottom of my retinas, targeting software pops up, along with critical information about my new weapon's diagnostics. *Energy charge, firing capability, range.*

"Blast me, this is so cool," Nadia whispers beside me, flexing her grip on her blaster. Her vision comes unfocused. She must be checking out the new targeting software. Excitement jolts through our ranks. This is the first time we've been armed. Suddenly, Basic feels very real.

"Not all of you will make it through this," the drill sergeant continues. "This is the most grueling test you will ever endure in your military career. Trust me, I remember it vividly."

She pauses to let that sink in. Heavy silence falls over our unit. We all feel the significance. This is what we've been training for these last brutal weeks. Today determines if we graduate and become Space Force guardians or wash out and ship back Earthside.

I glance around at my platoon, wondering who will pass—and who will fail. Of course, we lost a few recruits in those terrible early weeks. Nobody who I had grown close to, thankfully. One day, they were there, and the next, their racks were stripped and empty.

My core group has hung in there, against all odds. I scan their faces, my comrades, my fellow recruits—and really—my friends. Me and Nadia, of course (she drives me crazy, but I love the stars out of her). Percy and Genesis (who are still totally attached at the hip, not just as battle buddies). Anton and Luna (an odd couple if there ever was one, but it works).

I hope we all graduate.

I hope we all get to serve together.

I hope.

"One final thing," the drill sergeant says, glaring at us from under her wide brim. "If your battle buddy fails, then you fail. You trained together—now you need to pass together."

Hushed whispers ripple through our ranks. I glance at Nadia. Her expression looks solemn and unsmiling. I know what she's thinking—*Skye, don't fuck this up for me.*

"Good luck, recruits," the drill sergeant says. "You're gonna need it."

Then she orders us into our sim chambers with our battle buddies. We're geared up with enhanced Space Force suits and armed with blasters. However, we still don't know anything about the test itself. We have no idea what environment we'll face in the sim—or what dangers lurk behind those doors. And we know better than to ask. That would be speaking out of turn.

The *unknowing* rattles me as much as anything else.

Ma and Bea's faces flash through my mind. I miss them to the stars and back. Our short communications have been a lifeline. They have better housing and rations now, thanks to my enlistment. Ma finally retired from the factory, and Bea can go to college when she graduates high school. I can't take that away from them. I'm doing this for them—for all of us.

I can't fail, I think to myself. *I have to pass this test.*

"Now get your suits booted up—and get in those chambers," the drill sergeant says. "And on a more personal note, it's been an honor training you. Don't embarrass me in there."

Shock emanates through our unit. That's the nicest thing she's ever said to us. I'm pretty sure I hallucinated that. Did we hear her right? But there's only one proper response—

"Drill Sergeant, yes, Drill Sergeant!"

Our voices echo out, then fall silent.

On command, we boot up our suits, making sure they're synced with our blasters and neural implants. I marvel at this high-tech fighting gear. It must have cost a fortune.

I snap off a salute to my friends. "Good luck in there! See you on the flip side."

Luna grins through her visor. "Don't worry, I won't let him flunk out." Her voice comes out distorted. "Not after I've been dragging his ass for four long weeks."

"Don't I know it." Anton grins sheepishly, flexing his still puny biceps. He turns to his sister. "Good luck, sis. Make our parents proud . . . well . . . just in case I don't."

"Shut up already," Nadia snaps. "You're the one who's already made them proud. Trust me. You should've seen the last exchange they sent me. Anton did *this* . . . Anton did *that* . . ."

"Sheesh, quit your sentimental lollygagging," Percy quips, flexing his grip on his blaster. Then, he slips into his best impersonation of the drill sergeant. "And get in those sim chambers, or your ass is grass!"

We all break into laughter.

"What he really means is . . . break a leg in there," Genesis says, stifling a laugh. "Uh, maybe . . . don't actually break a leg. More like, metaphorically break one . . ."

"Jeez, you're making it worse," Percy cuts in with a dramatic eye roll.

But the affection between them is clear, despite their banter. With that, we bid our final goodbyes. It feels both celebratory—we made it to the end of basic training—and like a funeral.

"Speed your ass up," Nadia barks, gesturing to our chamber. I hear her voice in my head. "Seems my number one job of keeping you on schedule applies even to our last mission."

"Thanks, Battle Buddy—" I start, but she cuts me off.

"Don't thank me yet. Just get in there and pass this *blasted* test," she says, slipping back into her usual salty persona. "I don't need another black mark on my record. Stars, I've got enough already after getting paired with the likes of you."

"Well, it's been an honor serving with you, too," I reply, suppressing a grin. I know she cares, even if she can't come out and say it. I've learned to read between the lines.

As a duo, we march into our sim chamber.

The door shuts behind us with a *thud*, then seals with a *hiss*.

We find our marks on the floor and wait for the brain-sucking feeling as the sim boots up. That's when my vision zeros out. Blackness overtakes me. It feels like I'm falling down a deep, dark hole that has no bottom. I'm falling and getting sucked down at the same time.

I want to scream, to cry out.

Then suddenly, it stops—

Searing sunlight blazes into my vision. It stings my eyes. I blink rapidly, trying to adjust. I'm completely disoriented. I glance down at my feet—*grass*. I nudge it with my boot.

Not real grass.

Turf.

Black sludge leaks through it. Gradually, my vision clears.

I'm standing in the Park back home. The shock ripples through me. How is this possible? I don't wait for Nadia to appear in the sim. Instead, I lose all sense and start running at full speed, all thoughts of Basic and my final test forgotten. I push my legs to run faster.

"Bea!" I scream. "Bea! Ma! Xena!"

I bolt through the rows, heading for our trailer. It stands there, looking just like it did when I left home. I burst up the creaky metal steps and inside the trailer. The rusty screen door claps with a *thwack* behind me. I yell for them again, rushing into my bedroom.

But the trailer is . . . empty. My heart sinks.

Desperately, I glance through the dingy window, spotting Xena's trailer. She was my bus driver. But really, she was more than that. Xena was like family. She always looked out for us.

"Xena!" I scream at the window. "Are you home?"

But *nobody* answers me.

I charge back outside, realizing that it's not just my family who's vanished. The whole place is deserted. Usually, it's filled with life. Stray dogs barking and chasing feral cats. Retirees drinking hooch out back. A shudder tears up my spine, breaking cold sweat on my skin.

Where is everybody?

"Bea! Ma! Xena!"

Dead silence.

Then a low whine starts up. I jerk around—then recognize the sound. It's the stray dog I used to feed scraps, whenever I could spare them. I named her Daisy. She slinks out from under the nearest trailer, only her entire body is riddled with tumors. Big, fleshy, and leaking pus. I stagger back in horror. She bares her teeth, looking more like a demon than my old friend.

Suddenly, she snaps and lunges for me, but I grab her jaws and wrestle to keep her teeth away from my skin. I draw my blaster—

I fire one shot.

She yowls, then goes limp.

I stare in horror as she slumps to the turf. Her body starts decaying in fast motion, flesh drying out and flaking away from chalky bones, maggots consuming her sinewy muscle—until she's just a sack of leather and dry bones.

Tears drip down my face. I bolt down the row, looking through the rusty screens into the trailers. *Skeletal, irradiated bodies.* Slumped on ratty sofas, over kitchen sinks in the middle of making dinner. Overhead, the sky glows an eerie orange color like a polluted sunset.

The glow intensifies—

No, like a nuclear attack!

"Noooooooo!" I scream, circling back to my trailer. And there they are, crawling through the front door, Bea and Ma. Their faces are withered into skeletons. Weeping blisters erupt on their skin. Their mouths cry out with their silent screams. They're lifeless, frozen . . .

I'm too late.

I sink to my knees, feeling completely gutted. *This isn't real,* I whisper to myself, shaking with shock and grief. *This isn't real. It can't be real. It's a trick, part of the sim. They're trying to break me down. This is part of my test. They're showing me my worst fears—*

I crack my eyes open. I clutch my blaster. I take aim at Bea and Ma.

"You're not real," I say, and blast them.

Suddenly, the whole place collapses around me like the crumpling of a picture. Everything goes dark in my vision again, then light spills back into my retinas, blinding me.

Slick ice appears under my boots. I recognize this place. I'm back on Ceres. It's daytime. Suddenly, I hear a scream behind me. It's shrill and panicked, but utterly familiar.

"No, Anton! That's not you. You'd never do that!"

Nadia materializes into the sim beside me.

She looks distraught. Her blaster smokes, recently discharged.

It takes her a few moments to adjust and come out of the hallucination. Finally, her eyes focus and she meets my gaze. Even through her visor, she looks about as freaked out as I feel.

"You're late to the party." I try to sound snarky, but it comes out shaky. "Where have you been?"

"Home *sweet* home," she mutters. She frowns at me. "You?"

"Same. Let's never talk about that again," I say with a shudder, remembering Ma and Bea irradiated. How I blasted them and then reappeared here.

Nadia kicks the ice with her boot, almost slips. "Are we on Ceres?"

"Yup, the base is over there," I say, pointing to the small docking port. The tip of the iceberg, I remember Anton explaining when we first made our approach. Most of the base is buried underground. *Harold, ice picks*, I order my implant. They shoot out of my boots.

Nadia follows my lead, as I scan the area with my sensors. I'm on edge, expecting them to throw anything at us. Another Raider ambush or Siberian Fed attack. But the skies and icy surface remain deserted and undisturbed. I listen closer for anything, but it's quiet.

"Hey, hear that?" I say, still sweeping the area on recon.

"What?" Nadia says, whipping around with her blaster. She's on edge, which makes sense given what they just put us through. But then, she relaxes—

"I don't hear anything."

"Exactly, that's the problem," I say. "I don't trust it."

Nadia lowers her blaster. "You're right, Skye. I don't like it. Seems like a trap."

Suddenly, out of nowhere, a metal canister drops out of the sky.

It rolls, bounces, and lands at our feet.

"What in the asteroid fires—" Nadia starts.

But then it explodes.

Blinding green light rips out of the canister and expands, encasing us in a translucent dome. I bang on the shimmering barrier, but it's solid. We're trapped inside it.

"Looks like it's some kind of forcefield," I call to Nadia.

"But who deployed it?" she asks, whipping around.

Before I can respond, the canister starts rocketing around on the black ice by our feet, pumping out plumes of green-tinted gas. The poisonous gas clouds the air, filling the dome.

It's fear gas.

"Watch out, it's a gas attack," I yell, losing my senses for a moment and forgetting what to do. More gas hisses from the canister, obscuring my vision. My eyes sting, and my throat burns. I can taste it on my tongue. That snaps me into action. "Get your filters on! Now!"

Harold, help! I implore my neural implant, waiting for them to activate and protect me from the gas, but instead, a warning light pops on in my vision, accompanied by an alarm.

FILTER MALFUNCTION

The simple message flashes in my vision, accompanied by an alarm ringing in my ears.

Simple, but deadly.

The alarm blares louder, as the fear gas infiltrates my helmet. I cough and choke. My lungs feel like they're burning. I flash back to the gas chamber exercise.

"Blast it, filter malfunction—" Nadia starts, but violent coughing cuts off her voice.

Both our suits are malfunctioning at the *exact* same time. That can't be a coincidence. They're brand new. Clearly, it's another head-screw, courtesy of our sadistic drill sergeant.

Nadia doubles over, then starts clawing at her helmet as the fear sets in.

"Kari, help me! Don't let the gas get me again . . . I can't take it . . ."

I want to help her, but I'm choking on the gas, too. Blackness creeps into the edges of my vision. Any second now, we're both going to pass out—or worse—fall into a deep psychosis and murder each other. That's when the fear component kicks in full force. I'm helpless against it.

Nadia's features morphs into that Raider's face. Blackened, broken teeth. Wild eyes. Grimy face and stringy, greasy hair. He raises his electrified mace with glee lighting up his beady eyes.

"Now, who do we have here? Guardian scum!"

"No, you're not real," I scream, trying to fight back against the fear and paranoia. Desperately, I try to cling to some semblance of reality and will Nadia back into my vision.

But the Raider stays put. His filthy teeth and putrid breath assault me as much as his visage. He looks and smells so real. I blink hard . . . but still, Nadia doesn't reappear.

The Raider raises his mace to strike me down.

"You got away once," he sneers. "Time to finish the job."

CHAPTER 34

DRAE

L ook, this is where it happened," Rho says with a soft gasp. "The attack . . ."

I follow her gaze to the clusters of flowers, burned-down candles, and spray-painted messages scrawled on the pavement commemorating the GGA. It's strangely festive and whimsical, with petals strewn on the cold, wet concrete, while the air hangs heavy with fog.

I've never actually been to the memorial before. The marble columns stand before us like solemn guardians, engraved with the initials of every kid who died and the heroic bus driver. Beyond the memorial, the famous rust-red trellises of the iconic bridge arch over the white-capped bay. The fog has blown in, giving the whole area this eerie, haunted quality.

I pull off my fleece and pass it to Rho. She drapes it loosely over her shoulders. We don't talk; we don't need to. She takes my hand, leading me toward the shore. The water is dark and cold year-round, and the beach is rocky and equally uninviting.

This is the spot where the bus crashed into the bay. Down here, people have erected their own makeshift memorial with flowers, toys, and candles burned down to waxy nubs.

My heart catches when I spot a pink teddy bear. It's damp and smeared with grime. I picture the little girl who it was left for. The *dead* girl. I wonder who was responsible for the attack—the Siberian Fed? The Arctic Fed? Were they working together like the secretary-general insinuated? They both deny responsibility, but that doesn't mean they're innocent.

Anger overtakes my sadness like the sun burning off the fog. Whoever did this—they should pay for their terrorist actions. Killing kids? That's pure evil. It's not that I'm pro-war exactly. But I agree with the secretary-general that somebody needs to be held accountable.

"I know . . . it's terrible," Rho says as if reading my mind. She squeezes my hand tighter.

Beyond the bridge, the skies begin to lighten with pale lemon-yellow light. It's subtle, but a clear signal of what's coming. The sun will rise at any moment. That's our deadline.

We pull our gaze away from the beach and focus on finding the next—and likely final—clue. We scour the whole area, starting with the official memorial itself, then inspect the rocky beach, even the collection of flowers and toys, but come up empty. Both of us can feel it.

This is a dead end.

"But I don't understand it," Rho says, rereading the riddle for the hundredth time. "What if we got it wrong?"

"But it's the only answer that makes sense," I say, sharing her frustration. "It has to be here."

"But we looked everywhere," she says, sitting down on a stone bench in a huff. Tears prick her eyes. She's not used to losing or failing tests like this. It's not in her nature.

We watch while the sun eclipses the horizon, spilling through the fog.

Now it's official—

Time's up.

I shred the last clue card in my hands, discarding the thick paper. So much for the secret society. A hard lump catches in my throat, though I try to clear it away. I guess I was clinging to the faint hope of something going right in the middle of this horrible week. But then—

A roaring noise reverberates through the foggy morning air.

Rho cranes her neck toward the sound. "What is it?" she asks.

The rumbling grows louder. Headlights clip the bench where we're both sitting. An old school bus rips up the road, materializing from the fog like a yellow ghost.

"A school bus?" I say in disbelief. "And looks like it's headed right for us."

"But what's a school bus doing way out here?" Rho says. Her hair and eyes shift to an eerie white color. "Think it has to do with our initiation test?"

"Maybe it's a mistake?" I say uncertainly. "Or maybe the driver got lost?"

"Bus drivers don't get lost. Look . . . it's not slowing down either."

The headlights bear down on us, growing brighter and brighter. The acrid stench of diesel taints the air. I taste it on my tongue. It's not slowing down. I start to worry that it's going to plow us over, but then, at the last second, it skids to a halt with a screech, kicking up gravel.

And then—

Hiss. Pop. The door snaps open. I peer inside the bus, but I can only make out the driver's form in dark silhouette. "Friend or foe?" Rho whispers, following my gaze.

I blink at the driver. "Not sure, but buses are for . . ."

I trail off. I don't say *Park kids* out loud. But we both know it's true. Kids like us use transports. Mine is still parked back by the official memorial where I left it.

Suddenly, a gravelly voice echoes out. "So, what're you waiting for?"

It sounds familiar. But I can't place it. But then, the sun rises higher and reveals the driver's face. Rho sparks with recognition. Bright yellow surprise lights up her nano implants.

"Wait . . . Xena? Is that you?" Rho says slowly. "What are you doing out here?"

"Uh, you know her?" I whisper to Rho, keeping my eyes trained on the driver.

"Yeah, of course. She was Kari's school bus driver," Rho whispers back. "Don't you recognize her? I think she was also her next-door neighbor, but I'm not certain."

"Hey, no need to whisper," Xena says in an amused voice, leaning over the steering wheel and peering down at us. "I can hear you—and you're right on both counts."

"Oh, right," I say, blushing fiercely. "Sorry . . ."

"Let me guess, you've probably seen me a hundred times?" Xena says with a toothless grin. She breaks out in a deep cackle. "But have you ever *really* looked at me? Or folks like me?"

I'm totally busted.

She's right. She was there at school every day, dropping off or picking up students. I've watched Kari board her bus a hundred times. My cheeks burn with humiliation.

"I'm sorry . . ." I mumble, feeling ashamed of my internalized bias.

"Let's see . . . you must be her *famous* Sympathetic?" Xena says with a cocked eyebrow. "Guess I expected more from you. Though I suppose she did hate your stars-lovin' guts."

"Wait, how do you know about that?" I say, feeling totally exposed.

But Rho snorts. "Uh, like everyone at school knew about that. And *hate* is too kind."

"Okay, I get it," I cut her off. "But how does Xena know?"

"Oh, I know a great many things," Xena says. "You'll catch on quick, kiddo. I also know that you've been having weekly exchanges, while she's stationed out on Ceres Base."

"Wait, that's classified," I say in shock. "How do you know her location?"

"This is all NTKB . . . need-to-know basis," Xena says with a toothless grin. "And all you need to know right now is . . . I'm driving . . . and this is a one-way trip."

"One-way trip?" I ask in confusion. "To where?"

"Yeah, what does this have to do with our initiation test?" Rho adds. "Like to the Berkeley secret society? That's why we're here," she finishes, holding up the clue.

"Like I said, so many things you kiddos don't know," Xena replies. "All your inquiries will be answered in short order. That's all I can say. So, are you coming?"

Her question hangs in the air. I exchange a pointed look with Rho. The bus door gapes open to us like an invitation. But an invitation . . . to where? All those clues and tests led us all over campus, and now here to this bridge. But how does it all connect? And more importantly, how does it involve Xena? This can't all be a coincidence. We're all from the same small town.

Rho catches my eye, making it clear—we're both thinking the same thing.

"I don't know . . ." I hesitate, still feeling torn.

"Well, would you prefer to wait for Jude's father to come," Xena says, "and arrest you for assault? It won't take him long to find you."

I look up with a start. "You know about that, too?"

Xena smirks. "We have folks everywhere. Trust me, you're in big trouble. We know everything that happened last night. Jude already called his daddy first thing this morning."

"That means," I say, taking a step back. "My father . . . can't protect me this time . . ."

"Correct," Xena confirms. "The warrant for your arrest has already been issued. But maybe, if you're lucky, we can help you. And you can help us, too."

Rho looks equally stunned. We both absorb this information.

"Listen," Xena goes on. "The feds are already on their way to campus. Soon, they'll discover that you're gone and your transport is missing. That will result in an APB going out through the whole Federation. They'll lock down campus and put checkpoints on all major roads."

She pauses to let that sink in. And it does . . . big time.

"I'll have nowhere else to go . . ." I stammer.

"That's right, kiddo," Xena says. "Right now, we're your best shot at clearing your name. And helping the people you love. So, what do you say? Do we have a deal?"

Her words hang in the air like the fog quickly burning off the bay. Soon, it'll be gone—and Xena and her bus along with it. *Arrest . . . APB . . . checkpoints on all major roads.*

"Look, I don't want to disappoint the Old Lady," Xena says impatiently. "But we're on a tight schedule. Can't wait around forever. So, are you coming . . . or not? Final chance . . ."

My heart lurches. She's right. I don't have any other options.

Still, I hesitate and look to Rho. I hate that I dragged her into all of this.

"Should we trust her?" I whisper. None of this adds up or makes any sense. Not to mention, Xena keeps shrewdly dodging all of our pointed questions. Rho thinks it over.

"All I know is . . . Kari trusted her like family. So, that means . . . we can trust her, too."

That hits me, and it's what I needed to hear. Plus, Xena is right—I am in *big trouble*. And I'm quickly running out of both friends and options. This is my last chance.

"Fine, for Kari," I agree, turning to Xena. "Let's go."

"WARNING: TOXIC RADIATION" and "KEEP OUT: FORBIDDEN ZONE" signs appear everywhere. We're approaching the Forbidden Zone. That's the area destroyed in the last war. Bombed-out houses and singed foliage line the side of the road. Nothing grows here.

"Where're you taking us?" I ask, studying the signs. Rho's hair and eyes turn ghostly.

"Patience, kiddo," Xena says, shooting us a look through the rearview mirror. "Good things come to those who wait."

"Fine, but when will we find out?" Rho adds.

We're both annoyed . . . and more than a little tense.

"All will be answered by—"

"*The Old Lady,*" we both finish for her. "Right, we know."

The whole bus ride north from the city, she's had the same answer for every question. We sit in frustrated silence, jostled around by the bumpy roads. I'm used to my smooth transport, so I start to feel a little carsick. But Rho keeps my hand clasped tightly. That helps a little.

A few minutes later, we lurch onto a gravel trail. "WARNING: TOXIC WASTE" signs are posted on the roadside. They're rusted out and weathered with time. But they still rattle me. The bus doesn't have air filtration like my transport. We're completely exposed to the toxins.

In the distance, I spot an old military bunker. At first sight, it looks abandoned. Rusty, barbed wire fencing encircles the squat, concrete buildings. The signs explicitly say to keep out and that it's highly radioactive. We drive right past them without slowing down. Xena seems downright cheerful to be driving into a toxic wasteland. She spies our worried looks.

"Great for keeping folks away. Don't you think?"

"You mean, they're phony?" I say, staring at the foreboding signs.

I swallow hard. They don't look phony, that's for sure.

"Once, they were real," Xena says. "But now they're just used to control people. The radiation faded away long ago. The toxins are minimal. About the same levels as back in Lompoc, actually."

"But why would they lie?" Rho asks with a skeptical frown.

"Keeps everyone living in fear," Xena says with a shrug. "So you don't question the federation—or the need for Space Force. Also, keeps our kids enlisting and shipping out to die in the stars. Works like a charm."

With that, we roar up to a rusty gate in front of the military building, which looms in the distance. A guard stands in a booth at the gate. He's wearing faded military fatigues and has a blaster at his waist. He looks official—and my heart catches in my throat . . . he could report me.

But then, he grins when he sees Xena. He circles his hand over his heart.

"Disarm the stars," he says when we pull up.

"*Disarm the stars,*" Xena repeats, leaning out the driver's side window.

Rho and I exchange a shocked look. That's the slogan used by Resistance terrorists, at least according to the newsfeeds. I've never even heard it uttered aloud. Before we can object or ask any questions, the guard hits a button to open the gate. It retracts with a rusty squeal.

"Say howdy to the Old Lady for me," he says, waving us through the gate with a sharp salute. Xena returns his salute, then guns the bus away from him, kicking up dust and gravel.

Rho finally finds her voice. It comes out strained. "Wait . . . are you the . . . Resistance?"

Her words hang in the air. Xena smirks in response and she jerks the steering wheel and barrels into a gravel parking lot by the military bunker. Other buses are parked here, along with military vehicles, and even some personal transports. That's surprising.

What are they all doing out here in the Forbidden Zone?

Xena pops open the bus door.

"Last stop," she declares, cutting the engine. It rumbles to silence.

Then, she hops from the bus and heads toward the base. She doesn't wait for us. We have to scramble after her down the dusty gravel path. We approach the first building—which evidently isn't so deserted after all—where there's another armed guard and a security detector.

It lets out a shrill *beep* the second I walk underneath it.

Xena rolls her eyes, then jerks her thumb at me.

"Neural implant," she says. "He's a Sympathetic."

"Then he's a . . . *threat*." The guard looks me over. His hand inches toward the blaster at his waist. "He shouldn't be here! He could blow the whole operation—"

"Old Lady's orders," Xena shoots back.

"Oh, sorry," he says, looking contrite. "Apologies to the Old Lady."

"But you heard him . . . I'm a threat," I whisper, feeling singled out.

"Right, that's why we have to disable your implant," Xena says with a frown. "And we need your tablets and devices. Can't have anyone eavesdropping or tracking us."

The guard holds out a thick silver bag. It clearly blocks any incoming or outgoing signals. Rho doesn't look thrilled about it, but she deposits her tablet and devices into it. I didn't bring any. They seal it up and carry it away. Now, we both feel more vulnerable.

But my device is . . . well . . . *inside of me.* Courtesy of the Sympathetic Program.

"Yuri, we've got an implant," Xena calls out into the building.

She signals for the man in a lab coat. He's short and clean-cut with a pencil-thin mustache, which also doesn't reassure me. He pulls out what resembles a large wand, like at security checkpoints, and holds it over my neck. I back away, feeling assaulted. Plus, it hits me—this is my only link to Kari. If they disable it, then I'll lose our connection, too.

"Uh, is this necessary?" I stammer. "I already disabled the GPS . . ."

"Yup, they can override that and reactivate the GPS," Xena says. "They'll do that as soon as they discover you're missing. This is our last chance—or you really will be a security threat."

"Yeah, kiddo, trust me," the guard says in an ominous voice. "You don't want that."

"Don't worry," Yuri says, moving the wand toward my neck. "This won't hurt a bit."

That's how you know it's gonna be painful.

He waves the wand over my implant stub. A burning, stinging sensation starts at the base of my neck, then quickly radiates through my entire skull like liquid fire. Estrella starts talking.

Draeden . . . what are . . . you doing . . . stop . . . against regulations . . . deactivate . . .

Then her voice warbles and falls silent.

The stinging stops. The wand beeps and turns green.

"Neural implant disabled," the lab coat guy says with a crisp salute to Xena.

She salutes back, while I rub the base of my neck. I search inside my head, but feel only the absence of something. I've become so used to my implant that it makes me feel alone and disconnected. Xena doesn't seem to notice my discomfort. She leads us inside the base. The building itself is concrete and utilitarian. Everything looks like federation castoffs that have been repurposed. Meanwhile, the walls are spray-painted with the slogan, "Disarm the Stars."

This must be their headquarters.

And it's packed with Resistance fighters. Some rush around, carrying supplies and weapons, while others man desks with monitors and speak into old-fashioned headsets. The whole operation feels organized and focused, yet full of urgent, frenzied energy.

Rho reaches for my hand and clasps it. We both keep our mouths shut, taking it all in. But Xena appears undeterred. Moving at a fast clip just like her driving, she leads us toward the back office. We hurry to keep up with her. The door is blocked by two burly armed guards.

"I've got company for the Old Lady," she barks.

They salute her—clearly Xena has authority here—and wave her through without question. Fear jolts me to attention as we follow her. So, this is the Old Lady's office.

The one who will answer all our questions.

Xena raps on the door, then pushes it open.

A figure sits behind the desk. My eyes land on a familiar face, though she's dressed in faded military fatigues, so unlike the frumpy suits that she always wore on campus.

I can't believe my eyes.

It's Professor Trebond.

CHAPTER 35

KARI

No, don't touch me!" I scream and stagger back from the Raider in terror. His lips curl back from his blackened, broken teeth. I can smell his putrid breath from here. He raises his battle ax to clobber me. Scraggly hair and a thick beard obscure his face, which is smeared with grime. But I can see wild, murderous intent in his black eyes.

I draw my blaster and aim.

But my heart screams—*it's your battle buddy!*

I blink hard. *I'm still in my graduation test*, I remember suddenly.

The Raider blurs into Nadia in my vision, then snaps back to the Raider. But I saw a glimpse of the truth through the fear gas causing me to hallucinate this nightmare.

"No, you're not here," I whisper, as much to him as myself. I back away and hold my hands up in surrender. "You're my battle buddy. I won't hurt you. We're hallucinating from the gas. Come on, Nadia! Snap out of it! Listen to my voice. It's not real . . . it's a nightmare."

But the Raider charges at me.

My back hits the barrier.

I'm trapped.

The fear gas continues leaking from the canister, poisoning my eyes and lungs. I shut my eyes and hold my breath, counting to ten and trying to block out the hallucination. I know the stale air in my lungs is the last clean breath I'm going to be able to take for a while if we're both going to survive this. Surrounding us, the translucent dome keeps us trapped with the gas.

Fighting back, I hold the air in my lungs and grab Nadia's arm.

"Come on . . . we've got to break through . . . this barrier," I choke out, blindly dragging her behind me. "Before the gas . . . incapacitates us . . . and we both fail the test—"

"Raider scum, no!" Nadia says, flailing at me with her fists. At least it's not her holstered blaster, thank the stars. She's too disoriented from the gas. But her fists still hurt like the blazes.

"Nadia, calm down," I say, raising my hands in surrender and trying to block her punches. "I'm not a Raider—I'm Kari! Your battle buddy! Don't you recognize me?"

"No, it's a trick," she screams. "You're Raider scum. You want to eat me."

"Eat you? Stars no, I want to help you!"

That's the last thing I get out, wasting my precious breath that's quickly dwindling, before she leaps at me like a wild beast and starts pummeling my body with her fists. Fear starts to creep back into my mind too, quickly overwhelming my capacity for rational thought.

But I push back against it.

I summon my weeks of training. Good thing we had all those sparring sessions, so I've learned her fighting style and how to best her in hand-to-hand combat. I never thought I'd be thankful for those endless, repetitive drills. But now, it's going to save me.

Actually, both of us . . . I hope.

With a few deft moves, I put Nadia in a tight hold and pin her to the icy crust, then I whip out wire ties from my suit to restrain her. I snag her wrists with one hand and work fast. "Sorry, Nadia," I grunt back when she kicks me hard in the side. "But you'll thank me later."

"Get off me, Raider!" she shrieks in an inhuman voice. Her eyes are wild and spittle flies from her lips. The fear gas has total control over her. "Deserter, you'll pay for this!"

I feel a sharp stab at that slur. It makes me think of my father.

Suddenly, as my buried emotions swell, the gas threatens to get to me. My lungs are burning—*more like screaming*—for fresh oxygen. I don't have much time left.

I have to get moving.

Despite her frantic struggles, I finish binding her wrists and ankles. Then, with Nadia still flailing around like a crazy person, I hoist her over my shoulder and charge toward the barrier. Black spots start to encroach on my vision. My lungs and eyes burn like the blazing suns.

This is my last chance.

I'm about to pass out.

Here goes nothing, I think, aiming my blaster at the translucent barrier and squeezing off a round. The blasts hit the barrier in rapid succession, making it flicker with emerald light.

For a second, it holds fast. We remain trapped with the poisonous gas.

I'm sorry, I failed us, I think in despair.

But then the dome shatters like glass, the shards dissolving the second they hit the ice. The gas oozes out in the low atmosphere and quickly disperses. I stagger a few steps away, weighted down by Nadia, who is still thrashing and cursing like a Raider. I drop to my knees.

Only then do I finally breathe deep.

The fresh air tastes like sweet, cold water. My eyes and throat are raw and still tearing, but I can breathe again without feeling like I'm about to suffocate. I set Nadia down like a sack of potatoes—*a very angry sack of potatoes*—but I don't release her restraints.

She stares daggers at me.

"Get off me, dirty Raider," she swears, writhing on the ice.

"Just breathe," I say in a gentle voice. "It's the fear gas. You're hallucinating. I'm Kari—your battle buddy. No Raiders around these parts. It'll wear off soon. Just breathe."

It takes a few minutes before she comes back to her *stars-loving* senses. First, she stops writhing and panicking, trying to escape. Her breathing slows steadily and deepens.

And then—*all at once*—she comes back to herself.

She blinks at me through her visor.

"Kari . . . is that you?" she manages, her voice raspy and raw from the gas.

"Yup, it's me . . . and welcome back," I say with a relieved laugh. My eyes tear up. It's from the gas, but also I care about her. *Stupid emotions.* I blink back and try to keep my voice from choking up. "Now, if I let you out of these restraints . . . do you promise not to blast me?"

She gives me a horrified look. "Blast you? Wait, why would I do that?"

"Uh, 'cause a few minutes ago, you thought I was *Raider scum* trying to kill you," I say with a shake of my head. "Don't worry. It was just the gas screwing with you."

"Right, sorry," she says with a sheepish grin. "I plead temporary insanity."

"Apology accepted," I say, stumbling to my feet. My lungs still burn, but they're getting better. I suck down a few more cool breaths. I release her restraints. "Now let's get out of here. The sooner we finish with this hellish graduation test, the sooner we're real guardians."

"Deal," Nadia says. "Now what?"

I scan the horizon, using my helmet and sensors. The only thing out here on this icy rock they call a dwarf planet is our base. *No signs of life were detected.* The enclosed, domed structure gleams under the night sky, lit up with exterior illumination that reflects off the icy crust.

The only part visible aboveground is the docking bay. It's essentially a port for combat and postal ships to land. It has these big elevators that lower, carrying the vessels belowground.

"Ceres Base?" I say after finishing my recon. "It's the only thing out here."

Nadia nods. "Unless you count us."

"Yup, and stay sharp. We're still in the sim."

Trust me, it feels so real that it's easy to forget.

"No shit," Nadia shoots back. "Like I could forget. Only our whole military careers are on the line."

"That about sums it up," I say in a solemn voice. "Situation normal . . ."

"*All fucked up*," Nadia finishes for me. I detect a faint sense of humor, which is normal for her. That makes me worry less. She's back to her old self; the fear gas is losing its grip.

We cover the distance in leaps, due to the lighter gravity and our assisted suits. It's kind of fun, actually. I catch myself smiling as Nadia bounds ahead of me, then I push myself to leap farther and race ahead of her. We near the base like that, in quick suit-assisted bursts.

This is where we first landed as green recruits fresh off the ship. This was our first glimpse of the base that would become our new home. Now that feels like a million years ago.

We reach the concrete barrier that encloses the perimeter.

"Look, over there," Nadia says. "I've never seen those doors before."

"What doors?" I say, following her gaze along the wall. Sure enough, two doors are set into the side of the base, next to the docking bay.

We tramp over to them to investigate, our boots clutching the ice. When we get closer, I can make out the writing on them. My mouth drops open. The words stare back at me.

The first door reads: "Private Nadia Ksusha."

The other one reads: "Private Hikari Skye."

I shoot Nadia an uneasy look. "What do you suppose this means?"

"Probably another fun head-screw," she mutters, inspecting them.

"Roger that," I say, appreciating her sarcasm. Somehow, it makes this less scary.

"Should we switch identities and try to throw them off?"

But when she tries my door, partially as a joke, it won't budge.

After a few seconds of her tugging on it some more, electricity shoots through the door and zaps her, throwing her flat on her back. She lands a few feet away.

I rush over to help her up, but she pushes me away and gets up by herself. "Stars, that hurt like the blazes," she says belatedly, making me laugh. She brushes ice crystals off her suit.

"Hey, my pain isn't funny," she adds with a frown.

"Uh, it's sort of funny," I say, still chuckling a bit.

She scowls at me, but then she can't help laughing too.

"Yeah, maybe we should try the doors with the *right* names on them," I say, approaching my door. I reach my hand out to inspect it. *Whoosh.* The door dematerializes the second I touch it. But I can see a flicker of electricity cascade across the entrance like a selective forcefield.

Nadia follows my lead. *Whoosh.* Her door also vanishes at her touch.

"You see that?" Nadia asks, as electricity flickers like a warning across her doorway.

"Without risking it," I say, catching her eye. "I'm guessing you'd get zapped again if you tried to cross my threshold, and vice versa. We can conduct another experiment—"

"Nope, not worth it," she says, rubbing her arm, where her suit is singed and still smoking from where the electricity blasted her. "I'm sticking to my door this time."

"That means, we have to separate," I say after a moment.

Nadia grimaces. "That's clearly what they want—and trying to go against the rules results in major shock therapy. Even if splitting up sucks like a black hole."

I study my doorway, feeling my heart pound faster. I can't see anything beyond the electrified threshold. Just blackness, deep and penetrating as the Ceres sky at night.

"What do you think is back there?" I say, staring into the black abyss.

"I *think* . . . we don't have a choice. Even if I don't like it," she adds in frustration.

"Right, isn't *thinking* a bad trait in a soldier?" I say with a teasing lilt to my voice, remembering all the times Nadia drilled that phrase into my hard head during training.

"Exactly, so let's stop thinking already and take the plunge," she says, locking onto my eyes and holding my gaze for a long moment. "See you on the other side, Buddy?"

"*The other side*," I repeat. "Take care of yourself in there . . . wherever *there* is."

She gives me a crisp salute, like we've been trained, then punches my shoulder.

"Don't fuck this up for both of us," she says in a stern voice, but I can tell she cares, too. Her eyes give it away. She takes one step through the threshold, half her body disappearing through it.

I hear a faint voice echo out from beyond the field of her doorway.

It sounds frail . . . and masculine.

And also familiar.

"Help me . . . please help . . ."

It's Anton, I realize with a start.

It sounds like he's in pain. Panic flashes over Nadia's face, then she bolts the rest of the way through the doorway, disappearing into the void beyond. It seems to swallow her whole. The door rematerializes and seals shut behind her—but not before I hear Anton's voice cry out again.

"Nadia, help me! I'm hurt!"

Adrenaline kicks in hard. My first instinct is to run after Nadia to help him. But before I can act on the impulse, her door sizzles with electricity one more time, and then vanishes altogether, as if it had never been there at all. Only the solid concrete wall remains. Nadia is gone.

That leaves my doorway.

My heart is thumping with adrenaline. My lungs and eyes still burn from the fear gas. Anton's frightened voice rings in my ears like blaster fire. I taste metal on my tongue.

It's fear, I realize. Fear tastes like aluminum.

I'm afraid of what horror show lies behind my door. This test is clearly designed to mess with you—mind, body, and soul. But I don't have a choice. Like Nadia said—if we fail, then it's a one-way ticket back Earthside for both of us. If it was just my life on the line, it might be tempting to flunk out. But it's Nadia's life—her future—her dreams of becoming a guardian.

I can't screw this up for her.

Not after everything we've been through together.

"Here goes nothing," I mutter under my breath.

Then I plunge through the doorway like I'm stepping off a cliff.

CHAPTER 36

DRAE

"Professor Trebond?" I say, unable to believe my eyes.

Shock ripples through me like an electric current.

She's not dressed in her usual frumpy suit with her curly, black hair tousled in a messy bun. She's wearing faded military fatigues and scuffed-up, black combat boots. They look like they're from an old Space Force uniform, except the logo has been ripped from the lapel. Her sleeves are rolled up, displaying her uncovered forearm prosthesis in all its mechanical glory.

Trebond rises and approaches us, her boots *thwacking* against the brushed concrete floor. Her gait is sharp and staccato as her boots march forward with military precision. At that moment, I realize that it's not just her appearance that's different—but her whole demeanor. She projects authority and confidence, but also an icy calm. I almost don't recognize her.

"Welcome, Draeden and Rhodiola . . . to the Resistance," Professor Trebond says, offering her hand. It's her prosthetic one with metal joints and phalanges.

But when she speaks, familiarity rushes through me. Her voice is warm and inviting, lilting and rich, just as I remember it being when she lectured in the great halls of our university. But I'm still in so much shock that I freeze and stare at her like she's an alien, while Rho gapes at us both, at a loss for words. If her nano extensions could turn any whiter, they probably would.

Xena frowns and nudges me. "Kiddo, show some respect," she says in a low voice, gesturing for me to shake Trebond's hand. "She's the head of this whole blasted operation."

"Wait, you're the head of the . . . *Resistance?*" Rho says, unable to believe her ears.

"Bet you didn't think I was taking you to see your old professor?" Xena says with a raspy chuckle. Even Trebond cracks a mischievous smile. "As I said, so much you don't know."

"But . . . how?" I say, still trying to grasp it all.

My words hang in the air

Trebond exchanges a freighted look with Xena, gesturing for her to stand down. Xena seems protective of Trebond. But it's more than that—she respects her as their leader.

"Now, that's a very long story," Trebond says, turning back and pointing to the hard plastic chairs positioned in front of her desk. "Please, make yourselves comfortable."

We settle into the chairs, though my heart is still racing. Rho's hair and eyes remain freakishly white. Trebond's desk is metal and rusted, with impressive dents clunked into the sides, while the floors are unadorned concrete, giving the whole place a cold, utilitarian vibe.

Her desktop is laden with notes scrawled on actual paper, crumpled federation maps, and even an old-school compass and ruler, along with scrawled-out equations and astronomical units. One thing is clear. Something important is being planned here. Maybe many somethings. I remember Jude's father saying how they suspected that Trebond wasn't working alone.

But something else stands out. What's weirder is what's *not* here.

There's no sign of a computer or e-tablet in sight. In fact, the only thing electrical in the whole place is the overhead light fixture sizzling with a stark, fluorescent glow. Oh, and the twin blasters strapped to both of their waists.

Trebond takes a seat behind her desk and levels us with her penetrating gaze. "After my medical discharge," she goes on, lifting her prosthesis and flexing it. The mechanical fingers ripple and grasp with perfect coordination. "I felt pretty disillusioned and depressed. My whole life, I'd dreamed about enlisting in Space Force. Protecting our federation from Proxies and Raiders. Maybe returning a war hero. But the reality wasn't anything as I expected."

"Your injury?" I say, fixing on her arm.

She hardens. "Any good soldier expects they could sustain an injury in the course of their service . . . or worse. That's what we sign up for. Plus, the good docs fixed me right up," she says, contracting her palm into a tight fist. "We've got great tech for battle injuries."

"What was it then?" Rho asks. "What changed your mind?"

"It went far deeper than that," Trebond says. "The Proxy Wars, for starters. The skirmishes constantly breaking out. Flyovers and saber-rattling. The military industrial complex . . . and for what? Why were we fighting all these *blasted* wars? Why were we shipping our kids to the stars and training them to kill? And sending them back Earthside in body bags?"

"*To protect our federation,*" I say automatically, as it's been drilled into my head my whole life. "*We make a sacrifice of blood and stars to prevent another great war on Earth . . .*"

As soon as the regurgitated words leave my mouth, they fizzle out and dry up. Dizziness sweeps through me. It's like my whole world is rearranging itself around a new gravity field.

"Then why didn't we disarm completely back then?" Trebond asks with a shrug. "If you want to *prevent* wars, then why not dispose of our weapons of mass destruction?"

"Good point," I admit, wondering why I never considered that. *Space Force keeps us safe*. That's been drummed into our heads since birth, along with the belief that we need those weapons to protect us. But what if they're the very thing that threatens us with annihilation?

"You're right. Why didn't we disarm after the last war?" Rho asks with a puzzled expression. "Why export our militaries to space at all? What was the point of that?"

"Profit motives, control, power . . . and worse," Trebond says with a dark expression. "After I rehabbed from my injury, my real education began. I decided that going to grad school on the Space Force bill would enable me to effect positive change from within the system."

"Let me guess," Rho says with a frown. "They didn't like what you were teaching."

"Exactly. They censored my syllabus," Trebond says. "Told me what books were federation-approved. They even sent deans to observe my lectures under the guise of *helping* me. But really, they were reporting back to the government to make sure that I wasn't threatening their power. It quickly became clear that I didn't have a choice. If I wanted to change things—*really change them*—I had to go outside the system to achieve what I most desired."

The slogan of the Resistance shoots through my head.

"That's to . . . *disarm the stars*."

"Guess you did learn something from me?" Trebond says with a proud smile. She walks over and pulls down a map of our federation. Different colored routes run up and down the territory, through the cities and bisecting the coastline and mountains. They don't look familiar, but then with a start, I realize that they're the bus routes. They connect the whole federation.

"So, you recruited the bus drivers?" I say, glancing over at Xena, who stands guard by the door with one hand on her blaster.

"Actually, it was the other way around," Trebond says. "They recruited me. It turns out the feds weren't the only ones who had been monitoring my activities."

"Yeah, we targeted your old professor here," Xena says. "The drivers had already been organizing for generations. We found out about the good professor's little side interests."

"Side interests?" Trebond scoffs. "More like . . . *obsessions*."

Xena grins. "Exactly, so we followed her, observing her movements . . . and then eventually, we recruited her to our cause. Basically, the same way that we recruited you."

"Back then, I didn't know anything about the Resistance, or how organized they were," Trebond says. "I believed the newsfeeds. That they were Earthside terrorists with space trauma. Until I woke up one morning to a little embossed card on my pillow. The same as you."

She opens a desk drawer and pulls out an envelope. It looks tattered and frayed around the edges. It reads, "Professor Lilly Trebond," in ornate calligraphy.

My breath catches at the similarity.

"I keep it as a little reminder," Trebond goes on, tucking it back inside her drawer. "So I always remember the day my whole life changed . . . for the better."

"But why play all these games?" Rho says, frowning. "Why put us through tests?"

"Simple. We needed to push you," Trebond says, turning stern and businesslike. "To see how adaptable you were under pressure. To find out how much you wanted something that you didn't even fully understand. To see how far you were willing to go . . . for a cause."

"And . . . did we pass?" Rho says, unable to help herself. She sits on the edge of her seat . . . literally. *Type A* all the way. I bet she's never failed anything before in her life.

"With the *highest* honors," Trebond replies.

"But why pick us?" I interject, unable to help myself. "Out of all your students?"

Trebond nods to me. "Draeden, if I'm being honest, you were the initial target of this operation. But you had certain . . . *weaknesses*. Your family history, for starters. Your mother's political beliefs. Your father's a high-level fed agent. Not to mention, your connection to Jude Luther. His father is one of our biggest threats. But after I observed Rho interacting in my class with you, I realized that was the answer. You needed her . . . she could help you find the path . . ."

"I knew it! He needed the nerd," Rho says, her hair gushing out bright pink to match her eyes. "If it weren't for me, he would've failed that first test in the Campanile."

"Precisely," Trebond says with the barest hint of a smirk. "Although I must admit, much to our surprise, he performed better on the initiation tests than we anticipated."

Now it's my turn to feel smug. "So, you were watching us?" I say, absorbing this. "The whole time? In the Campanile? In the library? The scavenger hunt all over campus?"

"Of course," Trebond says. "We had to observe how you withstood the increasing pressure. We were testing you to find out if you could handle the next phase of the mission."

"And we passed?" I ask, the wheels turning in my head. I think back through all the tests. The hidden clues. The riddles in the dark. But now, it all seems different through this new lens.

"With high honors, remember?" Trebond says. "Otherwise, you wouldn't be sitting here."

"Well, what would you do if we failed?" Rho asks, her visage turning curiously blue.

"Oh, we'd simply have informed you that you didn't make the final cut," Trebond says. "Let you go on believing that it was just some college secret society, and you didn't make it through to the final initiation. And that would've been the last you ever heard from us."

We passed. The concept hits me all at once and finally starts to sink in.

It's actually real.

"Were there others you tested?" Rho asks, still radiating blue. "Students like us?"

Trebond pauses, then nods. "Yes."

"Who were they?" Rho presses.

"Right, I can't tell you their identities," Trebond says, turning stern. But I see files scattered across her desk. Other targets probably. "That's classified—you're both NTKB."

"Fine, did they pass?" I ask.

Trebond exchanges a pointed look with Xena, then shakes her head once.

One simple . . . *no.*

"Not even close," Trebond adds. "You're the only successful candidates who completed all of the trials. And that means one thing—a lot is riding on you. More than you know."

Dark shadows cloud her face, shrouding her complexion. I want to bask in her praise and the knowledge that we passed all her tests, but instead, I shrink down, wanting to disappear.

"Draeden, what's wrong?" Trebond asks, picking up on my shift.

"It's just that . . . I think you made a big mistake," I say in a soft voice.

"How so?" Xena asks. She perks up, alert.

Rho shoots me a hard look, but I won't meet her gaze.

"I'm really . . . a coward," I say after taking a deep breath. My words come out barely a whisper. "I've always been a coward. I used to pick on kids with my friends. I knew it was wrong, but I was afraid to speak up. I'm nothing more than a bully . . . I don't belong here."

Shame gushes through me. I remember Kari's words most of all. Trebond takes that in and nods. "Well, then a lot has changed . . . hasn't it? Even in the last twenty-four hours?"

But still, I shake my head.

"Like I said, you made a mistake. I don't deserve to be here."

If I had nano implants like Rho, I'd be sprouting pale red hair right about now. *Deep shame.*

Trebond regards me with a serious expression. "Draeden, all people are capable of growth and change. That includes you. I saw you come so far in our time together in the classroom. And now through these tests. And even here today."

"What . . . do you mean?" I say.

Trebond smiles. "Think about it. You just walked into a top-secret Resistance hideout and didn't panic. Most people in the same situation would freak out, or run the other way . . ."

"Like Jude?" I say, remembering last night. That makes me wince.

Trebond nods. "Yes, like your old roommate. Don't worry . . . we located his victim. The one you helped last night. As we speak, our associates are offering her protection. We'll keep her safe, somewhere his family can't get to her—and do what they did to his other victims."

"Other victims?" Rho says. "So, there are more then? We suspected as much."

"Sadly, that wasn't the first girl he assaulted on campus," Trebond goes on. "We did some investigating and discovered his pattern of abuse. And, well, it dates back to high school."

Her words hit me hard, puncturing my heart. My whole demeanor deflates. Like crumpling a can. Rho pats my arm. "It's not your fault. You didn't know. And when you found out . . ." Her hair shifts to volcanic red like her eyes. "Well, I'm glad you broke his face."

Xena snorts. "Oh, we'll do more than that if he tries anything again."

"But hopefully," Trebond cuts in, "with our intervention, that will be the last time."

Xena nods. "Yup, boss. I'm handling it."

Judging by her tone, I wouldn't want to be Jude right now. I feel slightly better knowing that she's on it and that he won't get away this time like he has his whole life.

I notice something odd on Trebond's desk—it looks like old-fashioned calligraphy tools. Black inkpots. Quills. Thick, cream-colored cardstock and matching envelopes. Wax for the seals. Suddenly, I remember how my father found the feather and pot of ink in her room.

"But why go to all this effort?" I ask, pointing to her desk. "Writing all those cards? Planting them in our dorm rooms? The riddles? Why not message us electronically?"

"For starters, it's the safest way to communicate," Trebond says. "The feds monitor all the digital networks. Hard communications are safest now. We use the bus drivers to deliver them. Their routes run all over the state. Not to mention the tunnels we dug out in major cities like San Francisco, and the abandoned subway lines down in LA. Ever notice how nobody pays attention to the buses? They're practically invisible. Or as close to it as you can get."

"You're right," I say, thinking about how most people don't notice them, except when they break down and block the streets. They really are invisible, for all practical purposes.

"That's genius," Rho says. "Absolutely brilliant. You're operating in plain sight."

Trebond nods, then glances at the analogue clock on the wall and turns more serious. "But back to why we targeted you in the first place. Time is running short. We can't waste it."

"Why did you pick us?" Rho asks, leaning forward with blue curiosity.

"Yeah, of all the students at Berkeley?" I add, joining her.

"You have a shared history with each other," Trebond says, rapping her fingers on the desk. "But more importantly . . . with someone else . . . who may be the key to everything."

"Someone else?" I say, exchanging a confused glance with Rho. "What . . . do you mean?"

There's a long pause.

"Should we tell them now?" Xena says, turning to Trebond. "Think they're ready?"

Trebond sighs. "I don't know. It's a big risk . . . but we're out of time. We don't have a choice. They're the best shot we have at reaching the main target and getting this intel out."

I level my gaze at them. But still, they clam up.

"Just tell us already," I demand, rising to my feet. "You went to all this trouble. Put us through all those tests. Brought us all the way here. Disabled my implant. Who is it?"

That's when Professor Trebond meets my gaze—and says two words that change how I feel about everything.

"*Private Hikari Skye.*"

CHAPTER 37

KARI

I'm in the jungle.

Vines, trees, humidity, and loamy earth stomp under my boots. The steady *drip, drip, drip* of light rain pattering my shoulders and splattering my visor. I march through the trees, pushing the tangled vines away, careful not to trip over the outstretched roots that threaten to snag my boots. The last thing I remember is stepping through the door with my name on it . . . and then . . .

Utter, soul-sucking blackness.

And now, here I am. But where is here?

This is a new sim environment. Probably modeled on some secret interstellar planet. I've never been in a jungle before—real, simulated, or otherwise. I push through the edge of the thick trees, stumbling upon a clearing. *A man-made clearing*, from the looks of the tree stumps and singed foliage. Boot prints mar the mud. Lots of them. But where are all the guardians?

I continue my recon into the campsite, spotting pop-up tents and firepits, even a dug-out latrine near my boot. I'm careful not to step on that. It's a campsite, and not just any campsite. It's one of ours. I recognize the California Fed markings on the tents—the grizzly bear symbol is unmistakable. Not to mention, the Space Force gear strewn around the muddy swamp.

"Anybody here?" I call out, clutching my blaster and scanning the area like I've been trained. It's silent. Too silent. That puts me on high alert.

I tramp deeper into the swampy clearing. On closer inspection, it's not a campsite—it's a blaster-torn battlefield. I register these details all at once. Dead bodies half-drowned in the thick muck, clutching at wounds. Blood mixing with rainwater. Faces contorted into masks of pain.

This sends an electric shock through me. I clutch my blaster tighter.

What happened here?

I plod through the remnants of the camps, stepping over the bodies. The mud tries to suck my boots down just like the corpses. All this carnage, all this blood. I'm guessing that it's the aftermath of an attack. They've been dead for a while. I kick a facedown body over—

Then flinch back, aiming at it.

It's a dead Raider, which makes my heart race. He's clutching an electrified mace. His chest is blackened with blaster shots. He looks just like the one from the combat sim.

"*Raider attack,*" I hiss under my breath.

I kick the body over, revealing more of the face.

I spot a glimmer of metal in his fist. The fingernails are blackened from frostbite and neglect. I peel them away, stiff with rigor mortis, and pry out the metal. The dog tags chink in my palm. I scrape the mud away from the embossed tags and read the name stamped into the metal.

"Captain Rache, Fifth Platoon."

It's Drae's mother.

That makes my heart race faster. This is a head-screw, that's for sure. They're expecting me to panic. I fight to stay calm and follow my training. I scan the clearing, but I don't see her body anywhere. Then I remember—she got wounded but escaped. She was the commander of this platoon. She managed to get some of her guardians out. She saved my drill sergeant's life.

That means . . .

This is what my father did.

That thought stops me dead in my tracks like I got blasted. I survey the battle-field again, feeling more disturbed. This is the aftermath of what happened when he deserted his watch, leaving his platoon vulnerable to the attack. Maybe even led the Raiders to them.

The horror of it sinks in deeper when I take in the smaller details.

The severed legs and arms strewn over the muddy earth. The dead guardians, their bodies intermingled with those of their attackers. The raided campsite, pillaged of supplies and then set ablaze. Some of the tents are still smoldering.

Suddenly, I can't breathe. I feel like I'm suffocating. I claw at my helmet, ripping it off and throwing it down. I collapse to my knees in the mud, feeling the rain start to fall and soak my hair. Without the filters, I can smell the burning. I breathe in ash and soot and charred flesh. It makes me retch in the mud. Then, I jerk my gaze up. In front of me, the mud bubbles and steams.

Something stirs and rises from the ground like a spike, filling out and growing taller. It's a monolith—obsidian, polished to a high shine. It rises from the mud like a monument to death.

I stare at the smooth surface, smooth like black glass, like a dark mirror. My reflection gazes back at me impassively. My cheeks look slick with rain and mud and worse.

Who are you?

I think it.

My lips move. No sounds emerge.

Suddenly, my face in the reflection dissolves into my father's face. The same brown eyes and black hair. It's like he's standing right there in front of me.

"Kari, what are you doing here?"

His deep voice comes out startled. His eyes lock onto my uniform. He jerks around, paranoia flashing in his eyes. "Did *they* send you? Answer me . . . who sent you?"

I can't find my voice. I know that I could talk once, but now that feels like a distant memory. Suddenly, something cuts through the jungle. It sounds large and terrifying. I whirl around, catching glimpses of silver metal and red blazing through the vines at high speed. I lock onto it for a split second in a clearing—it's a Raider attack ship, blazing through the jungle.

When my father sees it, he turns and runs.

Wait, come back!

I try to scream, but my voice still doesn't work. Nothing comes out.

I give up yelling and chase after him, tearing through the jungle. Vines whip at my face, drawing pain and fresh blood. Sweat pools on my brow, mixing with the rain and mud slicking my cheeks. He's just ahead of me. I try to run faster and catch him, forcing my legs to churn.

I burst through the trees into a clearing, cornering him on a ridge with a sheer drop-off. My father skids to a halt just in time, flailing around to face me. In one smooth motion, he produces a blaster from his hip. I'm caught off guard—and a second too late to draw mine.

He could blast me dead.

But he doesn't.

Instead, he throws the blaster down and crumples to his knees. The heat and noise of combat rise behind us. Blaster fire makes this red-tinged dusk appear bright as day.

"Kari, I'm sorry . . . I ran away," he says, whimpering as tears stream down his cheeks. His chest convulses with sobs. "I'm weak . . . I couldn't handle it . . . I was afraid . . ."

"Shut the stars up!" I spit back, feeling black hate rise in my heart. "Your apologies mean . . . *nothing*. I'd never do what you did! I'd never abandon my platoon to die like that. How could you desert your watch? How could you let the Raiders attack them without warning?"

He gives me a pitiful look. He isn't a man; he's a coward.

"Please . . ." he says. "I had to run away. I didn't know they would die. Don't you know the feeling? Like you're suffocating . . . like you're dying . . . like you can't breathe?"

"No, I'm *nothing* like you!" I say without pity. "And I'll never forgive you."

He peers at me with mournful eyes. I remember them looking down at me as a child—soft brown and almond-shaped and so full of love. Then when he shipped back to space after his leave, I remember them staring at me through warp mail messages. Our only connection to him.

Suddenly, he looks like the father I once had, before my whole world shattered into a million tiny pieces, before he vanished all at once, and I was left trying to clean up the mess.

"Kari, I love you," he goes on. "I'm so sorry, I didn't mean to hurt you—"

"Liar!" I scream at him, injecting all my darkest emotions into my voice. "You're deserter scum. You ruined my life . . . all of our lives. You destroyed our family . . . how could you?"

"I didn't have a choice," he says, shaking his head. "They made me enlist. It was the only way to take care of you. But I wasn't cut out to be a guardian. I love you . . . I'm so sorry."

Unbidden, tears spurt from my eyes, spilling down my cheeks. I hate that he can still affect me this way. He reaches for me through the mirror, stepping out of it and onto the muddy ground. His combat boots sink into the muck. He takes another step toward me with his arms outstretched to hug me . . . like when I was a child, and he was still my beloved father.

But I swat his hands away as if they're radioactive.

"Don't you *dare* touch me." I bite off each word like it's a curse. "You're nothing to me . . . less than nothing . . . I hate you."

"But I'm your father," he says. He takes another step. "I love you . . . I swear it."

"You lost the right to call yourself that the second you deserted." I stare him down, gesturing around. "Look at what you did! They were defenseless . . . you left them to die."

"Kari, please . . ." Another step toward me. Arms extended, pleading. "Forgive me—"

"Never," I say, drawing my blaster with shaky hands and aiming it right at his chest. "And I'm taking you into Space Force for deserting . . . you're a traitor . . ."

His eyes dart to his blaster in the mud. He lunges for it, but I'm faster.

I pull the trigger like I was trained.

The blast hits him square in the chest. He staggers backward, shock exploding in his eyes. His chest blooms with fire and smoke. One more step backward, and he pitches over the cliff.

"No, wait—" I yell, staggering after him. But I'm too late. I can only watch as his body plunges into the ravine. *Splash.* It hits the river, quickly submerging beneath the water.

Horror washes through me.

I just killed my dad.

And probably threw away any chance I had of passing my graduation test. I've never killed anyone before. Dread rushes through my veins like ice water.

"No, please," I scream, staggering up and whipping around toward the jungle. "If you're listening, I want to start my test over! I made a mistake. I need another chance—"

This concludes your test, Harold communicates.

I feel that brain-sucking feeling. Like I'm being pulled into a black hole.

Then everything goes dark.

CHAPTER 38

DRAE

Hikari?" I say, feeling my heart drop.

Shock cascades through me, then my protective instincts flare up. "What do you want with her?" I demand. "Is *that* why you chose me? Because we're paired together?"

I feel violated. Vulnerable. Manipulated.

They were just using me to get to Kari.

I jerk my gaze from Professor Trebond to Xena, searching for some explanation that doesn't make me feel completely . . . *used*. They exchange a look.

"Kari trusts you," Trebond goes on after a moment. Her dark eyes search mine. "She'll listen to you. We need someone on the inside at Space Force who can help us."

"Well, that's your mistake," I say, looking down. "Kari barely stopped hating me . . . and that's *before* I disappeared on her. Sorry, but you should've dug deeper before you went to all this trouble."

"Draeden, you're standing here for a reason," Trebond says, holding my gaze. "It's not an accident or a mistake that we recruited you. We know what you're capable of—"

"Yeah right, I'm a coward! I was totally freaked out when I got here. I just hid it—"

"No *coward* ever made it through our tests," Xena cuts me off. "Plus, you think you're the only one who feels afraid? We all feel fear, but that doesn't keep us from acting."

"That's right," Trebond says. "When Xena first floated the idea of recruiting you and Kari, I thought it was risky. We'd never conscripted a Sympathetic before. They watch you closely. But you're bonded to a guardian. And your guardian's a fresh recruit. That means they haven't brainwashed her yet. She can still think for herself. Plus, Xena trusts her."

Xena nods. "Exactly. We needed a way to infiltrate Space Force. We've got agents inside the federation government down here, but we've never been able to penetrate Space Force. The security's too tight. This is our last chance. Kari is our best shot."

I still feel uncertain. *This is a big mistake.*

"Look, I'm flattered. Really, I am," I force out, feeling inadequate to the challenge. "But I think you're mistaking me for my mom. She's the war hero . . ."

"No, we need you," Trebond says. "And we need you now. Time is short."

"But for . . . *what?*" I say, looking at Rho. "You still haven't told us anything."

Trebond lets out a long sigh.

"It's simple, really . . . to avert the next great war. Because if we don't act now . . . if it starts in the stars now . . . then it will be the last war that we'll ever live to fight."

"What makes you think that?" Rho asks, cutting in. "Sure, the Proxy tensions have been ramping up, especially with that flyover. But that's happened before. Saber-rattling and more. They're probably bluffing. It always calms down."

"No, this time is different," Trebond says, shaking her head. "The tensions won't die down. In fact . . . as we speak . . . the war is already starting . . ."

She trails off. This chills me.

"What . . . do you mean?" I manage, trading a look with Rho.

"In only a matter of days," Trebond goes on, "the secretary-general will declare war on the Siberian Fed. But it won't just be war in the stars. He's also going to issue a declaration to rearm Earthside for our protection. Then, all the Proxies will follow suit."

"But the Siberian Fed deserves it," I say in a rush of emotion. "For killing those kids. You know, maybe the secretary-general is right. We're vulnerable without an Earthside military force. There could be another terrorist attack . . ."

"Exactly," Rho says. "And all the evidence points to them. I've seen it on the newsfeeds. It makes sense, too. They're our biggest adversary."

"Oh indeed, that's what they're saying," Trebond says. "I've seen the newsfeeds, too. They claim we have evidence that implicates them."

I exchange a wary look with Rho. Her hair and eyes are pensive gray.

"Wait, are you saying . . . *they're lying to us?*"

"Not exactly," Trebond says with a shrug. "They just see what they want to see."

She produces a digital package and slots it into the projector on her desk. The overhead lights dim automatically as familiar images of the Golden Gate Attack light up the screen.

"Our inside informants leaked this data to us," Trebond says, projecting images of the explosive device. It shows markings on the bomb—the familiar red sickle that we've all come to recognize and fear.

"That's pretty clear," Rho says, her eyes flashing over it. "That's the Siberian Fed symbol. What more proof do you need?"

"Sure looks that way, doesn't it?" Trebond says, flipping through more angles of the bomb. The sickle flashes over and over. "It's obvious . . . a little too obvious, don't you think?"

"What do you mean?" I ask, squinting at the images.

Trebond sets her lips. "The real actor behind the attack planted these markings, knowing that we'd find them and declare war on our biggest adversary without questioning it."

"But *who* rigged the explosive and planted evidence?" Rho says in frustration. "Who would want us to destroy ourselves? The other Proxies would suffer equally. It's called *mutually assured destruction* for a reason. Why would they want that? It doesn't make sense."

"She's right," I agree. "Why would someone want deterrence to fail now?"

"You're both correct," Trebond says. "But those in charge are too reactive and power-hungry to stop it. It's a vile and dangerous situation. If you look closer, the real evidence is right there—buried under the fake evidence. But you have to *want* to find it. Unfortunately, that's not the case now. Secretary-General Icarus has been waiting for a reason to rearm Earthside."

I remember him from our Pairing Ceremony. His polished suit and security detail. The way he spoke in a way that provoked both respect and a healthy dose of fear.

"What're you saying?" I ask in confusion. "They don't want to find the truth?"

"The military industrial complex," Trebond says, flipping through more slides of the rebuilding efforts after the war. "More like, they're willfully blind. Our whole government, society, economy, our entire way of life—*our everything*—all depend on one thing."

"Space Force," Rho says in a soft voice.

"That's right," Trebond says. "Without it, the people who run our government wouldn't have jobs, power, and control over our federation. Think about their cushy lifestyle and perks. They don't want to give that up. Why would they?"

"Right, they want the opposite," I say, thinking of Jude and Loki. How they're guaranteed to run this federation one day. And also my parents. My dad with his cushy fed job, and my mom with her benefits and war hero status that lets her think she's better than everyone else.

Why would they want to give that up?

"Exactly. Secretary-General Icarus doesn't see declaring war as a negative," Trebond goes on. "Quite the contrary—he sees it as an *opportunity*. Not only to control Earthside . . ."

"But to take over the stars, too," Rho says, glancing at the screen.

"That's right." Trebond nods. "Our sources on the inside tell us that he will proceed with his war declaration. As we speak, it's already being decided. It will happen any day now."

Trebond clicks through images of the bus detonating in a fiery explosion. The small flaming bodies plunging into the dark, watery abyss. I've seen these replayed a million times on the newsfeeds. It's hard to believe it wasn't the Siberian Fed.

"Then tell us the truth . . . who's behind this attack?" I demand, tired of her games and riddles. "Somebody planted that bomb on the bus. Somebody killed those poor kids."

Tension hangs in the air, thick and suffocating. Trebond clicks to the next image. It's another forensic analysis of the explosive device. Only, this one looks different.

"Our operatives gained access to the device itself," Trebond says, pointing to the screen. "Or what was left of it. We snuck into the lab and examined it. These chemical signatures all pointed to the Siberian Fed initially. This also matched their patterns."

She points to the screen and the chemical signatures. "But it was a decoy, planted there for us to find."

Fear flashes over Rho's face. "What're you saying?"

Trebond points to the forensic report. "The weapon was rigged up to *look* like Siberian Fed tech. But if you look closer, it's far too advanced for them. Plus, see these other chemical signatures? Well, quite frankly, we've never encountered them before . . . anywhere."

"Then who did this?" I ask, studying the screen.

"Unfortunately, we're not entirely sure," Trebond says with a deep frown. "But we do know one thing for certain. It wasn't the Siberian Fed. Or any other Proxy, for that matter."

"Raiders then?" I say in a low voice.

"No way," Xena says right away. "This is way too advanced for them. They only pirate our tech and modify it. Plus, let's just say . . . we'd know if it was them."

Rho frowns. "How can you be so sure? What did you find?"

Trebond gives us a hard look. "This technology . . . well . . . it's unlike anything that we've ever seen before. I recruited some top university scientists to double-check our findings."

Those words stun me. "What do you mean?"

Trebond holds my gaze. A long moment passes. The light from the projection casts her face in stark light and shadow. She leans forward and finally speaks the truth—

"This weapon isn't human—it's *alien*."

PART 4

DEPLOYMENT

But a kingdom that has once been destroyed can never come again into being; nor can the dead ever be brought back to life.

—Sun Tzu, *The Art of War*

CHAPTER 39

KARI

The lights blaze back on and pull me out of the simulation.

I hear screaming and crying.

My neural implant stub feels hot and stings to the touch. I don't even realize it—but I'm the one who's screaming and crying. I clamp my mouth shut, biting down on my tongue hard. I taste blood in my mouth. I blink hard to clear my vision, then scan the sim chamber.

I'm alone.

Nadia isn't here.

That's probably a bad sign. The memory of the sim races through my mind, replaying like a horror movie. The fear gas attack, the two doors with our names . . . then the jungle.

I blasted my father.

I remember him pitching over the cliff with his chest still smoking from the blaster shot. The one discharged from my weapon. Devastation washes through me like a black wave. Not because I care about him—or more accurately—the simulated version of him. Good riddance, I think.

There's another reason that I feel my stomach churning with acid, and bile retching back up my throat. It's obvious—*I failed my graduation test.* I'm pretty sure you're not supposed to blast your own father. That's gotta be some kind of bright line, right? Like a major black mark on your record? Don't murder your immediate family in there?

Well, I know my fate now. *Dishonorable discharge*, and I deserve it. My knees buckle, forcing me to sink down to the floor. Even my enhanced suit can't keep me on my feet.

Suddenly, a voice reverberates through my chamber.

"Private Skye, you've just faced your greatest fears," the drill sergeant says in her stern voice. But today, it sounds like condemnation. "How do you think you fared in there?"

"Stars, you don't have to rub it in," I mutter from my knees. Tears prick at my eyes. "I know I failed. Just get it over with already. Kick me out and ship me back Earthside . . ."

There's a long pause. Too long. Probably another part of the torture.

"Failed?" she says in an even voice.

"Well, I did blast my father in the sim," I say, tasting bile at the fresh reminder. "And a dog . . . I killed a poor, helpless stray dog. So . . . I'm pretty sure I failed the test."

Another long pause, during which I feel like I'm being sucked into a black hole. It's that same crushing, obliterating feeling. Then the drill sergeant finally speaks again.

"To the contrary, Private Skye," she says, unable to contain the delight in her voice. "Though I must say, that was a pretty entertaining sim. Your mind is rather creative. Your instincts are sharp. You stayed calm under pressure. You saved your battle buddy from the gas."

"Yeah, but I blasted the stars out of my dad."

"Private Skye, you didn't have a choice in there," she says, turning more serious. "Your father deserted his watch and betrayed his platoon. His actions caused them to be massacred by Raiders. He would've blasted you if he had the chance. You had to kill him."

"Yeah . . . but there must've been another way," I stammer. "Maybe . . . I could've saved him . . . apprehended him and brought him in, so he could be rehabilitated. I failed him."

My mind races, trying to find an alternative narrative, one that doesn't result in me killing him. I come up empty. But still, nothing about this scenario feels right. My stomach churns.

But the drill sergeant cuts me off.

"No, he *failed* you. The second he betrayed his platoon. He failed all of us."

"Please, stop mind-screwing with me," I say, angry this time. "I'm sick of it. Look, I took your stupid test. Put up with your sadistic torture and insults for four *long* weeks. The least you could do is get it over with and discharge me already—"

"Recruit, shut up."

"Wh-what?" I say, too shocked to say anything else.

"Shut *the blazing stars* up," she says, sounding infuriated now. "And let me finish for once. With your complicated family history, we had to test you. Don't you understand that? We had to see how you'd react to your father. I'm pleased to inform you that . . . you passed."

"Wait, I did what?" I say in surprise. I can't believe it.

"Private Skye, you passed," the drill sergeant says. "Don't make me say it again. Unless you want me to think you're fishing for compliments."

"Wait, I passed?" I say, still in disbelief.

"Sure did, Private." She softens her voice. "And on a more personal level, that was one of the toughest tests I've witnessed in all my years as a drill sergeant. I've seen many recruits crumble and fall apart when facing less daunting obstacles. You should be proud of yourself."

"I passed," I repeat, no longer a question, but still not able to believe it fully. "You're certain? This isn't another weird test to mess with me? Or some aftereffects from the fear gas?"

She chuckles through the connection. It unsettles me as much as anything else. She rarely laughs. "Nope, this is the real deal. Congratulations, Private Skye. You've just graduated from basic training. Report first thing tomorrow morning for your MOS orders."

I can't believe my ears.

I graduated from basic training. And tomorrow, I'll receive my MOS orders, also known as Military Occupational Specialty. And I'll find out where I'm being stationed . . . or even deployed. *I requested front lines,* I remember, making my heart jitter at the idea of combat duty.

Right on cue, the chamber unlocks and slides open. *Hiss.* I stagger out to find my platoon waiting for me. They fall silent the moment I step into the corridor. Clearly, my test took the longest. That must have them all really worried. My eyes sweep over our little mismatched group. They each peer back at me expectantly. Nadia's eyes lock onto my face.

Her fate depends on mine.

"So?" Nadia says. I can hear the strain in her voice.

"Did you pass?" I ask her first.

"Yup, thanks to you saving me from that fear gas," Nadia says. "We all passed, thank the stars. Even my little bro. We've just been waiting on your slow ass. So, what happened in there?"

"Right . . . about my test . . ."

I wait a long beat, just to mess with them. Everyone looks freaked out. Nadia shoots me an impatient look. "Asteroid fires, spit it out already," she says. "You're killing us."

"Sorry to disappoint you . . ."

I can feel the energy in the corridor deflate. So I quickly add—

"But you're not getting rid of me that easy! I passed—"

I barely get those words out, before they all start jumping on me and cheering wildly. We pile into a group hug. Their hooting and jubilant voices fill the corridor.

"Congrats, you jerk," Nadia says, clapping me on the shoulder.

"Yeah, you really had us going there for a minute," Anton says, flashing his signature crooked smile. "Especially when you took so long to come out of that chamber."

Percy hoists me onto his broad shoulders—which feel even broader after these weeks of training—and parades me around the corridor.

"Put me down, you big lug," I grunt at him, pounding on his back. But he refuses and hobbles around faster. I laugh at his silly antics anyway.

From my bird's-eye perch on his shoulders, I study my friends—celebrating, applauding for each other, basking in how far we've all come—and feel like the luckiest guardian in the whole galaxy. And I know with certainty that the future of our federation is in good hands.

For one simple reason—
It's in our hands now.

Send exchange to my Sympathetic, I instruct my neural implant, after sliding into my favorite pod. I can't wait to record messages for Ma and Bea, but for some reason, the person I want to tell about my news first is Drae. My heart pounds faster, telling me not to question it.

But nothing happens.

My neural implant doesn't connect. Nor do any warnings pop up.

"Harold, what's going on?" I ask audibly, wondering if the pod is malfunctioning.

I wait for his voice to pipe up and reassure me. But instead, there's only silence. I shift around uncomfortably. I hit the button to open the pod door and summon the postmaster, but it stays shut. Now, I start to feel claustrophobic. I jam the button again . . . harder. Still *nothing.*

"Harold, not funny. I need an update ASAP."

Hmmm . . . that's strange, Harold finally says, coming back online.

"Uh, what's strange?" I say, not liking the sound of that. I jam the button again to open the pod, but to no avail. The door remains sealed.

Let's see, it appears your Sympathetic Pairing has been . . . temporarily suspended, Harold reports. Even he sounds puzzled by this turn of events. *Awaiting further information.*

"What do you mean . . . *suspended?*" I choke out, feeling a rush of fear. Horrible thoughts flash through my head. "Is Drae . . . okay? Did something bad happen to him?"

Stand by . . . preparing for incoming communication, Harold communicates, not answering my questions. That's highly unusual. I feel confusion mixed with fear and frustration.

That's when another face pops onto the screen.

One I never expected to see in this pod.

It's the drill sergeant. And she looks worried. No, not just worried. But downright troubled. She locks onto my gaze. I spot fresh worry lines around her eyes.

"Private Skye, I'm sorry to report this news," she says, glancing down at her tablet and scanning it quickly. "But due to the lag time . . . I just received the report myself."

"What news?" I say, feeling my heart thud like a rock.

"As you know, it concerns your Sympathetic."

"Draeden?" I say, barely able to force his name out.

"That's right. I'm sorry . . . but it appears that . . . he's missing."

"Missing?"

"Please understand, we don't have much intel yet," she says, tapping on her tablet. "We're still investigating . . . talking to key witnesses, piecing the events together. It seems that he vanished from his dorm room sometime late last night."

She gives me a moment to process that. "Now, is there anything you remember from your last exchange with him? That might help us figure out why he'd simply disappear?"

"No, nothing." My mind races at high speed, trying to process it. "He seemed fine during our last exchange. Better than fine, actually. His classes were going well. He was in good spirits. His grades were improving. He'd made a new friend . . ." I trail off.

I don't mention the whole *declaration of love* situation. Pretty sure that could get us both in major trouble. Tears spring to my eyes as my thoughts spiral darker. But maybe that's why . . . I'm the reason. Maybe he's running away from me. The tears spill down my cheeks unbidden.

"Private Skye, these things happen sometimes. People can be fragile. They can also hide when they're in trouble, so those closest to them don't suspect anything is wrong."

"*Trouble?*" I repeat. "Why would you think he's in trouble?"

She presses her lips together.

"Because right before Mr. Rache went missing last night, he assaulted his room-mate. For no reason, according to the roommate's statement. It's backed up by the other witness."

"Blast him . . . was it Jude?" I ask right away.

"That's right—Jude Luther," the drill sergeant confirms. "The other roommate is the witness. He reported that Draeden lost his temper and attacked Mr. Luther . . . unprovoked."

"Loki, of course," I say with derision. Their smug faces flash through my head. "Look, they were the biggest bullies back in high school. Trust me, Jude probably instigated it. I'm just surprised it didn't happen sooner. Loki must be lying. He's known for that. I'm sure Drae had a good reason for punching him—"

"Well, it wasn't just a punch."

She tilts her tablet, and that's when I see the image of Jude's face.

It looks like raw meat.

His nose is broken, maybe shattered. Dark bruises mark his eyes, which are swollen shut. His cheekbones are scraped and battered, too. The whole mess renders him almost unrecognizable. Almost, except for that cruel twitch to his lips that passes for a smile.

"*Asteroid fires,*" I gasp, realizing how bad this looks. Sure, he was the biggest bully in high school . . . but still . . . he got the stars beat out of him. "Drae . . . did that?"

"According to the report," the drill sergeant confirms, snapping me out of my morbid thoughts. My brain feels foggy and can't make sense of it all. "So, you knew the victim?"

"Sure did," I say, feeling a rush of memories, none of them positive. "And his roommate Loki. Though I wish I didn't. Like I said, we're all from Lompoc. Jude was the worst, along with his virtual shadow, Loki. And there's more. They were Draeden's two best friends."

"*Were* . . . past tense?" she says, picking up on this right away.

I nod, remembering everything I learned through our recent exchanges. "Right, Drae wanted to get away from them and have a fresh start at Berkeley. He tried to sign up for new roommates. But Jude pulled some strings to have them housed together. His father is majorly connected. I guess it can be hard to leave your past behind . . ."

I trail off, remembering how I blasted the stars out of my father not two hours ago in my test. The drill sergeant types all that down on her tablet. Then she looks up. "Thank you for that. I'll share it with the investigators back Earthside. Maybe it'll help us locate him."

I stare at her calm face on the monitor.

For some reason, it makes me feel more frantic.

"But can't you track his neural implant?" I ask, grasping for solutions. "Plus, with all the travel restrictions, he can't have gotten very far . . . even if he does have a transport."

She nods grimly. "Right, they've already tried that. His transport was also missing from campus. This morning, we located it outside of San Francisco. It had been abandoned."

That hits me. *Abandoned?* He would never do that . . . unless it was serious.

"What about his neural implant?" I say, tapping the stub on the base of my neck. It's always with me, almost like another brain. "Can't you use that to locate him?"

She sets her lips. "We tried tracking his neural implant, of course. But it appears to have malfunctioned . . . or maybe it was deactivated."

"Deactivated?" I say, but it comes out as a gasp.

That shocks me. But how . . .

Not to mention, that's highly illegal. Enrollment in the Sympathetic Program is not optional. We signed hefty agreements after we got paired together. You can't just back out. Plus, that's his link to me. Why would he want to sever our only connection?

"Listen, this all has to be a big misunderstanding," I say, racking my brain for any useful information that could help find him. "I'm sure he'll come back online soon—"

"Private Skye, you don't understand," she cuts in. "His neural implant isn't just offline . . . it's *dead*. First, the signal went dark just after midnight. We accessed the archives and it appears that he turned his GPS off . . . intentionally. And now, it's completely dead."

"Midnight . . . right after the assault?" I manage to choke out, staring at her face on the screen in shock. I realize how bad that sounds. "Does that mean . . . what I think it means?"

"Afraid so. Right now, the working theory is that he did it on purpose . . . that it was an intentional act to flee from the scene of a crime. They're treating him as a fugitive."

"Like a deserter?"

"Yes, the civilian version of that."

The idea hits me harder than a thousand blaster shots. *Deserter.* How could he abandon me like that? After I trusted him and told him everything? I'm sure he had a good reason for *beating the stars* out of Jude. He's not the only one who's wanted to punch that jerk in the face. I remember my last day of school. But still, I can't help the black emotions engulfing me.

Drae isn't just running away from Jude and school . . . he's running away from me, too. We were supposed to be on this adventure together—him at college, and me at basic training. Paired together. For the rest of our lives. No matter what happened. But now, I'm suddenly all alone.

I wrap my arms around my chest, trying to contain the sense of intense loneliness erupting in my chest and threatening to crush me into oblivion. It doesn't work, not really. The craziest part is that only a few short weeks ago, something like this would've been my greatest wish in the whole blasted universe. And now strangely, it feels like the worst thing that could happen.

The drill sergeant sets her lips. "I'm sorry to tell you this . . . but it appears he's not the only student who disappeared last night. Someone else has been reported missing."

My stomach drops. "Another student . . . is missing?"

"That's correct—and there's more. She also attended your high school. So, we think it's all connected. Maybe he kidnapped her . . . or she could be aiding and abetting him . . ."

"Wait, who is it?" I gasp. My heart pounds harder.

"*Rhodiola Raven.*"

"Wait, Rho's missing, too?" My voice strains over those words. I can't contain the distress that rockets through me as I struggle to process it. Drae and Rho. Both missing. Together.

What does that mean?

"How well did you know her?" the drill sergeant asks, jerking me out of my shock. Her eyes bore into me, studying my reaction. It takes me a long moment to find my voice.

"Rho is my best friend," I say, feeling a wave of sorrow wash through me at the thought. "Or rather, she *was* my best friend. But I haven't talked to her since I shipped out to Basic. We're only allowed to communicate with our immediate family and our Sympathetic."

"Very interesting," the drill sergeant says, tapping at her tablet. "And yes, our postal system is underfunded and already stretched thin. Unfortunately, we have to prioritize resources. So then, you were close to both of them? I'll alert the investigators back Earthside right away."

"Wait, what does it mean? That they're both missing?"

"Well, it's too early to say for sure," she says, looking more worn than usual.

But I can tell she's hedging and not telling me everything.

"Do you think . . . they ran away together?" I manage, hating the sound of my voice. Jealousy isn't going to help anything. But I can't stop it from flaring red hot in my heart. "Please . . . listen . . . you have to tell me . . . if there's something you know . . . I'm begging you."

My voice sounds thin and strained, tinged with anger. From my exchanges with Drae, I know that they'd been spending a ton of time together. First, they made a deal to be study partners, so he wouldn't flunk out and she could get info about me, but then as actual friends.

Another dark thought blasts through me. *But what if their feelings became something more? It's too horrible.* I try to stop the thoughts from spiraling. But memories assault me. The two of them bent over steaming pizza together. Flirtatious glances. Sneaking touches.

Even walking back to their dorms and kissing . . .

No, Rho would never betray me like that.

But emotions are fickle creatures that defy understanding, and despite our fierce loyalties and history, they often rebel and disobey us. I know that better than anyone. Plus, Rho is smart and beautiful and privileged and experienced with . . . well . . . romance stuff. And there's one bigger thing—she's not millions of kilometers away in the asteroid belt. She's right there.

I can't hide my dismay. It stretches my face, pulling it down like a lead weight, as tears cascade down my cheeks in twin rivers this time. I can't stop the outpouring of emotion.

The drill sergeant gives me a sympathetic look. "That was our first hypothesis. Some kind of romantic entanglement. Maybe Mr. Luther got jealous? These things happen sometimes. Especially with their shared history. But I assure you, we're investigating every possible angle."

"Please, you've got to find them," I say, trying to push my own jealousy away. Besides, it's not like Drae was my actual boyfriend . . . *ugh, I hate the word* . . . or anything like that. "Besides Ma and my sister Bea, they're the only two friends I've got in this whole universe."

That's when the bottom drops out.

My ears ring, drowning out the drill sergeant's voice.

Black stars dance in my vision, threatening to consume me like a supermassive black hole. Everything gets sucked in. Nothing can escape that gravitational pull. A thousand scenarios rush through my head, each more terrible than the last. Are they injured? In trouble? Fugitives?

Or worse . . . dead. That last thought makes me almost lose it completely. Drae. Rho. Both missing. Together. How could this be happening?

CHAPTER 40

DRAE

"Did you say . . . *alien?*"

I stare at Trebond. We're still sitting in her office, but it feels like all the air has been sucked out of the room. "That's right. This weapon is alien in origin," she confirms. "These chemical signatures. This tech. We've simply never encountered anything like it before."

I struggle to keep up, but it feels overwhelming. A million questions tumble through my head, one right after the other. Rho looks equally shocked. Her hair and eyes turn eerily white.

"But why attack a school bus?" I ask, exchanging a glance with Rho.

"Wait, he's right," she chimes in. "Sure, it's a terrible tragedy, but it's so small scale. If these aliens have such advanced tech, then why not just launch a full-on attack?"

"Well, we can't be sure," Trebond cautions. "Or even if they think like we do. They're *aliens* for a reason. We know very little about them. But my analysts have one solid theory."

"What's that?" I ask, still struggling to process everything.

"Remember it's only a working theory at this point," Trebond says in a solemn voice. It reminds me of her lectures about books, only far more serious. "We believe that they've been studying and analyzing us. They've concluded that we possess violent tendencies, so it wouldn't take much for them to trigger another great war. In short, they want us to destroy ourselves."

"But why would they do that?" I say, feeling a stab of fear.

Trebond stands up and pulls a slim paperback from her shelf. It's a real book with dog-eared pages and a worn-down spine. She flips through the weathered pages to a passage. Her handwritten notes pepper the prose.

"When you enlist in Space Force, they give all new recruits this book of philosophy. Sun Tzu's *The Art of War*. One quote jumped into my head when I got this analysis back. He writes, *The supreme art of war is to subdue the enemy without fighting.*"

I try to make sense of the enigmatic philosophy. "But how do you win without fighting? It doesn't make sense. It's some kind of riddle. Like something from *The Hobbit.*"

"Well, it's philosophy, which has a lot in common with riddles," Trebond says. "It's simple really. They're carrying out a few small-scale attacks so that we go to war and destroy ourselves. Then they can sweep in and take our planet without much resistance."

"That's genius," Rho says. "Why waste their time and energy attacking us, when we can do it for them? *Mutually assured destruction.* Professor, isn't that what it's called?"

"So, you're saying . . . they planned the Golden Gate Attack," I say, putting all the pieces together. "And planted evidence that implicated the Siberian Fed, hoping that the terrorist attack back Earthside would trigger another war between the Proxies?"

"Yup, but it's not just the GGA," Xena jumps in. "Our intel indicates that they're also the real actor behind the recent flyover of Ceres Base. The Siberian Fed denies it—"

"Yeah, but they always deny responsibility," I say on reflex. "The newsfeeds say they're lying. That they were the ones behind the attack."

Xena frowns. "That is what they're saying. But . . . what if they aren't lying this time? What if the aliens did it? And made it *look* like it was the Siberian Fed?"

Her words hit me hard. I remember how worried I was about Kari after the flyover. How it increased the Proxy tensions and threat level, pushing us closer to the brink of interstellar war. And worse, Earth rearmament. The newsfeeds chatter about it almost nonstop now.

"Asteroid fires," Rho curses with wide eyes. "Sorry, Professor . . . but that would mean their plan is working. We took the bait, didn't we? We're blaming them for both attacks."

"She's right," I say, thinking through everything. The riddle unravels in my mind. "You said the secretary-general plans to declare war on the Siberian Fed in the next few days?"

"That's correct," Trebond says. "The plans are already in motion. They're just working on the best time to make the official announcement. We don't have much time left."

"They're coming for us," Xena says. "They're just waiting and watching for their opening, once we destroy ourselves and our Earthside defenses are obliterated."

"But how do you know they're destructive?" Rho asks. "Aren't we jumping to conclusions here? You said so yourself . . . we don't know much about these aliens."

Trebond flinches at the question. "Well, based on their actions so far . . . blowing up a school bus of kids . . . it's heartless and calculating. Their intentions can't be good."

Nobody argues that point. I can't think of a more heinous act.

"But what can we do?" I say, gesturing to the projection and feeling completely inadequate in the face of this threat. "How can we stop a war if it's already happening?"

My words hang in the air.

Everyone falls silent. The only sound is the gentle *hiss* of the air vents.

"Well, it's a long shot," Trebond says, loading the forensic analysis onto a portable drive. It's tiny, unmarked, and fits easily into the palm of her hand. "We have to deliver this evidence to your Sympathetic, so she can disseminate it to those she trusts inside Space Force."

She holds out the digital package to me.

I hesitate, feeling afraid. But then I force myself to take it.

"So, what's the plan?" I ask, accepting the package. It's sleek and cold in my palm. The device weighs practically nothing, but I feel the heaviness of what it contains. "Kari is stationed way out in the asteroid belt. Any messages we send to her would be heavily monitored."

"That's right," Trebond confirms. "We can't use the usual communication methods. They'd be intercepted—and worse, could lead them back to us. Many in power at Space Force have been clamoring for Earth rearmament for years. That makes them blind to the truth."

"Exactly," Rho says, chewing her lower lip. "Power and profit are powerful motives. But why not just go public with the evidence? Send the evidence to the official newsfeeds?"

"Answer this . . . who controls the newsfeeds?" Xena says with a shrug. "Who controls all the media? The social networks?"

"The federation government," I reply without thinking. "There's no free speech."

Trebond nods. "Exactly, they won't report on it. They'll think it's a hoax. Worse, they'll discredit and bury it. Then even if it is made public, nobody will believe it. That's called confirmation bias . . . when you reject proven facts that don't conform to your beliefs."

"But what if we leak it out another way?" Rho says, trying to solve the problem like always. "An underground broadcast? Printed leaflets like back in the old days . . ."

"Same problem. They'll just deny it," Trebond says. "Call it *fake news*. You must understand, they want another war to happen. The secretary-general thinks it will increase his power, consequences be damned. History repeats itself, especially when we forget the past."

I realize that sounds like what happened leading up to the Great War. Everything I've learned today swirls through my head, each detail more worrying than the last. My whole worldview struggles to shift and realign itself, like a snow globe shaken around. The flakes swirl down, landing in a whole new formation and reshaping the landscape.

"Look, we've already made other attempts to get this intel out," Trebond says. "Last week, the Raiders tried to deliver the package to Hikari directly—"

"Wait . . . you're working with the Raiders?" Rho says with a frown.

"They're not our enemies?" I add in alarm. "They're helping us?"

"So much you don't know," Xena said. "The Raiders are allied with the Resistance. They're pacifists who have seen war firsthand. We both want the same thing . . ."

"To disarm the stars?" I ask, remembering the slogan.

Trebond nods. "They made a valiant attempt to deliver the package, but the Ceres Base defenses proved too robust and held them off. They couldn't get close enough to sneak the intel onto the base. We had to abort the mission. We couldn't risk our friends getting hurt—"

Just then, there's a rap on the door.

"Come in, don't be shy," Trebond calls out.

The door cracks open to reveal—

Trevor.

Another wave of shock cascades through me. He's the kid who I used to bully back in high school. What in the blazes is he doing here? He's part of the Resistance, too? He shoots me a wary look. Suddenly, I feel a stab of guilt for teasing him over his contraband comics.

But he quickly turns to the professor. "Old Lady, it's almost time," he says in an urgent voice. "The Cap sent me to fetch you. He doesn't want to miss our launch window."

"Launch window?" both Rho and I say in unison.

Trevor smirks. "Cap says, if these yellow-bellied recruits are late, then he'll have to blast off without them. He said . . . *the stars-forsaken' window is shorter than a blaster shot.*"

"Wait, what does he mean?" I ask, glancing nervously at Rho.

"Without them . . . as in . . . me and Drae?" Rho chimes in.

"You heard the kiddo," Xena says, rising to her feet. "You're hitching a ride to the stars. On a Raider ship, no less. They've agreed—*reluctantly*—to smuggle you off Earthside."

"Wait, I'm sorry," I say, still trying to wrap my head around this new twist. "Did you just say . . . we're going to space? On a Raider ship? Like . . . right now? That's crazy."

"Exactly." Rho nods. "Don't you have operatives trained for that?"

"Well, it's your choice, of course." Trebond regards us both with a grim expression. "We believe in that around here. But Hikari trusts you—and that makes you our best chance."

She locks her gaze on us and holds it for a long second. A heavy moment of silence passes, then she asks, "Do you understand what's at stake here? Both of you?"

The implications race through my head, each more frightening than the last. "But . . . why us?" I manage to choke out. "We're just two college kids. Why can't the Raiders deliver it?"

"We already tried that, remember?" Trebond says. "Plus, Kari will treat them as enemies. In basic training, they brainwash you and teach you that the Raiders are savages and cannibals . . ." She trails off, making it seem like there's another other reason. But what is it?

What isn't she saying?

"Okay, but what about Xena?" Rho says. "Kari trusts you."

"Wish I were up to the task," Xena says in her raspy voice. "But my ole ticker can't handle the strain of warp travel. Too many fed-issued smokes did a number on my heart."

"Professor, I hate to interrupt," Trevor says, shooting the professor an impatient look. "But time is tickin' away. Cap said . . . with or without them. And not in a friendly way."

I'd almost forgotten the kid was still there.

Trebond snaps to attention and rises from her desk, heading for the door.

"He's right—we're on a tight schedule. They have to slip through federation airspace at the exact moment our agent on the inside has programmed a clear launch window, so it'll look like a blip on the sensors. Just a minor gravity pulse. Trust me, we sacrificed a lot to set this up."

I exchange a look with Rho. I'm holding the digital package in my sweaty hands.

"So what's your decision?" Trebond finishes, turning back toward us.

I glance at Trevor and study his young, freckled face and scrawny body, probably from undernourishment due to ration scarcity. I haven't always made the right choices, but this is my chance to prove that I can do better. That I'm not like Jude. That I'm not a bully and a coward.

Plus one thought gives me strength and makes me take action—

Kari's in danger.

It really is that simple. What else is left to think about? All my other worries drain away. If I love Kari—*if I really and truly love her*—then I don't have a choice. I have to do this.

I take a deep breath and tighten my grip on the package.

"Fine, let's do this," I say, and I mean it.

I glance at Rho for her answer, but she beats me to it.

"Me too," she says without any hesitation. "Count me in for this whole *save the universe . . . blah, blah, blah . . . aliens are invading . . . and the fate of humanity rests on our narrow shoulders* situation. It's kind of like my favorite books. Especially the pirate stuff. "

Her hair sprouts out deep crimson to match her simmering eyes—*bravery.*

"Welcome to the Resistance," Xena says. "For real this time." She breaks into a toothless grin and pats us both on the backs, harder than necessary. I wince and grin at the same time.

"I'm pleased to say, you've made the right choice," Trebond adds with a warm smile. "And you've made your old professor proud."

With that settled, she thrusts open the door and marches through it, all business now.

"Now, let's get you two suited up," she adds, waving for us to follow her into the bustling Resistance headquarters. "Everything hinges on this—we don't have any time to waste."

"Time to blast off to the stars," Rho says with a little skip, following Trebond through the door. Her hair gushes out bright pink. *Infectious* pink. *Excited* pink. *Space* pink.

"To the stars," I repeat as I follow them from the office. But it sounds less enthusiastic coming out of my mouth. My feet feel leaden, while my head swims with worry and doubts.

The truth is—I'm scared out of my mind.

Kari, I say and keep repeating in my head like a mantra. She's the reason I'm doing this. Just thinking of her gives me strength. Maybe that's the answer. Maybe she's my courage.

"Kari, I'm coming for you," I whisper as the office door slams shut behind me with finality, and I step into my future. I know with certainty—there's no going back now.

CHAPTER 41

KARI

I remember that old nightmare I used to have before I shipped out, where the black hole sucks me in and crushes me into nothing. That's how I feel as I stagger back to my barracks after learning about Drae and Rho both going MIA.

Thankfully, it's empty. Everyone else must be out to celebrate graduating. All those grueling weeks of PT and classes under the drill sergeant's careful watch paid off. Everyone from my platoon made it through Basic. The base has one bar on the top level with glorious views of the stars, but it's only for official guardians. It's tradition to go after you pass. Plus, it's the last night before you get your MOS orders. Technically, that makes it your last night of semi-freedom. But celebrating is the last thing on my mind right now.

My chest is imploding. My head is imploding. My whole body is imploding.

I can't think straight with all this extreme pressure crushing my insides. The drill sergeant's words run through my head over and over again. I can't make sense of them.

How could Drae and Rho both go missing?

I fling myself on my rack, disrupting the crisp covers (made with perfect corners, just as Luna taught me). More questions stampede through my head. Why did Drae attack Jude? Aside from the obvious fact that he's a total jerkface? I can't count the number of times I've wanted to punch Jude in the face myself.

He probably deserved it, I think . . . but then I remember the pictures of his bruised and broken face. Drae didn't just punch him—he pulverized him. From the looks of it, Jude is lucky that he's alive and not in a coma. Or worse . . . dead.

That doesn't look good.

Plus, there's more. If he's innocent, then why did Drae flee the scene? And disconnect his neural implant? That makes him look guilty . . . like a fugitive. There's also a witness . . . Loki. No matter what really happened, that creep will lie and have Jude's back. That means that even if he's innocent, Drae is still in serious trouble. I shudder at the implications.

And worse, how is Rho involved in everything? Why did they run away . . . together? Is she just trying to help Drae escape and prove his innocence? Or is it . . . something else?

Romantic entanglement.

I can't stop the words from blasting through my head. The drill sergeant mentioned it, and now I can't think of anything else. A sharp stab of jealousy pierces my heart. *No way,* I tell myself. *Rho would never betray me like that.* She's my best friend in this whole blasted galaxy.

But then I remember her colorful dating history. How she dives into relationships headfirst without considering the consequences. How many times she's fallen in love with *THE ONE,* all caps, only to come to me sobbing about her breakup the next day. She's the smartest person I know. Heck, one of the smartest people in the whole federation. But when it comes to crushes and dating and her love life, she's impulsive and reckless. She always has been.

From our exchanges, I know they'd been spending a ton of time together. She was helping him study in exchange for secret updates about me, which is why I couldn't inform the drill sergeant about that. It could get them both in trouble. At first, it was a simple arrangement for their mutual interest, but Drae admitted that it had evolved into something more . . . something deeper . . . something like friendship . . . but did it become something deeper than that?

The way the exchanges work, I experience his emotions and thoughts, even the ones he doesn't voice. His feelings for Rho had turned warm and caring. Plus, she was right there in front of him. Meanwhile, I'm millions of kilometers away from Earth.

I can't stop the terrible thought—

What if . . . she and Drae . . . started to fall in . . .

I prevent myself from going down that black hole, banishing the thought. I hate dealing with feelings, especially ones like these, which have always confounded and confused me. Hence, my total lack of any love life.

I slip back into soldier mode, fighting back against the swirl of emotions storming in my brain, and worse, my heart. No matter what they did, I remind myself, the most important thing is finding them. I can deal with the rest of it later—whatever the rest turns out to be.

I try to refocus on that piece of the puzzle.

Where did they go?

Even with a transport, they can't have gotten far due to the travel bans. There are checkpoints everywhere. So, why haven't the authorities found them yet?

In the onslaught of unanswerable questions, I feel like I'm being crushed into nothingness. My first instinct catches me by surprise—*I need to talk to Drae about all of this.* It comes to me without thinking, as natural as breathing. He could help me figure this out . . .

But then I stop, knowing that's impossible.

Before this moment, I never realized how much I depended on our communications. Now that he's gone, it feels like that black hole is swallowing me and slowly crushing me to death.

I can't believe it . . . *I actually miss Draeden Rache.* But it's more than that. This doesn't feel like normal missing. This feels like *heartbreak.* Like my heart is shattering into a million tiny pieces. They rattle around in my chest like shards of glass, causing a raw, burning sensation.

Does that mean . . . I *really* do love him?

I can't stop the thought. The moment it blasts through my head, I realize it's true. I can't deny it anymore. But then, another terrible revelation stabs me in the heart—

But Drae deserted me.

Just like my dad.

Everyone I love leaves me. I can't believe I was that stupid. To let him in. To trust him. To fall for him. I feel a white-hot burst of rage. And the most twisted part—I both hate and miss him at the same time. Yeah, that's gotta be some kind of major psychological malfunction.

Again, I circle back to the central mystery. Why can't they find them? All of a sudden, a crazy idea occurs to me—one that I know is impossible. I sit up in bed, stunned by it.

"What if they're not on Earth anymore?" I whisper to the empty barracks.

But I dismiss it right away. Space Force is the only ticket off Earthside. And the only way to get on one of their spaceships is to enlist. I think back to what the drill sergeant said.

I cling to it like a lifeline.

They'll find them soon.

But another long day passes, and they still haven't located them. Even the drill sergeant admits that it's highly unusual when I ask her for an update first thing in the morning—and she excuses me from training today. Also highly unusual. Even though we graduated from Basic, that doesn't mean we can slack off. Our MOS orders are coming any day now. We have to stay ready.

Alone in the barracks, I sink into a black hole of despair, gently then suddenly. Another day passes like that without any news on their whereabouts. Even getting out of bed starts to feel impossible. How did I survive basic training, and now I can't even get up?

"Skye, get your stars-lovin' ass out of bed," Nadia finally orders on the second day. She's already showered and in the middle of pulling on her uniform. She sounds worried.

I haven't told anyone in my unit what happened with my Sympathetic, partially because we're not supposed to talk about the program. But mostly, I haven't been able to voice it.

For one reason . . .

That would make it . . . *real.*

"What's the point?" I grunt from my rack and flip over. I bury my head under the pillow.

"You're the one who enlisted," Nadia says in exasperation. "You also made it all the way through Basic *and* graduated. And now you want to get your stupid ass tossed back Earthside?"

"Blast off and leave me alone," I mumble, burying my head deeper into my pillow. That horrible sucking feeling pulls at my chest. "News flash—basic training is over. That means you're relieved of your battle buddy duties. My *stupid ass* isn't your problem anymore."

"Fine, message received loud and clear," she mutters as she tugs on her boots and laces them up. "But don't complain to me when the drill sergeant is your next wake-up call."

That threat is supposed to cajole me out of bed, but it doesn't work.

Just one short week ago, it would have been different. I'd have shot out of my bed like a comet, but now I just don't care. Whatever motivation I had, whatever drove me to wake every day and get on my feet and power through training, has completely deserted me.

From the door, Nadia exchanges a worried look with Anton. They mouth to each other, but I can make out their sibling exchange. I've spent enough time around them.

"Stars, what's wrong with her?" Nadia whispers. "Shouldn't graduating make her happy?"

Anton shakes his head and mouths back—

Front lines.

Oh, that's right. They think I'm freaking out because I requested combat duty. We can request different specialties, but they make the final decision. This will dictate the nature of our service from this moment forward. Everyone has been nervously anticipating our assignments.

"*I wish it were that simple . . .*" I mutter into my pillow.

But my voice is muffled, and they can't hear me.

At least then I'd have something real to focus on. I wouldn't feel so helpless and lost. I'd rather be doing something, anything to get out of my head, even if it's reckless and dangerous—so I can escape the maddening question that loops through it nonstop with each breath.

Rho . . . Drae . . . where are you?

"Privates, it's your lucky day."

The drill sergeant charges into our barracks. Hushed whispers ripple through our ranks, for one reason. She's clutching a stack of crisp envelopes. Sealed. Names printed on the exterior.

"MOS orders," Nadia whispers to me, catching my eye. "Shit just got real."

For this, I don't have a choice. I struggle out of bed at long last. I'm badly in need of a shower and a change of clothes, but again, I don't care. I force myself to line up in alphabetical order as instructed. Thankfully, we've gotten good at this little exercise.

The drill sergeant hands out the envelopes. I shuffle forward, feeling a prick of interest amidst the crushing despair. But it's faint and fleeting. Finally, I reach the front of the line.

She hands me the envelope.

"Good luck, soldier," the drill sergeant says. "You earned this."

Private Hikari Skye is printed on the exterior. Despite the black hole sucking at the center of my chest cavity, I feel a small thrill. Though duller than usual, it's there. My heart thumps a little bit faster, reminding me that I'm still alive. And this is really happening.

This is it, I think as I open the seal and remove the orders.

Front lines.

I got my request. That means combat duty. I scan the orders quickly—but then I flinch back. I deploy in forty-eight hours. My stomach drops. That's only two short days.

It doesn't say where I'm going to be deployed, only that it's an interstellar assignment. The locations of our bases are kept closely guarded secrets to protect them. All I know is that it's likely many warp factors away from our solar system. That means farther away from . . .

Drae and Rho.

I stare at the letter, unable to accept it. I should feel elated. This is what I've wanted my whole life since my father deserted, what I've trained so hard for these last many weeks, what I've dreamed about since I was a little kid and able to dream about anything. Or maybe I should be scared out of my mind to deploy to the front lines when we're on the brink of another war.

Those would all be perfectly normal reactions.

But I only feel numb.

A deep numbness that terrifies me.

All around me, I hear gasps and soft cheers. I rise out of my depressive haze for a moment and glance at Nadia. She holds up her MOS orders, and I see the assignment.

"Front lines," she says softly, all bravado gone from her voice. It's one thing to think about combat duty, another to live it.

I nod slowly. "Same. Front lines."

Percy gives us a grim nod. "Engineering Corps," he says with a shrug. "Only downside is . . . a lot more school and training."

"Field medic," Genesis says in an excited voice. But then she gives me and Nadia a worried look. "Don't make me patch you up. You'd both better stay safe out there."

"Special forces," Luna says with a sheepish smile. "Actually, I didn't choose it. They recruited me." Of course they did. Those are the most elite of the elite guardians. They execute special missions. Top secret assignments. Very few soldiers get tapped for this duty. It also carries a ton of extra training. Like Basic times a hundred. But I know Luna will do fine.

That she's meant for this. And she deserves it. She's the best of us.

That leaves Anton. He grins a huge, lopsided smile.

"Postal Service," he says, holding up his MOS orders. "I'll serve under Postmaster Haven at Ceres Base. Since I don't have to deploy anywhere, unlike you crazy people, I start tomorrow. Never thought I could fit in up here, but turns out I found the perfect assignment."

"Oh, you're such a nerd," Nadia says with a roll of her eyes. "Postal Service? Really? Guess it does suit you." But underneath the jab, it's clear how much she loves him.

"That's actually pretty cool," I say, giving his shoulder a squeeze.

Anton blushes. "You know, the Postal Service is the backbone of Space Force. We have the most sophisticated mail system of all the feds. Without it, we couldn't communicate. We'd be like a snake with its head cut off, wriggling but unable to think and coordinate—"

"There he goes on another rant," Nadia cuts him off. "Front lines. Now, that's the backbone of Space Force. Blasting Proxies and Raiders. Not a bunch of boring postal officers sorting mail and packages."

Anton shakes his head. "Don't dismiss it. We're critical to Space Force Operations. And Ceres is the communications hub. Trust me, the Postal Service might save your life one day."

"Mail ships to the rescue?" Nadia says with a derisive snort.

"Well, they happen to be the smallest, fastest ships in the galaxy," Anton says proudly. "Fitted with our most advanced warp drives and defenses in case of Raider attacks . . ."

The twins are at it again, but it's needed. It deflates the tension in the barracks—and the realization that our little crew, who made it through training together, who came in as mostly strangers, even enemies at times, is about to disperse into the cosmos like so much space dust.

"Stars, I'm gonna miss you crazy kids," Luna says in her soft-spoken way.

It's what we're all feeling.

Tonight, the drill sergeant lets us stay up a little later than normal. The whole platoon is charged with our news. *Front lines.* It hasn't sunk in yet. I turn the word over in my mind.

Forwards. Backward. Around. But something nags at me.

It doesn't feel right that I'm deploying alone.

My Sympathetic was supposed to be with me for every step—every boot fall and warp jump—of this journey. That's the point of the Sympathetic Program. But now, I'm going to have to deploy without Drae listening to my worries, anxieties, thoughts, feelings, and doubts.

At lights out, I climb into my rack, ready for the black hole to crush me into sleep. The old nightmares are back now. I shut my eyes and wait for hopelessness to descend.

The next thing I remember is Harold pinging me.

I blink in the semidarkness of the barracks. It's still pre-dawn by our military clock. It's not time to get up yet. He must have made a mistake.

"Shut up," I mumble and try to get back to sleep.

But Harold pings me again.

My first thought is—*Drae and Rho.*

Did they find them? I bolt upright, now fully awake and charged with a pure shot of adrenaline. This time there's a message for me. Even Harold signals that it's urgent.

The order flashes in front of my eyes—

Report to the drill sergeant's office immediately.

CHAPTER 42

DRAE

Xena pulls up to the blacktop airstrip and cuts the engine.

The bus rumbles and then goes silent, but the headlights remain illuminated. They shine on the dilapidated buildings and air hangars. Burned-out husks left from the Great War. A rusty sign clings to one such crumbling façade. It's faded and barely legible, but I make out the words.

SAN FRANCISCO INTERNATIONAL

"Isn't this airport contaminated?" Rho says, pointing to the radiation signs posted everywhere. Her hair and eyes turn sharply blue, icy blue, worried blue. *Apprehension.*

Her emotions match my own hammering heart.

"Oh, is it really?" Xena says, catching our eyes in the rearview mirror.

"Everyone knows SFO was a prime target during the Great War," Rho says, repeating our Federation History teacher's boring lectures. "It got hit hard by the Proxies."

Xena grins. "Hear that on the newsfeeds? Or maybe at school?"

Rho flinches. "Another lie?"

"Shortly after the war, the Resistance seized control of SFO," Xena says, countering the narrative that's been drilled into our brains. "We knew it would be a critical asset. Then we planted fake news that it got hit hard with nukes . . . when actually the site tested clean."

"Really?" Rho says. "And nobody questioned it?"

"Worked perfectly," Xena replies with a smirk. "Kept the feds away. They wrote it off as another casualty of the war. They were too overwhelmed at the time to verify the story."

"And all this time," I say in wonder. "It's been a secret Resistance base."

"Occasionally, the feds send some low-level grunt to check the radiation levels." Xena nods to meters installed around the airport's perimeter. "We just make sure to juice the readings, so the site tests off the charts. Besides, they've got Vandenberg for Space Force. They don't need this old airport. It's just a worthless relic to them."

Rho grins. "But for the Resistance . . ."

"It's how we get off this stars-forsaken planet," Xena says, jamming the lever for the old bus door. It hisses in complaint, then folds open. "Now, let's get moving. We've got a tight launch window," Xena starts, but then we all hear something—

There's rustling in the back of the bus.

It's faint but audible.

"Watch out, get down!" Xena orders in a commanding voice.

She pulls out her twin blasters. They glint in the light. Her face goes hard as she scans the bus. Rho and I duck under our seats like we've been taught. We've been through enough drills at school.

"Stay down and don't get up," Xena hisses to us. "One more thing . . . if I start blasting . . . run for it and don't stop . . . not for nobody and nothing. Do you understand?"

We both nod nervously. Rho grabs my hand, pulling me lower under the seat. Cold sweat slicks her palms. They're trembling. Her hair and eyes turn ghostly white to match.

Xena charges past us, clearing the aisles with her blasters raised and fingers on the triggers. As she nears the back, there's movement in the shadows. It's subtle—a slight shifting of light and shadow—but unmistakable. It looks like it's coming from under a seat.

Somebody is hiding back there.

Rho clenches my hand tighter, cutting off all circulation. I taste bitter metal again. "Show yourself," Xena barks, aiming her twin blasters under the seat. "Or I'm gonna blast the livin' stars out of you! I'm counting to *five* . . . then I'm squeezing this trigger. Got that?"

There's silence. Xena starts counting.

"One . . . two . . . three . . . four . . ."

Suddenly, a soft voice echoes out—

"Please . . . hold your fire."

That's when a small figure wriggles out with her hands raised. The dim light catches her face. Wild, untamed curly hair. Warm almond-shaped eyes. Thin, willowy frame.

"Wait . . . Bea . . . is that you down there?" Xena says in surprise. She shakes her head, then lowers her blasters. "I almost blasted you! What in the blazes are you doing on my bus?"

Now, I identify her—it's Kari's little sister.

I recognize her from Kari's memories in our exchanges. She loves Bea more than anything—and would do anything to protect her. But what's she doing here?

Bea scowls back. "Seriously? Took you long enough to find me. I've been stowed away for over twenty-four hours. I super-duper gotta pee. I've been holding it . . . like *forever*. Oh asteroids, is that a Raider ship?"

She points to the window. I look over—and that's when I see it.

A Raider ship rolls out of one of the hangars and idles on the airstrip. So, that's our ride to the stars. It looks like an older model Space Force vessel that's been heavily modified.

"Anyway, what did I miss?" Bea goes on. "Let's see . . . I heard you talking on the bus . . . something about . . . blasting off to space with the Raiders? And saving the universe from . . . aliens? Do I have that right? Well, I'm definitely coming—"

"No, you're going straight home," Xena cuts her off. She gives her an incredulous look. "You conniving, sneaky little stowaway. Your ma must be worried sick—"

"No way," Bea shoots back. "You send me home . . . and I'll rat you out to everyone from here to Lompoc. Oh, I heard you talking all about your little secret mission."

We're busted. She's right—we were talking about it on the bus ride here.

Xena's mouth drops open in shock. "You wouldn't dare, you little scoundrel."

"Just try me," Bea says. Mischief flashes in her dark eyes. "Also, Kari trusts me. She'll listen to me. Seriously, you're gonna need my help for this plan to work."

"*Blazing stars* . . ." Xena curses under her breath.

But Bea flashes a stubborn look like Kari always gets when her mind is made up. I can't help but like her. She reminds me so much of her older sister. They both have that same fiery spirit that could power a hundred thousand suns. It only makes me miss Kari more.

"Hey, newsfeed alert," Bea says, undeterred. "I'm not letting you find my sister and save the whole world without me." She crosses her arms. "This is like some real-life Estrella Luna space junk. Either you're taking me with you, or I'm blowing your cover. It's your choice."

"Not on my watch," Xena says in exasperation. "Before your sister shipped out, I promised to look out for you. That's why you're staying Earthside, where it's safe."

"But . . . it's not safe here anymore," Bea says in a small voice. All the fight drains out of her. Her shoulders sag forward. "You said those bad aliens want us to destroy ourselves. And I've heard the newsfeeds talking about Earth rearmament. That means it's already working . . ."

This reminder sends fresh shivers up my spine. Bea is right. This new war won't leave Earth unscathed. Not with the secretary-general about to declare war, while calling to rearm Earth. We're all in danger now. Not to mention the imminent alien invasion coming next.

"Jeez, kid, you heard that part, too?" Xena says in a defeated voice. "Well, that doesn't change anything. The safest place for you is still back at home with your ma . . ."

"Please," Bea says. "Don't send me back there. I hate that stuffy 'hood. It's always freezing in that giant house. Ma's always worried about Kari and barely even notices me. Everybody there hates me. They call me *deserter spawn*. They say . . . they can *smell* me coming."

Her eyes tear up. She looks down at her shoes. "Plus, I miss Kari. And I know she's in danger up there. She needs our help. If you're going to save my sister, then I want in."

"Blast it, the Old Lady will kill me," Xena curses. She frowns, thinking it over. "But *he* has been asking to meet you. Not just asking . . . begging . . . he would be thrilled . . ."

Rho leans into my ear and whispers, "Uh, who wants to meet her?"

"No clue," I whisper back. "But sounds important."

"Fine. It's too big a risk to send you home," Xena says, glaring at Bea. "Even if I threaten to have the Raiders eat you alive if you tell on us, you can't keep your blasted mouth shut."

"Exactly," Bea says. "That's what Ma always says. I have *no filter*. I blurt out every little thing that pops into my head. No telling when I'd tell someone about your secret plan."

I've only spent a little bit of time around this kid, but I can tell it's true. My head is already throbbing from her nonstop, rapid-fire chatter. Whereas Kari is stoic and reserved, hoarding her words and then deploying them like heat-seeking missiles, Bea throws her words around like confetti, sprinkling everyone in sight with her colorful banter.

"Just don't make me regret this," Xena says as the ship powers up, going from a soft hum to a deafening roar. "And don't get yourself blasted up there, or your ma will murder me."

"Roger that," Bea says, popping off a military-style salute. Then she skips up the aisle toward us like she's going on a fun field trip. Her backpack bounces on her shoulders. I recognize the character printed on the back—it's Estrella Luna. She wields twin golden blasters.

I wouldn't be surprised if her bag is stuffed with comics, a perk of her new status. She rushes over to hug Rho, then comes up for air and alights her dark eyes on me with a shy smile.

"Pleased to meet you," Bea says, sticking out her hand to me. She looks me up and down, then grins a gap-toothed smile. "I'm Kari's sister . . . and you must be her Sympathetic."

"Uh, *was* her Sympathetic," I say, tapping the nub of my neural implant. Without Estrella, my head feels quieter, but also lonelier. "That kind of got put on hold when I went AWOL."

"Right, got it," Bea says. "Well, you're way cuter in real life. I dig how you grew your hair out. Is that a whole new look? Or just 'cause you're too lazy to get a proper haircut?"

Rho snorts out a laugh. "Kid, you're a trip."

Feeling self-conscious, I run my fingers over my head, feeling that it has indeed grown out. I hadn't even noticed since I've been so caught up with school and the secret society.

Before I can respond, Xena chimes in.

"Alright, enough loitering around my bus," she says, herding us through the door onto the tarmac. "We've got a tight launch window to make. It's time to hitch your ride."

I climb out after Rho and Bea. Xena pulls up the rear. Together, we make our way toward the Raider ship. The skull and crossbones symbol—their sigil—marks the hull. I try to keep my heart steady, but as we near the rumbling spaceship, it rebels and flutters wildly in my chest.

"Now, be extra nice to your new hosts," Xena goes on, catching our eye. She has to speak up to be heard over the roaring engines. "Mind your manners. You're their guests, remember?"

"What do you mean?" I ask, not liking the sound of that.

Xena frowns. "Well, let's just say . . . they don't exactly like your kind."

"Our kind?" Rho says. Her eyes ripple aquamarine.

Apprehension.

"Ringers," Xena says. "Friendly piece of advice. Don't provoke them. They're only doing this because the Old Lady insisted. And, well, they can be a tad bit . . . sensitive. Oh, and don't mention the word *deserter* around them. Unless it's the last thing you ever want to do."

"Of course," I say, swallowing against the bile that threatens to singe my throat. The closer we get, the larger the ship looms over us. It's probably crawling with Raiders.

"Truth be told," Xena goes on with a dark look, "they'd prefer to jettison you out the trash chute with the other garbage. If you catch my drift . . ."

With that final admonition, she marches ahead with Bea to greet the ship. But Rho hangs back and catches my eye. "The trash chute? Think it's true?" she says in a low voice.

"Uh, I'd prefer not to find out," I say with a shudder, imagining that they must have all sorts of colorful ways to dispose of their enemies over even the smallest slights.

As we approach the ship, the hull splits open with a sharp *hiss*. Steam gushes out of the engines, clouding the air. Then a plank unfurls like a mechanical tongue, touching down on the pockmarked runway and releasing another thick blast of smoke that obscures our view.

At this moment, standing on the precipice of boarding, my newfound courage deserts me like a soldier in the dark of the night. But that's not what keeps my shaky, rubbery legs moving forward. It's not why I push these fears to the back of my mind. It's not why I don't desert.

There's only one reason—

Kari.

Every beat of my heart chants her name.

A minute later, the smoke disperses to reveal a tall man striding down the gang-plank, dressed in faded fatigues adorned with bits of metal, colorful pins, feathers, and skull-and-crossbones patches. He has long, dark hair tied back into a loose pony-tail and almond-shaped eyes. I look him over, taking in the Raider's visage. He's taller than me by a good foot, and quite imposing with his athletic build and confident gait. Twin golden blasters hang on his narrow hips, holstered on a fancy, bejeweled belt, while a thin mustache and goatee frame his full lips.

He clambers the rest of the way down the gangplank, coming to a halt right in front of us. I feel panicky, but then he breaks into a warm smile. Even his eyes seem to be smiling at us.

"Captain Skye, at your service," he says in a deep voice.

His dark eyes fix on us. They're bright and filled with amusement. And I almost recognize them . . . but I can't quite seem to place them. But then he turns to greet Xena.

"You old bastard," Xena says, thumping his back. They guffaw and hug like old friends. "How're the star-seas treatin' ya? And your rangy crew?"

"Not half as good as your navy-proof rum," he thunders back. "But I miss the cold expanse. Blasting through the void at warp speed. Earthside doesn't feel like home anymore."

"Spoken like a true Raider," Xena says with a nod. "Well, I've got good news. The Old Lady threw in a crate of vintage rum for your trouble. A little extra to sweeten the deal."

This man's voice sounds so eerily familiar. Something about the tone and cadence. Not to mention . . . his name . . . Shock rockets through me as it clicks into place. I fumble for words.

"Captain Skye . . . wait, are you . . ." I trail off, unable to finish.

But I don't have to.

Bea steps forward, adjusting the straps on her backpack. She peers up at the dark stranger. He looks down at her—suddenly, his face twists with recognition, followed by astonishment.

Bea returns his gaze and speaks.

"Uh, are you . . . my dad?"

CHAPTER 43

KARI

Any updates on Drae and Rho?" I say as I burst into the drill sergeant's office. The words fly out of my mouth before I can stop them. I'm speaking out of turn, but I don't care.

I scan the room. Like everything else at Ceres Base, it's utilitarian in every sense of the word—basic desk, ergonomic chair, harsh overhead lighting. The desk itself is barren, except for a tablet and a battered paperback copy of *The Art of War*.

Dimly, I register these details, but my mind is focused on one thing—

My missing friends.

"Private Skye, you should sit down," the drill sergeant says, using her typical emotionless tone. Adrenaline thumps my heart, setting off a cascade of sensations. Metal blooms in my mouth. Blood drains from my extremities, making them feel numb and shaky.

"Why . . . what happened?" I stammer. "Are they okay? Did you locate them? Are they . . . in danger?"

"Private, it's not about your friends," she says, folding her arms in front of her.

My thoughts slam to a halt. I blink at her in confusion.

"Then . . . what's going on?"

Another long pause, before she finally speaks words that stab at my heart.

"It's your little sister."

Thump, thump, thump goes my heart.

More blood drains away. My ears ring and my sight blurs. Black stars dance in my vision. I feel like I might faint. I collapse into the hard plastic chair in front of her desk. My lips move—

"*Bea* . . ."

It comes out like a choked gasp.

The drill sergeant nods. "I'm sorry to inform you, but it appears she's also gone missing. The report came in last night when she didn't come home."

I grip the arms of the chair so hard that pain shoots through my hands. My head spins. I can't make sense of it. "Drae . . . Rho . . . and Bea? They're all . . . missing? How's that possible?"

"Correct. That seems to be the situation. According to the authorities, your mother reported her missing. That's our morning here. But we suspect she's been gone longer."

"Ma reported her missing?"

"Yup. The night before, she told your mother she was staying over at an old friend's house. Your mother wasn't worried until she didn't show up after school the next day. She spoke to the family of the friend. A kid named . . . Travis. And found out that your sister had lied."

"Let me guess," I say, trying to focus. "No sleepover."

"That's right. It turned out to be a total fabrication," the drill sergeant says with a frustrated shake of her head. "They also searched your old trailer. Sometimes kids get homesick after relocation. Your mother said she'd been having some trouble adjusting. But it was empty. The new occupants haven't moved in yet. However, we did find evidence she's been there . . ."

"Our older trailer?" I say in surprise. "But why?"

The drill sergeant nods. "More than once from the looks of it."

"What did you find?" I ask, my head spinning.

The drill sergeant scans her tablet. "Food wrappers. Comic books. Footprints. A sleeping bag. An old pair of binoculars. We investigated further and discovered she's also missed school on several occasions. She had a note from your ma. But it was forged, we now believe."

"Skipping school?" I say in disbelief. "But she loved school . . . she never did anything like that before . . . well . . . before I shipped out. I'm the one who always struggled."

Guilt stabs at me like the sharpest of knives. That's part of why I enlisted. My service bought her a full ride to college. This worries me—it's so unlike her.

"We scoured the area and found her transport," the drill sergeant replies. "Parked out back behind your old trailer, hidden in the bushes. But there was no sign of her . . ."

That hits me hard.

Then something worse occurs to me.

"Are the disappearances . . . connected?" I say, fearing the truth.

"At this point, we can't rule anything out," the drill sergeant admits. "It does seem like a stretch, given the distance and age disparities. But people don't go missing very often, not with the travel bans. And certainly not *three* at the same time . . . all from the same town."

"But then why haven't you located them?" I can't keep the anger out of my voice. "We're talking about three civilians here. One who's only eight years old. How could they evade the authorities and vanish like that?"

The drill sergeant shoots me a steely gaze. "Lower your voice, soldier. I invite you to exercise your training. Directing your anger at me won't improve your situation. I'm on your side, remember?"

But I don't want to take a deep breath—I want to *scream*.

"Fine, then put me on the next transport back Earthside," I demand in a heated voice. "I'll help them find Bea . . . and my friends. I know them better than anybody. I can locate them. Just give me a chance . . ."

"I'm sorry, but I can't allow that," the drill sergeant replies. "We're handling the situation. I'm certain that they'll find them soon. It's probably just a simple misunderstanding—"

But I cut her off, rocketing to my feet.

"Didn't you hear me? The next transport back Earthside. I want transfer orders."

I level my irate gaze on her. I've never been more certain of anything in my whole life. I have to go back home. I have to find my sister and my friends. I don't have a choice.

"Sit down, Private Skye," the drill sergeant barks in a cold voice. "And exercise some respect. I give the orders around here, not the other way around. Is that clear?"

She stands up from her desk and towers over me. She's a veteran of two deployment tours. She's a trained guardian. She's killed for our federation. Under her wilting gaze, all the fire snuffs out inside me. Still smoldering, I slump back down and mutter under my breath, "*Fine then, I quit.*"

"Dishonorable discharge?" she says with a bitter laugh. "You haven't completed the terms of your service agreement. Remember that contract that you signed? And the pledge you swore? You belong to us for the next eight years—that's two service tours. No exceptions."

Her words hit me hard.

Dishonorable discharge.

"Might I remind you, your family would lose everything," she goes on. "All their new privileges. The house. The transports. The stocked pantry. Your ma's retirement. Your sister's admittance to college. You'd be signing yourself up for a life in the Park and a job in a factory."

I swallow hard as that sinks in. My greatest fears, all packaged up and tied together with a neat little bow.

The drill sergeant goes on. "And what a shame that would be, since you just graduated from basic training. Oh, and with the highest test score of your whole platoon. Did you know that? We're counting on you to deploy on combat missions—even lead other guardians."

"Wait . . . the highest score?" I repeat, knowing that can't be right. "Don't you mean Luna or Nadia? Or even Percy? They were our strongest recruits. I was just trying not to wash out."

"They'll make excellent guardians. But you had the highest score. I administered your test myself. Like I said, it was one of the hardest I've ever seen. And I don't make mistakes."

I try to absorb this information, but it doesn't quite sink in yet. I've never thought of myself as the best at anything. Everyone else had something important to offer. I never felt special, or like I was excelling, more like failing. Mostly, I was trying not to flunk out.

"Right, I didn't know that," I say in a soft voice. "I thought I was on your shit list?"

"You were . . . but it appears that things have changed."

The drill sergeant slides her tablet toward me. On the screen are my new orders. I blink in surprise. They're granting me a promotion in rank to specialist. That's highly unusual.

"Listen, I wasn't supposed to tell you until the day of your deployment," she goes on, giving me a stern look. "But I figured you should know . . . before you make such a rash decision. We need guardians like you to lead our forces, especially in these difficult times."

I realize something right away. This is a bribe. So I don't desert. They want me to stay here and fight. It's no secret that enlistment numbers are lagging. They need dedicated guardians to serve and protect our us.

They need . . . *me*.

Two warring thoughts tug at me. On the one hand, my sister and friends are MIA, a situation too awful to comprehend. But on the other hand, my federation needs me.

She picks up on the shift in my mood. "Private, I know that I rode you hard in training," she admits with a sympathetic look. "But that's only because I knew the guardian you could become with proper training. I'm pleased to report that my instincts were correct. We need you at Space Force. I promise—we'll find your sister and friends. You have my word."

"But what if something . . . happens to them . . . while I'm deployed?" I say uncertainly, still hesitating. "My orders specify an interstellar posting. I won't even be in our system."

"I'll keep you briefed . . . *personally*," she says with a firm nod. "As you know, we have the best postal service in the galaxy. Also, we'll put you on the first transport back home if . . . well . . . if anything happens to them. But I highly doubt it will come to that," she adds quickly.

I bite my lower lip. "How can you be sure?"

"Because I used to live in the Park, remember?" she says, dropping her stoic facade for a moment. Real emotions leak over her face. "Look, your sister's probably hiding out there. There are lots of little nooks and crannies. Plenty of secret places to hide. Lompoc had a similar case last month." She flicks at her tablet, scans it. "A kid named Trevor Barnaby went missing—"

I look up sharply. "Trevor went missing?"

I remember him suddenly. He's the kid who Drae and his friends bullied back at school. I protected him from their antics, though his poor comics didn't fare as well.

"Just for two days," the drill sergeant goes on. "He turned up safe and sound, though in serious need of a bath. Turns out, he'd been hiding out in an old, abandoned shed by the bus routes. A driver named Xena Starsforth found him and brought him home. You know her?"

"Yeah, I know them both," I say with a shrug. "Xena was my school bus driver. She also lived next door to us. Also, that kid probably needed a bath *before* he went missing."

She cracks a smile. "True, I'm sure."

We share a smile, though my stomach still churns with unease. She's right though. The trailer park is full of great hiding spots. I know firsthand. I made use of them to avoid getting beaten up after we moved there. Plus, Bea knows the area as well as I do . . . better even.

That makes me relax slightly. She's probably just hiding out somewhere. She was having trouble adjusting and likely felt homesick. She's good at staying hidden, being so small and skinny. Just like Travis, I bet that she'll turn up when she gets hungry—or misses Ma.

I study the drill sergeant's face. She's the only person I trust here, aside from Postmaster Haven. "Drill Sergeant, do I have your word?" I ask, though worry makes my voice warble.

"My word is my bond," she says right away. No hesitation. "And you have both. I've got your back, Private. You'll be the first person I'll brief when they turn up safe and sound."

When, not *if*. . .

That's a good sign. She believes they'll find them.

I cast my gaze down at the tablet with the shiny new orders and rank. It's everything I've always dreamed of. If I quit now, there will be a black mark on my record for the rest of my life. And my family will suffer, too. I'll be just like my father. There's no coming back from that.

"I accept your offer," I say finally. "Please, just find them. Promise me."

"I promise," she says with a solemn look.

I prepare to stand up and leave, but she stops me.

"Private Skye, one more thing," she says. "We apologize for the unsuitability of your original Pairing. Our system and algorithms are good, but they're not perfect. Regardless of what happens, we plan to pair you with a new Sympathetic who can support your deployment."

Unsuitability of your original Pairing.

Those are words that would have been music to my ears just a few short weeks ago. Now, they're the last thing that I want to hear. They hit me like a blast to my heart, ripping it open.

"Thanks," I mutter before she dismisses me from her office.

I stagger back to my barracks in a haze.

I don't remember putting one foot in front of the other. I don't remember taking the elevator down to the lower level. I don't remember how it's dark and deserted because the rest of my platoon is at dinner in the mess hall. I don't remember throwing myself onto my rack and burying my head in the scratchy pillow.

But that's exactly what I do. A sob escapes my throat. Deep and primal. It doesn't sound like me at all. It sounds more animal than human. Right now, it feels like my whole world is imploding. Just like that black hole nightmare that has crept back into my dreams every single night lately. Graduation, MOS orders, deployment . . . nothing seems to matter anymore.

Not if Bea isn't safe.

She's the whole reason that I came here. How could she be missing? Along with Rho and Drae? I can't think straight. Too many opposing thoughts are setting off explosions in my head. It's a war zone in there. I barely think of one thing before another terrible thought blasts it out of the way. The questions loop through my head nonstop. But something nags at me . . .

I try to identify what it is . . .

Trevor went missing . . . but turned up safe a few days later . . . Xena found him . . . Bea was hiding out in our old trailer . . . with a pair of binoculars . . . That detail jumps out at me.

What was she watching . . . or maybe it's . . . who?

The only things outside our dingy windows were other trailers. Xena lived next door to us. She was also our only real friend there. But why would Bea want to watch her trailer?

I grasp at the thoughts flying around, fumbling for any clues. Trevor was the neighbor on Xena's other side, and he also went missing. But he turned up safe two days later, claiming that he'd been hiding out in a shed. But what if he was somewhere else that whole time?

What if the hiding in a shed story wasn't the true story? That thought rings true to me. So then . . . what if it's the same place where my sister went? And also Rho and Drae?

What's the connection between them?

All of a sudden, I remember another detail. Xena is the one who found Trevor. She's also a bus driver, so she does have more range and ability to travel than most people. But she's also completely harmless. She drives the school bus route, for stars' sake. And, well, Trevor's just a clueless kid with a penchant for contraband comics. Bea might know him a little, as they're closer in age. Even so, they weren't really friends. They weren't even in the same grade.

And also, how are Rho and Drae connected?

They were hundreds of kilometers away at Berkeley, for starters. Rho might be my best friend, but she never set foot inside the trailer park. Not once. Only waited for me on the outskirts in her transport. Drae's probably never been there. I can't help but roll my eyes at his privilege.

Bea. Trevor. Xena. Rho. Drae.

They're all so different, aside from being from Lompoc. That's when it hits me like a sun flare. There's only one thing they have in common—*one big thing*—and that's me.

I'm the connection.

It hits me all at once. I'm linked to each of them in different ways. But still, that doesn't explain why they'd all disappear at the same time, or where they could have gone. The travel bans make it nearly impossible to disappear off the grid anymore. None of this makes sense.

My mind struggles to piece everything together, but comes up . . .

Empty.

Before I can ruminate more and drive myself crazier, Anton rushes into the barracks. He looks ashen. That's the only way to describe it. Like all color has drained from his face.

"Anton . . . what happened?" I sit up in my rack, wiping away my tears. "What's wrong?"

"It's the secretary-general . . ."

That's all he gets out before I see the newsfeed alert flashing in my retinas. Somehow, I missed the pulsing red light while I was busy sobbing into my pillow. I snap to attention.

Harold, show me.

The alert ticks past my retinas.

Secretary-General Manual Icarus was assassinated at a press conference . . . bomb exploded the podium . . . Federation on lockdown . . . stay-at-home orders . . . second terrorist bombing Earthside since the Golden Gate Attack . . . war declared on the Siberian Federation . . .

That's accompanied by gory footage of the press conference explosion. Bodies are strewn everywhere. Severed limbs. Several reporters were maimed in the attack. Blood, smoke, shrapnel, rubble. I scan the disturbing images as the headlines tick past my eyes.

Bomb linked to the Golden Gate Attack . . . same explosive device . . . Siberian Federation held responsible for both terrorist attacks . . . emergency war cabinet convened . . .

Anton stares at me when I finally refocus. He looks terrified. We both know this means only one thing. He finds his voice first, though it comes out barely a whisper.

"The next great war . . . it's already starting."

CHAPTER 44

DRAE

That's my dad?" Bea repeats, turning to Xena with a shocked expression. She lowers her voice, but not nearly enough. "That Raider guy . . . that's him?"

"You got it, kiddo," Xena says and nods her head at the handsome Raider captain standing before us. Now that I study them, they do bear a striking similarity to each other. Bea scrunches up her forehead, scrutinizing his face.

"Guilty as charged," Captain Skye says as his shock subsides. He has a faint accent, almost folksy and colloquial. "Xena's brought me pictures of you over the years. Not that I'd need 'em to recognize my own flesh and blood. You're taller than I expected."

"And you're . . . shorter," Bea shoots back, provoking laughter from everyone.

"Well, you're definitely my kid. No question 'bout that," he says, exchanging a proud look with Xena. "You did warn me. This one has spunk. You weren't kidding."

Behind him, the pirated ship rumbles on the runway, getting ready for blastoff. I know that anything related to the Raiders is supposed to scare the living stars out of me.

But Captain Skye projects so much intelligence and warmth that it's hard to summon up any fear. Plus, he resembles Kari . . . and, well . . . I'm hopelessly in love with her . . .

"So, let me get this straight," Bea says, giving him a probing look. "My father is a Raider captain with a spaceship. Wow, I thought you were dead! That's what Ma always said."

"Well, sorry to disappoint you," he says. "But I'm very much alive and kicking, at least last time I checked." He bends down on one knee, lowering himself to her level.

"*Beatrice Anne Skye*," he says, using her full name. "After what happened, I wanted to smuggle a letter back to your ma. Tell her the truth about everything. 'Cause I never stopped loving that gorgeous woman—or you kiddos."

"Then why didn't you?" Bea asks accusingly. "I grew up thinking my father was dead. Kari was the lucky one. At least she got to meet you and send messages. But I was too young."

He looks crestfallen. "I'm so sorry, but it was too risky. I didn't want her to get arrested—*or worse*—for protecting a deserter and wanted fugitive." His voice chokes up. He's talking about the space prison camps, supposedly a fate worse than death. I've heard suicide rates run high there and for good reason. "But you're right. I never got to meet you," he goes on. "Not even as a baby. That was the worst part. You were born while I was deployed . . ."

Tears glisten in his eyes. This tough Raider captain now sounds like a big softie. Bea sticks out her hand. "Nice to meet you, Captain Skye."

He starts to shake but then stops.

"That's so formal," he says awkwardly. "How about . . ."

"Dad?" Bea ventures. Another awkward moment passes. But something else starts to happen. His expression shifts, almost like a warm spring breeze after a long, cold winter.

"Yeah, how about that?" he says with a somber nod. "Wanna test it out?"

Bea scrunches up her face. "Nice to meet you . . . *Captain Dad?*" she says, though it still sounds stilted.

She sticks her hand out again. But instead, he wraps her up in a fierce hug. "Nice to meet you, too," he says, patting her back. "*Captain Dad* has a nice ring to it, don't you think?"

Even I feel tears pricking my eyes. Rho reaches over to squeeze my shoulder. I notice Xena tugging a grimy handkerchief out of her back pocket.

But Xena clears her throat. "Look, I hate to interrupt this little family reunion, but you've got a launch window to make. You miss this chance, then our whole mission goes up in flames."

Captain Skye throws Xena a salute. "Do we have the package?"

Xena nods to me. "Yes, Draeden has it. Our intel confirms that Kari is still stationed on Ceres Base for another twenty-four hours . . ."

Captain Skye frowns. "Until she deploys? MOS orders? Interstellar?"

Xena nods. "Front lines."

"Stars *blast* her," he mutters. "Why couldn't she request a safer assignment?"

"'Cause I hate to inform you, but she's just like her old man," Xena says, clapping his shoulder. "Stubborn and foolhardy, but also selfless and brave. It's a powerful combo."

He smiles. "Now you're making me blush."

"Once she deploys, it'll become much harder to get this package to her. Plus, we know the secretary-general plans to declare war any day now. So, time is not on our side."

"Aye," he says. "Let's get this show on the road—*or rather*—to the stars."

We all clamber onto the gangplank. Steam gushes in billowy tendrils out of the engines, which are revving up for blastoff. Before we board, Xena throws us a wave.

"Stay safe up there," she calls out. "Remember, stick to the old commlink channels . . . it's safer that way. They're a bit glitchy, but the feds don't monitor those old radio signals."

As I turn away, I feel a surge of newfound respect for her courage—and all the bus drivers. Then, to the sound of Bea's happy banter with her father, we follow them into the ship. Rho reaches over and clasps my hand. In my other hand, I'm clutching the package.

"Hey, look," Rho says, nodding ahead. She points to Bea. She's still talking Captain Skye's ear off, peppering him with questions about the Raiders, but it's super cute.

"Nice seeing her happy like that," I say with a smile. "But does that kid ever shut up?"

"It is nice. And no, she doesn't." Rho laughs but then frowns. "Only . . ."

"Only . . . what?" I ask, catching her shift in mood. Her eyes ripple with navy hues, matching her iridescent hair, which cascades down like the deepest ocean waves.

"I've got a bad feeling—Kari won't be so easy."

"No, she won't," I agree, watching Bea with her father.

I remember our exchange when she confessed everything about her father. And it wasn't good. Bea was only a baby back then, so she doesn't remember any of it. All she ever knew was life without her dad in the trailer park. But Kari remembers. She remembers . . . *everything*.

On that ominous note, we board the ship. The interior deck resembles other vessels—my mom took me to Vandenberg as a kid to tour one—but it's been refurbished with colorful graffiti and tapestries of vibrant cloth. The Raider crew rushes around, preparing the ship for launch.

"Captain Skye, you're late!"

A slim girl with punky, short pink hair rushes over to him and Bea in the corridor. She's dressed in her uniform—old Space Force fatigues decorated with patches and feathers.

"And you're insubordinate!" he growls back. "Should've had the crew ditch you at port by that last nebula. Or better yet, dumped you down the trash chute into zero-g."

"Not a chance, Old Man," she replies. "You'd miss me too much."

They both break into ribald laughter. "And where are your manners?" she admonishes him, turning toward Bea. "Aren't you gonna introduce me to your new crew members?"

"First Officer Gunner, meet my daughter," he says. "Her name is Bea."

"Pleased to meet you," Bea says, then adds with a smirk, "Are you Raider scum?"

That makes everyone laugh.

Next, Captain Skye turns to us. "And these are our esteemed civilian guests. Careful, they're probably the sensitive types. Not exactly used to our kind . . ."

"Sensitive, huh?" Gunner says, giving us a steely look. "I'll see about that."

I find myself stepping in front of Rho protectively, though I know it's futile. They both have twin blasters strapped to their waists. And they're trained to use them.

But everyone bursts out laughing. She's just messing with us.

"Don't worry," Gunner says. "I'm vegan and a pacifist."

With that, Captain Skye leads us into the cabin, which is similarly adorned to the rest of the ship, and shows us to our sling chairs. We all buckle up and pull on the headsets.

"Gunner calculates that it's about twenty-four hours to Ceres Base, where we know Kari is stationed, thanks to the Resistance intel that the Old Lady provided," Captain Skye says, helping Bea into her harness. Once she's buckled, he gives us a salute. "Prepare for blastoff . . ."

He heads to the bridge with Gunner. I peer through the port window, where I can still make out Xena on the tarmac. She's standing in front of her bus, in the halo cast by the headlights. She salutes the ship as the engines rocket louder. The whole cabin vibrates from it.

I feel my sling chair respond, cushioning me against the friction. My heart jumps into my throat, making me grab Rho's hand. But she looks thrilled. Her nano implants turn excited pink. Bea bounces excitedly in her sling chair next to us. But I feel rattled down to my bones.

Then, with a great thrusting of rockets, we accelerate down the bumpy runway and abruptly lift off. Before I know it, we've left Earthside and the atmosphere far behind. Everything turns miniature, then transforms into breathtaking swirls of white and blue.

I hear Captain Skye's voice in my headset.

"Hold on, kids! Warp drives engaging."

The warp drives kick in, rocketing us away from our home planet. My sling chair and headrest respond, keeping me comfortable despite the insanely strong g-force. I hold on tight, as advised, and focus on the thought running through my head on repeat. It keeps me strong.

Kari, I'm coming for you.

Once it's safe to move about the cabin, Captain Skye comes to retrieve us. First Officer Gunner accompanies him, pushing a cart that floats on thin air, suspended by some kind of magnetic field. It's loaded down with a veritable feast. And sure enough, it's all vegan.

"Hey, hope you're hungry," Gunner says, pointing to a large salad on the tray. It glistens with dark, leafy greens and red seeds. "That's a kale and fresh pomegranate salad."

"How'd you get this?" I ask, poking the salad with my fork. I stare at it in awe. That's because I haven't seen fresh kale or pomegranates in . . . well . . . ever.

"Oh, we have greenhouses on the ship," Gunner says. "Since we're vegan, we have to work extra hard to raise sustainable crops for our diet. Keeps us healthy, too."

I study her visage. She's pretty, in a Raider-ish sort of way. Underneath the bedazzled fatigues and spiky, punked-out hair, she's got an elfin vibe accentuated by bright green eyes.

Off my impressed look, Gunner explains. "If kale blows your mind, wait 'til you check out our chocolate stash."

"Wait . . . you have *chocolate?*" Bea cuts in. Her face lights up with pure joy. "Like real, actual chocolate? Not that gross carob stuff that we have back home?"

"Sure do. Contraband farmers in the Bolivian Fed trade us for it. Our hydro farm is pretty fantastic. Like I said, that kale is home . . . err . . . space grown. I'll take you on a tour of the gardens later if you want. They're on the top level of the ship, one of our many modifications."

"I've never had chocolate," Bea says. "Well, not the real stuff."

"Oh, kiddo, you're in for a real treat then," Gunner says, patting her head.

"This salad is amazing," Rho says, eating it in big forkfuls. "Who knew a leaf could taste so good?"

"Fresh citrus is the key," Gunner says. "Florida Federation, if you can believe it."

"Those religious zealots?" Rho asks in surprise. Everyone knows Florida became isolationist and fanatical in the wake of the Great War. They don't even have a military.

"Yeah, but they're great farmers," Gunner says. "Garden of Eden, or something. It's pretty utopian there if you can ignore all the Jesus talk. That does get kind of old."

"Ha, really?" Rho says. "You know so much," she gushes, as her hair and eyes flush bright pink. "And you've traveled, like everywhere. Asteroid fires, I've never been out of California."

That makes Gunner blush. Her cheeks turn bright pink.

Is it my imagination—or is Gunner crushing on Rho?

She hasn't taken her eyes off Rho since we first boarded, and from Rho's coy reactions and flirtatious banter, I suspect that the feeling might be mutual. They share a heated moment.

But then, Gunner looks away, flustered.

"Somebody's gotta help Cap steer this ship," she says before she hurries off to the bridge.

Eventually, after we eat, I doze off for a bit.

I wake up disoriented, forgetting where I am. I look over expecting to find Rho, but instead, my eyes land on—

Captain Skye.

Bea is cradled in his lap. She's fast asleep, snoring faintly.

"Where's Rho?" I ask in a sleepy voice. The cabin is empty, except for us.

"Gunner's giving her a tour of the bridge and the hydroponic greenhouses," he says with a knowing look. He hugs Bea a little tighter, smiling down at her.

"Mr. Skye . . . I mean . . . *Captain* Skye," I start, already tripping over my words.

"You can call me Akio," he says, saving me from myself.

"Draeden Rache," I reply. "But you can call me Drae."

"Yes, I know who you are," he says in a serious voice. "The Old Lady told me. But there's more. And, well, it's time you found out. I'm sick of secrets. They always cause more pain."

"Found out . . . *what?*" I ask, suddenly more alert. That sounds ominous.

"Better I tell you now . . . I knew your mother."

Shock ripples through me. "My mother?"

He nods solemnly. "That's why I came back here to have a little chat with you. We served in the same platoon. She was my commanding officer on my second deployment tour."

"Wait . . . does Trebond know?"

I can't keep the surprise out of my voice.

"Yes, the Old Lady knows," he says with a frown. "Xena knows, too. But we aren't sure about Kari . . . though likely it was a factor in your Pairing."

"That means my mother knew, too . . ." I trail off. "But she didn't say anything about it. Though she did seem pretty upset after the ceremony. But why would they do that?"

He shrugs helplessly. "Nobody knows how the SPT and algorithms work. Or what factors they weigh. But it can't be an accident, right? Their records would reveal my complex history with your mother. And it's a rather sordid tale, I'm afraid. How much do you know?"

I lower my head. I can't make eye contact. "Right . . . from my exchanges with Kari . . . I know you deserted. And what she thinks happened that night. You're right . . . it's not pretty."

He snorts. "Those stars-lovin' bastards sure cooked up a good story."

"So, it's not true then?" I study his reaction. "That you deserted?"

"Right, I'll put it this way. Was anything they told you about Raiders true?"

His words resonate with me.

"No, far from it," I'm forced to admit.

"Then you'll believe me when I tell you that I didn't desert?"

"Then what really happened up there?" I ask, remembering the story as Kari laid it out for me. That he deserted his sentry post, so the Raiders could sneak up and kill his platoon.

He gives me a sympathetic look. "Look, you seem like a real nice kid. Even for a Ringer. Are you sure you want to hear it? The truth can set you free, but it can also become a painful burden. This concerns your family, too."

"You mean my mother?" I say, feeling trepidation creep into my voice.

He nods sharply. "Choose wisely."

"No, I want to know the truth," I say, not caring if it hurts me. I have to know the truth. I hate that I've been lied to my whole life. "Please, tell me. Who really attacked your platoon?"

"Fine, it wasn't the Raiders," he says. "It was one of our own—our commander."

"Your commander?"

Captain Skye nods. A dark look passes over his face. He takes no pleasure in delivering this news. Silence hangs heavily, but then he continues.

"Her name was . . . *Captain Rache*."

My head spins, trying to make sense of this. I fumble for words.

"My mother?"

But in my heart, I already sense the veracity of his accusation. I picture her sitting on her recliner, numbing herself with federation whiskey, chalky pills, and newsfeeds. The pain that she carries—more than her physical scars—cuts deep. Apparently, deeper than I realized.

"That night at our encampment," he goes on. "I guess she just snapped. That's the only way I can describe it. One second, she was our normal commander, who graduated with top scores from Basic. And the next, she pulled out her blaster and turned on her own guardians."

"She . . . blasted you?"

He nods as tears prick his eyes.

"It was like she was hallucinating from fear gas, only there were no chemical weapons. She opened fire, picking us off one by one. She kept yelling—*Proxy scum, die!*"

"She thought you were the enemy? But why would she think that?"

He shakes his head. "I don't know if it was a fear gas flashback. They subject recruits to it in basic training. They force you into a gas chamber, pump it full of fear gas, then make you remove your masks and inhale." Off my shocked look, he plows forward. "Trust me, that stuff does a number on your head. But I guess she thought that Proxies had attacked our encampment when really we were her platoon. In her twisted mind, she thought she was saving us."

I listen in horror. It takes a long minute to find my voice. "Captain, I'm so sorry," I say, somehow feeling responsible for my mom's horrific actions. Even though it's not my fault.

He shakes his head. "Look, I don't blame your mom. I want to make that crystal clear. The pressures up there can drive anyone crazy. I tried to stop her rampage and disarm her, but she blasted me in the chest."

He pulls up his tunic, revealing a nasty scar that wraps all the way around his torso. The tissue is rippled, knotted, and raised. I flinch back, even more shocked.

"In the chaos of the massacre, I managed to slip away and save myself," he continues, tugging his shirt back down. "I was badly wounded and bleeding out. After a few minutes, I stumbled upon a secret Raider hideout nearby. They were planning to raid our supplies later."

"They were gonna attack your platoon?"

"Nonviolently," he says with a shake of his head. "That's our code. We just take from those that took so much from us. Anyway, not only did they save my life, but they stopped your mother from killing the rest of our platoon. Of course, that wasn't the official story."

"Let me guess," I say, knowing enough of my mother's history to fill in the rest. "The attack got pinned on the bloodthirsty Raiders, while she got awarded a medal of honor."

A bitter look crosses his face. "Exactly, kiddo. I escaped with the Raiders. They patched me up and saved my life. From that moment forward, I was branded a deserter, and she was named a war hero. End of story. They even said that I was a traitor. That I didn't just desert my watch, but instead led the Raiders to where we were stationed."

"Of course they did," I say, thinking it all over. "Space Force couldn't have a story like that leak out about their commander. It would have been bad press, like in the first waves of deployment with the high rates of PTSD. Enlistment numbers have been lagging for decades."

"Federation History?" Captain Skye says. "That's right. They always need more guardians to enlist and feed into the space military industrial machine. That's their priority."

"Well, if it makes any difference," I say after a long moment. "My mom never really recovered from everything. She's probably still carrying the guilt."

"Maybe deep down," he says with a pained expression. "Though, guilt doesn't serve anyone. The past lives in the past. It's only a memory now. The present is what matters. But it does make me sad to hear she's still suffering. I want you to under-stand—it wasn't her fault."

I meet his dark eyes. There's so much genuine kindness buried in them that it almost stops my heart. My whole life, people have envied me for having a war hero mother, when really my daily life at home was complete misery. But now I realize this incident—*this one event*—robbed me of my mother and Kari and Bea of their father. Only one thing is to blame.

And it's not our parents.

It's Space Force.

Professor Trebond and Xena and all the resistance fighters are right. They ship our young people up to the stars to die. And now they're about to declare another great war and break our peace treatise by doing something that violates everything we supposedly believe in—

Rearm Earth.

Another question pops into my head. "Why do you think they paired me with Kari? Given that complicated family history, wouldn't they want to keep the story buried?"

He frowns. "I don't know everything, of course. But maybe you needed each other . . . to make this right. If you ask this old Raider captain, I think your Pairing makes perfect sense."

Something else occurs to me suddenly. "But shouldn't we report my mom? Set the record straight? It might not be too late to clear your name. You could come back home—"

He frowns sharply. My words dry up instantly.

"That won't bring those guardians back to life, will it? Or fix the years I've lost with my family, watching my kids grow up? Besides, I forgive her. She wasn't in her right mind. I saw the crazy look in her eyes when she blasted me. She was ranting about Proxies and enemy fire." Sadness washes over his face. "We all suffer, sooner or later. That's why this has to stop."

I study his face. "But are you sure? It can't be easy living in the shadows, knowing that you did nothing wrong. That in fact, you're the real hero . . . not my mother."

"First, there's no way the federation will admit to their cover-up. I reckon they'll take it to their graves." Then a mischievous look passes over his face. "Besides, it kind of adds to the whole Raider mystique. How do you think I became captain of this surly, rowdy bunch?"

"Good point," I say with a nod. "You sure that's what you want?"

"Kiddo, I'm sure. More wrongs don't make a right," he says with the solemnity of a man who has spent years thinking about it, but who has also stopped fighting and come to peace with the past. It's hard not to respect that. "I'm happy with my life on the star-seas. Especially now that I've got my little girl back—and hopefully her sister soon, too. Only one thing is missing . . ."

"Your wife." It hits me all at once, and I feel his ache for her.

"Aye, I still dream of her . . ." he says with a twinkle in his eyes. "She was a handful. Spirited and strong-willed. The kind of spark that can ignite a thousand dormant stars. Always arguing with me about the littlest things. I probably deserved it back then. I was foolhardy and reckless. But those sparks that burned between us are what made me fall in love with her."

"Well, then she's just like her daughters," I say with a shake of my head.

That makes him chuckle. Bea continues sleeping in his lap, but she stirs and wraps her arms around him, murmuring, "I love you . . . Captain Dad."

I wonder if she's really sound asleep, or if it's a bit of an act to eavesdrop on our little conversation. That kid is sneaky, that's for sure. Maybe it's a little bit of both.

"Look, I believe you," I say to Captain Skye. "But will Kari? She kind of . . ."

"Hates my guts?"

"Yup, that pretty much sums it up," I say softly. Our exchanges are supposed to be kept private, of course. I won't share the details of what she's confided in me, but I know it's bad.

"I hope so," he says. "Otherwise . . ."

He trails off. But we both know what's riding on this mission. It's not just repairing his relationship with his daughter, but the fate of our federation—and possibly the whole galaxy.

And the key to all of it is . . .

Kari.

Suddenly, an alarm goes off, followed by Gunner's voice over the comm system. She sounds panicked. "Cap, incoming commlink from the Old Lady—it's urgent."

"Put her through to the cabin," Captain Skye says, shedding his sadness and donning his Raider captain persona again. His voice turns serious and deepens a whole notch or two.

"One sec—they're trying to jam our signal," Gunner reports.

"The feds?" I ask in alarm.

"Blast them," Captain Skye curses. "Gunner will reroute the signal."

Abruptly, the screens in front of our sling chairs light up with Professor Trebond's face. It's drained of color. I've never seen her look so afraid. She snaps in and out of focus suddenly, as static interrupts the feed. But then it stabilizes for a second—and her message comes through.

"Captain Skye, it's urgent. The secretary-general has been assassinated."

"Wait, what . . . ?" I start, as Bea bolts awake. She clings to her father like a lifeboat. He hugs her back fiercely, shifting her to his hip and standing up. He focuses on Trebond.

"Old Lady, are you sure?" Captain Skye says, sounding stunned.

"I'm afraid so . . . been trying to reach you . . . signal was jammed . . ." Trebond says, going in and out. "Moves up our timetable . . . mission in jeopardy . . . that means one thing . . ."

The signal drops out again. There's a long pause. Nobody dares to speak or make a sound. Then she pops back only for a quick second and finishes—

"We're officially at war."

CHAPTER 45

KARI

The secretary-general . . . he's been assassinated?" I say in shock. "He's dead?"

My eyes scan the newsfeed ticker for any details. The words whiz past my retinas, blurring together into a collage of suffering. I want to look away, but I can't. Each update is more disturbing than the last. I struggle to wrap my head around this sudden turn of events.

Anton shakes his head in disbelief. He's scanning the feeds, too. He looks up and shoots me a grim look. "You know, World War One started the same way . . . with an assassination of a world leader, then all the countries had alliances that dragged the whole world into the war."

"You're right," I say, feeling a rush of dread. "It's like whoever did this studied history and knew it would trigger a war . . . maybe even like they wanted it to happen again."

That hits us both hard. The air feels heavier suddenly, thicker.

"Siberian Fed bastards, probably," Anton says with a sharp nod. "They've had it out for us for centuries. Icarus was right. They're probably behind the Golden Gate Attack—"

He's cut off as another emergency alert pops up.

I scan the ticker.

"The Arctic Federation backs their alliance with the Siberian Federation . . . declares war on California . . ." I read aloud, then look up at him. "Oh no . . . it's already happening . . ."

"Those who don't know history . . ." he starts the familiar phrase.

"Are doomed to repeat it," I finish his thought. Then I feel a surge of fiery anger. "But the whole point of Earth disarmament was to prevent something like this from happening!"

Anton doesn't say anything, but we're both thinking the same thing. Yet here we are, standing on the precipice of another great war, only this time it would also engulf the stars.

That's when the drill sergeant pings us.

Her voice broadcasts over my neural implant. "Privates, report to your barracks immediately for an emergency briefing."

Anton and I sit on my rack in stunned silence, refreshing our newsfeeds and doom-scrolling, until everyone starts trickling in from the mess hall. The jovial banter that usually hangs over our platoon after meals has evaporated, replaced by gloomy silence. Nobody speaks while we wait for the drill sergeant to arrive. What is there left to say? We're officially at war.

A few minutes later, she marches in, wearing her usual stoic mask, as I've come to think of it. For that, I envy her. My brain is a jumble of warring thoughts. My face must be painted with every single thing I'm feeling right now—panic, terror, confusion, worry.

Nadia meets my gaze from her rack across the aisle. Even she looks . . . agitated. *Stay strong,* she mouths.

If only she knew what I was really going through right now. Not just this recent shocking turn of events, but also with my sister and friends missing back Earthside. The timing of everything seems like such a coincidence. *Could it all be related?* I think suddenly.

Before I can consider this crazy idea, the drill sergeant starts the briefing.

"Privates, I'm sure you've seen the alerts by now," she begins darkly. "Our secretary-general has been assassinated. This terrorist attack leaves us no choice. We must defend ourselves from those enemies who seek to destroy us and take away our freedoms."

Mostly murmurs, but also patriotic chants ripple through the barracks. A familiar cheer breaks out. I can't help it; I mouth along, though the words feel like rocks in my mouth.

"California Fed! Home of the free, home of the brave!"

The drill sergeant lets it go on for a moment, then signals for silence.

"Some of you may have already guessed by now what this means for you," she goes on, scanning her tablet as if wishing it would change our fates. "This alters your orders."

Nervous whispers rustle through our ranks, but she plows forward. "All eligible soldiers are being called up for front lines duty," she confirms our worst fears. "As we speak, the transports are being prepped for combat zones. It also moves up the time frame for deployment.

More shocked whispers erupt. She frowns, then speaks—

"Privates, you will each deploy to your postings tonight."

That hits me hard.

This can't be happening, I think with a stab of panic. I was supposed to have another twenty-four hours. Maybe it was wishful thinking, but I was hoping my sister and friends would turn up before I left. The reality of this hits me like blaster fire. But I'm not the only one feeling panicked. I was already headed to the front lines for combat duty. For those with other military occupational specialties—safer ones, like postal or engineering—this carries a bigger shock.

Percy looks like he just got punched in the gut, while Genesis and Anton both look equally dismayed. They didn't expect to be called up for combat. At least, not so soon. Of course, we all knew this was a possibility when we enlisted, but it's been so long since the last war. Most of us didn't truly believe this could happen again in our lifetimes. But I guess that's how it always goes, right? We never think it'll happen to us . . . until it does.

"Privates, use this time to strip your racks and pack your things," the drill sergeant says, sweeping her gaze over us. "And to say goodbye to your platoon. This is a difficult time for everyone. But remember why you enlisted in Space Force. This is your chance to prove your worth as guardians—and to defend our federation from these heinous terrorist attacks."

"*Drill Sergeant, yes, Drill Sergeant*," we echo together, one last time. She tips the wide brim of her hat forward in acknowledgment. She knows it's for the last time, too.

"Guardians dismissed."

With that command, she marches off, leaving us alone to carry out her orders. We glance nervously at each other. Just because we're all going to the front lines now, doesn't mean we're deploying to the same bases, or even the same systems. This really might be our final . . .

Goodbyes.

I start going about my duties on autopilot, packing up my meager possessions into my duffel bag and stripping the sheets from my rack, but I feel anxious and overwhelmed.

Nadia spies the look on my face. "Chin up, soldier. This is what we signed up for."

"Ugh, I wish it were only that," I say with a grimace, shoving my spare uniform into my duffel bag. I don't bother to fold it, though I know that's bad form for a guardian. "Deploying to the front lines I can handle. I signed up for that . . . but I didn't sign up for this . . ."

"Wait, did something else happen?" Nadia says, exchanging a worried look with Anton and Luna. They close ranks, coming over to support me. Percy and Genesis, too.

I can't stop the tears that prick my eyes.

"Maybe . . ." I sniffle.

"Right, we noticed you've been acting a little off," Anton says. "That's why I left dinner tonight and came to check on you in the barracks. But we thought it was your MOS orders."

"*Front lines*," Luna says, shooting me a knowing look. Her orders put her in a similarly perilous situation. "We figured it was sinking in. But you're saying it's something else?"

They wait for me to respond.

Silence hangs while I gather my words. My tongue feels thick and clumsy.

"Yeah, I've been meaning to tell you," I say as my knees wobble. I sink onto my bare mattress. "But I didn't want to worry you. You've got enough on your minds—"

"Cut the crap," Nadia interjects. She trades a concerned look with the others. "We're in this together. I don't care what they say—we're still battle buddies. So, spit it out already."

I take a deep breath, then force myself to tell them everything that's happened over the last two days. It all comes out in a jumbled rush, filled with my emotional turmoil and despair.

"I'm so sorry," Nadia says after I finish. "That's a lot to handle . . . for anyone. No wonder you've been wandering around looking totally shell-shocked."

"Let me get this straight—your closest friends and sister?" Luna says. "All missing? At the same time? Right as you get your frontline orders . . . and now we declare war?"

I nod glumly. "It's like my whole world is imploding into a black hole."

Anton bites his lip. "Well, everything has to be connected, right? Like Occam's razor?"

He glances around, expecting us all to get it right away and follow his logic. But we stare back with confused faces. Nadia glares at him. "Why do you always use such big words?" she chides him. "Seriously, what's . . . *Occam's razor?*"

Anton shrugs. "Oh, it's this philosophical principle. Essentially, the more assumptions you have to make, the more unlikely it is. Or put another way, the simplest theory is usually correct . . . they ran off together. Their disappearances are likely related to the recent events, too."

"So, you're saying . . . it's not a coincidence?" I say, trying to understand the theory.

"Exactly," Anton says. "For all of these big events to be purely coincidental and unconnected requires a lot of major assumptions. The simplest theory—it's all related."

"But why would her little sister run off with them?" Nadia asks. "I get the two friends at college thing. A sordid little affair makes perfect sense. Maybe he attacked the roommate over jealousy or some lover's quarrel. But how is her sister connected? She's only eight, right?"

"Yeah, that's correct," I confirm, feeling another stab of worry.

"Forget motive—let's talk logistics," Genesis says, picking up the tangent. "Where would they feasibly go? With all the travel bans? Even with a transport, they wouldn't get that far."

"They've got to be even stricter now, too," Luna chimes in, leaning over her rack to peer down at us. "The threat level has been RED since that flyover. The timing is pretty crazy."

"Again, if we go by Occam's razor," Anton says. "Then it's all connected. Their disappearances. The flyover. The Raider attack. The assassination . . ."

"Are you suggesting that they knew something big was about to happen?" I say, my mind racing through the crazy possibilities. "Maybe even . . . that they were involved in it?"

Anton frowns. "Okay, that does seem pretty far-fetched. A big actor had to have pulled that stuff off. Not that they're involved exactly. But maybe, they knew something about it?"

"But Drae and Rho are college students," I point out. "And my sister is just a little kid. We're from a small town. How could they know anything about these terrorist attacks?"

"Yeah, they're just civilians," Percy agrees. "How does that compute? This Occam guy sounds like a crackpot to me."

Nadia looks up at me. "But my brother might be right. There must be *something*. Come on . . . think hard . . . did anything unusual happen in the days leading up to their disappearance? Anything out of the ordinary? You had exchanges, right? Did anything stand out?"

"Let's see . . ." I say, thinking back to our last exchanges. "He did mention something about a professor who disappeared suddenly. He loved her literature class, but apparently, she was teaching unapproved books. Then before they could arrest her, she vanished, too."

That's when it occurs to me.

Yet another mysterious disappearance.

"Wow, so that's *four* unexplained disappearances," Anton says. "In a short period of time. All people who know each other. Well, except the professor didn't know your sister. But still, doesn't that sound suspicious? And let me guess—they never located the professor either."

I shake my head. "Not that I know of . . . she was his favorite professor, too." As soon as I say it out loud, I realize how crazy that sounds. It's hard for anyone to vanish off the grid.

That's when Luna speaks up, keeping her voice low. "I'll wager anything that the professor was part of the Resistance. And maybe that's the link to your friends, too."

"*The Resistance?*" I hiss in shock. "You mean, the lunatics who want to *Disarm the Stars*? But they're just a bunch of vets with space trauma. They're completely harmless."

However, I can't stop thinking back to the protestor who attacked me at my shipping-out ceremony. He grabbed my arm, I think with a shudder. The way the secretary-general and his security team reacted and tackled him didn't make it seem like he was harmless.

"Look, I shouldn't be saying this," Luna goes on, lowering her voice to barely a whisper. "But that's what our government wants you to believe. They're more organized and sophisticated than you know. I've overheard my parents talking about it. My dad works in military intel."

I perk up. "Wait, so you think the professor recruited Rho and Drae to join the Resistance?"

"It's possible," Anton says, thinking it through. "But it does sound a bit far-fetched. The universities are full of Ringers nowadays. Most Resistance folks come from the Park."

"That's true," Luna agrees, reluctantly. "I've heard my parents talking about it. The Park is a hotbed for Resistance activity. The universities used to be like that, before the Great War. But when they changed college enrollment to only privileged kids, that pretty much quashed that."

"Okay, fine, I'll bite," I jump in. "That sounds like a dead end. But even if that theory was correct—and she recruited them to join the Resistance—then how is my sister involved? She's never set foot on Berkeley's campus. Starfires, she's never even been outside Lompoc."

That puzzles everyone. Nobody has a theory, not even Occam himself.

That's when the drill sergeant pings us to *hurry our asses up*. We can't waste any more time. We have to finish packing ASAP and prepare for immediate deployment. In a few short hours, we'll be split up and warped to the front lines, scattered like stardust across this universe.

Percy and Genesis sneak away from the barracks. We all know where they're heading. The nature of their relationship has become an open secret in our platoon. These are their last precious moments together before they're likely to deploy for separate combat postings.

I'm shoving my last item into my duffel bag—a battered pair of shower slippers that I've grown quite fond of, and for some reason, can't bear to leave behind—when suddenly, the floor shudders under my feet. I glance down at my boots. At first, I dismiss it as minor seismic activity. Ceres plays host to regular cryovolcano eruptions that spew out ice and mud.

But then . . . it happens again.

"Hey, did you feel that?" I turn to ask Nadia.

Before she can respond, the alarms go off—

Ring! Ring! Ring!

That's followed by another rumble. This time, it's so strong that it throws me off-balance. I reach for the top rack to stop my fall. *What in the stars is happening?* Before I can react, another tremble tears through the base. Chaos erupts in the barracks as we struggle to brace ourselves. The alarms keep blaring—while an urgent voice echoes over the comm system.

"Ceres Base is under attack!" the drill sergeant barks. "Repeat . . . Ceres Base is under attack! Guardians, report to battle stations. All other personnel down to the bunker!"

CHAPTER 46

DRAE

"Brace yourselves," Professor Trebond says after Gunner stabilizes the signal. Trebond types on her tablet, triggering images from the press conference to transmit to our screens.

From my sling chair, I watch in disbelief as the grisly scene unfolds. Secretary-General Icarus is speaking in front of the capital in Sacramento about the threat of terrorism and the need for Earth rearmament, then suddenly—

An explosion rips through the podium.

The camera cuts out, then pops back to the massacre.

Once the smoke clears, I feel revulsion at what materializes on the screen. *Severed arms and legs . . . torn-up bodies strewn over the ground . . . dust and rubble . . .*

Rho and Gunner rush into the cabin and crowd around my screen. Rho's hair and eyes look shock white. Trebond comes back on the screen after the footage finishes.

"The newsfeeds are reporting the explosive device bears the same markings as the one used in the GGA," she says, freezing the screen on the bloody assassination scene. "They're blaming the Siberian Fed. They've officially declared war. This is playing nonstop on the official newsfeeds. Public support has reached a fever pitch in support of Earth rearmament."

"Asteroid fires, it's everything we feared," Captain Skye curses. Bea clings to him tighter, wrapping her arms around his neck. But for once, she remains silent.

Trebond leans closer to the screen. "That's correct. The chain of events has been kicked into fast motion. But we all know what those markings mean really happened . . ."

"The aliens," I whisper. "They *did* this. This is what they've been planning all along. This is what tips us into war. Now our federation has no choice. We have to retaliate."

"Exactly, I'm afraid so," Trebond agrees. "The aliens studied us well. They know our warlike tendencies. They hatched this nefarious plan, and sadly . . . it's working perfectly."

"So, what now?" Rho asks. "How does this affect our plan?"

"This moves up your timetable," Trebond replies. "Exponentially. You have to find Kari ASAP and get her that package to disseminate . . . before it's too late . . . to stop . . . war . . ."

The screen flickers, threatening to cut out.

"Sorry . . . have to go . . ." Trebond says with static coming in and out. "The feds . . . hacking our signal . . . can't let them trace . . . to Resistance . . . or we're all in great danger . . ."

The screen goes dark, then pops back one last time.

"Good . . . luck . . . all is riding on you . . ."

With that, it goes dark and cuts off. The silence feels louder than the talking.

Nobody speaks for a long moment.

"What are we gonna do?" Rho says, glancing at Gunner. "You heard Trebond? We don't have much time left. But we're still a good distance from Ceres. Isn't that right?"

"Yup, that's true," says Gunner. Clearly, Rho has been spending time with her. "We're about halfway there. Approximately twelve hours are remaining. Cap, should we risk it?"

She catches his eye, but he frowns deeply. "Extreme emergencies only."

"Doesn't this qualify?" Gunner says. "End of world and all that fun?"

"Risk what?" I ask, glancing at them. "Captain Skye, what aren't you telling us?"

"Well, I hoped it wouldn't come to this," he says with a grimace, hugging Bea closer. "Our chief engineer rigged up special warp boosters a while back. But we've never tested them out . . . because it's risky."

Rho frowns. "Right, just how risky?"

"They're supposed to be used only in cases of . . . *extreme emergency*." He glances over at Gunner with a rebuking look. "Like if Space Force was about to intercept us and we had to outrun them. And even then, only if we'd exhausted every other possible defense."

"Why only extreme cases?" I ask, fearing the answer.

"Let's just say, there's a reason they're illegal," he replies. "Space Force banned them due to their instability and tendency to go into hyperdrive and tear the whole ship apart."

"Cap's correct," Gunner confirms. "That's why they're banned. But you can scavenge booster parts on the black market. Our engineer jerry-rigged them up just in case . . ."

"Translation?" Rho asks. "How dangerous are we talking?"

"Well, it's about a fifty-fifty shot," Captain Skye says with a helpless shrug. "Either we get there in half the time and have half a chance at stopping this blasted war—or my poor ship rips apart from the g-force . . . and us along with it. No way to tell really. Mrs. Smee's a brilliant engineer, but she washed out of Space Force on account of her affinity for rum."

"Just great, she's a drunk," Rho snorts.

"Hey, lots of great leaders were alcoholics," I say, remembering my history classes. "Winston Churchill. Ulysses S. Grant. Alexander the Great." I run out of names there.

Rho scowls at me. "Since when were you paying attention?"

I smile ruefully. "Uh, just the interesting parts."

"Cap's right," Gunner says. "Mrs. Smee is the only reason the ship's still star-worthy. I'd trust her with my life. But we never tested those boosters. They're unpredictable."

"Yup, plus my ship's already running on borrowed time," Captain Skye says with a sorrowful expression. "Space Force decommissioned these before you were even born."

Gunner nods. "Yeah, I'd have Mrs. Smee weigh in . . . only . . ."

"Only . . . what?" Rho says.

"Uh, she's belowdecks sleeping off a bender," Gunner says. "Usually, nothing can wake her from that stupor. Figured we'd rouse her when we got closer to Ceres Base."

"Well, if you're trying to reassure us," I say, feeling my stomach churn, "it's not working."

Silence falls over the cabin. We're all contemplating the terrible choices that face us, each more harrowing than the last. But then, Bea hops up and shoots us a chastising look.

"Now, just listen to yourselves! My sister's life is in danger . . . war officially declared . . . and you're all being total cowards! Snap out of it, right this second."

Captain Skye grins from ear to ear. "That's my girl! No doubt about it, kiddo." He fixes her with a proud expression. "Come on, she's right. Where's your sense of adventure?"

"Not sure I've ever had one," I say, feeling fear in every part of my being.

But Bea skips over and tugs on my arm.

"What would Estrella Luna do?" she asks softly, pointing to her backpack with a drawing of the comic hero. She knows I'm a major fan. I made a point of admiring it before blastoff.

I swallow hard against my dread. I know exactly what Estrella Luna would do—but I also know that's not the right question. Estrella Luna is a fictional hero, but I know a real one.

"I think you mean . . . what would Private Hikari Skye do?" I say, catching Bea's eye. "Your sister's the real guardian. She's the one up there fighting to save our universe."

Bea nods in agreement. "So . . . what would Kari do?"

I meet Captain Skye's steady gaze, realizing that I admire him more every nano-second. Right now, he looks every bit like the war hero that he's always been denied.

"Let's do it—let's use the boosters," I say, despite my fear. "For Kari."

That decides it.

Everyone murmurs their agreement. Gunner rushes off to the bridge, while we climb into our sling chairs and buckle our harnesses. Captain Skye claims the chair next to Bea. Rho shoots him a nervous glance. "Shouldn't you be on the bridge? To like pilot the ship, or something?"

"Or something," he says with a frown. "Trust me, Gunner's a far better pilot than I'll ever be. She's gonna run this whole operation one day. And, well, if these are my last moments alive, then I'm spending them with my daughter."

"I love you, Captain Dad," Bea says, reaching over to clasp his hand. She squeezes his hand. "And by the way, this is, like, so cool. Don't worry, you've totally got this."

Suddenly, the ship rumbles and shudders. I wait for my usual fear response to kick in. My heart does thump a bit faster, but I don't feel jittery and anxious. Instead, all I can think about is Kari. My love for her burns like the heat of a thousand blazing suns and steadies my nerves. But I also know that for once, she'd be proud of me. And that's what gives me courage.

"Warp boosters *engage*," Captain Skye says into his comm unit.

Gunner's reply echoes back. "Roger that! But Cap, you sure? Mrs. Smee's one heck of an engineer . . . when the ship's dry. But we've had one major rum haul after another. The hull's stacked full of kegs and she's been hitting them like it's her job. I got her up and on her feet . . . sort of . . . and to the bridge—"

"Gunner, am I the captain?" he asks in a stern voice.

"Yes, Cap," Gunner replies.

"Blast it! Then follow my orders . . . for once," he mutters back. "Or I'll have to ditch both of you at the next port. And it's not friendly territory either. Am I making myself clear?"

He smiles at us and whispers, "It's just for show, don't worry."

That makes Bea giggle. But I can't believe we're joking about ditching his crew when we're on the brink of being torn apart by a drunken Raider engineer's contraband warp boosters.

"Oh, and tell Mrs. Smee when she perks up," Captain Skye goes. "Either she's dead—no pun intended—or she's getting an extra case of the good stuff the Old Lady threw in."

"Yes, Cap," Gunner replies, then, muffled, "You hear that . . . Mrs. Smee?"

"Yup, I heard the Cap," a slurred voice comes over the comm unit. "Don't worry, Cap . . . those warp boosters are rock-solid . . . Space Force only wishes they had them . . ."

That's followed by a lengthy burp.

"That's not exactly comforting," I whisper to Rho. I get the feeling that discipline doesn't run high on the list of Raider priorities. Then Gunner hops back on, as the ship rumbles.

"Okay, everyone, hold on to your sling chairs," she says excitedly. "Mrs. Smee fired up the boosters. I locked in the coordinates. Warp boosters engaging in *three* . . . *two* . . ."

I don't even hear *one* as the boosters engage.

All I feel is a great sucking sensation, like my guts are being smashed and pulled out through my skin at the same time. My sling chair struggles to counteract the extreme g-force, but it's not cut out for this. Outside, stars streak by the windows like comets. The edges of my vision blur. It's so painfully beautiful, I think for an instant as my vision closes to a faint pinprick.

Then, I black out.

CHAPTER 47

KARI

The base rocks with the explosions. Alarms sound everywhere.

A second later, our drill sergeant's orders for our platoon pop up in our retinas. "Privates, suit up with blasters and evacuate to the bunker!"

Chaos breaks out in our barracks as everyone rushes to follow orders. A strong blast tears through the base. I stagger, trying to keep my footing. Anton stumbles next to me, while Nadia and Luna brace themselves against the racks until it subsides.

"Siberian Fed!" Nadia yells over the alarms. "Those Proxy bastards are blasting us!"

My head's spinning as I blurt out the first question that jumps to my mind. "But why . . . attack Ceres? We're a training and communications base in the middle of nowhere."

"Oh, that's just it," Anton says, looking up sharply. "To take out our most critical communications hub. I had my first training session with Postmaster Haven yesterday. All communications to and from Earth pass through Ceres Base. If they take out our ability to communicate, then they cut off our interstellar bases. They'll be lost in the dark."

"You're right," Luna says. "Like chopping the head off a snake. It's a brilliant plan."

"Asteroid fires, don't call them brilliant," Nadia cuts in, with hatred blazing in her eyes. "Call them . . . *child murderers.* Call them . . . *terrorists.* They blew up that bus of kids."

The truth of that stuns us into silence—and action. We rush to put on our newly issued deployment suits. They're high-tech and made for exterior missions, where there's less gravity and little to no breathable air. They're also reinforced, making us faster and stronger.

Now I'm grateful for all those endless drills that make putting on my suit as automatic as breathing. Despite the blasts and general panic, I get mine on fast and seal it up.

Next, I reach for my blaster, which conforms to my grip and syncs with my neural implant, then strap it to my waist. Finally, I snap on my helmet with the golden shield and power my suit up, feeling it clench around my body. The electronics boot up. The lightweight, blaster-proof material shimmers and ripples black and silver.

The alarms continue to blare, along with the evacuation orders. Abruptly, another explosion hits the barracks—but this time, I'm ready. I brace myself using my new suit until it subsides. The reinforced strength makes it easier. I don't even stumble once.

"Alright, should we head down to the bunker?" Anton says. He's suited up with his blaster at the ready. He gestures for us to head out. "Drill Sergeant's orders."

The barracks empties around us as our platoon evacuates to the bunker, leaving the whole place in disarray with half-packed duffels and half-stripped racks. Our little crew makes up the last ones left. But Luna straps on her blaster, then gives us a steely look.

"Well, are we trained guardians—or aren't we? I say . . . we should go fight."

"Don't talk crazy. We're still grunts in all but rank," Nadia says. "We're green as the radioactive turf. We would be disobeying direct orders. We could be court marshaled."

"Yeah, what can we do?" Anton says, sounding helpless. "My sister is right . . . for once. This isn't a combat sim. We're not ready. The drill sergeant's orders make that clear."

But I hesitate. Those are our orders, plus it's true that the bunker is our safest bet. We rode out the last two incidents down there. But something about it doesn't sit right with me.

Not anymore.

"We're guardians, I repeat," taking Luna's side. "Not recruits. We're about to deploy on combat missions. We can fight for our federation. So, what're we waiting for?"

"This is what we signed up for," Luna says, her voice firm. "Our base is under attack. This is our sworn duty. I'm not hiding out down there. I want to fight."

She joins me by the door. We look back at Nadia and Anton. I can't help remembering when I first met the twins on the transport, back when we were green. Since then, we've been through so much together. But is this the moment that divides us? It's risky to disobey direct orders. But we're at war—our base could fall into enemy hands. This could be our last chance.

"Fine," Nadia says, flashing her classic eye roll. "Count me in with you crazy grunts."

Anton hesitates. "But what about Percy and Genesis?"

Nadia makes kissy noises, making us crack knowing smiles. "They snuck off, remember? They're probably down in the bunker with everyone else. Let them have some time together . . ."

I hate leaving anyone from our crew unaccounted for. It goes against all of our training. But Nadia's right. They probably evacuated and joined up with the rest of our platoon.

"Okay, that's settled. Is everyone suited up?" I ask, as another explosion rocks the base. I feel my suit brace my stance. "Sync up our commlinks—and then let's head out."

I pull down the golden blaster shield on my helmet, which displays my neural link. Harold comes online and speaks up. *I detect an elevated heart rate,* he says. *Is everything okay?*

Pretty fucking far from okay, I think back. *Thanks for asking.*

You're welcome, Harold says brightly. *May I recommend meditation exercises?*

Not now, I think with a grimace.

Clearly, he's new to combat situations. We both are.

With our new combat suits and golden visors, we rush into the corridor—but it's chaos. Guardians and other personnel pack the hallways, rushing to evacuate or get to their posts. The alarms are also louder out here. For a split second, I'm rattled by the confusion. Harold comes online again, asking about my heart rate. I swallow hard and think back—

Harold, show me the route to the battle stations.

A holographic map of the base flickers onto my retinal screen. It shows the route to the battle stations—but also displays the bunker per our orders. They're divergent routes.

The bunker is down on the lowermost level of the base. But if we want to fight, then we have to head for the upper level. Either way, we have to find the elevator bank first.

"Come on, hurry!" I say over the commlink. "This way to the elevators."

My voice is piped into their helmets. We charge down the corridor at a fast clip, weaving through bodies. Some are only half suited up, while others are strapping on blasters as they run.

When we reach the elevator bank, the confusion has deepened. People jam the elevator buttons in frustration, but nothing happens. Not to mention, with this many people waiting, we'll never make it anywhere. *Harold, what's wrong with the elevators?* I think to my neural implant.

Elevators are offline, Harold says after a moment.

"Dead end," I say in frustration. "They're down."

"Looks like . . . power outage on this sector," Anton chimes in. "They must have blasted out the generators on the surface. Probably part of their attack plan."

I feel deflated. This was our chance to fight back.

But then Harold pings me and shows me another route.

"Quick, the stairs," I say, pointing to a door set in the wall. It says—*Emergency Exit.*

We charge up the flights—too many to count. Thanks to all the PT and our suits, we fly up them in record time, emerging into a plant-filled atrium with domed skylights. Outside, it's night by Ceres time. I jerk my head up. Cracks span the ceiling, threatening to collapse.

Up here, the explosions rock the base harder. It feels like an earthquake every time blaster fire rains down from above. I catch sight of the battle zone through the skylights.

Swarms of Siberian and Arctic Fed fighter ships hurl past, spewing fire with each bombing raid, bringing up tufts of dust and ice crystals from the barren surface. I recognize the insignia on their hulls, if there was any question about who was behind the attack. They look like insects swarming toward a nest. They're the smaller, faster attack ships. Looming just beyond the thin atmosphere, I spot the larger warships—like aircraft carriers—that transported them here.

Our ships have also taken to the skies to fight them off, while our anti-spacecraft defenses hurl brutal round after round at them, but we're outnumbered and taking on too much damage. The surprise attack did its job. They got the jump on us before we could raise our defenses.

But then something worse occurs to me—

We're going to lose.

I can't stop the thought. But then I remember something else. It's above my rank to worry about that. I have to focus. My job is simple. Find a battle station where I can help fight back. And also, prepare for a ground invasion and breach of the base should it come to that.

My fingers twitch for my blaster, feeling the reassuring shape of the handle slot into my gloved hand. This is the moment I've trained for, and if I die in the line of duty, then so be it.

That doesn't scare me. My only regret . . . well, my biggest fear really . . .

Bea, Drae, Rho. They're still missing.

But I push that from my mind. There's zero I can do for them right now. I have to compartmentalize my feelings and focus on the present. I have to protect my bandwidth.

I have to forget them for now . . . even if it kills me.

All of this flashes through my head in mere seconds, like the blasts whizzing at our base. After I calm my emotions, stuffing them down, I turn my attention to my neural implant.

Harold, which way to the battle stations?

A map flashes in my retinas, highlighting the route.

"This way," I yell, leading my crew down the corridor to the right. We've never been to this part of the base. The tunnel is utilitarian and narrow, without any windows. Artificial lights span the ceiling, generating long shadows. Our boots thump the concrete floors in lockstep.

Nadia flanks me, like when we were battle buddies, while Luna and Anton bring up the rear. Suddenly, another explosion hits—and this time it's stronger than anything before.

"Watch out—fire in the hole!" I scream. We all brace ourselves.

Under the force of the blast, the corridor starts to collapse around us. The floor buckles under my feet, while the ceiling starts to cave in. Concrete, rubble, and dust rain down from overhead. I struggle to break my fall and remain upright, but everything feels unsteady.

When the explosion finally subsides, dust clouds line the air like thick smoke. Thankfully, my filters click on automatically, preventing me from choking on it. I'm still standing . . . on something unstable . . . but it's nearly impossible to see anything. That means . . .

I can't see my friends. Panic sets in.

"Guardians, check in," I call out, grateful when they identify themselves one by one over the commlink. Thanks to our new deployment suits, we're all still in one piece. Barely.

"Asteroid fires, we're trapped," Nadia says, waving away the dust and inspecting the solid barrier of rubble now blocking the corridor. "This is completely blocked."

"And we can't go back," Luna reports from the rear. "It's blocked back here, too."

"Hurry, look! We have to find a way out," I call out, trying to see through the dust. We're stuck in a small pocket of safety in the middle, but not for long. Another blast shakes more dust and rubble down on us. "The corridor is highly unstable and could collapse at any moment."

I feel for the wall, skirting it to orient myself.

"Mayday . . . mayday . . ." I try over my commlink, broadcasting our distress signal with our location. "We're trapped . . . top level . . . the corridor collapsed . . . Harold, call for help . . ."

But all I hear through the open link is static and chaos on the other end. So many calls for help, so many guardians in trouble, making one thing clear—*nobody's coming to rescue us.*

I have Harold switch it off. Fanning out into the smoky air, we inspect the small pocket where we're trapped. Power flickers in and out, creating staccato bursts of light. The air starts to clear, but only a little before the next bombing pass hits. We don't have much time.

Finally, Anton speaks up.

"You might want to see this."

He points to the outline of a door. It's almost hidden under a thick layer of dust. "I think it's manual in the case of a power failure," he goes on, inspecting it closer. "Probably installed way back when they first built this base. With any luck, we might be able to pry it open."

"That's great," I say, glancing at the exposed wires sparking and dangling from the ceiling. We make our way over to it. "Since the power lines have clearly been damaged."

"Looks like our only way out," Nadia says. "But . . . where does it lead?"

"The surface," Luna says, sharing the neural projection of our current location. "Near the south side . . . by the docking bay. I'm guessing it's an emergency evacuation route."

"But the surface is worse," Nadia says. "Their ships are blasting the whole base! We'll be completely vulnerable and exposed. What good are four little guardians in a big war?"

More blasts rain down, as if emphasizing her point. The tunnel shakes hard— and threatens to give way as dust and debris rains down. Our time and options are fading fast.

"We don't have a choice," I say. "This tunnel's going to collapse—better to risk the surface. At least up there, we'll have a chance. Otherwise, this corridor will be our coffin."

"Fine," Nadia says. "What's the plan once we get out there?"

"Stay low to the ground and move fast," Luna replies. "Use the natural formations—rocks, craters, ice rivers, anything you can find—for cover. If we're lucky, they won't even notice us. As Nadia said, we're just four little guardians. But we can use that to our advantage."

No wonder she's been tapped for special operations. I give her a nod of respect.

"Great, but we can't stay out there forever," I point out. "The longer we're exposed, the more likely they'll spot us. Time is our enemy. Plus . . . our oxygen reserves."

Our suits have air units. But we'll be on a ticking clock once we get out there. These are deployment suits—not space suits. And Ceres doesn't have breathable air.

"Yeah, and one more little problem . . . how do we get back inside?" Nadia says. "Not like we can just saunter up and knock on the front door, right? The whole base is locked down."

"The docking bay," Anton says. "Where the postal ships take off. That's our target. It's not far from our current location. Remember those freight elevators that carry them up from the post office? I'll bet we can slip inside and hitch a ride on one back down to safety—"

That's when more blasts hit, cutting him off.

The ceiling buckles and more alarms blare. The tunnel is on the brink of collapse.

"Quick . . . over here . . . I think this unlocks it," Anton says, indicating the spoked wheel attached to the airlock door. It looks like a relic from military history. "Let's hope it still works."

"How long since it was last used?" Nadia asks, examining the lock and sounding concerned. "The metal looks corroded . . . not a good sign."

"Only one way to find out," I say, gripping the wheel and trying to turn it.

But even using all my suit's reinforced strength, it remains stubborn and stuck. I feel defeated as more shocks tear through the corridor. Maybe this will really be our coffin.

But I see other hands grip the wheel around me . . . *six of them.*

"On the count of three, we put everything we've got into it," I say in a strained voice as I lean forward and grip the wheel. "It's our only chance! One . . . two . . . *three!*"

On three, we put all our combined strength into turning the lock. Finally, with a great shedding of rust, the lock gives way and cranks open. Stale air rushes out of the old airlock.

We dash inside, quickly shutting the door behind us. More blasts hit, shaking the airlock. Then, with all of us cranking the next door's handle, we open the emergency exit and stagger through it as—behind us—the corridor crumbles and collapses. We got out just in time.

That was close—too close.

When we get outside and our boots clomp down on icy dust, it's worse than I thought. Arctic and Siberian Federation ships swoop overhead, coming in low for bombing raids that unleash death and destruction on the base, while our defenses fire back. The battle rages on, full of fire and fury. But now that I'm out here, I can see just how badly we're losing this fight.

Anything exposed has been blasted. Only a few of our anti-spacecraft artillery weapons are still operational, while more and more enemy ships keep materializing out of warp.

But I snap my attention back to the more immediate problem. Not getting blasted out here on the surface. I signal to my team. We dive behind rock outcroppings and natural formations to avoid getting blasted or hit by shrapnel, and inching our way toward the docking bay.

More bombing runs, more diving for shelter. The Proxies continue their aerial assault without relenting. Still, reaching the docking bay remains our best chance to make it out of this catastrophe alive. So far, Luna's plan works beautifully. The enemy ships don't zero in on us—four tiny figures creeping along the desolate surface. They have bigger targets in mind.

"Sorry to report," I say into my comm as we continue worming our way across the surface, keeping low to the ground. It's slow going. "But looks like we're losing. It's not even close."

"The surprise attack did its job," Luna says in a dark voice. "We weren't prepared."

"Had to play the hero?" Nadia gripes. "Couldn't wait it out in the bunker?"

"Admit it, you wanted to fight, too," I reply with a knowing smirk.

"Yeah, seconding that," Luna says, joining in on our banter. "You've been itching to punch something since you first got here."

"Fine, guilty as charged," Nadia says. "But my poor brother. He wanted postal service."

"Just wait, you'll see," Anton says with a laugh. "The mail system will save your life one day. I already did my first day of training. Postmaster Haven even gave me a mail key."

"Mail key?" I ask. "What does that mean?"

He nods as we crawl forward over the frozen crust. I hear everyone's voices piped into my helmet. "Yup, it's like a private way for us to communicate directly with the postmasters."

Anton raises his wrist, pointing to a device strapped to it that I hadn't noticed before. It does look incongruous with the modern tech on the deployment suits. In fact, it resembles an old wristwatch, the kind I've only seen in movies with a bronze metal ring, a glass face, and hands.

"Like a magic wizard key?" I say, studying the ancient-looking device, though looks are deceiving. It's clearly wired with modern technology. "How many postmasters are there?"

"Oh, hundreds," Anton says. "At our bases all over the solar system and beyond."

"Always a nerd, to the bitter end," Nadia says with a snort.

It's crazy how in the middle of a war—with enemies on all sides, including the terrain—your friends can still make it all seem okay somehow. I wonder how I ever got by without them. I guess I always had Rho and my sister. And then after the Pairing, I had Drae, too.

That thought gives me a sharp pang, but I push it away.

He abandoned me, I remind myself. *Just like my father.*

"Almost there," I say instead, and motion to my team. I have to remain focused.

We spring from behind the jagged rocks, keeping low to the ground, and slide down a steep crater and into the basin. Down here, we're more exposed and have to move fast.

Rivulets of ice cut into the basin from cryovolcanism, making it clear what created this crater in the first place. There are also fewer natural outcroppings to hide behind. I spot the next one about a hundred meters away. We move together as fast as we can and jump behind it.

And that's when I feel a low rumble.

My boots vibrate, but it grows stronger. The surface starts to ripple and convulse. But it's not like the bombing explosions. This feels different, like it's much deeper. In horror, I realize what's causing it. It's likely triggered by the blasts—and I signal frantically to my team.

"Watch out—cryovolcano!" I scream.

CHAPTER 48

DRAE

We come out of warp into the middle of a war zone.

I pop back to consciousness—jerking my neck to the window and the crazy scene below. Siberian and Arctic Fed ships make coordinated bombing runs over Ceres Base, raining explosions down on the dwarf planet's dusty, icy surface. Beyond us in low orbit, the larger enemy warships loom and wait for the smaller attack ships to take out the main defenses.

"Oh no," Rho says, stirring next to me and following my gaze.

Cap and Bea also come back to full awareness right as—

A Siberian Fed ship rockets past us, trailed by two of our Space Force fighters. They break away from the surface and lock onto the enemy ship, blasting it into fiery oblivion—

But then they double back and focus on us now.

They start firing—

"Cap, we're under attack!" Gunner yells over the comm. "Cloaking shields damaged from warp!"

Why are they attacking us? I think, still jumbled. But then I remember—we're on a Raider ship. We're technically the enemy of our own federation. That's why they're blasting us to hell.

"Blast them, Gunner!" Captain Skye yells into his commlink, unbuckling his harness.

He lurches up, then pivots back to us.

"Stay put!" he orders. "And keep your harnesses on! This is about to get bumpy." Before he rushes off, he points to his daughter. "Especially you. Do you hear me, kiddo?"

"Aye, Captain Dad," Bea says with wide eyes.

With that, he heads for the bridge, as our ship rocks from a barrage of blaster fire. The Space Force ships whip past in a blur of motion, then arcs back around to make another run.

I grip Rho's hand. "Hang on—Gunner will fight them off."

Our ship shakes and lurches again, but this time I'm relieved it's because we're returning fire. Meanwhile, below us on Ceres, the battle rages on. And worse, it looks like we're losing and our base is about to fall. With a stab of fear, I reach into my pocket, feeling the package.

How am I supposed to get this to Kari . . . in the middle of a combat zone?

Bea fidgets, struggling against her harness. "I hate . . . *staying put*," she says with a defiant look. "Drae . . . Rho . . . can't we do something? Can't we help Kari?"

"Uh, like what?" I ask. "I admire your spirit, kid. But there's a war out there."

Bea rolls her eyes. "Like, I'm aware. But we're on a secret mission, remember?"

"Yeah, a *secret* mission you hijacked. You're not even supposed to be here."

"Stop dwelling on the past," Bea says. "And let's do something already."

"Exactly what do you have in mind?" I ask as the ship quakes from more blaster shots. My harness pulls hard against my chest, keeping me securely in my sling chair.

"Well, first we have to find my sister," Bea says, thinking it over. "She's down there . . . in the middle of that . . . probably in danger. Any ideas?"

"You're right," Rho says, her hair turning deep blue . . . *serious blue*. Then she perks up. "Oh, I do have one idea . . . but . . . uh, it's super dangerous."

"What is it?" Bea says. "Come on, tell us."

"Drae was her Sympathetic, right?" Rho says.

"What's that got to do with it?" I ask, not liking where this is going.

"Your neural implant," Rho says, pointing to the base of my neck. "It's deactivated, but it's linked to Kari's implant. Maybe if we reactivate it, then we could use it to track her."

"Yeah, but one *big* problem," I point out. "Then the feds can also use it to track me. They're waiting for me to come back online. I'm a dangerous fugitive, remember?"

"But that will take them a minute," Rho says. "They think we're still back Earthside, right? They're not expecting us to pop up in the middle of the asteroid belt. If we're lucky, they'll think it's a malfunction at first."

"You might be right," I say, but hesitate. "But how would we reactivate it?"

"Oh, I have an idea," Bea says in excitement, unfastening her harness and jumping up, as the ship plunges and lurches sideways. "Stay put like Captain Dad said. I'll be right back."

Despite the instability and being in the middle of a dog fight, she moves quickly and keeps her footing. Before we can stop her, she takes off and disappears through the door toward the bridge. This is her first time off Earthside, but it's almost like she was born to be in space.

"Kid's got fighting spirit," Rho says with a smirk.

"Yeah, she's related to Kari," I agree with a wry expression. "And her dad's a Raider captain. It all makes a strange sort of sense, doesn't it?"

A few tense minutes later, Bea reappears—but she's not alone. She's got a Raider with her. The woman has gray tufts of hair sticking out from a black bandana and big, ruddy cheeks.

Bea holds her hand, leading her back to us, while she wobbles on her feet . . . and it's not on account of the blaster fire. She's lugging a toolbox behind her that rattles with each step.

"Mrs. Smee, at your service," she says with a theatrical salute, then staggers into the seat next to me. Her breath stinks like gasoline. Sweet gasoline. That's probably rum, though I've never tasted it. She's the drunken engineer who rigged up the warp boosters that nearly killed us.

"Bea, you sure this is a good idea?" Rho whispers. "She seems a bit . . . impaired."

"Her warp boosters worked, didn't they?" Bea says. "We made it to Ceres. She's the best engineer in the universe. I told her about Captain Dad, so she has to do what I say."

"Yup, that's true," Mrs. Smee says with a bewildered sigh. "Cap's got a kid. Who knew? That man's full of mysteries, ain't he?"

"Yeah, and now we have to find his other kid—ASAP," Rho says. "Can you help us?"

I nod and tap my neck. "We need to reactive my neural implant so we can locate her."

"Roger that," Mrs. Smee. "Might sting a little bit. Once you're back online, we'll have to work fast, or the feds will latch on to you . . . like Raiders on a fresh bottle of rum."

She chuckles then reaches into her toolbox and starts pulling out some draconian-looking instruments. They look like torture devices. I swallow hard, feeling like this is a terrible idea. I'm about to back out when suddenly she grips my neck—and she's much stronger than she looks.

"Ouch," I cry out and squirm. *A little bit* was definitely downplaying the pain.

"Don't be such a wimp—hold still!" she demands, digging into the base of my neck with her tools, even though it stings like crazy. "Don't wanna accidentally give you a lobotomy."

That makes me freeze with fear.

Right when I start to think that we should've had a longer discussion about the risks of this procedure, I feel something sharp and tingly. It's that familiar sensation of my neural implant booting back up. My vision blurs and then clears. I see the display in my retinas again.

Draeden, how can I assist you? a soothing female voice echoes in my head.

It's Estrella.

"Back online," I report right away, though my neck still throbs.

"Jackpot!" Mrs. Smee declares in triumph.

I rub my neck, as the pain slowly recedes. But then, it's replaced by another feeling—a leechlike, brain-sucking feeling. I realize what that means—the feds are tracking me. With any luck, they'll think it's a glitch for now. Rho is right. That should buy us time, but not much.

That jolts me to action. I turn back to Mrs. Smee.

"Okay, let's find Kari. The clock is ticking."

But she's already on it. She's pulled out some wiring from her rig, which she connects to the base of my neck and then plugs into a small tablet device. The screen shows static, but then a geographical map displays on it. A little green dot appears on the screen . . . and it's moving fast.

"Look, there she is," Bea says excitedly. "My sister."

Mrs. Smee nods. "Right you are, kid. But, uh . . . that's strange."

"What is it?" I ask, not liking her tone.

"Well, that's her all right," Mrs. Smee slurs, jabbing at the screen. "*Hikari Skye.* Pretty name. Yup, Cap's kid . . . and your Sympathetic. Well, that must've been an interesting Pairing Ceremony," she says with a snicker. "Oh, bet that ruffled some feathers—"

"You bet it did," Rho says with a snort.

"Uh, can you both focus, please?" I cut in, pointing to the screen.

"Right," Mrs. Smee says. "I hacked into your implant to find her location . . ." She zooms in on the blip that's blinking across the screen. "And looks like she's moving. But that's a bit unusual . . . appears she's on foot . . . but not inside the base . . . she's on the surface . . ."

"The surface . . . like out there?" I say in shock. My eyes dart back to the window, as barrages of blaster fire and explosions pummel the surface. "Why would she be on foot?"

"Locking on to her neural feed," Mrs. Smee says. "Generating visual footage."

She pulls up the footage on the tablet. It's from Kari's POV. We've hacked into her visual sensors. She's running in a panic, making the feed look jerky and erratic. Her breath hisses in and out, fogging the view. Blurrily, I spot three figures running beside her in Space Force suits.

But the strange thing is . . . I don't just see her . . . I can *feel* her. I've never been in such close proximity to her with our neural implants connected like this. Her fear and adrenaline flood through me in a terrible rush of emotion. The sensation is altogether out of body and inexplicable, but also so much stronger at the same time. It threatens to overwhelm me.

"Watch out . . . run!" Kari screams to the other guardians.

She sounds terrified. Her fear hits me like blaster fire. Then she glances back— and I catch sight of something behind them. It looks like it's exploding from the ground . . .

That's what they're running from.

But what is it?

"Oh no, it's a cryovolcano," Mrs. Smee says, squinting at the screen. "Instead of lava, they spew out ice and mud. Still, they're quite dangerous . . . nothing to trifle with—"

Abruptly, a direct blast hits our ship and throws us around.

I grab onto Bea, making sure she doesn't fall. My harness catches and yanks me back into my sling chair—and her right along with me. Somehow, Mrs. Smee ends up splayed out across Rho's lap, but she doesn't seem to mind. She's still clutching the tablet with Kari's visual feed.

Then—

Alarms go off. That's a bad sign.

"Incoming!" Gunner yells over the comm. "Hold on to your harnesses!"

"*Frigid bastards*," Captain Skye curses over the comm. "Caught another blasted Arctic Fed ship on our tail. Stand aside, Gunner. I'm dealing with this one . . . *personally*."

Then, the comm cuts out.

A few seconds later, the captain returns fire. Blaster explosions fly about in the void of space. There's no sound in zero-g, but there is light and impact. We lurch around to avoid enemy fire, pivoting and careening, then unleashing a slew of missiles that sail out like comets.

The Arctic Fed ship takes a hit—but avoids serious damage.

They zoom back to attack again. But I tear my eyes away from our skirmish and back to Kari. Her emotions flood through the neural link and force me to only focus on her.

I breathe with her lungs; I think with her mind.

And my heart hammers in rhythm to her own.

I am me—but I am also her at this moment.

She scrambles up a steep crater to the higher ground away from the sludgy river of ice and mud gushing after her. The footage is shaky, jerking around with each movement. I struggle to make out what's happening. It's not easy, especially with her adrenaline engulfing me.

We're locked together.

Then I hear something in my head . . . her voice.

Draeden . . . Draeden . . . Draeden . . .

I sit up with a start. *Does she know I'm here?*

"What is it, Drae?" Bea asks in concern.

"Kari . . . she can feel me . . . watching her."

Hikari . . . Hikari . . . Hikari . . . I think back in rhythm to her heart.

To our hearts. They beat as one now.

Kari and two of the guardians scramble up the crater and make it to safety—but one flails below them. She turns back to help her friend. He's the smallest of the bunch.

It's so like her to always help those in need. I feel her deep relief, but then—

Something worse happens.

Kari freezes—and jerks her gaze to the sky, which is black as sin but illuminated by staccato bursts of blaster fire that flare the vista. She focuses on what resemble tiny black dots parachuting out of Siberian Fed ships, drifting down to the surface. They're dressed in black suits and helmets with the red sickle insignia. They clutch blasters, which are aimed down.

They start firing—right at Kari and her friends.

"Incoming!" Kari screams to her friends. "Get your heads down . . . now!"

That's when I bolt to my feet, yanking the wires out of my neck. I feel searing pain, but I don't care. The images flicker off the screen, but remain in my head. I can still see and hear her.

In a panic, I reach for Rho and grab her arm.

"Drae, what's wrong?" she asks as her hair and eyes turn black.

She fears the worst . . . black means death.

"The Siberian Fed's deploying foot soldiers after Kari and her friends," I yell, pointing through the window to the surface. "We have to help her! They're trapped on the surface."

CHAPTER 49

KARI

We barely escape that cryovolcano eruption.

Anton stares back at the sludge, catching his breath.

"The bombing raids probably triggered the eruption," he says, always the scientist. "All that seismic disturbance combined with pressure that had built up underground."

"Yeah, death ice volcanos are so fascinating," Nadia quips. "Hurry up—we've gotta keep moving. That eruption could draw enemy attention to our position. We can't risk that."

"Yup, she's right," Luna says, patting Anton on the back. "Roll out, Guardians."

We start covering the rest of the way to the docking bay, moving low and stealthily. Suddenly, I feel the strangest sensation again—hear him calling my name.

Hikari.

I first felt it when we were running from the cryovolcano, but dismissed it as part of my panic reaction. But now, Draeden's voice is back inside my head—and stronger than ever. But how is this possible? He vanished back Earthside a few days ago, and his neural implant was deactivated. Suddenly, his voice reverberates through my head again . . . calling my name.

My ears ring, and my vision doubles and blurs. I think back to him—

Draeden.

That's when I'm engulfed by that same brain-sucking feeling as when I jack into the mail pods. But that's impossible. How can we link together without the tech? But that doesn't mean that it's not happening. And for a quick moment, I glimpse something as if through his eyes.

It's hard to make out at first, but it looks like the interior of a ship. All of a sudden, I hear a laugh—light and airy, tinkling like metal tapping on glass—and I recognize it right away.

That's Bea's laugh.

There's no mistaking it. That's my little sister.

But just as quickly as it appeared, the vision vanishes from my mind—and I snap back to the present. Everyone is laughing at something Nadia said to tease her brother. I try to join in, but still feel completely disoriented. However, this small moment of levity is short-lived.

"Incoming bogey!" Luna yells, pointing to the sky. "Get your heads down!"

Out of nowhere, a Siberian ship flies low overhead.

We don't have time to duck as it coasts right over us. I'm sure they spotted us. Luckily, they don't open fire. That's weird, I think. But then I remember we're small targets.

"That was close—" Nadia starts.

But she's cut off as the ship doubles back and does another low pass, exposing their hull. They still hold their fire, but then I understand why. That's when their bay doors retract—

Foot soldiers parachute out clutching blasters—too many to count.

They're clad in black deployment suits and helmets with tinted visors, emblazoned with their sigil, the red sickle. They drift down like little black specks, growing larger as they fall.

They're headed straight for us.

They aim their blasters—

Now, they open fire on us.

"Incoming!" I scream to my friends.

The sky blisters red with the ambush. It's all noise and explosions. Before I enlisted, I thought that combat would be like the comic books, orchestrated and organized.

But the reality is—it's complete chaos.

"Hurry, run!" I scream, and we all break for it.

We have to get away and find cover, where we can dig in and return fire. That's our only chance. My suit plus the low gravity makes me bound over the surface faster than normal. Luna and Anton bounce-run ahead of me, but we're missing—

Nadia.

I turn back in horror.

She's panicked and frozen—and completely exposed. The Siberian soldiers have almost finished their descent. She has to get out of there and find cover fast, or they'll pick her off.

"Nadia, hurry and get down!" I start screaming.

But it's already too late. The next cascade of enemy fire rains, drowning out my voice and shattering the thin air. I have to dive down to save myself. Once it lets up, I stagger up and try to go back for Nadia. I spot her silhouette right over the next ridge. I start running for her.

Before I can reach her position, I hear the sharp whistle of more blaster fire.

"Incoming, duck now!" I scream.

I dive behind the rocks, but I keep my eyes pinned on the ridge ahead. She hears me this time and drops down into the icy dust, despite her panic. But the next round of fire stuns us both.

My ears ring, my head spins. I feel nauseous. I want to puke.

I don't take a direct hit—but Nadia gets blasted and crumples to the ground. I scramble to my feet and rush over to her. I see blood, too much blood. I struggle with the weight of her prone body—so much heavier than when she was conscious—and drag it over the blaster-torn landscape, feeling the hot, wet slick of blood dripping down my shoulder. It's not slowing.

It's gushing.

Harold, check vitals, I tell my neural implant, even though I already know it's dire.

I can feel her blood now on my skin, but also I can see the reality of her status in my sensors. The erratic throb of each weak heartbeat. The rush of looming unconsciousness clouding her brain like cotton—and also mine. The dampening of eyesight that comes right before . . .

Death.

I know with certainty. It's about to claim us both. I crest the next ridge with a staggering limp, dragging her body with me. We create twin rivulets in the dust. Ice crystals cling to our suits. I try to call for help, but my comm unit crackles uselessly. It must be damaged.

The rain of blaster fire pauses, but I only register briefly how strange that is. Then I understand. The faceless enemies land in crouches surrounding us. There is nowhere to run, nowhere to hide now, not with her body weighing me down. And even then . . .

I won't leave her, I think, hugging her closer. *I'd rather die than abandon her.*

The Siberian soldiers encircle us closer. Their tinted visors shield their faces. Their breath hisses out through the air filters in smoky tendrils. Their boots kick up icy dust. Twenty of them. Maybe thirty . . . I can't tell . . . they blur together. They retract their parachutes and raise their blasters. Dimly, I see another swarm of enemy soldiers ambushing Luna and Anton in their hole.

They tramp closer to us. I hear them speaking. The strange language whispers out of their helmets. The leader, I'm guessing, signals to his comrades. They aim at our chests. Our suits have body armor, but that will offer little protection from that many blasters at this close range.

We're done for, I know with certainty. This is the end for us.

They start to pull the triggers.

I shut my eyes and wait for death to claim us, when suddenly—

Another ship appears in the sky over us, coming down fast for landing. The pilot is expert level, I notice despite my panic, able to descend quickly in the middle of a combat zone, as if out of nowhere. I may not speak the enemy's language, but I recognize this—

The accented word sounds like . . . *Reyder!*

There's no mistaking what that means in any language. They're right—it's the Raiders. The skull and crossbones sigil on the hull makes that clear. The Siberian soldiers yell and regroup, turning to face the new threat. Their panic reflects my own. The Raiders touch down only fifty yards from us, setting off a cloud of icy smoke. The skyjacked ship looks more like space junk but somehow seems to handle itself better than our newer federation vessels.

I flash back to the savages who attacked us in the combat sim. Panic washes through me like I've been fear gassed. If there's one saving grace, I'm glad Nadia has drifted into unconsciousness. I try my comm again to call for help. "Mayday! Mayday . . . help!" But all I hear is static, peppered by other guardians' screams. It's unnerving and means one thing.

Ceres Base is about to fall.

I pray that we find a way to turn the tides, that the casualties aren't too steep, and that this isn't a bad sign that means we're about to lose the larger war. But all that matters right now is—

Nadia.

She's still breathing. But it's shallow at best. I hear her ventilator hiss in and out . . . Weakly.

Meanwhile, the Siberian soldiers are the only thing standing between us and the Raiders. They kneel in tight formation and open fire on the Raider ship. The blasts hit the shell, but the shields are too strong and deflect the shots. They spark and ricochet into the icy crust.

The Siberian soldiers stop firing. They chatter to each other in confusion.

But then, the Raider ship comes alive, tilting its blasters down and returning fire, taking them down one by one, skillfully picking them off. They scream and crumple like dominoes.

Blast. Blast. Blast. Blast.

I flinch with each shot.

I'm still clutching Nadia, her blood leaking onto me and soaking the ground. I have my blaster, and hers. But what use will they be in the face of this new—and worse—threat?

In the chaos of the standoff, Luna and Anton sneak over and rush to our side. "Oh no," Anton says when he sees me cradling his sister's unconscious body.

"She's still alive," he says, checking her vitals. "But barely . . ."

Luna raises her blaster, hunkering down next to us. "Don't look now," she says grimly. "But our situation just went from bad to worse."

"Raiders," I mutter like a slur. "Guess it's our lucky day."

Suddenly, out of nowhere, they deploy from their ship, grappling down like gymnasts. That's the only way I can describe it. They let out fearsome war cries as they land, just like in the combat sim. They're wearing helmets and scavenged suits. My heart hardens. I might despise the Siberian soldiers. They blasted my friend. But what I feel for the Raiders burns much deeper—

It's pure hatred.

Belting out savage war cries, they fall on the remaining Siberian soldiers with their rudimentary-looking weapons, including electrified sabers, axes, katanas, spears, and crossbows that fire blaster shots. Despite their eccentric appearance, their weapons prove deadly and pierce through armor. The Siberian soldiers don't stand a chance. But they still put up a solid defense.

That buys us a chance to escape.

"Come on . . . hurry!" I hiss to Luna. We shoulder Nadia, dragging her behind a rocky outcropping. Then we hunker down while Anton tries to stop his sister from bleeding out.

"Filthy pirates," I curse, rechecking my blaster to make sure it's still working, then taking aim at them. "Probably sweeping in to scavenge what's left after our base falls."

"Yup, that's their MO," Luna agrees. "But stars, they sure can fight."

She's right. Their combat style is impressive.

In short order, they dispatch the rest of the Siberian platoon. The few left alive flee back toward their ship. Weirdly, the Raiders let them escape. We were taught that they never leave survivors alive, and they don't take prisoners. So, why'd they let them go?

Now, nothing stands between us and the Raiders. They regroup and turn on us. This will be our final stand. We're prepared to fight to the death, rather than being taken captive.

But then, that strange sucking feeling stampedes through my head again—

Hikari.

It's Draeden again. My vision doubles and blurs. I push back against it, trying to focus on staying alive. I take one last look at my fellow guardians—more like, my friends.

"If I'm going to die, then I'd rather die with you," I say, clutching my blaster tighter. Luna and Anton nod grimly. "And I'd rather go down fighting."

With that final missive, I leap out and point my blaster at the first Raider. He's their captain, from the looks of his uniform. But then, he tilts his visor up—revealing his identity.

I stop in my tracks when I make out his face.

It's not just any random Raider.

He's my father.

"You bastard," I scream when I make out his features. He's got a trimmed goatee and wavy black hair, and he looks decades older. But there's no mistaking his visage, so like my own.

I'm about to squeeze the trigger when—

"Kari, don't blast him!"

I'm so shocked by the familiar voice that I freeze.

It's Drae. He bounds out of the Raider ship, wearing an air mask.

My mind struggles to understand the situation. But then I switch into rescue mode. The Raiders must have kidnapped him from Earthside . . . that's the only possible explanation.

"Deserter scum, let him go!" I scream at my father.

My finger feels for the trigger again, but then something else happens—

A smaller figure darts out from the ship.

Bea throws herself between me and the Raider captain.

"Kari, don't blast him!" my little sister begs, wrapping her arms around our father's legs. "I just got Captain Dad back! And I'm not losing him on account of your dumb actions."

Confusion overpowers me. I struggle to process it but fail miserably. Tears prick my eyes and blur my vision. I feel the trigger . . . my finger strokes it . . .

But finally, I lower my blaster.

"Bea . . . Drae . . ." I stammer through my tears and confusion. "You're alive . . . and you're in space. And what in the blazing stars do you mean by . . . Captain Dad?"

Drae approaches me cautiously. He keeps his hands raised in case I decide to blast him. My hand is shaky, but I hold my fire . . . of course. Our eyes meet—and something happens. Our neural links fire up and lock together. I can't explain the sensation, it's so otherworldly. But I don't just see him now—I feel him. His fear, his worry, his excitement, and . . .

His love for me.

It overpowers everything else. He can't make out my face through my helmet. But he reaches out and places one hand on the golden visor. No words pass between us, only feelings. I can't believe he's here; I never thought that I'd see him again. Especially not on Ceres, so far from Earth. And certainly not with my sister—and a whole Raider crew. That's led by my dad.

How in the stars did this happen?

"Kari, listen . . . we need your help," Drae says in a soft voice. Through our link, it echoes inside my head, too. "To save everyone . . . actually the whole universe."

I frown at him. I can't believe what I'm hearing.

"The universe? What do you mean? And where's Rho? Did she come with you, too?"

"Miss me that much?" Rho says, emerging from the ship right on cue. She always did have great timing. It's like some kind of crazy reunion. She comes over to Drae's side.

I can't believe this is happening. But time is running out.

"Listen, we have to hurry," I say, snapping back to my senses. I gesture to Anton, who's cradling Nadia behind the rocks. "My friend . . . she's wounded. Can you help us?"

My father steps up. But I raise my blaster.

"Stay back—not so close!" I cry out.

What happened in my test flashes through my head.

My father raises his hands. "Look, I know you must have a lot of questions," he says in a steady voice. "But we've got a top-notch medical bay. My crew can save your friend."

"Kari, please . . . you can trust him," Bea says in a pleading voice. She looks up at me with her big eyes, still gripping his legs. "He's not what you think. Just give him a chance."

My dad is right. I still have a hundred—no, more like a million questions. But we're out of options. I have to let my father save her life. Plus, if I don't trust Rho, Drae, and Bea—

Then who can I trust?

That makes up my mind. I drop my blaster and signal to Anton and Luna to let them through to help. My father doesn't waste time. He signals urgently to his crew.

"Gunner, get her to the medical bay!"

Led by a young woman, they load Nadia onto a floating gurney and rush her to the ship. Despite her diminutive size, she carries sharp authority.

"You heard Cap—get her inside ASAP," she barks.

I watch helplessly as Nadia's body convulses on the gurney and then vanishes inside the ship. "Please, don't let her die," I whisper to my dad, praying that I made the right choice.

Anton and Luna stand up when I emerge from the medical bay. I just spoke to the lead medic. They've been working for over an hour to stabilize her and treat her blaster injuries, including two synthetic blood transfusions. Luckily, the Raider ship does have a top-notch facility.

"Thank the stars," I say in relief. "Nadia is going to make it . . . barely."

"She's really . . . okay?" Anton says. I nod, and then he whispers, "But are . . . we?"

"Yeah, out of the lion's den into the mouth," Luna hisses to us, glancing around suspiciously. "Didn't think our situation could be worse. Think we can trust them?"

"Well, not like we have a choice," I say, thinking it over. "Nadia is stable—but too critical to move. Plus, they just saved her life. If they wanted to harm us, then why go to all that effort?"

While we were waiting, I already briefed them that the Raider captain is my long-lost father, much to their shock and dismay. And the others are my friends and sister, who went missing. For good reason, their trepidation at being on a Raider ship remains . . . as does mine.

"But why are they here?" Luna says in a low voice. "How are they connected to the Raiders? Not to mention . . . where has your dad been this whole time?"

"Exactly," Anton says. "Something feels . . . fishy."

Suddenly, Gunner reappears in the corridor.

"Fishy, huh?" she quips. "Too bad we're vegan. Not much fish 'round these parts. Just loads of kale . . . and rum. All your questions will be answered. Just come with me."

"Where's my dad?" I ask, hesitating.

"He's on the bridge with your sister, making sure our cloaking shields hold up," she replies. "He felt that maybe it's better if you speak to the others first."

I nod at that. It makes sense.

We have no option but to cooperate and follow her. Nadia's life remains in their hands. Gunner leads us through the ship, weaving past other Raiders, some who are swigging from corked bottles and seem quite tipsy, to the main cabin where Drae and Rho are waiting.

He looks the same as our last exchange, maybe a little weary, while Rho's nano implants turn a vivid pink fading to dark blue. She's thrilled to see me, but also apprehensive about it.

Gunner quickly bids goodbye and scurries off to the bridge, leaving us alone. We sink into the sling chairs facing my friends. I can't help feeling my heart lurch when I see Drae. Warring thoughts erupt in my head. He abandoned me, so why do I still feel so drawn to him?

"*How . . . what . . . when?*" I choke out a series of jumbled questions. I fling my arms up in the air. "Blast it, I don't know where to start. What in the *blazing stars* is going on?"

Drae sets his lips, which creep into a slight smile.

"Of course I'll tell you everything," he promises me. He leans forward and holds out his hands. I stare at them in confusion as he says, "But first, let's try this . . . hold my hands."

"Hold your hands?" I scoff, thinking this feels inappropriate. "Really, now?"

"Just trust me, okay?" he replies with a smirk. "For once? Mrs. Smee said this might work—and help you believe me. If all goes well, then it should be like our exchanges."

"Mrs. Smee?" I ask in skepticism. "This is her idea?"

"Yeah, she's their head engineer," Rho says. "Uh, she's a bit unorthodox. But her warp boosters are the reason we got to Ceres in time. She helped us locate you on the surface."

"And save your friend," Drae adds. "So, do you trust me?"

"Fine." I reach out and grasp his hands—

Suddenly, I feel our neural implants link together.

That brain-sucking feeling takes over. His memories cascade into me . . . and I learn everything . . . about what really happened with Jude . . . my father and his mother and the cover-up . . . what brought them out here . . . but before that finishes transferring . . . he breaks our grip.

I exhale sharply, coming out of the connection. I saw quick glimpses—something about a digital package—but then the connection broke and the memories vanished from my mind.

"Oh my . . ." I stammer, disoriented. "So much has happened."

He nods. "But now you know . . . everything. And that I'm telling the truth, too."

I can't deny it. That's part of the magic of the neural implants. They have built-in lie detectors. Plus, I don't just hear his thoughts—it's like I experience his memories.

"I know it's a lot to absorb," Drae goes on apologetically. "And you probably still have a million more questions. And need to talk to your father. But there's something more pressing."

"Okay, care to brief us?" Luna asks. "Since we aren't mind-melded to your Sympathetic?"

"Yeah, what's really going on?" Anton says. They both sound frustrated.

Drae nods. "Of course. We're all here for one simple reason."

"Oh, and what's that?" Anton asks, sounding skeptical.

Drae gestures to the windows, where below our ship, the battle for Ceres Base rages on, before continuing, "We have to stop this war . . . before it spreads across the universe."

"And back to Earth, too," Rho says, picking up the tangent.

Their words stun us. We glance at each other.

"Stop the war?" I say in disbelief. "That's why you're here?"

"Listen, you seem like nice civilians, so I hate to break it to you," Anton says with a shrug. "But we're just a couple of grunts. What good are we against all the federation forces?"

"Exactly, it's impossible," Luna agrees. "Plus, this war is a necessary evil."

"Yeah, she's right," I jump in. "The Siberian Fed assassinated our secretary-general. We have to defend our federation from terrorists. You saw it! They killed all those little kids!"

Now I'm feeling heated. It's all over the newsfeeds. It's everything I believe in. It's why I enlisted. But Drae takes a deep breath. I can sense that he's weighing his next words very carefully. "You're right. That's all over the newsfeeds. But what if . . . it wasn't them at all?"

"Then . . . who did it?" I ask, exchanging a baffled look with Luna and Anton. I trail off. Drae holds my gaze for a long moment, then utters words that change everything.

"It wasn't them—and I have proof. The attacks were alien."

CHAPTER 50

DRAE

"Did you say . . . *alien*?" Kari says with a shocked expression.

Our eyes meet—and she holds my gaze. The back of my neck tingles and burns as we sync up. My emotions ricochet back to her just as strongly. My heart thumps in rhythm to hers. This is the moment I've been dreaming of . . . all I want is to hold her and take her in my arms and whisper in her ear that everything is going to be okay. Even though I don't know that at all.

But I can't right now. Time is running short . . .

Too short.

I force myself to stay focused on the immediate threat and not get distracted. But that's easier said than done, when all I've wished for is to be close to her. Now, we're sitting mere inches apart, but I can't even touch her, let alone kiss her. It's not the right time.

Time never seems to be on our side, I think woefully.

I drag my gaze off Kari and look down. I don't relish what I'm about to say.

"Yes, the threat is alien," I continue. "And I have evidence."

Then as quickly as I can, I explain everything that Professor Trebond told us about the alien threat. I broke our connection earlier before Kari could learn this through our link because I knew her friends—the other two guardians—needed to hear it, too. This part affects all of them, and it's their right to know the truth. The more I talk, the more outlandish it all sounds. But Kari and her friends listen to every word, their expressions growing more and more astonished.

But I keep talking and talking.

"The Resistance discovered the truth about the GGA," I continue, turning more serious. "They still don't know much about these invaders. Aside from the fact that they were able to infiltrate our defenses and plant the explosive device without being detected."

"Yeah, that's alarming," Luna says. "It means we're completely vulnerable."

"That's right," Rho says, picking up where I left off. Her hair and eyes turn jet black , , , *serious*. "We don't know what they look like or where they come from. We're still very much in the dark about everything. They do have superior tech. But Professor Trebond has a theory."

"What's her theory?" Kari asks with a frown.

Rho sets her lips. "They studied us and realized we're militaristic and prone to violence. We have powerful weapons that can destroy us many times over. They plotted to use this against us. Essentially, their plan is to trigger interstellar war to break out, so we destroy ourselves."

"Destroy ourselves?" Anton repeats. "But why would they want that?"

But Kari puts it together first. "Asteroid fires, that way they can invade Earth and capture our planet without even fighting. Actually, it sounds like something Sun Tzu wrote."

Anton trades a look with her. "*The supreme art of war is to subdue the enemy without fighting*," he quotes. "Of course, it's ancient battle strategy from *The Art of War*."

I nod in recognition. "That's exactly what the professor said."

"Oh no, but that means it's working," Kari says, gesturing to the window. The night is as bright as most days. The whole dwarf planet looks like an inferno engulfed in explosions.

"Yup, we took the bait," I say with a mournful shrug. "But the aliens are really behind everything. The GGA, that Siberian Fed flyover, probably the assassination of our secretary-general. Oh, but the Raider attack? That was your father trying to get the drive to you."

"The Raider attack was . . . my father?" Kari says in surprise. "Only our defenses must have chased them off before he could sneak onto the base and get the intel to me."

"Yup, exactly," I say with a nod. "So, unfortunately, we're like plan B."

That's when I pull out the drive and hold it out. The tiny metal device catches the light, refracting it. Everyone's eyes fix on it. The fate of our whole universe depends on it.

Kari studies the drive. "What exactly is on it?"

I close my fist over it. "Forensic evidence proving that the GGA explosive device was alien in origin, only that it had markings to make it look like the Siberian Fed to throw us off. We've got to find a way to disseminate the evidence to Space Force, so they'll halt the war."

"Yup, before we destroy ourselves," Rho says. "And the aliens invade and take Earth."

"But why come all the way out here to find me?" Kari asks, catching my gaze. I feel her probing deeper into my neural synapses. "Why me of all people? I'm green as the stars."

"Right, Professor Trebond said they needed to get the evidence to someone they trusted," I explain. "Back Earthside, they want this war to happen. They've been hoping for it . . . well . . . for a long time. The interstellar war industrial complex. But the Resistance doesn't have anyone inside Space Force. They also wanted someone who wasn't yet . . . brainwashed . . ."

"Yup, and Xena suggested you," Rho adds. "All the bus drivers are aligned with the Resistance. She vouched for you, which led them to target your Sympathetic. I just happened to get caught up in everything somehow. And, well, the professor thought he needed my help."

"Please, you needed *my* help," Drae shoots back.

"Or maybe, we needed each other?" Rho finishes with a smirk.

"Fine, I get that," Kari says, raising her eyebrows. "But how does this involve my sister? She's just a kid. I can't believe Xena would recruit her for such a dangerous mission."

"Oh, Bea wasn't part of the plan." I smile at the memory. "That little rascal stowed away on Xena's bus. Xena tried to get Bea to go home, but she refused and threatened to bust us."

"Of course she did," Kari says, shaking her head. "That little snitch. That also explains why she kept going back to our old trailer . . . she must have been spying on Xena."

All the pieces seem to fall together. But then Kari frowns.

"Look, if you're right about these aliens," she says, looking troubled. "Then this is serious. I'm sorry to disappoint you, especially after all this effort . . . but what can I do to help? We need to get that drive out ASAP. And not just to Space Force, but to all the federations."

"We haven't figured out that out yet," I say with a grimace. "If we go to the newsfeeds, then they'll just bury the story and call it fake news. There's no free media back Earthside anymore. Our government wants this war to happen. We need another way to get it out."

"Guess we're the plan B for a reason," Rho adds, as her hair and eyes blush light pink. *Embarrassed.* "We didn't even know if we could find you. We also thought we had a little more time, but then the assassination happened . . ." She trails off in defeat, her visage tinting black.

Silence falls over the cabin. We're all stumped on what to do next. Feeling frustrated, I look through the window again at the fiery battle down below. Every second is another life lost.

But Kari brightens suddenly. "Wait, I think I've got an idea! It's obvious really . . ."

She looks at her friends, the other guardians. I can tell that she's become their leader. I'm not surprised at all. After all, I've been following her for years too . . . even to space.

"Well, what is it?" I ask, saying what we're all thinking.

Kari points to Anton's wrist.

"We use the postal service," she says. "And he's got the key."

"Of course!" Anton says with a lopsided smile. "I'm just mad I didn't think of it first."

"Think it'll work?" Luna asks. "The mail to the rescue? Kind of has a nice ring to it."

I exchange a confused glance with Rho. "The postal service?"

"Please, allow me to explain," Anton says, standing up and speaking with great pride. "Space Force has the fastest, most dependable postal fleet in the galaxy. Not to mention, Ceres Base is a huge communications hub. If anyone can get this intel out and fast . . . they can."

I think it over. Before I became a Sympathetic, I never fully understood the value of our postal service. But after my exchanges with Kari, I've gained tremendous respect for them. Without it, our whole federation would fall apart . . . literally. We'd fragment to pieces.

"Of course," I say, taking that in. "The only way to prevent a cover-up is if we get the message out to everyone at the same time so it's undeniable. They don't have time to bury it."

"Yeah," Rho agrees. "They won't be able to cover it up."

"But a few low-level guardians?" Luna says. "Who went AWOL in the middle of a battle? And a bunch of fugitive civilians and a Raider crew? Who's gonna believe us?"

Hearing it said out loud like that deflates all of us.

"Well, it would only work," Rho says finally, "if there was someone you trusted inside the postal service. Otherwise, to put it bluntly . . . like Luna said . . . we're screwed."

But Kari doesn't look worried.

"Postmaster Haven," she says, turning to Anton. "I trust him completely."

Anton flashes a grin. "Me too. He's probably down in the bunker with the other postal workers, waiting out the attack. With any luck, I can reach him directly."

"But how?" Rho asks. "Communications must be restricted. The base is on lockdown."

"Behold—my new postal key," he says with a flourish. "The device syncs up with my neural link, but it uses an independent communication network." Anton flashes his wrist with what looks like an antique watch fastened around it, only housing advanced comm technology.

"Oh, it's like some magical wizard tech," Luna says. "Except it lets postal workers communicate directly with the postmaster, kind of like a secret commlink."

"That's perfect," I say. "That way they can't hack us."

"Amazing!" Rho looks impressed. "Wow, now I regret not enlisting."

Anton nods. "It's only for postal workers. Guess we're like the wizards."

"And thank the stars for that," Kari says. "This might save us after all."

We're scattered around the cabin—two civilians and three newly minted guardians on a Raider ship. A ragtag bunch, if there ever was one. Doubt creeps into my heart, along with my familiar cowardice. *What chance do we stand to save the universe?* I feel a rush of dread.

But then Kari speaks up in a strong and steady voice. It reverberates through the cabin. "It's decided then?" she says, sweeping her gaze over us. "We trust Postmaster Haven?"

Everyone voices their agreement.

With that settled, Anton starts cranking the hands on his postal key. It reminds me of an antique wristwatch, the kind from the olden days. They spin wildly. Then they lock into place, as the whole face of the watch lights up and lets out a chime. Luna was right—it definitely reminds me of wizard tech. He waits for it to connect. I hold my breath as my heart hammers.

"*Postmaster Haven?*" Anton says through his neural link to the key. "*It's Anton . . . I know this is going to sound crazy. But we need your help to stop this war—*"

Suddenly, the cabin rocks violently as blaster fire hits us, throwing us around. I'm thrust forward as we all struggle to stay in our sling chairs. Then, another blast hits directly—

Smoke and flames erupt outside the windows, billowing and extinguishing into the void. Alarms blare . . . the scary emergency kind. Gunner's urgent voice pipes over the comm. I struggle to hear it over the alarms, while outside the window flames lick the stars.

"Incoming attack!" Gunner yells. "Those Siberian bastards don't give up. They broke through our cloaking shields!" There's crackling and static—and her voice cuts off.

Then Captain Skye comes on the comm.

"Blast the stars! And looks like they brought some Arctic friends this time."

CHAPTER 51

KARI

W atch out!" Captain Skye barks into the comm. "Arctic Fed . . . incoming!" he finishes in a growl. More blasts hit our Raider ship, threatening to destroy it. We're under attack.

The ship shakes again as we struggle to hold on. Then I rush over to Anton. He's struggling to connect with Postmaster Haven, using the postal key fastened to his wrist.

"The drive . . ." Anton says urgently. "I need it . . . now!"

I signal to Drae, but before I speak the words aloud, he hears my thoughts. "Here, catch!" he yells and chucks it through the air. It arcs toward us. Anton grabs it—but then frowns.

"Asteroid fires, this is old pre-war tech. Not compatible. We need a way to upload it."

My heart sinks, but then Rho brightens to yellow.

"Oh, I know!" she says, hopping up. "I'll fetch Mrs. Smee. She'll know what to do." I'm about to ask who that is, but then I remember she's their engineer with an affinity for rum.

Despite the ship's violent lurching and flames erupting just outside the window, quickly extinguished by the cold expanse of space, Rho unfastens her harness and bolts from the cabin.

"Wait, it's not safe—" I yell after her.

I'm used to needing to protect her. But she turns back and grins at me.

"Kari, you worry too much!" she shoots back. Then she skips from the cabin as if we're on a fun field trip, not in the middle of a combat zone. The door seals shut behind her.

Before I can worry about my best friend, more blasts rain down on our ship. I hold on to my sling chair. Outside, I spot the sigils on the attack ships as they whiz by—

"Siberian and Arctic Fed," Luna says with a steely look. "It's only a matter of time before all the other Proxies call up their Star Alliances, and they all jump into the fray. Then . . ."

I know what it means. "All-out interstellar war."

That chills me. We hold on as the attacks rain down on our ship, blast after blast ricocheting off. We fire back, but there are too many of them. Suddenly, the cabin door opens—Mrs. Smee staggers through it, though I can't tell if it's from the blasts rocking our ship, or too much rum. Rho rushes after her, looking fiery. They both head for our sling chairs.

"Upload . . . you said?" Mrs. Smee says with a sharp hiccup. Her cheeks are ruddy, while her eyes look a bit glassy. Not a good sign, I think. "Gimme the drive . . ."

Anton looks unsure, but she snatches it from his hand and starts working to upload it. She connects wires to Anton's key, then back to her tablet. She looks like she knows what she's doing, but I'm still concerned. Abruptly, the ship rocks and drops. My harness digs into my shoulders. More blaster fire hits us, and more flames erupt outside. The alarms turn shriller—

That's a bad sign. Our deflector shields must be failing.

"So, what's our plan?" I say, looking around and waiting for someone else to take charge. But then I realize something crazy—I'm the one in charge. This is my decision now.

"Right, we need to buy more time," I say, answering my own question and unbuckling my harness. "For the drive to upload and the transmission to go through."

"Time to fight back," Luna agrees, unfastening her harness too.

"Plus, you know how much I hate sitting around doing nothing," I say, jumping to my feet. "We graduated from Basic. We're trained guardians. Maybe we can help my dad."

"Are you sure?" Drae says, sounding apprehensive.

But he knows better than to talk me out of this.

"It's pretty dangerous . . ." Rho starts. But she knows better, too.

Once I've made up my mind like this, I don't like to change it. And there's more—this is my sworn duty. Even if I'm protecting a Raider ship, technically our enemies, I'm doing it for the good of our federation. I get the feeling the drill sergeant would approve. A good guardian doesn't just blindly follow orders but uses their best judgment. I've come to realize that.

I charge toward the door with Luna on my heels, but then turn back. "Once Mrs. Smee uploads the drive, then Anton . . . you know what to do. Right?"

"Of course," Anton says with a salute. His eyes light up like I've never seen before. "Time to deliver the mail to the stars. Who knew postal work could be so riveting?"

"The fate of our universe is in your hands," I reply. "Don't let us down."

I salute back, then rush through the door with Luna trailing after me. Our boots thump on the smooth floors of the corridor in tandem. The door whooshes shut behind us. Raiders scurry around, some looking jubilant and exhilarated by the explosions, others more panicked.

Using Harold, I zero in on the right direction as we dash through the twisting, maze-like passages of the ship. It's been renovated and expanded, making it hard to navigate. But my neural implant finds some old blueprints of the original ship, and it's not that different. The core structure remains the same. Finally, I spot the way to the stairs that lead to the bridge.

Abruptly, the ship takes a bigger blast.

If not for our reinforced suits, we'd be hitting the deck.

"This can't keep up. We've gotta buy them time," I say to Luna, once the shaking subsides. "Come on, this way!"

We find my father on the bridge, where he's in command and directing their response to the attack. Several Proxy ships trail after us, firing off blasts that light up the skies.

"Gunner, get us out of here!" my father barks. He sits in the captain's chair, every bit the Raider leader, while Gunner sits at the controls and pilots the ship.

The bridge resembles our Space Force vessels, only with the same embellishments, and what looks like some illegal warp tech and other black-market modifications. The Raiders have certainly made it their own. "Disarm the Stars" is emblazoned across the ceiling.

"Aye, Cap!" Gunner works the switches and switches to manual, and we bank right, then left, then right again. We twist around again as Luna and I struggle to stay on our feet.

At first, it looks like Gunner's moves worked and we lost them—

But then they swoop back around. More blasts sail out and hit us.

"Asteroid fires," my father curses, then speaks into the comm to his ship. "What're you waiting for? An invitation? Blast them to the stars already!"

Our ship fires back from the blaster pods, but they miss the Proxies. Frustration surges through me. The ship can't take much more damage. I don't need to be a pilot to know that. Alarms are beeping everywhere on the bridge. Gunner can't flick them off fast enough.

"Dad . . ." I start, knowing how strange and awkward it sounds coming from my lips. But I push through it. "We want to help. We want to fight . . ."

"I don't know . . . it's dangerous," he starts, but I wave him off and affirm my wishes. "Fine, down the corridor. Find the blaster pods . . . climb in one . . . and have at it!"

That's all we need to hear. Luna and I bolt down that way, rushing past Raiders darting around in the chaos. One even clutches a case of rum as if it's a life raft, albeit one that won't get him very far. "Guess rum is . . . vegan," Luna quips as he staggers past us.

"Well, at least part of their rep checks out," I say, realizing that it might be the only true thing that we knew about them. Rum . . . and I wonder if they have real chocolate, too.

"Over here," I say, looking for open blaster pods not occupied by angry Raiders. They're rigged up with spherical-shaped ball turrets for maximum range and versatility. Luna climbs into the first one and straps herself into the sling chair, which pivots and swings around, allowing her to target the enemy ships with precision. I clamber into the one right across the corridor.

We lock in our commlinks, and then—

"Let's blast those Proxy bastards!" Luna says. "We need to buy Anton more time."

"For Nadia," I say, and then I grip the trigger.

The Proxy ships bank around—Siberian and Arctic Fed—but we return fire. I use my targeting sensors to unleash a slew of blaster shots. My chair swings around while I pull the trigger, tracking the enemy ships through the void. The first few shots don't connect.

But then, getting the hang of it, I hit the thrusters on a Siberian attack ship. The twin engines explode as the ship somersaults and loses control, falling away behind us. They'll recover, probably without casualties, but I took them out of the fray. I didn't want to kill them.

Now, thanks to Drae and the Resistance, I know that they aren't our real enemies. Same as the Raiders aren't brutal savages. But we need to buy time for Anton—and avoid getting blasted to pieces. They are trying to kill us, after all.

"That felt great," I say through my link to Luna.

"Nice shot, Kari!" my dad cheers over the comm. "Don't look now, more *incoming*—"

Our ship lurches to avoid the detonations, flipping upside down and diving fast. Gunner's skills appear to be unmatched. But we're outnumbered. More Proxy ships join the dogfight.

How long can we hold them off? And stay in one piece?

Anton needs to hurry with that upload.

I reach out through my neural link to Drae. I can sense him vaguely, somewhere on the ship, through the chaos and damage and shaking—then suddenly—I catch a quick flash through his retinas of the cabin. Mrs. Smee is working on the upload . . . but it's going slow.

It says only twenty-five percent.

More time . . . more time . . . please!

I hear his plea through our connection. Then I block out everything else and focus on combat. I don't have a choice. I swing my chair around, pulling the trigger rapid-fire.

I target a stealthy Arctic Fed ship that's snuck up on our tail—

Blast. Blast. Blast-blast.

It's a direct hit.

The ship spirals out of control and falls away as we rocket past. I feel a moment of elation, but then more keep coming at us, one after the other. Luna takes down another Siberian Fed ship, but they won't stop blasting us. And worse, a few seconds later, more enemy ships materialize out of warp, swarming our airspace. They've called for reinforcements.

Gunner does her best to evade them. But there are too many.

Draeden, update? I think urgently to him.

I catch another glimpse . . . *seventy-eight percent.*

I wince at that. I don't need to hear the shrill alarms on the bridge to know we're taking on too much damage. But we still have a chance, and that's what keeps me going. Plus, I'd rather go down fighting than sitting around in the bunker. *I don't regret anything*, I realize.

Except for one thing . . .

And that thing surprises the stars out of me. *Drae . . . I regret not kissing him in the cabin . . . when I had the chance.* Like a real kiss, the kind where I don't fight it like I fight everything in my life, but where I finally give in and surrender to him. *His lips crushing mine. His strong arms pulling me closer. Breathing him in.* The thought shoots through my head before I can stop it.

The wrenching of my heart tells me something with certainty . . .

Drae, I love you.

The truth of it thumps my heart and sends deep chills surging through my entire body. Then, I hear his voice in my head, too.

Message received . . . I love you, too.

I sense his amusement, but also the seriousness of his heart's desire. Even at the end of all things—on the brink of death—this steadies my nerves and gives me what I need to keep going.

Luna and I blast a few more, but reinforcements keep appearing out of warp— one second there's empty space, the next a Proxy attack ship—all joining the melee. We heave and drop sideways as one engine goes out, and the other one looks like it's on life support. It's smoking and stuttering out flames. We're jerking and lurching through space. I check in with my dad.

"Don't stop blasting them!" he orders me. "Gunner, give them a run for it!"

Somehow, his first officer digs in, executing a series of complicated evasive flight maneuvers that leave the Proxies in our dust. But we're limping through space with one engine out and the other about to die. But we keep fighting and whipping around, not giving up.

I cling to the last vestiges of hope. Suddenly, another strong blast hits us.

"Dad, what's our status?"

There's a long pause, too long. Then he comes on the line. "We're finished . . . prepare to abandon ship!" my father orders. "Hurry, the escape pods. Our only chance . . ."

Another blast hits us and the comm drops out; our ship drags even more. We're helpless, drifting in space. The Proxies maneuver into tighter formation to come in for a final attack run—and terminate our vessel. Even if we abandoned ship now, they'd just pick us off in space.

There are too many of them.

This is it. This is the end.

I close my eyes. I grip the controls and prepare to trigger my last shots before fiery blasts and then oblivion takes us. My one regret thumps my heart . . . *I wish I kissed him . . .*

But then—

Out of nowhere—

The Proxy ships disengage their targeting locks. They fall back, breaking formation, and cease firing on us. We're dragging through space with barely one functioning engine.

"What's happening?" I stammer, watching in shock.

"They just stopped," Luna says in disbelief through our comm. "They let us go."

Suddenly, Harold pings me with an urgent communication that pops up in my retinas. It's from the drill sergeant—but transmitted to all of Space Force. She's forwarding the order to our platoon. I scan it, unable to believe my eyes. But the words stand out clear as day.

"Space Force guardians, stand down. Ceasefire ordered. Repeat. All guardians, disengage from combat operations. That's an order. Effective immediately."

I burst through the door and into the cabin, with Luna on my heels. My gaze sweeps the room—spotting Drae, Rho, and Anton. Mrs. Smee slumbers softly, haphazardly draped over a sling chair. How did she fall asleep in the middle of a battle? But then I remember . . . rum.

"Did our plan work?" I say, holding my breath. I scan their expectant faces for some clue. "The Proxies stopped firing on us. They disengaged. Space Force ordered a ceasefire."

"By the stars, it worked!" Anton says with his lopsided grin. "Postmaster Haven broadcast the message out to all his postal workers . . . both here and back Earthside."

"I knew we could trust him," I say with a relieved smile.

"They stopped firing on Ceres Base, too," Drae says, pointing to the window. Indeed, our base is badly damaged, but the Proxies have withdrawn. The ceasefire worked . . . for now.

"And what about our interstellar bases?" I ask, knowing how lag time works.

It would take forever for a regular signal to reach those positions. We need our Space Force Postal Fleet to warp to our bases with the communication packages. That's the only way to get them the intel. The war is already breaking out across the universe, not just here.

"Look, down there," Anton says. "It's happening now."

We crowd around the thick windows with clear views of the dwarf planet below. A few rounds of anti-spacecraft defenses fire off in cascading waves to clear the way, even though they're unnecessary. The Proxies have left the airspace and withdrawn from our base.

And then the most beautiful sight unfolds.

Our fleet of postal ships takes off like comets streaking across the dark sky. They fan out and reach orbit quickly, then one by one, they vanish as they engage their warp drives. They're bound across the universe to disseminate the truth about the emergent alien threat.

"It's really . . . over?" I ask, not quite believing it. I sink into a sling chair on weak knees.

"Well, there's still the little matter of the aliens," Drae says, catching my drift. "Oh, and some definite red tape that we'll have to clear up about where we've all been this whole time. And how this all happened. Guessing we'll need to get our stories straight. That's for sure."

"But if all the federations join forces, we can fight off the aliens," Rho points out. "And better yet, we can also protect Earthside. However, it'll take us working together for once."

"But how do you know that will work?" I ask, still in guardian mode. It's hard to relax when adrenaline is still flooding through my body. "That hasn't happened in a thousand years."

She grins, her hair and eyes turning clear blue. "Oh, simple logic. That's why they couldn't attack us directly. Ever heard of Occam's razor?"

"Oh, I love Occam's razor," Anton says. "One of my favorite principles."

"Right, me too," Rho says, turning flattered pink. "They needed us to destroy ourselves—otherwise they'd just have invaded. That means, together we have a chance to fight them off."

"But make no mistake, they will try again," I say, my mind already whirring with dark possibilities. "They won't like that we thwarted their plans. We will have to be prepared."

"Right, but that's a bit—" Luna says.

"Above our pay grade?" I quip back the familiar refrain, thinking of Nadia and hoping she's still recovering in the sick bay. And with that, we all laugh. But it's true.

Our part made the difference today, but we're still as green as the stars, to quote the drill sergeant. We did what we had to do. We got that intel into the right hands. There's a ceasefire declared. But now, a bigger mission lies ahead for everyone. Not just us.

"Stand down, Guardian," Drae says, approaching with his hands raised. He's taller than me, and his dark eyes find mine. He lays his hand on my shoulder, and it's like electric sparks go off, zapping my whole body. I feel him inside my mind—and he feels me inside his.

Suddenly, I regret my crazy near-death urge to kiss him that he clearly heard. That is so embarrassing since we didn't actually die. But luckily, I'm saved by Mrs. Smee.

"Oh my, did we win?" she says, popping awake after letting out a loud snore.

She blinks at us in bewilderment. She unwittingly broke the awkward moment. I breathe a sigh of relief, though sparks still simmer between us.

"Yup, thanks to you," Anton says. "Well, actually . . . thanks to everyone. But we did it!"

"This calls for a drink!" Mrs. Smee says in a jubilant voice.

And with that, she produces a corked flask from inside her uniform and starts passing it around. On first pull, I grimace at the burn of the rum, but then I taste the sweetness and richness and marvel at the smooth finish. This is not low-level hooch; it's a finely crafted liqueur.

"Well, that'll grow you up," Mrs. Smee says when she sees me wince at the burn.

That's when my father and sister join us in the cabin. Everyone partakes in a celebratory drink . . . or two . . . or three. Except for Bea, of course. Gunner also appears in short order.

All over the ship, cheers and toasts break out. They may be vegan pacifists, but they sure know how to party. It's an amusing sight.

A few minutes later, the cabin door bursts open.

And Nadia limps through on crutches. She winces with each little hop. She's still in a hospital gown and looks a little banged up, but like she'll recover. Maybe with a few scars, but nobody escapes this life unscathed. While scars can be visible, like her blaster injuries, they can also be invisible, but just as painful, like with Drae's mother. She fixes us with a scowl.

"Oh, you just had to fight them without me?" she says with a groan. "And I heard my little bro saved the world? That can't be accurate." She tries to look irate but fails.

Anton grins at his sister. "Told you the postal service might save your life one day! Nadia, admit it. You were wrong . . . for once."

"Being distrustful doesn't mean I'm wrong," Nadia fires back. "So, I've got nothing to admit. Ever hear that skepticism is healthy?"

"Well, now I know you'll live," Anton says. "You're still in verbal sparring shape."

"Jeez, and I heard a bunch of Raider savages patched me up," Nadia goes on, shaking her head and looking down at her bandages. Her eyes sweep over the cabin, landing on my father.

He's got Bea bouncing on the sling chair next to him, a cheerful grin plastered to his face, and a pint of rum in his fist, but he still looks every bit the fearsome Raider captain.

Anton follows her gaze and smiles. "For starters, they're not savages," he says, slipping into his nerd lecture voice. "They're pacifists. And for another, they're our friends now."

"You got that right, kiddo," my dad says. He breaks into a grin and raises the pint. "Glad to see you're back on your feet and in fighting shape. To your health . . . and to the stars!"

We all repeat the toast to Nadia.

"To your health—and to the stars!"

Then everyone takes a swig, except for Bea, of course. "One day," our father promises. "When you're old enough, else your ma will make me regret my entire existence."

"Yeah, she can be scary," Bea whispers. "But she means well."

He chuckles past her head. "Soon, we'll be back together." I overhear that, and it warms my heart more than the sun emerging from the clouds on a foggy day.

Nadia even accepts the flask from Mrs. Smee. She drags a long pull, then coughs.

"That burns like the asteroid fires," Nadia says, after taking another careful sip. "Guess I missed a lot. You'll have to brief me. But for now, I'm glad we saved the stars."

We all cheer. The exultant atmosphere on the Raider ship is infectious. We're still AWOL, of course. But for once, our duties can wait. There will be plenty of time to clear the air and return to base. With all the damage and chaos, we've bought ourselves a respite.

As I gaze around the cabin, I can't believe how this all ended up. I watch Rho flirting with Gunner, her hair and eyes hot pink . . . total *crush* mode (she did always want to date a space pirate, after all). Bea giggles on my dad's lap as he regales her with colorful tales of his Raider adventures on the star-seas. Mrs. Smee sings a drinking song and dances a little jig, pulling Anton in for a slower number. She's got a thing for him, which makes me smirk. Nadia and Luna watch them dance and clap along to the beat as Gunner fires up some music over the comm.

I can't help it. I smile in a way that melts the panic that had lodged itself into my body. We still have a lot to figure out. I know that much. This isn't the end, only the beginning . . . of a larger war for Earth. But for once, I let myself stay in the moment . . . this moment . . .

On a Raider ship . . . drifting on the star-seas . . .

With Drae.

I catch his eye, and he gets my hint. Our neural links flare together—it seems Harold and Estrella are getting well-acquainted. And then, when nobody is looking, we slip away from the cabin. We dash through the corridors, giggling and blushing. The whole ship is in full-on party mode with music and drinking. The Raiders all toast us when they spot us in the corridors. News of our part in this victory must have reached them. Gossip always travels faster in zero-g.

We find the officers' quarters below deck. Still giggling and a bit tipsy, we peek inside one of the rooms. It's deserted, as everyone is off celebrating. Drae grabs my hand and pulls me inside. The rum has warmed up my stomach and loosened my mind, but just a little bit. I feel sparks sizzle through me at his touch. I don't pull away. I give in to him this time.

It's time to stop fighting.

He shuts the door and gazes deeply into my eyes. His are dark like the void. The quarters are cramped and narrow with basic furnishings—a metal slab with a mattress and single, flimsy pillow, drawers in the walls, overhead lights, and no windows. But they're private and much better than the barracks where I've spent the last two months and had zero privacy.

I feel his emotions like electricity channeling through me—adrenaline, fear, desire, love, concern—a strange concoction, but wildly alluring. My heart thumps harder.

His thumps back.

Thump. Thump.

Our hearts beat together, as one.

"Private Hikari Skye, we just saved the universe," Drae says, pretending to interview me for the newsfeeds and making me laugh and play-punch him. His eyes never leave mine. They probe them like a telescope examining the stars. "What do you want to do next?"

I gaze up at his dark visage . . . his shining eyes . . . longer hair since college . . . lush, full lips. Things that I never noticed . . . well, before I really knew him as a person also and what he was capable of becoming. He's not just a spoiled kid anymore . . . he's a hero now.

But there's more. He's kind and sensitive, generous; a great friend to Rho; and he took care of my little sister in a crisis. I realize now that maybe he could be something more for me. That passionate urge seizes ahold of me again, stronger this time. I reach up and run my hands through his tight, wiry curls, feeling the softness brush against my palm. I like his longer hair.

"Sorry, I should get a haircut," he says, apologizing, but I brush him off.

"Oh, I prefer it this way. It suits you," I say in what I hope is a flirty voice, though I'm way out of practice. Come to think of it, I've never had any practice. I'm pretty much a novice in this arena, which makes me feel vulnerable, unprotected, almost naked . . .

Though I am clothed, for the record. And I don't plan on changing that, despite the racing of my heart . . .

Yet.

"So, got any ideas?" Drae says, leaning into my touch. It's not like before in the hall at school. He's letting me lead; he's surrendering control, too.

"One thing," I say, stroking his soft hair. Mischief lights up my eyes. "I've been thinking about it a lot actually. You could say . . . all the time lately."

"Oh, and what's that?" he asks in a faux-innocent voice. Now he's acting coy, and I'm the one being forward (even though our neural connection spoils any chance of surprise or deception). It's a total role reversal, but I kind of like it. I savor the moment.

"I want to *kiss* you," I say, unable to believe my directness. I'm not like Rho, who throws affection around. Punches, yes . . . but the touchy-feely stuff? Well, I tend to keep it to myself. But I realize suddenly that he isn't the only one who has changed. I've changed, too.

We've both changed . . . together.

"Oh . . . do you, Private Skye?" he says, pulling back and acting like he's hard to get.

But I can feel his heart racing to match my own, and I know it's an act. His true feelings broadcast out to me, and I echo them back. He gives me a smoldering look as a sexy smile spreads across his face, complete with full-on dimple action. That makes my heart pound harder. Moving slowly, he tilts his head toward me and his lips part . . . but then he hesitates.

"Only if you consent," he says in a flirty voice. "Last time, you socked me pretty darn good. I totally deserved it. But I'd rather avoid offending you like that again."

"Oh, I'm sure that's true." I giggle, feeling my whole body relax and tense at the same time, then nod. "One hundred million percent . . . yes . . . you have my permission to land."

And that's when he tilts in—

And he kisses me, long and deep like it will never end, his gently tilting planet orbiting around my fiery sun, finally right where it always belonged. I feel his desire, but also his love and care. He leans into my gravity, while I lean into his elliptical rotation, and I know I'll be safe from black holes, for in this universe—*our own special universe*—there are none.

Only peaceful planets circling a steady, yellow dwarf star that's singular and life-giving, like the one that belongs to our Earth. We kiss, orbiting each other for a long spell. Each time our lips touch, time itself seems to bend and change, like it does when warp drives kick in.

He kisses me harder, deeper—

I detect elevated heart rate, Harold pipes up. *May I suggest meditation exercises?*

Mute, please! I think back in embarrassment. My cheeks flush. But he falls mercifully silent and stays that way. For once, it's like he got the hint. Maybe he is learning, after all.

Minutes pass, maybe an hour, maybe two days. I don't know and I don't care. His lips become my whole universe and time bends to us, as we kiss deeply and our minds remain forever linked. Finally, breathless and swept up in each other, we come up for gulps of air.

My whole body tingles and vibrates, wanting more, but also wishing to enjoy every little moment and not rush anything. He gazes back at me and feels the same way.

"Wow, so incredible," he marvels. "Especially when it doesn't end with you punching me in the jaw."

"Careful," I tease him back. "There's still time. And I hit much harder now, thanks to my drill sergeant." That's when I lean in and kiss him more, pulling him onto the bunk and twisting the lock on the door. "Now you're at my mercy," I say, unable to keep the smile from my voice.

"Private Skye, time for some *private* time?" he jokes in a cheesy voice.

But it makes me love him all the more. He wraps me up in his warm embrace. Our breathing synchronizes. He's tall and strong, but so am I. Somehow, it works and we fit together perfectly, like two puzzle pieces. The mattress is thin and on the hard side, but we don't care.

I melt into his lips, and then into his body. Gradually, and then all at once, like proto-planets colliding. And he doesn't stop holding me and kissing me, all through the artificial night. Even if he tried, I wouldn't let him. He's caught in my gravity now—and I won't let go.

I wake in his arms.

I don't even remember falling asleep, but the crash after the adrenaline rush of combat is so real. Not to mention, the few swigs of rum, and the best drug of all . . .

His sumptuous kisses.

Drae cracks his eyes open next to me and smiles sleepily at me, roused by that thought. Our neural links spark together, bringing us even closer and adding this extra element.

"*The best drug?*" he says, reading my thought.

"Ugh, you weren't supposed to hear that," I say with a grimace, play-punching his shoulder.

"Ouch . . . I surrender!"

"Oh, please. You didn't even feel that."

He acts wounded, then he breaks into a grin and plants another kiss on my lips. I feel that tingly rush all through my body again. I'm secretly mad at Rho for never properly explaining *this* to me. I make a mental note to tell her later, and probably fill her in on all the gory details. If I can get her away from Gunner and Bea and everyone else, that is. I imagine Bea is following our father around the ship like a chatty second shadow, peppering him with a million questions.

That makes me smile, but then concern seeps into my heart, making me blush. I'm guessing they're all feeling quite nosy after we pulled that disappearing act last night.

"So, back to my burning question. What now?" Drae asks with a mellow smile. "Do we become space pirates? Go on the run together? Have grand adventures around the galaxy?"

He props his head up on his elbow and stares back at me. That does sound tempting, especially now that I finally got my dad back, not to mention lying here in Drae's arms is the best feeling in the universe. But my heart sinks. I know my oath, and I don't intend to break it now. Plus, more than ever, Space Force needs guardians to face this new alien threat. This fight might be over, but the real war for the fate of our universe and humanity is only just beginning.

He feels this before I speak the words. His face falls. He can't help it, any more than I can. We can't hide our true feelings from each other either, thanks to the neural link.

"I've chosen a life in the stars," I say, reaching over to stroke his face. I run my finger over his full lips, memorizing the outline and each indentation, the perfect curvature. "You've chosen one back Earthside. How does this . . . whatever *this* is . . . make any sense?"

"Well, nothing about us ever made any sense," he says with a wistful smile that turns into a grimace. "What did you say when we got paired? Remember, after the ceremony?"

"Uh . . . that the powers that be lost their stars-loving minds?" I say with a wince. "Something like that . . . and maybe worse."

"Exactly. And what do you think now?"

"That they're secret geniuses." I smile, but then I turn serious. "Look, I have to return to Space Force. It's just this new threat . . . the alien threat. It's not over. That was only first contact. But they're going to return." I pause, processing my thoughts and feelings. "And there might be more like them out there. I swore an oath when I enlisted—and I intend to honor it."

"I know. You're right. I just wish it could be easier . . ."

"And that we didn't have to keep fighting?"

He nods. "Yes, that . . . and dying in the stars." Those grim words hit us both. But it doesn't change anything. That's what I signed up for. I knew the risks when I enlisted.

"And what about you?" I ask, nudging his shoulder gently, lovingly. "You know my deal. Front lines. Four-year tour before my first Earthside leave. Eight-year contract."

Drae nods. "Right, I should go back to Berkeley and graduate. Our federation has problems, but I'm thinking . . . I want to try to change things from the inside out."

"What about that mess with Jude?" I ask, remembering their fight. But also why Drae did it. He was defending that girl from a predator. Jude deserved every punch.

"Oh, Xena and her friends offered to help out with that," he says with a knowing look. "She promised to pay him a little visit and make him see reason. They're also protecting his victims."

"Oh, did she now?" I say with a knowing look. "Bunch of Resistance fighters, maybe some Raiders? Bet that'll convince him to see your side of the story a little more clearly."

"She can be pretty persuasive! She got me to space, didn't she? And then . . . well . . . I'm thinking about maybe running for office. There's so much wrong, so much that needs fixing back home. Plus, someone needs to fight to keep Earth disarmament from becoming a reality."

"A politician, huh?" I say, raising my eyebrows. "You've certainly got the personality and charming smile part down." I point to his dimples, which he can't hide.

He blushes, then turns more serious. "Maybe even . . . secretary-general one day."

"Secretary-general?" I repeat with a bit of surprise. But then, the idea settles in—and I can't believe I didn't see it before. He's got intelligence and natural charisma, the kind that's needed for that sort of position, plus that full-on, irresistible, dimpled smile. It all fits . . .

But most importantly, he has a good heart.

I know that now.

"Just a local representative, at first," he backpedals. "Go back home after I graduate, build some grassroots support. Capitalize on my family's reputation and make sure my mother's mistakes are good for something. But also, maybe I can use my Resistance connections. But yeah, that's the plan. Oh, and there's one more important item on my agenda."

I bat my eyelashes at him, teasing him. "Oh, Mr. Secretary-General . . . what's that?"

"Shush already," he jokes, but then gives me a penetrating look that pierces my heart. "I'm gonna stay your Sympathetic . . . if they'll let me. Private Skye, you're stuck with me."

"I wouldn't have it any other way."

We savor the moment, knowing it might end soon. Too soon. But time has never been our friend. My mind is whirring now, thinking about our unspooling futures . . . all of them.

"I have a hunch that Rho and Bea are gonna stay up here with the Raiders," I tell him, feeling suddenly certain about it. "Rho's crushing hard on Gunner. Her heart always leads her, for better or worse. And, well, Bea lost out on our dad. I just have this feeling . . ."

Drae nods. "What about your ma?"

"At the party, before we snuck away, I chatted with my dad for a while . . . wow, it still feels so weird calling him that," I marvel. "He's not interested in clearing his name. I think he told you already? So, he can't return home. But they're gonna swing down and grab her."

"Raider abduction?" he asks, raising his eyebrows.

"Apparently, Xena and your professor promised to fabricate a cover story for Ma and Bea's disappearance . . . maybe fake their deaths . . . something like that. They deserve to be a family again. Even if I have to serve out my contract and can't join them yet."

"Yeah, I can see that. A life on the star-seas. Sounds nice, doesn't it? Plus, my mom staying a war hero—at least officially—will help me run for office one day . . ." He trails off with a grimace. I feel his self-consciousness. "Asteroid fires, does that sound terribly cynical?"

He looks ashamed.

"No, now you sound like a real politician, but the good kind . . . I know your heart."

I place my hand on his chest. Drae takes that in. But something troubles him. He stares deeply into my eyes. I feel his thoughts flow from his mind. "And what about us?"

"You'll always be my Sympathetic, of course."

"Oh . . . is that all?" I hear the strain in his voice, but I feel it, too.

He can't hide his disappointment.

"Well, it's a long wait. Four years before my first leave," I hedge in a careful tone. "I'm going to deploy to the front lines." I look down. "I'd understand if you didn't want to . . ."

"Kari, I love you . . . so shut the stars up."

"Are you sure? Think about it—"

"Waiting for you is the only thing I want to do in this whole blasted universe. You can go to the stars, and I'll be waiting back Earthside. I promise, I'll be there for you. No matter what happens."

"No matter what happens?" I repeat.

He nods solemnly. "No matter what. That's my oath."

I like the sound of that. I like his promise. Something about our impossible situation suddenly feels possible. Like we can make this crazy thing work. Maybe my head is swimming in dreams and starlight, or maybe I'm seeing clearly for once. And then he buries me in kisses again, while our Raider ship blasts through space with its cloaking shields back up, buying us a few more precious moments together, before we both have to come back down to gravity.

As Estrella Luna would say—

To the stars and back!

CHAPTER 52

DRAE

And just like that, I'm back at Berkeley.

I wake up in my dorm room to the bright California sunlight drifting through the window. I blink to make sure it's real. That I'm back Earthside. Sadness settles over me like a heavy blanket, but then I brighten, remembering her kisses, her bright eyes . . . her everything.

We're still connected, I think, tapping the back of my neck and feeling the stub of my neural implant. More than ever. And still, she's my last thought before I drift off. She haunts my dreams all through the dark of the night. And her name is the first breath to kiss my lips in the jarring blaze of morning light.

Kari.

Always Kari.

Captain Skye had a Raider ship drop me off at the SFO airstrip last week. There's a whole loose alliance of pirates, scattered in the stars. But first, I got to spend a few precious days with Kari on the Raider ship with our cloaking shield up, while the world struggled to realign itself and face the news that we're not alone anymore—and worse—we're in great danger. But all things, even the good things, must come to an end. We couldn't stay in limbo forever.

After we landed at SFO, Xena retrieved me in her bus and drove me back to my transport, waiting for me in the shadow of the Golden Gate Bridge.

Everything was working perfectly, like nothing ever happened. *Only everything has happened*, I thought as I climbed into the back seat and felt the familiar soft hum of the electric engine. It turns out that saving the universe did have some perks. The government didn't want to admit the truth—that it took two rogue college students and a bunch of Resistance fighters to uncover the truth about the Golden Gate Attack. So, they've settled for covering it all up.

The excuse for my disappearance?

A research project on the Golden Gate Bridge. My history professor signed off on the paperwork confirming my whereabouts. And what about Jude and that night? The same powers that be also quashed the investigation into my actions and cleared my record. My dad is even afraid to ask any questions, though he and Mr. Luther still have their cushy fed jobs.

I guess some things change, but others remain the same. They're not too worried about me anymore. They have a new mission to focus on—the alien invaders, or Astrals as they're now called. It's all my mom can talk about on our weekly catch-up vid chats.

Thanks to Captain Skye, I know the truth about what happened. But I also know that clearing his name isn't worth the pain it would cause my mother. War hero is her whole identity.

Besides, the past can't be undone; it can only be endured and accepted. She's mostly harmless anyway, ensconced on her recliner and fixated on the newsfeeds' constant chatter about the new threat to humanity. I guess it's brought us closer together—and I'm not dreading the holidays anymore.

At least we all have a common enemy now—my parents, Mr. Luther, all the Earthside federations, not to mention the Raiders and the Resistance.

You're going to be late for class, Estrella chimes in. My fall schedule flashes before my retinas. I still have to finish my first semester. Exams loom like ticking time bombs. However, all of it feels a bit mundane after everything. But my education is important . . . it will help me make a difference. Those who don't know the past are doomed to repeat it, I've learned.

So I climb out of bed, grab my backpack, and muss my long hair. College sweats will have to do for today. Then I rush through my common room, waving to my new roommates.

"Not a morning person, huh?" Sylvia says with a smirk.

She is the very definition of a morning person, sitting on the raggedy futon with an extra-large coffee and a set of scary-looking math problems proudly displayed on her tablet. She has thick black glasses and equally black, blunt-cut bangs that frame her round, freckled face.

"Nothing *fun* happens before noon," Theo groans, strolling out with messy, bed-rumpled hair. He yawns for dramatic effect. "Plus, it balances you out. You're like the crazy early bird who rockets awake at the crack of dawn, while he's the brooding night owl."

"Oh, is that so?" Sylvia smirks at him. "And what does that make you?"

"The *normal* one," he shoots back. "Stars knows, you both need that."

"Ugh, that's code for . . . *boring*," Sylvia says, pulling a face. Then she jerks her thumb at me. "At least the night owl has an air of mystery about him. Don't you think?"

I can't help but smile at their antics. "Brooding, did you say?"

They both nod emphatically.

"Don't worry. It only adds to your charm," Sylvia adds with a mischievous glint in her eyes. "Plus, we're thrilled to have you move in. I totally needed someone new to tease."

"Yeah, thank the stars for that," Theo says with a wince. "You saved me from her slings and arrows." Thanks to my reading list, I even catch her Shakespeare reference and chuckle.

With another smile at our banter, I hurry to class and weave my way across campus. I don't need Estrella to guide me any longer. I know the way by heart. As students swarm around me, filling the courtyard with happy chatter, the pure normalcy of regular life overwhelms me.

It's only been a few short days since I returned, but so much has changed. I have new roommates, of course. Our easy banter and fresh friendship, literary references included, are just what I imagined college life would be like. I don't miss Jude and Loki, that's for sure.

Officially, they're both taking the rest of the semester off.

Let's just say, that girl who ran off? She ended up filing a report with the dean after all.

Apparently, Trebond got to her and offered her protection from retaliation by Jude's family. Something else came out of her report. Loki slipped something into her drink and helped Jude lure her back to the dorm. They were offered two choices—expulsion, or take the semester off and find a quiet school to transfer to for the next semester.

They chose the latter. And while sweeping it under the rug doesn't sit right with me, I know that it's an improvement. And I know Trebond will keep her word and protect the girl. But it's also a reminder of how much still needs to change back here. I remind myself that it's the reason I want to get into politics after graduation. I even floated the idea to my mom, and I've never seen her or my father so excited about anything. Let's just say, they're on board.

Some things are different; much remains the same. But there's more they don't know. I'm still working with my old professor and Xena. For safety, we communicate the old-fashioned way. I'll find notes left under my pillow or slipped into my library books with that gorgeous handwritten calligraphy, specifying the date and time for our next meeting. I guess it's official. I'm one of their agents now. Our mission—to bring peace to the galaxy and eventually disarm the stars. But we also know that the alien threat looms and can't be ignored. We need our defenses. And we need good guardians to keep enlisting and preparing to fight this new threat.

Hardline ideas won't save us. Everyone is adjusting and bending to our new reality. They're also starting to work, cautiously, and share intel with the federation authorities. In some ways, my old professor thinks that I'll be the one who will bridge the gap between our government and the Resistance. I blush when she says it. I don't feel up to the task yet. But I'm grateful to have my teacher back to guide my trajectory through this life.

I pass the café where I used to buy Rho lattes. She's the one change that hurts the most. Once she caught feelings for Gunner, there was no going back. I knew better than to try to change her mind. The truth is—Rho was never really of this world anyway. She didn't forsake Kari when her family got evicted, like everyone else. She stuck by her friend to the end and hitched a ride to space. She's still riding that rocket somewhere up there on the star-seas.

The official story?

She's studying abroad, something being encouraged more now that the Proxy Wars have ended. And really, what's more abroad than space? Maybe she'll return next semester, or maybe the galaxy will be her new university, and the stars her new professors.

I tilt my head skyward, where a thin sliver of moon hangs in the sapphire blue skies, like a reminder of the night that fell, or maybe a foretelling of the one to come. We are all stardust, floating on these jagged rocks, orbiting around the sun, and basking in all the starlight of a billion, trillion galaxies. We are adrift at a great distance, yet still connected all at once.

And with that, I head into my class and settle in for the lecture, knowing that each day I'm learning more that will help me build a better future. And Kari isn't lost—she's with me every step of the way. Soon, she'll deploy, and our communications will go dark for a spell, but on the other end of that warp tunnel is another postal fleet waiting to carry her communications back to me, and my words, thoughts, kisses, and love back to her . . . just with more lag time.

But the good things—the best things—are worth the wait.

CHAPTER 53

KARI

The last thing that happens before I return to base—
Ma comes back.

It's a surprise for me and Bea. Our father summons us to the bridge, acting like we're in trouble. "What did you do?" I scold my sister, knowing it has to be her usual shenanigans.

"Nothing," Bea says. "And for once, I mean it."

Her tone is so earnest, I drop my scowl. "And for once, I believe you."

"You scoundrels," Dad bellows through the door. "Get in here . . . now!"

And that's when I see her—it's my mother. Her eyes water instantly and her lips wobble. She stands with my father, his arms entwined around her thin frame. She has her usual scarf wrapped around her hair, but she looks better than the last time I saw her, healthier and stronger.

"Girls, you heard your father," she says. "Give me a hug already."

We rush over and pile into a group hug, all four of us, united for the first time ever. My father was deployed when Bea was born, so he never got to meet her in person until last week. We stay like that, intertwined with arms and laughter and happy tears, for a long time.

"But . . . how?" I ask in amazement.

"Your father had a Raider ship scoop me up," Ma says with a twinkle in her eyes. "Nearly gave me a heart attack. I guess they had to drop someone off first in the general vicinity."

"Drae," I manage to choke out. His absence still hits me out of nowhere like a punch to the gut. I miss him that much already. "They took him back to college."

"Ah, yes . . . your Sympathetic?" she says with a nod. There's so much more I need to tell her about him. But for now, that's enough. He is my Sympathetic, and so we are bound.

"Surprised you, didn't I?" my dad jokes, swooping in for a kiss. He plants it on her lips, and like magic, it seems to age her backward a decade or more. She giggles like a kid.

"I always knew you'd come back for me." Then she turns to me and Bea. "I'm sorry that I couldn't tell you the truth sooner. I knew in my heart that he didn't desert, but I couldn't prove it. And that knowledge would have put you in danger. I couldn't risk it."

"It's okay," I say, tearing up again. "All that matters is we're together now."

"Yay for Captain Dad!" Bea adds, doing a happy dance.

"But won't they come looking for you?" I ask, feeling my familiar worry flare up. My need to protect my mother is so strong. But she shakes her head with a roguish grin.

"They're going to fake our deaths," Ma says, reaching down to Bea. "Looks like our transport crashed off a cliff last week. It burst into flames. That's the thing with transport fires. When the batteries catch that way, it's like an inferno. It leaves no trace. Anyway, it was in the middle of nowhere, so they won't discover the wreckage for another week or so . . ."

"Ma, is this what you want?" I ask, still feeling worried.

"Oh, my dear, it's the only thing I've ever wanted," she confirms. "Plus, with this new alien situation, the safest place for us is with your father and these seaworthy pirates."

I can't argue with that. For once, I drop my shields and put away my blasters. I let myself relax and bask in the reunification of my family, knowing this moment, like all moments, is ultimately fleeting and doomed to turn into the past, while a frightening new future awaits.

Where will it lead me? All I know . . .

The stars are calling for me.

Best not to keep them waiting too long.

A few days later, I have to return to base and everything that comes with my service.

Anton helps by "discovering" me stranded on the surface. He sends out a postal ship to rescue me. He grins his lopsided smile when I emerge into the post office. He's wearing his new postal uniform, emblazoned with the Space Force logo. But then, he delivers my orders.

"The drill sergeant wants to see you."

A million thoughts run through my head. But I know my official cover story. During the Ceres Base attack, I got kidnapped by the Siberian Fed. But when the ceasefire was declared and the intel broadcast out, they changed their minds and decided to ditch me back at base.

With that, I rap on her door with great trepidation.

"Come in," she says, giving me an appraising look. Her face is stone, as usual. I can't read it. But I figure I must be in some kind of trouble. Fits with the narrative, doesn't it?

"Sit down, Guardian," she says, then frowns at me. "So, let me get this straight. You disobeyed direct orders and went rogue? Then, you got stranded on the surface and kidnapped by the Siberian Fed? And they just . . . let you go?"

I nod sharply. "Exactly. When the alien threat was revealed, they realized that I wasn't their enemy. So they decided to let me go. I'm just lucky that postal ship spotted me."

"Ah, right," she says. "Private Anton Ksusha called it in."

"Like I said, I'm really lucky."

"In my experience, there's no such thing as luck," she says with a skeptical frown. "And this story . . . well . . . it's pretty ironclad. It all checks out. I interviewed everyone, including Private Ksusha. I can't find holes in their stories either. But I don't buy it. When you disappeared is the exact same time that this anonymous communication mysteriously got sent out."

"What do you mean?" I ask with a start. My heart starts to race. She's talking about the intel we sent to Postmaster Haven. He's claiming it arrived from an anonymous address.

"Also, your missing Sympathetic?" she goes on. "Well, he also just turned up out of nowhere back at school . . . with a perfect cover story. Apparently, he was working on a research paper? The report is even stamped and approved by the head honchos down at the fed."

"Yes, I'm so relieved he's safe," I say, starting to sweat.

"That's pretty high-level stuff for a missing civilian," she says, rapping her knuckles on the desk. "And his going AWOL and your kidnapping happen to sync up, too."

"Uh, yeah, that's super weird," I say through my dry mouth.

She clicks off her tablet and sets it aside.

"That's the official story," she says. "The one you told me. Don't worry. I already signed off on the report clearing you. Now, why don't you tell me what really happened?"

"Uh, I don't know what you mean," I hedge . . . badly.

"Kari, I'm not your enemy," she says, using my first name. That jolts me. "When will you realize that? And with this emergent threat, we're in more danger than ever. You're going to need all the help you can get. You can't fight this war on your own. None of us can."

I grimace and look down at my hands. My heart races, and I'm sweating more. I suck at lying. That's why I could never be special ops like Luna. My internal lie detector is too strong.

"You sure you want to know? And I won't get in trouble? Or anyone else?"

"*Yes, yes*, and *yes*," she says rapid-fire. "Now, spill your guts."

"You won't believe it."

"Just try me," she says with a smile.

That's when I start talking. And once I get going, I can't stop. I tell her the truth about my father and what happened that fateful night to her platoon. How he didn't desert, how it was Drae's mother who really betrayed them. Then, I tell her the truth about Draeden and the Resistance and the intel about the alien threat. I finish with the Raiders flying them to space.

And I'm right—the incredulous expression on her face tells me everything. She knew something was up, but she didn't expect all of this. The usual mask that she wears breaks into human pieces, betraying her turbulent emotions. Finally, once I finish with Postmaster Haven's role in everything, and give her a moment to process everything, she speaks again.

"Wow, that is some story," she says with a shake of her head.

"You believe me?" I ask nervously. "I'm not in trouble?"

"Of course I believe you! First of all, you're not creative enough to make that up. No offense," she adds quickly. "And second of all, I can feel it in my bones. You're telling the truth. Over these last many weeks, I've gotten to know you . . . the *real* you."

"That's true," I agree. "The head-screws had a purpose, right?"

She nods. "And that's also why I know . . . you're not a liar."

"My father . . . it doesn't feel right not clearing his name," I say, feeling tears prick at my eyes. "He was framed. He's the real hero. He stopped Captain Rache from blasting everyone."

She nods. "Sometimes the choices we have to make for the greater good require that we sacrifice," she says in a wise voice. "Plus, it's what your father wants. Isn't that important?"

I nod, but add, "The Raiders aren't our enemies."

"That's important intel that we need to know," she says. "I'm glad you confided in me. Off the record, not everyone at Space Force is ready for the change that's coming. But I'm more open-minded. I know that with the Astrals, we're going to need all the help we can get."

"Even space pirates?"

She smirks. "Yes, even them. Your father might prove a useful asset that we should explore, even though we can't clear his name. Space Force is more important than ever. A story like that would undermine faith in the very institutions we need to protect us the most."

"You're right, I know . . ." I say, finding myself grateful for her guidance. "But I feel like I'm living a lie . . . and I have to keep living that lie to honor my service . . ."

I trail off, but she meets my eyes.

"Yes, but now I know the truth," she says. "I hope we can continue our communications after your deployment. There's more. Your MOS orders are changing . . ."

"To what?" I ask in surprise.

"That's still classified," she says. "But trust that it relates to this intel. And the brand-new front in the war. How can we hope to fight an enemy when we know nothing about them?"

"Sounds like something Sun Tzu would say," I reply with a nod. "We can't fight a faceless enemy. We have to find out about their origins . . . how they think . . . what they want . . ."

"Still top secret, for now," she says, cutting me off gently. "But I know you'll be an asset to the new program. I recommended you personally—as my brightest star pupil."

"Yes, Drill Sergeant," I say, feeling a secret thrill.

"Viola," she says softly. "Just for today . . . you can call me Viola."

Her real name.

I never knew it before this moment. That's on purpose, to keep the drill sergeants shrouded in mystery and intimidation. But she's letting her guard down now . . . for me.

Before I know it, it's time to deploy.

My destination? Interstellar, that's all I know.

My mission? Top secret still. I'll be briefed when I arrive there in a few Earth days' time.

Still very much in the dark, I board the transport and settle into my sling chair. I'm surrounded by a bunch of jittery guardians, fresh out of basic training like me, and a handful of grizzled officers transferring to new postings. A lot is changing at Space Force to prepare for the new war. I glance at their faces—young and nervous, older and stoic—and realize that I fall somewhere in between. After everything, I'm not that fresh-faced newbie with a hot temper and something deep and dark to prove. But I'm still hopeful; I still believe in the core mission.

Even the corruption that we uncovered can't fully dim the fluttering feeling I get in my stomach when I gaze upon our logo on our fleet of ships, or hear the patriotic stirrings of our national anthem. Space Force is still an idea—that we can be better, all of humanity, and strive for something greater than us that lies in the stars. I feel my sling chair tighten and cushion me as we rocket away from Ceres and into the depths of space. The base grows smaller and smaller, while the black velvet vacuum engulfs us and bathes us in ever-twinkling starlight.

Before my sleep meds kick in, I keep my eyes trained on the view. I can't keep my mind from racing and speculating about my posting. I wonder if I'll run into Luna out there with her special ops assignment. I think of my other friends from Basic, scattered into the cosmos with their divergent specialties and orders. Except for Anton. He's staying on Ceres Base. For now. But the postal service is the core of our operations. I learned that—and I'll never forget it.

Regardless of the details, I'll be on the front lines fighting for our safety and security. Just where I've always wanted. I don't know the future. All I know is this.

Drae will be there for me each warp jump—each space bounce—each heartbeat of the way. I can feel it deep in my bones. In the desperate quivering of my heart, where he awakened something real and lasting. In my neural synapses that have absorbed his deepest memories, thoughts, and feelings. For what is a person anyway except the amalgam of those things?

Perhaps, then, I've uploaded him, and he lives inside me now—as I live inside him, too. We are bound together, our fates intertwined. For better or worse, until death do us part.

A very real possibility given the danger of my new mission.

We won the battle. But the greater war looms, the true fight for Earth and our people, finally united together for the first time in our war-ridden history, without faction or federation dividing us. Our only core mission now is to save humanity and protect our home planet. I hope that we can rise to this great purpose. But I fear the darkness of our history and true nature. The Astrals have already exploited it, exposing our weaknesses and deficits of character.

But for the first time since the Pairing Ceremony, I feel at peace. Even if I could go back in time, I wouldn't have it any other way. And I know that Drae feels the same way.

Draeden. Draeden. Draeden.

His name has become a familiar refrain in my head, as we ascend into orbit and leave Ceres in our dust. I stare out at the familiar expanse filled with stars, an impossible-to-fathom amount of them at an impossible-to-fathom distance—but despite all odds, their light reaches my retinas anyway, and they even twinkle like a trillion tiny diamonds. *Stars are hope*, I decide as I watch them and wait for the warp drives to kick in. But for now, we're floating quietly through zero-g's, tilting away from the base that's been my home for the last eight weeks.

The future awaits. I'm ready to meet it. I know that Drae won't let me drift too far into nothingness. That our hearts are tethered together. He will give me enough slack to explore the cosmos, doling it out inch by inch, then by leaps and bounds, but he'll never let me drift too far. Gently, lovingly, he will tug me back to him, as our gravities attract stronger and stronger, until all at once, we will collide together again with the heat of a thousand yellow dwarf suns—

And we can kiss once more.

That thought keeps my heart thumping as the warp drives thrust me back into my sling chair—and catapults me into the endless, ever-expanding reaches of the unknown.

I can't wait.

EPILOGUE

KARI

Sympathetic Exchange Transcription
From Space Force Postal Service Archival Records
Delivered via warp mail

From:	*Captain Hikari Skye (Earth Federation Space Force)*
To:	*Sympathetic Draeden Rache (University of California, Berkeley)*
Post Office:	*Ceres Base*
Subject:	*Safe (For Now)*

This will be my last message before I go dark for deployment.

My return to Space Force has gone mostly smoothly, after some stern interrogation from my drill sergeant. She grilled me pretty good, but playing a small part in saving the universe tends to grant you a little bit of leniency. This is my last communication I can send from our solar system before the long dark of the galaxy road, traveling to interstellar space. Warp drives shorten the duration, of course . . . but it's still a stars-forsaken long-haul journey.

I wonder if I might bump into some of our old friends out this way. You know who I mean? From what I hear, they're having some wild misadventures on the star-seas.

The Interstellar Federation Peace Treatise was signed by our new secretary-general Priscilla W. Andromeda last week, officially ending the Proxy Wars. Representatives gathered in Aries City, the planetary capital of Liberated Mars, which is neutral territory. The treaty also preserves Earth disarmament. But I heard that was a touchy subject at the negotiations, which almost broke down on several occasions. Apparently, Secretary-General Andromeda played a key role in protecting the provision. But I'm guessing, this won't be the last we hear of it.

Thankfully, we're all united against the emergent threat. They're calling them "Astrals," or "Interstellar Beings," if you're feeling more politically correct. They're still out there, of course. Even scarier, we know precious little about them. However, we can't rest easy, or wait for them to attack Earth again. Oh yeah, my new MOS orders also came through.

My mission remains top secret, but I have a hunch it involves our new little friends. I also got a fancy promotion. Guess saving the universe from aliens has some definite perks.

"Isn't that rad?" to quote Estrella Luna.

Too bad I didn't get twin golden blasters and bejeweled holsters to go with it. I can always dream, right? One day, I'll be back Earthside and can devour your comic collection. You'll have to show me your favorites. Just don't be mad if I take them out of the plastic, okay?

They'll redact this if I reveal any classified details about the Astral situation or my new mission. But Postmaster Haven gave me special clearance for this exchange. Besides, by the time this reaches you, most of it should be released on the newsfeeds. I can tell you this—

Earth is safe.

For now, of course.

However, our vigilance must remain constant and tireless. Mysterious and dangerous enemies flank us on all sides of the galaxy, but at least they're not coming from inside our planet anymore. Thankfully, the federations are finally united. Who knew that it would take a little alien invasion to make us stop fighting each other? I guess our crazy plan worked after all.

By joining our military powers together, we were able to reinforce our galactic defenses and hold off any incoming invasion. They're calling us the *Earth Federation Space Force* now.

Nifty new name, right?

I wanted to tell you all that, so you wouldn't worry. So you'd know that your family and friends and loved ones would be safe. The guardians are out here, still fighting to protect Earth.

Since our last misadventure, I've never had a greater appreciation for our postal service. I trust that they'll carry this exchange to you safely back Earthside. I'm sorry that I won't have time to receive your response before I have to catch my ride off base. But there's more.

I'm not always great with words . . . or feelings . . . or trite, sentimental stuff . . . you know that. But it took losing you, and then getting you back, to make me realize how much you mean to me. We might not have tomorrow; there might only be today. So, I'll get right to it—

I never gave you credit.

I never believed you could help me.

I never understood how much I needed to heal.

I never thought you could change, too.

I never realized you would prove me wrong.

I never knew I'd . . . fall in love.

Until you.

Acknowledgments

This book has been a journey! I'm thrilled to see it published at long last. This began as a simple short story concept that morphed and grew into this epic space opera—all set around the militarization of outer space. I started writing it *before* the president mentioned Space Force in a speech. I had to set the book on hold at many junctures, waiting for the world to catch up so I could adjust my worldbuilding. That's the thing about being a sci-fi writer, when we hit on a truth of what will be, the book's world can manifest into the real world.

This was supposed to be my follow up to the Continuum Trilogy, but so many books bumped their way ahead in line. In this time, I've written and published two graphic novels, a seven-book series for Disney called *Disney Chills*, and contributed countless stories to anthologies, including a canon Darth Vader story for *Stories of Jedi and Sith*, and "Elsa and The Frost Monster" for *All is Found: A Frozen Anthology*. It's been a busy few years!

Thanks to my editor Stephanie Beard, whom I began my career with on *The 13th Continuum*. Thanks for always being my champion, along with my agent, Deborah Schneider. Your notes were invaluable to getting this manuscript in shape! Thanks to my manager David Server for "getting" what I do and helping me continue to build it all, book by book, story by story.

I'm grateful to have a great team. Thanks also to everyone who has stuck by me through a tough few years, including a divorce, a COVID emergency move, then another. But all that has led me to the high desert—and I couldn't be more grateful to have found such a glorious, creative community nestled among the Joshua trees. Living here feels like I'm so close to touching the stars.

Finally, and most importantly, thank you to all the servicemen and women, both currently serving and veterans, including my partner, Andrew. This book wouldn't exist without everything you've sacrificed to keep us safe. I honor your commitment. I hope I did it justice.

Lastly, thanks to my readers for giving the chance to forge a life out of words and stories.

Book 2 will be coming in a year!

Best always,
Jennifer Brody
Joshua Tree, CA

About the Author

Jennifer Brody, also known as Vera Strange, is the award-winning author of the Disney Chills series, the Continuum Trilogy, and Stoker finalist *Spectre Deep 6*, which prompted *Forbes* to call her "a star in the graphic novel world." She is the coauthor of *All Is Found: A Frozen Anthology* and *Star Wars: Stories of Jedi and Sith*, in which she penned the Darth Vader story. A graduate of Harvard University, Brody is also a film/TV producer and writer and a creative writing instructor. She began her career in Hollywood working for A-list directors and movie studios on many films, including the Lord of the Rings trilogy, *The Texas Chainsaw Massacre*, and *The Golden Compass*. Brody lives and writes in Joshua Tree, California.

DISCOVER
STORIES UNBOUND

PodiumAudio.com